BY IVO ANDRIĆ

The Pasha's Concubine and Other Tales
(*1968*)

The Woman from Sarajevo
(*1965*)

Bosnian Chronicle
(*1963*)

THESE ARE BORZOI BOOKS

PUBLISHED IN NEW YORK BY ALFRED A. KNOPF

THE PASHA'S CONCUBINE

AND OTHER TALES

THE
PASHA'S
CONCUBINE
AND
OTHER TALES

by

Ivo Andrić

Translated from the Serbo-Croatian by Joseph Hitrec

NEW YORK: ALFRED · A · KNOPF
1968

Note on the Pronunciation
of South Slavic Names

Phonetic English transliteration of Slavic names—serviceable in the case of the Russians—does not work quite as well with South Slavic names, which are often built in groupings of velars, rolled r's, sibilants of varying hardness, and fixed vowel sounds. Applied with any consistency, this method would yield gargoyles such as Cherkhlintse and Kowkdzhich, for Čerklince and Kaukdžić. It seemed better, therefore, to leave them as they are in the original and to trust the visual memory of the reader to keep them in context as he goes along—as doubtless he often does with French, German, and Scandinavian names.

For those, however, who would not be fobbed off, here are a few rules of thumb: the Serbo-Croatian *a* is sounded as in f*a*ther (never as in fare, fall, fan). *E* as in th*e*re (not here, or herd). *I* as in s*ee*k (not ice, or bird). *O* as in m*o*re (not move, mode, or Mom). *U* as in tr*u*e (not tune, or thumb). *C* is always ts, as in ba*ts*. *Č* is always the hard ch, as in *ch*in. *Ć* is a softer ch, as in Italian *ciao*. *Dj* is the English j, as in *j*ar. *Dž* is similar but harder, as in bu*dg*e. *J* is always soft, the

v

English y, as in boy. *R* is rolled, often vowelized, as in Serbo-Croatian *mrk*, gloomy (similar to English mu*r*ky). *Š* is always sh, as in *sh*ine. *Ž* is always zh, as in seizure.

A few Turkisms—impossible of translation—have been retained in the text, and the reader, hopefully, will take them in his stride. Most are Bosnian usage of Turkish titles of rank, profession, landowning status, and traditional honorifics—as follows:

Aga: military title, used loosely of any higher rank. *Beg:* meaning one of the landed gentry. *Divan:* council or council chamber, also an audience or reception. *Effendi:* learned sir, your honor, sir. *Hodja:* muezzin. *Kavass:* Syce, groom, attendant. *Rayah:* subject Christian populace of Bosnia; sometimes meaning poor country folk, or town riff-raff.

Contents

THE PASHA'S CONCUBINE

AND OTHER TALES

THE BRIDGE ON
THE ŽEPA

In the fourth year of his term as Grand Vizier, Yusuf committed a political indiscretion and, falling victim to a dangerous intrigue, unexpectedly fell into disfavor. The struggle lasted a whole winter and spring. It was a wicked and cold spring, which refused to let the summer begin. But in May, Yusuf emerged from banishment as victor. And so life went on as before, glorious, peaceful, and undisturbed. But from those winter months, when the margin between life and death, glory and ruin, amounted to little more than the sharp edge of a knife, there remained in the victorious Vizier a sense of something fretful and subdued. It was something that could not be expressed, something that men of experience who have suffered harbor inside them like a hidden treasure, and which unconsciously, and only at times, is reflected in a look, a movement, or in speech.

While he had lived in confinement, in solitude and in disgrace, the Vizier's memories of his origins and of his old country had grown more vivid, for disappointment and pain

3

always turn the mind back to the past. He recalled his mother and his father. (They had both died while he was still a modest assistant to the Sultan's Master of the Horse; he had since ordered their graves to be edged with stone coping and marked by white tombstones.) He recalled Bosnia and the village of Žepa, from which he had been taken when he was nine.

It was pleasant in his unhappiness to think of that distant country and the scattered village, where tales of his success and glory in Istanbul were told in every house, and where nobody knew or even suspected the reverse side of the medal of glory, or the price at which success was to be attained.

That very summer he had had an opportunity to talk to people coming from Bosnia. He questioned them, and they told him what they knew. After many rebellions and wars, the country had been convulsed by riots, scarcity, starvation, and all kinds of epidemics. He ordered substantial help for all his relatives who were still at Žepa, and at the same time instructed the officials to find out what was most needed in the way of building work. He was told that the family Šetkić still had four houses and were the wealthiest in the village, but that both the village and the surrounding countryside had become impoverished, that the mosque had fallen into disrepair and become damaged by fire, and that the wells had gone dry; but their worst predicament was that there was no bridge over the river Žepa. The village stands on a hill right above the confluence of the Žepa and the Drina, and the only way of getting to Višegrad was over the Žepa, about fifty yards above the confluence. No matter what kind of plank bridge they threw across, it was always swept away by the waters; for either the Žepa would rise quickly and unexpectedly, as mountain streams are wont to do, and weaken the bridge and sweep away the logs, or else it was the Drina that swelled suddenly and rushed into the channel of the Žepa and backed its flow, so

4

that its level rose and bore the bridge away as if it had never been. Then again, in the winter the planks became iced and slippery, so that both men and beasts of burden came to grief. Thus, were anybody to build them a bridge, he would do them the greatest service.

The Vizier gave six rugs for the mosque and as much money as was needed to build a fountain with three spouts in front of it. At the same time he decided to build the villagers a bridge.

In Istanbul at that time there lived an Italian master builder who had put up several bridges near the city, and so had made a name for himself. He was now engaged by the Vizier's treasurer and sent to Bosnia with two men from the Court.

They arrived at Višegrad before the last snows of winter had melted. For several days afterwards the astonished people of Višegrad watched the master builder as, stooping and gray-haired but with a pink and youthful face, he inspected the great stone bridge there, knocking on it, crumbling the joints' mortar between his fingers and tasting it on his tongue, measuring the arches with his steps. Then he went to spend a few days at Bania, at the quarry from which the stone for the Višegrad bridge had come. He hired day laborers to clear out the quarry, which had become partially filled with earth and overgrown with bushes and hemlock saplings. They went on digging until they found a wide, deep vein of stone that was harder and whiter than that which had been used for the Višegrad bridge. Then the master builder walked down the bank of the Drina as far as the Žepa and determined the spot where the stone would be ferried across the river. Whereupon one of the Vizier's men went back to Istanbul with an estimate and plans.

The Italian remained behind to await their return, but he did not want to stay either at Višegrad or in any of the Christian houses overlooking the Žepa. He built himself a log cabin on a rise in the triangle between the Drina and the Žepa—the remaining Vizier's man and a Višegrad clerk acting as his interpreters—and there he lodged. He cooked for himself, buying eggs, cream, onions, and dried fruit from the peasants. He never once bought meat, it was said. All day long he dressed sample blocks of stone, made drawings, experimented with various kinds of rock, and studied the course and the currents of the Žepa.

In the meantime, the other official returned from Istanbul with the Vizier's approval and one third of the necessary funds.

Work on the bridge started. The people's wonder at the unusual spectacle knew no bounds. What was happening before their eyes in no way resembled a bridge. The men sank massive pine trunks diagonally across the Žepa, and between them a double row of piling, plaited together with brushwood and reinforced with clay, so that the whole thing looked like a trench. In this way the river was diverted and one half of the river bed was drained. But one day, just when this work was completed, there was a cloudburst somewhere in the mountains and in no time at all the Žepa changed color and rose. That same night it broke the middle of the newly finished dam. By dawn the following morning the water had receded, but the wattle was broken through, the piles torn up, and the beams knocked askew. Among the workers and the people it was whispered that the Žepa did not want a bridge thrown over itself. But three days later the master builder ordered new piles to be driven in, this time deeper, and the remaining beams to be repaired and secured. Once more the rocky bottom of the river bed echoed to the din of the mallets and workmen's cries and rhythmical blows.

Only when everything had been set and made ready, and the stone from Bania delivered, did the stone cutters and masons arrive—men from Herzegovina and Dalmatia. They built themselves wooden huts, in front of which they chipped away at the stone, coated with dust and as white as millers. The master builder went from one to another, bent down over them, constantly checking their work with a drafting triangle of yellow tin and a lead plumb bob on a green thread. When the steep and rocky banks had been cut through on both sides, the money suddenly ran out. The workmen began to grumble and rumor arose among the local people that nothing would come of this bridge. Some men who had just arrived from Istanbul reported having heard that the Vizier had had a change of heart. No one knew what was the matter with him, whether he was ill or beset by other troubles, but he was becoming more and more inaccessible and was neglecting or abandoning public works which he had begun in Istanbul itself. Yet a few days later one of the Vizier's men arrived with the remainder of the money, and the work went on.

A fortnight before St. Demetrius' Day, the people crossing the Žepa by the plank bridge a little distance above the new works noticed for the first time a white, smooth wall of hewn stone, decked with scaffolding like a spider's web, and jutting out of the dark-gray slate on both banks of the river. From then on it grew every day. Before long, however, the first frosts began, and work was suspended. The masons went home for the winter, while the master builder ensconced himself in his log cabin, from which he hardly ever emerged. All day long he pored over his plans and expense ledgers, and went out from time to time to inspect the bridge works. When, just before the spring, the river ice began to crack, he was often seen puttering around the scaffolding and the dams, a worried look on his face. Sometimes he would even do this at night, with a torch in his hand.

Just before St. George's Day, the masons returned and work was resumed. And exactly at midsummer the bridge was

7

finished. Gaily the workers took down the scaffolding, and from behind the maze of beams and boards there appeared a white and slender bridge, spanning the two rocky banks in a single soaring arch.

Few things would have been harder to imagine than such a wonderful structure in so ravaged and bleak a place. It seemed as if the two banks had each spurted a foaming jet of water toward one another, and these had collided, formed an arch, and remained thus for a moment, hovering above the chasm. Through the arch, at the farthest point of vision, one could see a small blue stretch of the Drina, and deep down beneath it was the gurgling Žepa, now tamed and froth-speckled. For a long time one's eyes could not get used to the slender and beautifully conceived line of that arch, which looked as if in its flight it had momentarily got caught on that prickly and harsh landscape full of bramble and hemlock, and that at the first opportunity it would take off again and disappear.

Country folk from the nearby villages flocked to see the bridge. Townspeople from Višegrad and Rogatica also came to admire it, regretting that it had been built in such a stony wilderness instead of in their own market town.

"The thing to do is to give birth to a Vizier," answered the people of Žepa as they passed their hands over the bridge parapet, which was straight and fine-edged as if carved from cheese, not hewn from stone.

Even as the first travelers, halting in wonder, were already crossing the bridge, the master builder paid off his men, packed and loaded his cases of tools and paper, and set off for Istanbul together with the Vizier's two men.

Tales about him now spread through town and village. Selim the Gypsy, who had carried the Italian's purchases on his horse from Višegrad, and was the only one ever to have entered the log cabin, now took his ease in the coffeehouses and recounted, Lord knew how many times, all he knew about the stranger.

"Truly, he is not a man like other men. This past winter, when there was no work, I went away for ten-fifteen days. But when I came back everything was in a mess, just as I'd left it. There he was, sitting in the freezing cabin, with a bearskin cap on his head and wrapped down to his waist—only the hands showed through, all blue from cold. He kept scraping those stones and writing. Scraping and writing, just like that. I'd unload the horse and he'd look at me with those green eyes of his, his eyebrows thick and dark, and you'd think he was about to snap my head off. But not a word, not a peep out of him. Never have I seen the likes of it. Ey, my lads, how that man worked his fingers to the bone during those eighteen months, and when it was all over, we took him across the ferry and off he went to Istanbul on that horse of his. You'd expect him to turn around just once and look at the bridge—but no, not him!"

The shopkeepers plied him with more questions about the master builder and the life he had led, and their wonder grew and they could not forgive themselves for not having paid more attention to him when he was still to be seen in the streets and alleys of Višegrad.

Meanwhile the master builder was riding home, and he was but two days' journey from Istanbul when he fell ill of the plague. He arrived in the city in high fever, barely holding on to the saddle. He went straight to the hospital of the Italian Franciscans. The following day, at the same hour, he breathed his last in the arms of a monk.

The very next morning the Vizier was told about the death of the master builder, and given the remaining accounts and sketches of the bridge. The builder had received only a quarter of his pay. He had left neither debts nor ready money, neither a will nor any heirs. After a long deliberation, the

Vizier ordered that one third of the pay still due to him should be given to the hospital and the other two thirds used as an endowment for the orphans' bread and soup.

Just as he was issuing these instructions—it was a fine morning in late summer—they brought him a petition from a young and learned teacher of the Koran who was Bosnian by birth, and author of some polished verses, whom the Vizier had patronized and helped on past occasions. He had heard—the letter said—of the bridge which the Vizier had built in Bosnia, and hoped that it, like all other public works, would bear an inscription making known when and on whose orders it had been built. As always, he offered his services to the Vizier and would deem it an honor if the attached inscription, which he had composed with great care, were accepted. On a separate parchment was the chronogram, in an exquisite calligraphic hand, with a red and gold initial.

> *When Noble Skill joined hands*
> *With Wise Administration,*
> *This wonderous bridge was born,*
> *A joy to men, and Yusuf's glory*
> *In both worlds.*

Underneath was the Vizier's oval seal, divided into two unequal sections; the larger bore the words *Yusuf Ibrahim, true servant of Allah,* and the smaller his personal motto: *In Silence is Safety.*

The Vizier sat a long time over this petition, his hands wide apart, one palm resting on the verse inscription, the other on the sketches and expense accounts of the master builder. Lately, he had been wont to spend more and more time deliberating over petitions and official documents.

This past summer it had been two years since his fall and banishment. At first, on his return to power, he had noticed no change in himself. He was at that age—the best of all—when a man knows and feels the full value of life; he had vanquished his opponents and was more powerful than ever before; the depth of his recent fall enabled him to measure the true height of his power. Yet, as the months went by, instead of forgetting his confinement he was nagged more and more by the memory of it. Even when at times he managed to shut his mind to such thoughts, he was powerless to prevent dreams. And his dreams were beginning to be haunted by the specter of prison, and from those nightmares the specter passed, like a nameless dread, into his waking hours, poisoning his days.

He became more sensitive to the objects around him. Certain things that he had never before noticed now began to offend him. He ordered all brocade to be removed from the Palace and replaced it by a light-colored homespun cloth that was smooth and soft yet did not rustle under the touch. He developed something akin to hatred for mother-of-pearl, since in his thoughts it was connected with a certain chill wilderness and his own present isolation. At the mere touch, or even the mere sight of it, his teeth would chatter and his skin would break out in goose pimples. All furnishings and weapons that contained any mother-of-pearl were removed from his quarters.

He was beginning to view most things with a concealed but profound distrust. Somewhere in the back of his mind there was lodged the thought: Every human act and word *can* bring evil. And this *possibility* was now found to be lurking in almost everything he heard, saw, uttered, or thought. The victorious Vizier had become fearful of life. Thus, without even being aware of it, he was entering that state which is the first phase of dying, when a man begins to be more interested in the shadows thrown by things than in the things themselves.

This evil rankled and seethed within him, and there was no person to whom he could even think of admitting or confiding it. And when, in the end, the evil had finally done its work and broken to the surface, no one would be likely to recognize it anyway; people would simply say: Death. For people have no inkling of how many of the great and powerful ones of this world die in such a fashion within themselves, silently and imperceptibly, yet rapidly.

That morning, too, the Vizier was tired from lack of sleep, but was calm and collected. His eyelids were heavy and his cheeks all but frozen in the radiance of the morning. He thought of the foreign master builder who had died, and of the orphans who would feed on his earnings. He thought of the distant, mountainous, gloomy land of Bosnia (he could never think of Bosnia without experiencing a sense of gloom!) which even the light of Islam had only partially succeeded in illuminating, and where life, devoid of finer urbanities and grace, was poor, brutish, and hard. How many such regions were there in this world of Allah? How many torrential streams without a bridge or ford? How many places without drinking water? How many mosques without decoration and beauty?

In his mind the earth stretched on and on, full of all manner of needs, poverty, and fear in all shapes and forms.

The sun shone brightly on the tiny green tiles of the garden pavilion. The Vizier looked down on the teacher's verse inscription, raised his hand slowly, and then crossed it out twice. He waited an instant, then struck out the upper half of the seal bearing his name. There remained only the motto: *In Silence is Safety*. He stood for some minutes gazing down on this, then raised his hand once more and crossed that out, too.

That was how the bridge came to have no name and no inscription.

But over in Bosnia, the bridge sparkled in the sun and glimmered in the light of the new moon, and men and cattle passed back and forth over it. Little by little, the crater of ravished soil and scattered objects that marks a new structure vanished without a trace. The people carried off, and the waters swept away, the broken piles, the remnants of the scaffolding and the rubble of the works, and the rains washed clean the last vestige of the work of stone cutters. But still the landscape could not fit itself to the bridge, nor the bridge to the landscape. Seen from the side, the white span of its bold arch always looked isolated and lonely and took the traveler by surprise like a strange thought gone astray and caught among crags in the wilderness.

The teller of this tale was the first to think of looking into the origins of the bridge. This happened one evening when he was returning from the mountains and, feeling weary, had sat down beside the stone parapet of the bridge. It was that time of summer when the days were scorching but the nights had a nip to them. As he leaned against the stonework, he noticed that it was still warm from the day's heat. He perspired, yet a cool breeze was blowing in off the Drina; pleasant and somehow unexpected was the touch of that warm hewn stone. There was an instant rapport between them. He then decided to write its story.

THE JOURNEY OF
ALI DJERZELEZ

Djerzelez at the Khan

The government way station at Višegrad, which lay adjacent
to the customhouse, gradually filled up with travelers. The
small tributaries of the river Drina had swelled, overflowed
their banks, and carried away the wooden bridge on the road
to Priboj. The highway had been washed away in several
places. Thus, while the bridge was being repaired by carpen-
ters, and the roads by workmen and prisoners condemned to
hard labor, all the travelers coming from Sarajevo and going
east were obliged to stop at the khan by the customhouse and
wait till the bridge was restored and the highway made passa-
ble again.

The huge khan, built in a square shape, was humming like
a beehive. The rooms were narrow and strung along the four
sides of the building like cells of a honeycomb, and all were
connected in front by a shaky wooden balcony that creaked
and echoed without letup to the footfalls of the visitors. The
whole place reeked of horse manure and roasting mutton, since
in the open courtyard down below men had been slaughtering

rams all day long and nailing the hides to the walls to dry.

The people who interrupted their journey here at the khan were of all kinds. There was Suli-aga Dizdar, accompanied by three tax collectors, on an official trip. Two Franciscans from Kreševo, on their way to Istanbul to lodge some complaint or other. A Greek Orthodox monk. Three Venetians from Sarajevo, with a beautiful young woman. Rumor had it that the latter were delegates from Venice taking the land route to the Porte; they had a *laisser-passer* from the Vizier in Sarajevo and a constable to assist them. Their manner was reserved and they looked distinguished, though there was a troubling air of mystery about them. Then, there was a Serbian merchant from Pljevlje with his son, a tall, slight young man with unnaturally flushed cheeks. A couple of merchants from Livno and their drover; some beggars from the lowlands near the Sava River; a pale-faced cadet from the military academy at Istanbul, with his uncle; three Albanian vendors of sweetmeats; a knife peddler from Foča; a degenerate who claimed he was a hodja from Bihać but who apparently roamed the world wherever his dark and morbid instincts took him; an Arab who sold medicines and prescriptions, coral ornaments and rings on which he engraved initials to order; and a whole crowd of drovers, horse traders and petty merchants, as well as Gypsies.

Besides these foreigners, there were also the local youths, idle and well-to-do Muslims who lounged around the coffee room all day long. And throughout the day one could hear laughter and the clapping of hands, sounds of a flute or a string instrument, the rattle of dice in a game called *šešbeš*, the yelling and shrilling of wanton folk who had nothing to do. The Franciscans never even came out of their room, while the Venetians emerged only for brief strolls, and all three of them together.

Among the last to arrive was Djerzelez. He was heralded

by his own voice, singing. Mounted on a white horse with bloodshot eyes, he rode up the level meadow in front of the khan; red tassels hung from the horse's forelock and bounced over his eyes, and the long sleeves of Djerzelez, embroidered with a thread of pure gold, flapped and glittered in the wind. His arrival was greeted by a silence heavy with awe and respect: he brought with him the fame of many battles and of a strength that inspired fear. They had all heard of him, although very few had actually seen him for he had spent his youth riding and fighting between Travnik and Istanbul.

A crowd of local people and foreigners quickly gathered at the courtyard gate. The servants ran up to hold his horse. As he dismounted and walked through the gate, it was noticed that he was was unusually small and squat and that he moved slowly and with a waddle, like a man not used to walking. His arms were disproportionately long.

He barked a greeting—*Merhaba!*—through the side of his mouth and entered the coffee room. Now that he had climbed down from his horse, as from some pedestal, the onlookers began to lose their awe and, recovering their sense of equality, attempted to engage him in conversation. He loved to talk, and now and then slipped into Albanian, for he had roamed around Skoplje and Peč for many years. He was not a smooth talker, however, and often paused for want of a word, as men of action are apt to, and would then spread his long arms and roll his pitch-black eyes in which, as in a rabbit, the pupils were indistinguishable from the rest of the eyeball.

In a few days, the forbidding magic that surrounded his name was completely dispelled; one by one the khan guests approached him with an unconscious desire to assert their equality with him, or even make themselves superior in some way. And Djerzelez drank with them, shared his meals, sang and gambled.

One morning soon after his arrival, he saw the Venetian

woman as she climbed to her quarters with her escort. He cleared his throat and slapped his knee hard, then shouted twice in her direction:

"Lo and behold! Lo and behold!"

He seemed to take fire. The mere thought of those tender limbs crushed under his fingers made him prance; he felt something akin to pain at all that softness and beauty so close at hand. He went into raptures and, of course, became ridiculous. The townspeople and loafers at once took advantage of this weakness of his. They began to ply him with advice, urging him to act, then warning against it and teasing him, and he countered all of it by spreading his arms beatifically and rolling his eyes.

Meanwhile, there arrived from Rogatica a certain Bogdan Cincarin, a singer well known through half of Bosnia. The minute he started singing, he delighted and captivated the whole guesthouse. Even the friars listened behind their closed doors. Djerzelez lost his head and all his restraints; breaking out in a sweat, he loosened his tunic and waist belt and sat among the local lads and khan guests, with cheese and brandy in front of him. While the others came and went, taking their turns, he kept drinking, calling for more brandy, and singing in his deep, heavy and off-key voice. The pranksters now made fun of him without the slightest fear or concern. Bogdan Cincarin, a young man but already gray-haired, threw his head back (his upper lip trembled slightly) and sang away. To Djerzelez it seemed as if the singer were tugging at his soul, and that at any moment now he would either burst from his own agonizing strength or else breathe his last in a deep faint. The knife peddler from Foča sat beside him and ragged him so much that they all guffawed, but Djerzelez only looked at him with glazed, rapturous eyes, then threw his arms about him and kissed him on the shoulder, while the former kept filling his head with ideas about the infidel woman. Suddenly

18

Djerzelez arose. He had a good mind to go for her, to snatch her away and seat her by his side, and the khan keeper already thought he had a scandal on his hands. But the man from Foča held Djerzelez back with a roguish, superior smile.

"Where are you going? She's not a barmaid from Metaljka—and no whore from Sarajevo either! She's a lady, my friend!"

Djerzelez sat down again, docile as a child, and went on drinking, smoking, singing and paying, until even the boy who served them made faces over his head.

Two whole days Djerzelez caroused with his friends and called loudly to the Venetian woman, sighing and telling everyone about his love, mumbling, thick-tongued, ludicrous; men would tap him on the shoulder and lie that she had sent him this or that message, and he would get up forthwith to go upstairs and fetch her, until the man from Foča, who by then had him completely under his thumb, would stop him and pull him down again, making an ass of him with all kinds of outrageous advice, so that the whole guesthouse would rock with mirth.

On the third day, about lunchtime, Djerzelez and the Foča peddler squabbled for no apparent reason, as men in their cups and with nothing to do are wont to. The peddler put on an air of mock seriousness.

"And why, may I ask, can't *I* have her?"

"No! By God, no!" yelled Djerzelez, and his face lighted up with rapture now that someone had challenged his claim and he could fight for the woman.

"By Allah, the one who gets to her first is the one she'll take," suggested one of the onlookers.

"Not if you had wings you couldn't! Not if you had wings!" Djerzelez retorted in a hoarse shout, glaring into the man's eyes and making his point more with his hands than his words.

"You'd better make a race for it. We'll put an apple some distance away, and the one who gets to it first gets the girl." This from a poker-faced stranger from Mostar, who was in cahoots with the Foča man and wanted to play the new joke.

Djerzelez at once leaped to his feet, swung his arms around him, ready to fight, race, or throw stones, not knowing any more what he was doing, or to what purpose, yet beside himself with happiness that the moment had come when strength would have the last word.

They went out to the flat field in front of the khan. The men hung a big red apple from the pole of a swing, drew a string in front of the two runners, and the rest of the crowd gathered around them, nudging each other and grinning openly. Some stayed close to the competitors, while others preferred to watch from a distance. The man from Foča rolled up his sleeves, causing everyone around him to burst out laughing, while Djerzelez loosened his clothes and tied a large kerchief around his head, making himself appear even squatter and smaller. Several men laid their bets on Djerzelez, others on the man from Foča. The stranger from Mostar gave a signal; the string snapped, and both runners surged forward.

Djerzelez flew like a man on wings, but the man from Foča, after the first ten paces or so, stopped in his tracks and simply stamped his feet, like a person egging a child on by pretending to race. He clapped his hands, and the spectators doubled with laughter. There was applause, yelling, glee.

"Hey, Djerzelez!"

"That's it, jackass!"

"Run, Djerzelez! Run, falcon!"

"Well done, ginger!"

Djerzelez raced on, looking shorter and shorter, as if his legs were being swallowed up by his body. He was borne along by a furious burst of strength and exhilarated by his own heady exertion, by the soft turf and the fresh stream of air. He

seemed to hear behind him the steady thudding of his opponent, and this spurred him and drove him on. When he
reached the swing, he snatched at the apple, but the pranksters
had deliberately hung it too high, so that he missed it at the
first try and had to leap up and pull it down together with its
thread.

Bedlam broke out among the onlookers. Some had to wipe
their tears, while others fell on the grass and just rolled helplessly. The fat beggar from Posavina laced his fingers around
his belly and guffawed. Even the dried-up official, Suli-aga
Dizdar, paused at the khan entrance and hee-heed through his
missing teeth.

For a moment Djerzelez stood there with the apple in his
hand, then turned around, and seeing that the man from Foča
was not there, screwed his eyes in the direction of the crowd.
They could not make out the expression on his face, but his
pose was ominous. In a thrice they all realized they'd gone too
far. The ground separating them seemed to reinvest him with
all the qualities he had lost when he was in their midst. Now
that he was some three hundred paces away and waddling back
toward them, sullen and heavy, the fast-narrowing space
brought them abruptly to their senses; even the most noncha-
lant bystander now felt ill at ease. There was no doubt any
more that he was angry and plotting something. The first to
vanish was the man from Mostar, and then, one by one, the
others began to retreat to their rooms. A few stole behind the
khan and lost themselves in the hazelwood.

By the time Djerzelez had returned, not a living soul was
left on the meadow. A kerchief shone white on the grass,
abandoned there in haste and fear. This emptiness made his
fury complete.

Panting and disheveled, still somewhat bewildered, he
scowled at the gate through which the men had disappeared. It
was as if under that thick, hard skull the first light of compre-

hension was beginning to glimmer: that someone here was being made a fool of and that the whole thing was an idle practical joke. The thought sent a fire racing through his veins and limbs. He felt a savage and fierce desire for the infidel girl—to see her, possess her, to settle this thing once and for all, or else to break and smash everything around him. And as he walked through the gate, pitching wearily from hip to hip and swinging his arms, he had a sudden glimpse, before his misted eyes, of a wide green skirt and a white veil at the top of the stairway. Bare-chested and wrought up as he was, he just had time to let out a groan and stretch his arms toward her, as if about to run up in a couple of leaps, when the green dress swayed lightly and vanished behind the door of her room, followed by a loud click.

Djezelez dropped his hands to his sides, inclined his head a little and, sweating profusely and exuding male force, stood still for a minute, sullen as a cloud and powerful as the earth itself. He didn't know what to do next, or whom to strike. Then he wheeled around, and the khan broke into a scramble and pandemonium. One child, not knowing what was afoot, had not managed to hide himself, and now he dropped the copper vessel he was holding and crawled under the nearest sofa, his bare and cracked feet showing from underneath. The horses neighed in their stables, and throughout the rest of the khan there wasn't even a cat to be seen; every living creature had taken cover and hushed up in fear. The stillness exasperated and inflamed Djerzelez even more. He banged on several doors, but all were padlocked, as if under a curse.

Unaware in his rage of what he was about, he began to saddle his horse and pack his saddlebags. Glancing around constantly to see if anyone was there, he got ready, and then, tugging viciously at the rein, led his jumpy white horse to the gate and mounted him from the stump that served as a butcher block. The animal bore him on; the metal flask and the strapped weapons gave out a clinking sound; and at once his rage began to abate. He spat, rode out of the courtyard and, as in a dream, moved down the meadow that a little while ago he had crossed at a run. After he had gone a short distance, he turned and saw, quite unwittingly, the recessed window of the young woman on the forward corner of the khan. Looking at those lowered shutters, enigmatic as a woman's gaze and cold as the human heart, he felt a powerful new surge of the all but forgotten wrath and misery; and seized by a mad impulse to strike and insult someone, anyone, it didn't matter whom, he raised his hairy fist at the window and shook it, then flipped his fingers as if hurling a spell.

"Bitch! Bitch!"

His voice was hoarse with rage.

Then he rode off at a gallop, striking out over soft ground and over short cuts; he would see what kind of ravaged highways and swamped bridges were there to stop him! Let him just see them!

The khan remained behind him, still voiceless with terror.

Djerzelez on the Road

At Uvac, Djerzelez swam the river and then spurred the horse so hard that by the time he got to Priboj every available syce and groom had to get busy; they put fresh manure compresses on the animal's hooves and bathed them with the urine of a male child, while Djerzelez said nothing and duly bent down to inspect the hooves, not daring to meet the horse's eyes. He offered old Turkish gold pieces to anyone who would heal the animal and make him gallop again as of old.

He was silent and fidgety, and, a rare thing with him, he could not eat. Since he had come from Višegrad, he had lost all appetite. He would sit down at the table and smoke himself into a nausea, but the very thought of food filled him with loathing.

On the second evening, he came out of the coffeehouse, looked over his horse and was pleased to see that he was improving. Taking a side path, he set out on foot toward the main road. It was a dark, cold night with a great many stars. He wandered around for a long time and, on his way back to the khan, overtook a monk on the road. The monk was bent over, or else affected the stoop in order to look older.

"Are you from these parts?"

"No, bey. Just spending the night," replied the monk softly, disconcerted to be meeting with so burly a Turk so late at night.

Djerzelez walked ahead of him, a little astonished to find himself talking to a monk.

"Tell me, priest, did you ever come across such a thing in your books, whether in your law it's a sin for a girl of your faith to look at a—Turk?"

The monk became nervous and began to squirm and hedge, until at length, perhaps sensing that the Turk was in some kind of a dilemma, he grew a little bolder and shrewdly wound up with a parable of how the good Lord had created all kinds of beautifully colored flowers, just as He did people of various faiths. Had He wanted us to be all of one faith, He would have, almighty that He was, done just that. But having settled the matter in this fashion, He now expects every man to pray to God according to his law, to follow and observe his own faith.

As always when he listened to someone else, Djerzelez had the impression that the man had spoken the truth. He continued walking in irritable silence, his mind in a haze. Suddenly he turned and faced the monk, as if to demand an explanation of something for which the man was personally responsible.

"Tell me, priest, why don't your women cover themselves?"

"Well, now—one of those customs, I suppose. Search me! Silly women's business. That's a thing we monks don't know anything about. We've no women, so we don't know."

"Hm!"

He studied him another minute, then turned coldly and quickened his step. In the stillness, only the creaking of his leather bandoleer and gaiters could be heard. The monk shuffled after him in wonder. When they reached the khan, Djerzelez went up the steps, turning once more.

"Good night!"

"May God help you, bey effendi! Good luck!" the monk called back, hastening on his way.

Early next morning, Djerzelez was roused by voices, laughter and singing. It was the Gypsy women. They were washing themselves by the water mill, splashing and switching each other with willow cuttings. It was St. George's Day.

In the coffee room he found the two brothers Morić. They were sons of the old Morić from Sarajevo, who had been famed for his wealth and his piety, and for having died while on a pilgrimage to Mecca. They, on the other hand, were idlers and wastrels, given to bullying and violence, known far and wide for their excesses.

The younger one had gone to school in Istanbul, then ran away after his father's death and started a life of dissipation and vagabondage, together with his brother; but he always wore the white band of hajji around his fez. And despite all his appalling binges and vagrancy his face remained as it always was, hairless and rosy, with the pouting lips of a spoiled child, and only his eyes, immodest and green, seemed to age and wither under their puffy lids. The older brother was tall and pale-skinned, and had once been the handsomest lad in all Sarajevo; he had thick black mustaches and big dark eyes that were always liquid with a golden glow; except that now his face was turning lackluster and fey, as he was secretly wasting away from a loathsome disease, for which no one knew the cure save a barber from Bistrik who treated him with pills and medicinal incense but refused to reveal their ingredients to anyone. In recent months, however, the brothers had not dared return to Sarajevo, for they'd heard that, in answer to the many complaints about their harassment and rough play, Istanbul had sent the final answer: Arrest the Morić brothers and cut them down—and so now the constables and the Vizier's Albanians were looking for them. They had come to the end of their rope, anyway. They had sold all their tenant holdings and the only thing left to them was the great khan in the city of Sarajevo and the famed Morić homestead in Kovači. In that house lived their old mother and their only sister, a small, hunchbacked and sickly girl.

Now they inquired about each other's health (they were old acquaintances) and ordered drinks. The brothers observed the change in Djerzelez and began to ask questions, some of them caustic in tone.

"What is it, why so glum? By God, you're getting old, Djerzelez!"

"Darinka from Pljevlje sends her greetings. Since you went away, she sleeps alone, she says."

Djerzelez said nothing. The older Morić spoke in the cheerless and almost kindly tone of a tramp who is past all hope; his manner toward him was amiable and familiar. The younger brother just smiled.

"You look as if you just came out of a woman's bed." The elder Morić laughed, thinly and briefly.

Djerzelez looked at them and kept quiet. Inside him all was calm, the pain had faded and the anger cooled down; the only thing he was still conscious of was a heaviness in his heart. He watched them and couldn't help feeling they were chil-

26

dren, ignorant and silly; to him, anyone was a child who had not seen the slender Venetian in her wide skirt of green velvet and her small head above the fur collar. He kept silent. They suggested that he go to see the fair in the afternoon, but he declined. It was only after lunch, when he began to feel the return of boredom, that he gave in and agreed.

At the top of a hillock, there was a small level plateau ringed by great and sparse pines, and open toward the west. Here the Gypsies held their fair. Fires were burning. Drums were beating, flutes and string instruments playing; the round dance—the kolo—never stopped. The gaudy colors of Gypsy skirts flashed brightly in the sunlight of the clear day; the red predominated. There was much drinking, eating, chasing, laughter, rolling on the grass, and singing without letup.

Djerzelez, the Morić brothers, and some lads from Priboj sat by the fire. They drank plum brandy. At first Djerzelez found the brandy sour; but they all pressed the jug on him, and the day was warm and clear, and so he drank; and whenever he tilted his glass up and drained it, he would see the tips of the dark pines swaying in the spring sky.

Presently, just as a local grocer addressed him—"The minute I heard you'd arrived, I closed the store. I'm going to see him, I said, and so—" he was interrupted by hand clapping and laughter. The music grew ragged and fitful: Zemka had climbed into the swing.

She was a woman thrice-divorced, with green-gray eyes and a slender figure, and fairer than all the other Gypsies. They said that no one had ever gotten the better of her.

The swing was hung from a wild pear tree and it soared high, with Zemka in it, pushed from behind by young Gypsy girls; with her arms above her head, she clutched the ropes hard and kept swinging higher. Her eyes were closed and her face paled as she rose above the line of the hill and was silhouetted against the horizon; her loose Turkish pants billowed and wreathed themselves in a hundred folds, fluttering and sweeping the sky, Squatting low by the fire, Djerzelez followed her swings with his eyes, and each time she sailed up and became outlined almost horizontally against the sky and then tumbled steeply into the depths, he would experience a pang of sweet anxiety and a tingling dread, as though he himself were on the swing. He drank with more animation and zest.

Zemka did not stop; one could see that her breath came in short gasps and that she had grown quite wan, but she kept rising and rising and every time she reached the apex she would open her eyes and glance in pleasurable horror at the ploughed field down below and the river at the foot of the hill. At first everyone watched her in admiration, but after a while there was again laughter and drunken clamor. The Gypsies and the lads from Priboj began to shriek and call to her, but she heard nothing.

"Aha! Look this way, Zemka!"

"Don't. She'll fall, the poor girl!"

"If she does, it'll be a soft landing!"

"Here's a pillow!"

"Hahaha, haha-a-a!"

"Yee-hee! Swing, Zemka!"

But Zemka had wearied of it. The girls had stopped pushing her, her swings grew shorter, now it was just her own momentum that propelled her, but less and less, slower and slower, until her feet grazed the turf and she jumped down, rapt and smiling.

Djerzelez sat and watched, melting inwardly, opening his arms—good-by to reason! He was delighted and charmed by those shining pantaloons that fluttered like a flag and mingled with the pine crowns and the clear sky; it was as if his gloom had suddenly decided to transform itself into complete and wanton joy. He felt a fleeting regret and shame at having so soon abandoned his sorrow and the fierce resolution he'd made back on the road never again to have near him "anything female—not even a cat, not even a cat!" But at this point, after a lengthy whispered consultation, the Gypsy women sang out in unison:

Djerzelez fell ill, what a pity, what a pity!

There was a burst of wild laughter and shrieking, they all looked at him, but he no longer saw anyone. His eyes were aglow and his face shiny; he felt himself helpless and light as air, yet couldn't get up.

That song had been made up by the Gypsies of Srebrnica in the year when Djerzelez had spent the whole spring lying in bed, after someone had wounded him badly one Friday when he came to serenade Nuri-beg's daughter under her window. He no longer remembered that Friday or that window, nor the daughter of Nuri-beg, whom he had long since forgotten. The only thing he recalled was lying there wounded and weak; under his window the swollen brook hummed and splashed, on the hill St. George's fair was in full swing, and the Gypsy women were singing about him for the first time. The song spread from hill to hill, the whole valley of Srebrnica echoed and rang with singing and brooks, while he lay in bed, feeling so weak that he was unable to lift the ornamented lemonade pitcher to his lips without help. He remembered, remembered, but was unable to separate this feast from the one he had listened to when he was sick, and everything became mixed up, the singing and the music and the drink and the people of that time and of this, and across it all Zemka was floating in a wide, bold arc, while he followed her with his eyes and tingled all over—with a tingle that was now cold, now in his very loins.

In the last few days he had eaten almost nothing, and now the liquor rapidly went to his head. The sun had set. A cold wind came up, the pines rustled; the smoke from the fires changed to blue, the dusk grew thicker.

Djerzelez ordered the Gypsy fiddler to play close to his

head, on the treble string, and kept swiping at him every other moment and felt like beating him, then cursed his violin and the man who had made it, while the elder Morić grabbed his hand and tried to pacify him. Then he got up and wanted to catch Zemka by the hand. The Morić brothers held him back, laughing; and those lads from Priboj also grew bolder and laughed. There was a roar of merriment, and Djerzelez's tongue moved thickly.

"She's—my enemy."

He wrenched himself free, threw up his arms, and started in the direction of Zemka, who was standing among the Gypsies and crunching on a piece of red Albanian sweetmeat. He had loosened his belt, so that his baggy pants slid lower in accordion folds and his already short legs appeared even shorted and stumpier; the cherry-colored silken cord of his waistband had come undone and dragged after him, soaked with brandy and smudged with fire ash. His feet could barely support him, and he tottered and wove now left, now right. The Gypsy girls shrieked with glee, and their menfolk threw the last of their restraint to the winds. The music stopped.

"Get hold of that cord! Pull it!"

"Hold him up, earth!"

"Y'Allah!"

And the Gypsy small fry, who had clambered up into the pines, pelted him with dry cones from their hiding places. He came back, slumped down, tossed back another glass of brandy and sang out mightily.

Darkness fell. Little by little most of the crowd went away, but the Morić brothers and their companions were only beginning to get down to serious drinking, to reveling and horsing around with Djerzelez, who was straining his eyes through the darkness to catch a glimpse of Zemka's figure, while everything in front of him rocked and floated. The musicians wanted to go home; the Morićes kept them back, first with friendly appeals and then by force, cursing their Gypsy mothers, offering money and then beating them, one after another.

"It's late, honored agas. Let us go home!"

"Our homes are far. It's a dark night, we'll come to a bad end."

At that the younger Morić sprang up unexpectedly and his beardless face blanched, taking on the wry and vicious cast of a man who is ready for anything.

"I'm going to make light for you, damn your Gypsy souls!"

He rose and picked up a chunky billet of smoldering juniper; holding it away from his body, to escape the smoke and the spark showers, he set off slowly down the flat meadow. On the open western edge there was a haystack, secured by a trellis of cut branches and plucked and eaten away from the sides as high as the cattle had been able to reach. He found the stack in the semi-darkness, but the hay wouldn't catch fire for some minutes; only after he had broken some dry twigs from the fence and placed them underneath did the fire spread all around the stack, rising ever higher, until it spurted into a tall column of flame that billowed in the wind and looked like a fiery sail. The hay crackled and the sparks shot up in a swarm, bathing the pines and the meadow and the lingering group of men in a red glow. Most of them began to slink away, each for himself. The musicians were horrified.

"In God's name, aga, what did you do? The judge will hang us all!"

"The devil take you and the judge!"

"It's not you he'll be after, no—he'll be after us Gypsies. They'll say, look, the Gypsies set fire to the judge's hay."

Several town merchants who were present also became alarmed; drunk though they were, they could see: too much was too much! Only the two Morićes sat on, firing their small arms, sipping brandy and staring, with blinking eyes, into the flames.

Farther away, in the semi-darkness, Djerzelez was lunging after the last of the Gypsy women and trying to corner Zemka. He forced himself to run as fast as his legs would carry him and was already gaining on her when she suddenly wheeled left and vanished on the path that led down between the ploughed fields. Djerzelez had not expected so sudden a turn; heavy, rigid, and drunk as he was, having started running he could not stop. He went over the rounded edge of the slope and ran down the high steep bank toward the brook. At first he managed to stay on his feet, but as the incline grew steeper he lost his balance and tumbled like a log all the way down and into the brook. Feeling wet stones and silt under his hands, he began to pick himself up right away. The glare of the blaze was still in his eyes, but down here it was dark. He scooped some water and cooled his hands and forehead. He sat like this for a long while. The night was wearing on.

After a time he felt chilly and was seized by an unpleasant shiver; collecting himself, he resolved in his fuzzy head to drag himself out of the brook. He clambered up the slope, holding on to grass and bushes, using his knees, bearing more and more to the left where the bank was less steep; and all this he did as in a dream.

After a lengthy and strenuous effort, he found himself on the edge of the meadow, which for some time now had been utterly deserted. It was dark up there. He felt the even, hard ground underfoot and only then gave in to exhaustion. He dropped to his knees, broke his fall with his hands, and felt something warm and soft under him; he had landed on the spot where the haystack had burned down. Nausea stirred in his gorge. Under him, in the heap of black soot, a spark glowed here and there. One could hear the dogs snarling and gnawing at the leftover bones. From one of the pines, a cone tumbled down and rolled toward him. He grinned.

"Stop pelting me, Zemka, you wildcat—come 'ere!"

Try as he might, he could not collect himself. He remembered he'd wanted to fight someone; he wanted to ask what happened . . . The night was late, the sky overcast; and there wasn't a soul around him: there was no one to ask, no one to fight with.

Djerzelez in Sarajevo

Unhappy, famed, and an object of derision, Djerzelez traversed half the province in this fashion. About his adventures that summer very little was known; and he himself promptly forgot them. One heard only that he had committed many follies over the widow of a tradesman from Ušćup, and that he'd been fleeced by a Jewish woman who kept company with some musicians from Selanik.

On the eve of Ramadan he came to Sarajevo.

Three days before his arrival, the two brothers Morić had been executed above Kovači, on that wide crossroad that served as a haymarket. They had been caught at an inn on the road to Trnovo, and then paraded through the city. They walked in chains, with a jerky and sharp step, like some marching Albanians, surrounded by constables and the Vizier's guard. Behind them was a small cloud of dust. People turned to watch. As the procession made its way through the lower market, the crowd became abusive. Merchants scrambled down from their shop platforms and, wiggling their bare feet, looked for their clogs on the ground.

"Ha! Look at them!"

33

"Bandits!"

"Ax for the swine!"

Thus were they led out to the drill square at Tašlihan.

They were not executed by the riverbank, below the Latin Bridge, where the poor people were hanged and remained hanging for two days while the idle passers-by would twirl the rope and then let go of it, so that the corpse would spin for a long time like a top. They executed them quickly, and buried them right after dusk at Bakije. Their mother had collapsed and died, without a cry, when she saw from her window where they were being taken.

Their large house, with its myriad of windows that overlooked the city and the hill of Igman, remained dark and desolate. A single candle burned in one of the lower rooms. There, wasting away with consumption, lay the sister of the Morić brothers, her blond head on the hot pillows, her eyes fevered; she was listening to the whisper of her old nanny, Andja, who was secretly planning to have her christened when the moment came for her to die.

After the first autumnal rains and winds, the streets of Sarajevo were clean and sparkling with that gay brilliance of September that made the air pure and sharpened the contours of buildings, and brought with it the first russet patches on the foliage of the steep hillsides. Thistles floated on the air like fine silk.

It was the month of Ramadan. During the day everything was at a standstill, but at night the town rang with music, parties, and serenades in the residential quarters. The stores, bursting with fruit, and the coffeehouses, jammed with people, were open all night. Acrid and stifling smells of roast meat and burnt sugar wafted from the inns. Groups of women came and went, each preceded by a man carrying a big lantern. In the more distant gardens one heard the overripe fruit hit the ground with a soft thud, while the heavy pear trees sagged and drooped over the fences and, in their autumnal exuberance, fell on the heads of the passers-by.

Djerzelez went around, tanned and light-footed, brimming with the great strength that filled every man just before autumn. Every place beckoned; many joys were in store for him; the people and the days to come were full of promise. He was regularly invited to break fast with friends. And one early evening, on his way to the house of Bakarević, as he passed between Kršlo and Turbe, he paused in front of a house on a street corner. An old woman, a domestic with shriveled hands, was scouring the courtyard door with fine sand when one of the door wings half opened and a girl in light pantaloons and a red waistcoat appeared. After giving something to the maidservant, she remained for a minute bent over her in the open door.

As always when he came face to face with womanly beauty, he at once lost all sense of time and proportion, as well as all understanding of the reality that separated people one from another. Seeing her so young and full like a bunch of grapes, he never for an instant doubted his rights; all he had to do was stretch out his hand!

With his right eye screwed and his legs apart, he looked on for a second, then chuckled softly and, opening his arms and all but skipping, started toward her. The girl saw him in time, tugged the old woman's sleeve and pulled her into the dooway. The lithe and ample movements of the ripe lass filled Djerzelez's eyes with dazzle—then, there was a bang and he saw nothing more except, before his very nose, the broad white surface of the outer door, behind which the lock clicked and the stanchion made a grating sound. And there he stood. On his face remained a ghost of a smile, by then quite meaningless. He turned around.

"See!"

In helpless wonderment, he repeated the foolish word several times, like a man who had accidentally bumped into something. In the meantime, it had grown darker. Beyond Kršlo, shaggy and bow-legged mounted constables were scouring their burned pilaf cauldrons in readiness for the breaking of the fast. Djerzelez walked up the hill toward the Bakarević house.

During supper, he talked loudly to drown out his memory. He ate, but the food gave him no pleasure. After the meal, as they lay on their cushions smoking and breathing heavily from overeating, he was unable to contain himself and confided in young Bakarević, a slim lad with green eyes, rosy cheeks, and a scornful smile. He told him everything, and as he spoke he was surprised himself that the whole incident, when related to another person, was so petty and insignificant. And, quite unwittingly, he embroidered it and blew it up and wove in the memories of other encounters, and some of the words became lumps in his throat.

The following day, he rose after noon and at once went to that house near Turbe. It was a bright September day, but his bitterness of the day before lingered on. There was that same high white wall, the massive shut door, and the vines peering over the edge of the wall. Opposite the house was a halvah shop, from which someone called his name. The stranger turned out to be an old acquaintance, an Albanian, who greeted him with quiet respect. The son of a merchant from Prizren, he virtually spent his life on the road, ostensibly on "business" but in reality wearing himself out in the pursuit of a single overmastering passion. Now, having been alerted by his compatriots, the halvah makers, about the girl in the white house on the corner, he was wasting his days here and did not budge from the sweetshop, vainly spying on her.

After Djerzelez had entered, the halvah makers came out of the back room where they'd been kneading sugar and dough, and spread a mat on the sheeted floor for them to sit upon. Both Djerzelez and the Albanian tried to face the door and the street. Since they were not allowed to smoke and were dying of thirst, they spoke very little at first and kept glancing outside. Djerzelez was the first to start confiding, and he told the man "everything." When the Albanian heard it, he showed a pleasure that was untainted by any jealousy; his sallow, deeply lined cheeks flushed and his dull eyes brightened up. They began to chat like old friends. Inclining his pale face with its trimmed whiskers, the Albanian spoke slowly, pausing between words:

"She's like a pear, smooth and soft. Truly, an infidel woman is more luscious than any other kind."

They launched into a long and impassioned conversation, in Turkish and under their breath. The Albanian spoke hoarsely and had a smirk on his face that was like a constant, unpleasant shadow. From him Djerzelez learned all there was to know about the girl.

Her name was Katinka and she was the daughter of Andrew Poljaš. About her beauty songs were sung all over Bosnia, but to her it was a source of unhappiness. Because of it, men besieged her house, and she dared not go out. On holidays, she would be led at daybreak to the early mass in the Latin Quarter, shrouded in a big shawl like a Turkish woman so that no one should recognize her. She seldom ventured even into her own courtyard, for right next to it was the military academy, towering above their own house by a whole floor, and the cadets, young men poorly fed and much whipped, spent long hours on the windows, wan with desire, hungrily watching her as she moved around. And whenever she did go down, she would see behind a certain window the leering face of the mad Ali, a yellow-skinned half-wit with missing front teeth, who was a janitor in the academy.

It happened sometimes, after a stormy evening, when the soldiers and local lads had whooped and coughed pointedly under her windows and banged on the front door, that her mother would scold her, blameless and upright though she was, and wonder aloud whom she'd "taken after" that the whole town should lose its wits over her and their home invite so much harassment, and the girl would listen to her, buttoning the waistcoat over her breast, without a ray of comprehension in her big eyes. Often she wept all day long, not knowing what to do with her life and with her wicked beauty. She cursed herself and fretted, and struggled vainly in her great innocence to fathom that "brazen and Turkish thing" about her that turned the heads of men and made the soldiers and tramps rut and prowl around her house, and because of which she had to hide and feel ashamed, and her own folk had to live in fear. And she grew more lovely by the day.

From then on, Djerzelez spent all his afternoons in the halvah shop. Several local men began to congregate there too. The young Bakarević also came, and so did Derviš Beg from Širokača, red-haired and bloated with drink, and now, because of the fast, bad-tempered like a lynx to boot; and Avdik Krdžalija, frail, haggard, and keen like a tongue of fire, a notorious manslayer and lady-killer. Here in the twilit halvah shop where every single thing had tarnished and become sticky from sugar and sweet vapors, they would wait for the cannon shot that announced the breaking of the fast, and would carry on long conversations about women in order to forget their thirst and still their craving for tobacco. Djerzelez listened to them, while his parched mouth felt bitter and every muscle twitched with a kind of aching restlessness; he laughed and sometimes joined in their chatter, but was apt to maunder and could not articulate his feelings. And in all that time Katinka's house, with its padlocked door and empty windows, loomed silently before him.

One afternoon, out of sheer tedium and peevishness, they beat up a Christian bread vendor who had walked past the shop smoking.* Later, to amuse themselves, the men tried to stir up a quarrel between Djerzelez and the Albanian over the girl, but all in vain, for the latter was not to be budged out of his smiling self-possession and showed not a trace of jealousy. On one occasion, they bribed a child to go and shout around the corner in his thin voice:

"Look, Katinka! How are you, Katinka? Where on earth were you? We lost track of you!"

Hearing the voice, the Albanian blinked just once and without a sound, like a weasel, slid toward the door. Djerzelez was right on his heels. He caught up with him at the door and the two of them stumbled into the street at the same instant. Outside, there wasn't a living creature: only the stealthy white house in the languid early dusk before the hour of fast-breaking and the patter of feet on the cobblestones, made by the bribed child who was running away. They all had a good long laugh. Even Djerzelez grinned.

Young Bakarević suggested that they call Ivka Giguša, an old and well-known peddler from Bistrik, who had free access to every house because she sold cloth and shawls but whose stock in trade was not so much her merchandise as the vices and gullibility of her customers. She was a tall and burly old crone with round brown eyes, and as she talked with Djerzelez she constantly touched his knees. She promised to see how the land lay, but didn't hold out much hope, since the girl was kept in strict seclusion. Then she took her leave and went away.

The afternoon of the next day, Djerzelez found the Albanian and the old woman together; the former was shaking his head.

"Hey, she's gone! Gone!"

"Gone away, by God, effendi, two days ago," averred the old woman. "They took her away, they told me, before day-

---

* Since during the month of Ramadan the Muslims were not allowed to smoke, eat, or drink during the hours of daylight, the Christians were not supposed to smoke or eat in their presence either, so as not to tempt them.

break. And now, lovey, who knows where she is. They watched you fidgeting around here, the lot of you, so they said, 'Let's hide the girl.' That's how it is, lovey. And now, just you try and find her."

She raised and lowered her voice in turns, rocking her head as if over a loss. The Albanian stared in front of him, and it was hard to tell what he was thinking.

Blood rushed to Djerzelez's head. This thing so clear and unbelievable and so irrevocably true—namely, that for some days now the house had been empty of the girl with the pale, lean face, luxuriant hair, and ample, lush body (he saw all of her once again)—stirred and churned everything inside him. It was as if the halvah shop had shrunk and grown dark; the sight of the old crone and the Albanian became intolerable; he reeled around and blindly went out into the street. He all but burst from wrath. Not to be able to reach that infidel wench— never, never to come close to her! And not be able to kill anyone or smash anything! (A fresh wave of blood broke over him.) Or was this some kind of a game! Were they using him as a fool? What sort of joke was this again? What sort of women were these that you couldn't get hold of, as if they were God? And at the same time, he had a clear intuition that these threads were too subtle for his mind, that he was utterly incapable—how often had he felt this in his life!—of understanding people and their simplest actions, that it was his lot to renounce and withdraw, and remain alone with his ludicrous wrath and unwanted strength.

He walked listlessly, shattered. There wasn't a thought in his head, just one crimson cloud after another, swelling and evaporating. He never once looked back. The silent white house and the dark, low-slung halvah shop were left behind him.

In Kršlo the trumpeters were holding their exercises; the monotonous tune of a march was broken off every other moment and then joined again. The sun beat down mercilessly. He felt a sudden contraction in his throat and a fresh wave of sweat. He walked down the bank of the Miljacka; below him were osier bushes and green willows, still bearing the marks of spring floods. It was just as well that the road along the river was so even and long; if only it would never end! Then he wouldn't have to turn left or right. He slowed down only after reaching Hiseta, and then swerved, with an intention already crystallized in his mind, toward Lower Tabaki. There, he entered a small courtyard with a high door. The stairs, worn by many visits, groaned and creaked under him. In a small and neat room, lighted softly by curtains of delicate white silk, sat Yekaterina with her placid eyes and white arms, as if waiting.

She was the daughter of a doctor who had originally come from Odessa. They said he had been a Georgian, but, in fact, he had been a Russian; and no one ever knew why he had fled from there. He used to wear a fez, and they called him Veli-beg, but just before he died he sent for a priest and died as a Christian. Alone and impoverished, his daughter first wanted to return to Russia and enter a nunnery there, but a local constable, a Greek, persuaded her to remain; and when he ran out on her, she moved into one of those small houses that stretched all the way from Hiseta to Lower Tabaki, in which lived, under government supervision, single girls and often pairs of them—known by their first names throughout the town. She had bought the house with what was left of her father's money, and now lived in it together with an old maid-servant, who also had once been a "Hiseta girl." During the day she would sleep or sew pillowcases in the shade of her courtyard, and nights she received wealthier patrons. She was short, stocky, and taciturn. Djerzelez had known her for some time.

She was taken aback by being visited in broad daylight;

she rose to her feet, and he said quietly from the door:

"Yekaterina, here I am."

"Good, good—welcome," she said, meekly setting the bolsters for him.

He lowered himself onto a short cushion, while she remained on her feet, bending a little. Without another word, he began to unbuckle and loosen his clothing.

Afterwards he lay with his head on her lap, while she stroked his sunburned neck. He pressed his face into the thin fabric of her pantaloons; behind his lids there was a steady throbbing of red rings sent up by his hapless blood and a shimmer of countless memories, now balmed and distant.

And this hand he felt on his body, was it the hand of a woman? Of the Venetian wrapped in fur and velvet, whose body, slender and aristocratic, was past imagining? Of the Gypsy Zemka, the bare-faced and crafty yet also loving animal? Of the fat widow? Of the passionate and devious Jewess? Of Katinka, the fruit ripening in the shade? No, it was the hand of Yekaterina. Just Yekaterina's! Yekaterina was the only one a man reached in a straight line!

And once more he pondered a thought with which he'd gone to sleep a hundred times, an unclear thought, never pursued to the end, yet humiliating and depressing: Why was the path to a woman so tortuous and mystifying, and why was he, with all his fame and strength, unable to traverse it, when so many men worse than him did? So many—yet only he, in his vigorous and laughable prime, for ever held out his arms as in a dream. What was it women were after?

The tiny hand did not stop caressing him, deftly and expertly, up and down the spine. And the nightmare thought faded again, settling heavy and unsolved within him. He spoke absently, not moving.

"What a lot of the world I've seen, Yekaterina! How far I've wandered!"

42

He didn't know whether he meant this as a complaint or a boast; and he caught himself short. He lay quietly in the dreamy silence, in which the days and events of the past overlapped, blended, and made peace with each other. He forced himself to close his eyes, wishing to prolong this moment that was free of thought and desire, to rest up as well as he could, like a man for whom a day was only a short pause and who had to resume his journey.

CONFESSION

Having set out from his house on the mountain when it was still dark, Peter Ljoljo had been waiting since early morning in the monastery courtyard for Brother Superior to finish his breakfast and see him. The farmer refused to talk to anyone else. He tapped his worn, soft-soled shoes on the frozen ground, blew on his chilblained hands, and waited. It was quite some time before he was ushered in to Fra Julian, guardian of the monastery, a man of considerable book knowledge and a decent sort but lazy and a notorious sleepyhead. This weakness of Fra Julian's was so well known, so storied and incurable, that he was no longer required to mention it in the confessional. It was certain that he would take it with him to Judgment Day, for on this earth there was no judgment or cure for it.

At length the visitor stood before the guardian, kneading his red fez and his head scarf in his gnarled hands. Ljoljo was a white-haired old man, neatly turned out, but bashful as a youngster. He had been widowed for some years, and lived alone on the mountain. His children, all girls, had long since

45

married; they lived in the village and kept him in clothes and sent him whatever he needed. A man of solitary habits, he drove the herds of the livestock merchants to spring pasture and seldom came down to the village, let alone to the small town nearby. Now he lumbered on his feet before the guardian, his face set in that countryman's expression that looked like a grin but which in fact meant that he was ill at ease. The steady gaze of the guardian's big eyes above their pallid and owlish twin rings forced Peter Ljoljo to lower his own gaze, to stare down at his feet every other moment.

"Well, your Reverence, there's this—um—there's this sick man—" he brought out hesitantly after some prodding.

"What sick man?" Fra Julian was losing his patience and was on the point of calling for his assistant, the monastery chaplain.

"Begging your pardon, Reverence—he ain't just any sick man, but—what I mean is—"

"What *do* you mean? Stop mumbling."

"What I mean, Reverence—" and here the peasant summoned all his eloquence and blurted out fitfully: "There's this bandit up on our mountain—Roša, you know—and he's took sick, if you please, and ain't long for this world—so I came to you like—"

The moment the guardian understood what it was all about, he wouldn't let him finish but at once called in two more brothers. Whereupon the farmer told them the whole story, bit by bit.

Ivan Roša, who had turned bandit some ten years ago and gotten himself a bad name in the valley of Kreševo, had recently been operating in Dalmatia and Herzegovina; and when the French had chased him out of there, he found shelter in neighboring Montenegro. Last fall, together with some Montenegrins, he had held up, at Senica, the French imperial courier who was on his way to the Porte at Istanbul. The French protested vigorously to the Turkish authorities and demanded that the culprits be apprehended and punished, and so the Turks began to hound him in earnest. Believing that his safest course was to hide near his own native village, where they were least likely to look for him, he then crossed back into Bosnia. Somewhere along the way he fell ill. And there he was now, lying sick on the mountain—about to give up his soul to the good Lord. But the good Lord wouldn't have it.

"So he sent you for a priest?" asked one of the brothers.

"No, not like that, uncles, if you please," protested the farmer, who evidently found it very hard to admit the truth yet dared not do otherwise. "One morning last week—Tuesday it was—I went out to cut me some fresh wood, when out of a bush someone calls my name, 'Ljoljo, Ljoljo!' I gets up closer and what do I see? A man lying on his stomach, all blown up and blue in the face. Couldn't tell right off who he was, as I ain't seen him in years. He gives me his name—Ivan Roša. 'Help me,' he says, 'if you're a Christian. Down there somewhere,' he says, 'there's a cave, only I can't seem to hit the exact spot. Put me in there, so the Turks won't catch me and I won't freeze to death tonight.' And he begs me in the name of God. So I go down and look—and sure enough, there's a hole in the rocks just as he told me. So I slings him over my shoulder—heavy as a corpse he was—and carry him to the cave. There's dung all over him and I can tell he's pretty well finished. I go and fetch him some bread and brandy. Well, it turns out he can't keep down the brandy. Then he says, 'I'm thirsty.' But water's no good either—he just gags on it. So then I want to make a small fire for him, but no, that don't suit him either. 'No fire,' he says, 'I can't look after it and the smoke's liable to choke me or give me away to the Turks, one or the other.' In the end I rake up some dry leaves and pile them around him to keep him warm."

The guardian cleared his throat, showing his impatience, but the farmer went on.

"Next day, I go and look him up—he's feeling better. 'Get

me strong brandy,' he says, 'and some honey and ground herbs, so I can make a poultice for this swelling.' And he gives me a Venetian ducat. Well, I go and buy those things and give him a couple of my sheepskins in the bargain, so he'll keep warm. I drop by again—he's on the mend. In this way three-four days go by. 'Better not see too much of him,' I says to myself, as somebody might spot me, but on the other hand I feel sorry for him, bandit or no bandit—"

Again one of the brothers glanced at the guardian and wanted to interrupt the farmer, but the latter, evidently all primed to speak his piece, would not be diverted.

"Well, that's how things were yesterday afternoon. I put together some cheese and bread and went to see him. There he is, moanin' his heart out like somebody stuck a pitchfork into him. 'What now?' I ask him, but he just grabs my blanket and gags—like his ghost's ready to leave him. Holds on to me and won't let go. Just rolls his eyes, like he's looking for something. 'You got the chills,' I says to him. He coughs a long time and bites the air, then says, 'No, no, Peter, brother, it's not the cold,' he says. 'There's a load of sin on my soul.' He mumbles like that and his fingers are on his throat. 'A great big load's pressing me down—I can't live and I can't die.' "

Here Ljoljo faltered as if in two minds.

"So he sent you for a confessor?"

He scratched the back of his head.

"No, he didn't, begging your pardon. But when I sees the man's dying and some kind of sin's holding back his ghost, I tells him he ought to see a priest. 'Let me go down to the monastery,' I says, 'and ask the uncles, and maybe one of them'll want to come.' "

The farmer paused again in confusion; now it was the brothers who urged him on. To deliver himself as quickly as possible of the unpleasant message, he blurted out:

"He says no, he don't want it."

"How do you mean? What doesn't he want?" the brothers asked scandalized.

"He's burning up, he don't know what he's saying. 'Don't need a priest,' he says. 'A priest can't help me. It's a powerful lot of sin.' "

"Why won't he? Does he say why?" the brothers shouted all at once, while the guardian sat with his chin on his chest, saying nothing.

For a while the farmer was silent, unwilling to tell them the rest; but the brothers overwhelmed him with questions and at length he admitted that Roša didn't want them because "A friar never fathered a child of his own, doesn't even know about puppies and kittens, so how'd he know about troubles and sin?" Or something to that effect. The brothers looked at each other. The farmer, squirming uncomfortably, went on.

"Don't know as I can tell you exac'ly what he said. He keeps babbling like that, a man in fever—you can't make no head or tail out of it. So last night I couldn't shut my eyes and kept thinking, What now, merciful God? I got scared. 'It's no joke,' I says to myself—'a man's soul is at stake! Well then,' I says to myself, 'let me go and see his Reverence and tell him how things are, not to carry this stone on my conscience—and let *him* do as the Lord and the holy books tell him to."

He gave a big sigh of relief. The brothers exchanged glances. With a firm wave of his arm, the guardian commanded them to keep silent and sent Ljoljo back to the courtyard, to wait there until he was called.

The older brothers immediately began to argue about what to do next. Fra Nikola, who was nicknamed Old Wolf, counseled the guardian, in his deep, unpleasant voice, to watch his step. The times were stormy and difficult, this Ljoljo was a strange duck and not too bright either, and a bandit, after all, was a bandit. If the Turks heard that the monks had gone up the mountain and consorted with the bandit, chances were that nothing would happen to Ljoljo or Roša and all the blame would fall on the brothers and the monastery. Others argued that someone should go up, for the dying man was a Christian, and a great and notorious sinner at that. The clean-shaven and sickly Fra Subašić, who had studied divinity in Italy, brought out several books; he passed around his volume of *Ritual* and a new copy of the Venice edition of *Rights and Duties of the Parish Priest*. Fra Nikola firmly declined to look at the book, even though Subašić held it up in front of his eyes and with a yellow nail underscored the lines that supported his opinion.

"I shall ask your opinion when the time comes to pay the fine, not before," said Fra Nikola.

As the guardian remained silent, the bickering might have gone on for some time had Fra Marko not entered the refectory at that moment. He had been occupied with something in the kitchen and had been the last to learn what was afoot. Now, having barged in with his sleeves still rolled up, he refused to listen to the arguments of Fra Subašić and the warnings of Old Wolf, but simply adjusted his habit, approached the guardian and, with a bowed head, said in a clear, firm voice:

"With your blessings, Father Guardian, I should like to go with Ljoljo to see the sick man."

As though he'd only been waiting for this to make up his mind, the guardian slowly raised his pale and shapely hand and blessed him. After this, the others began to shower their advice on Fra Marko—to be sure to leave the village from the side opposite to the monastery, to go first to Ljoljo's house to cover up his tracks, and to look out for any Turks who might be in the vicinity. Fra Marko paid them no heed and began at once to get ready. Hurrying as if there were a fire outside, he pulled on his black fox-lined coat and his heavy hobnailed boots, which promptly set the whole building reverberating. He looked even bulkier and heavier than usual. The small black monastery horse sagged under his weight; up in front, Ljoljo led the way with his measured peasant's step. And thus avoiding the center of the village, they started up the mountain.

After a three-hour march, all of it uphill and over stony ground, they began to descend along the steep bed of the Babin brook. Some two hundred feet below them the deep and almost waterless bed appeared like a dark gash filled with huge boulders. These had been washed down by the spring and autumn torrents, but now, contracted by winter frosts, the brook had all but disappeared among the boulders and dark driftwood. On a height above the path Ljoljo's house could be seen in a clearing between two trimmed spruces. There they stopped. The farmer once more glanced cautiously around him, then motioned to the friar to dismount. Impatient to get on, Fra Marko declined to go up to Ljoljo's house, and so they led the horse behind some boulders and tied him to an ice-coated juniper; then they climbed down the rocky slope below the path. The farmer walked with a light and careful step, but Fra Marko clutched at the sharp rocks for support and grunted irritably. They landed in a gray and sheer-sided gully, one that probably was bare of greenery and flowers even at the height of summer. Ljoljo halted under an overhang and waited until the monk caught up with him. Before them was a gaping hole almost circular in shape, slightly more than a yard in width; the last few steps had to be negotiated with extreme care, as at that spot the gully turned into a naked and smooth ledge that was still covered with morning frost. Ljoljo must have given some kind of a signal, for inside the cave there was a sound of rustle and movement, followed by the appearance of a greatcoat hem in the opening. After helping Fra Marko to approach the cave, Ljoljo backed up the gully, while the monk put his head to the edge of the opening. From inside, an appalling stench met his nostrils, rooting him to the spot. Never before, not in a cemetery, not even at the bedside of a sick peasant in the most wretched of hamlets, had he been assailed by such an odor. The lair stank both of a corpse and of a living creature festering in a tight, closed space.

Fra Marko squatted by the very edge of the hole, so that his fur cap grazed its apex. The cave was filled almost entirely by that greatcoat, out of which now a man emerged, hands first, big, bony, and quite dark, and then the face, half-hidden in a beard and long graying hair and marred by a dark, crusted skin that must have been the aftermath of high fever and the poultice of herbs and raw brandy. A pair of round brown eyes, with a lost and apathetic look in them, rested for a second on the monk, then dropped; his whole head seemed to sag a little. Fra Marko crossed himself and, after a short prayer, began to urge the bandit to confess himself.

Roša was more obstinate than one would have expected of a man in his situation. Denials and equivocation had apparently become second nature with him, for he kept shaking his head, which was propped feebly on the palm of his hand, to indicate that he did not approve of the suggestion. Whereas Fra Marko, after the first few quietly spoken words, soon grew excited and began to flip his hands, now one, now both. They saw each other intermittently through the air stream of his gesturing hands, sometimes through the earnest, pleading, outspread fingers, and then again behind a huge, wrathful, and pumping clenched fist. If a stranger could have observed them from afar, hudding so close to one another, he would have thought that they were highwaymen quarreling over the division of their loot. As he talked on, Fra Marko leaned his upper body deeper into the cave, forgetting his nausea and the stench. Roša acknowledged the monk's words, but doggedly refused to confess; his voice was slurred and his answers laconic and list-less, like those of a person who had no hope of being able to make himself understood, and who cared little whether or not he convinced his opponent. His tongue thickened; the words were barely audible in his gap-toothed mouth. And stronger than his voice was the rattle and wheeze in his cavernous chest, which accompanied his every word like an underground echo.

He admitted readily that he did not wish to confess and wanted no priest. "It's true, I told him," Roša went on strenuously. "You people in the monasteries who've no homes of your own, no trouble and no wives—you can't know these things. You've no idea what life is like outside—or what sinning is. I did say it, that's right. You don't know, so what's the use—"

Losing his self-control, the monk flared up.

"What? What do you mean what's the use? Have you lost your mind? You fool, don't you see that the Accursed One's putting these thoughts in your head? I don't have a wife! Are you any better off that you have? Where are these children of yours?"

Roša twisted his face painfully and tried to turn his head to the other side, like a patient in distress. His chest gave a hollow, reverberating sound, as of words he could not voice, or else did not consider worth uttering. Fra Marko calmed down and tried to moderate himself.

"My friend, it's not the priest who confesses you and forgives your sins but the mystery of God and His command."

And he continued in this vein, talking easily and with conviction about Jesus Christ and His innocent blood that washed away the evils of mankind, and about confessing one's sins and the forgiveness that no living man could afford to spurn. "Every day the Son of God is crucified as an innocent sacrifice," he said, "and this will go on happening as long as there's a single man left on earth. If we didn't have someone to relieve us of our sins, the ground under our feet wouldn't hold us up, that's the sort we are! So you'd better come clean, Roša, and show some humility."

Seeing how the bandit made no move, he began to describe Hell and threaten him with fiery punishment. Roša only shrugged apathetically. "I won't be the only one there," he said. But his strength and defiance seemed to leave him.

"What?" Fra Marko exploded again. "How do you know that? You might very well be the only one. Hear, hear—look at the brave man! Who was it told you he'll be waiting for you there? Alone, that's what you'll be, what else? Any man in sin and without God is alone—along through all eternity. But when he's with God, he is not alone, not on a mountain and not underground."

The bandit lay motionless and simply kept shrugging, which only incensed the friar more and caused him to lapse into his everyday manner of speech.

"Look at him! Don't talk like a fool. What's come over you?" he thundered, as if they were both in the monastery courtyard, unloading horses or trying to lift a cart out of deep mud. "The God of Kreševo is not a magistrate you can run away from by hiding in a cave. God sees and remembers much better than that!" And once again, as soon as he touched upon this exalted subject, his voice softened by itself. "Confess and humble yourself, dear Roša. See, God didn't forget you in your sins and your trouble. There's no desert or mountain in the world, and no mountain with that kind of secret cave, that the grace of God couldn't reach it. There isn't, my poor friend. You think: I'll rob and kill for fifteen years and then crawl into a cave and give up the ghost and that'll be that. Don't you know that God's grace is attached to you like a rope and will lead Him to you whether you're under the sod or under rocks? You forget that once, when you were no bigger than this, Fra Marian baptized you in St. Catherine's Church—so you carry the cross on your forehead and the rest of your body can't run away from it. And now God himself is warning you and telling you to confess your sins."

The chesty wheeze of a moment ago had ceased, or else

had grown inaudible. His face turned to the wall of the cave and his temple resting on dry leaves, Roša lay mute and rigid. Aware that his resistance was weakening, Fra Marko pressed his case, using all the blandishments and wheedling he was capable of. He spoke of great sinners whose transgressions had been forgiven because of a single good deed they had performed at the very end of their lives, and he came back again and again to God's grace, which could neither be seen nor recognized but which shone alike on a bandit's cave and a hermit's cell. "God doesn't wish to have a sinner's death on his hands," he added.

Roša listened to the speech as though it were a long tale delivered in a monotone that soothed his torment, both physical and spiritual, and he squirmed now and then and shook his head obstinately, hopelessly, which in turn caused Fra Marko once more to abandon his quiet and fervent reasoning and wrangle with the bandit in the fashion of a peasant—coarsely, stammering with indignation.

"Look at him, there he goes again! Can't see farther than his unspeakable nose—" and at once he would bite his tongue and try to control his temper. "Listen, my poor misbegotten friend. God is calling you and you toss your head like a pregnant mare!"

Yet the very word 'God,' the minute he uttered it again, would send him into his old transports, and that rich, fluent eloquence would pour forth of itself as it were; while Roša, for a while at least, would give him the benefit of docile and silent attention. This was repeated several times. The monk became more insistent, while the bandit flagged visibly, until eventually he grew quite subdued and in the end gave in. Fitfully and still unwillingly, without lifting his head, he began to mumble the preliminary prayer after the monk and then to talk about his sins, that is to say, about his years of brigandage and about his life as far back as he could remember. As he talked on, however, he lowered his voice every now and then and sometimes faltered altogether, as though wishing he didn't have to mention certain things, and hoping that the monk would sense them and guess them instead. Fra Marko helped him out and encouraged him with gestures and facial expressions, even though his own eyes grew misty and his throat tightened. Finally, no longer concerned with himself, he thrust the upper part of his body into the cave and held his ear to Roša's face, so that, huddling close together, they filled the entire cave like one single, weirdly contorted body.

At one point, Roša's whisper quickened and grew more urgent, almost unintelligible. At times he strained as if wrenching certain admissions out of the depths of his being, in order to make them as brief as possible if he couldn't keep them to himself. His chest rattled with a dire sound. Tense as a hunter, Fra Marko caught each rasp with the very cup of his ear.

Suddenly the monk raised his head, then abruptly his whole upper body. He turned to the cave opening and, gripping the edges with his hands, thrust out his head like a man choking and snapping for air and relief. He could scarcely go on; his face was green and bathed in sweat, which promptly began to turn icy in the winter air. But what utterly transformed the friar's usually ruddy peasant face was a new look in his eyes, frozen, almost squinty with terror, incomprehension, and helpless compassion. He stared ahead fixedly, unseeing, and his breath was short. But then he steeled himself again and went back to his sinner and clung to him as if to warm him. The confession continued. Fra Marko backed away in this fashion several times and stuck his haunted face outside, as if fleeing from what he had heard and looking for help and advice, as though imploring someone to guide him, make him understand, lead him out of the wilderness. His blinking eyes invariably met the leaden sky and the dead winter landscape in the valley below.

After he had accounted for every last and worst sin, Roša

lay back exhausted and fell silent; one heard only his rhythmical wheeze. Fra Marko just barely managed to coax him to
repeat a few words of repentance after him: "For these and all
the other sins of my life I repent with all my heart—" When
that was over, Fra Marko shifted back a little and, raising his
hand firmly, made the sign of the cross over the entire hole as
if blessing everything that was inside; then absolved the bandit
of "all sins and punishment." Taking his leave, he promised to
bring him Holy Communion and assured him that God's
grace, which he had now won back, would watch over him
and keep him safe. Not stirring, the bandit gave only a feeble
hand wave.

"Let Him do what He wants with me," Roša said.

The monk, too wearied and shaken, would not be drawn
into a new argument; he exhorted the bandit once more not to
lose hope in God's grace, and let it go at that. After which,
breathing hard and shivering from cold, since the sweat on
him was cooling rapidly, he clambered stiffly up the ledge and
to the path where Ljoljo was waiting for him.

They walked up to Ljoljo's dark, unswept, and depressing
widower's hut, and there Fra Marko slumped on a low stool,
flung his legs out, and let his arms dangle limply, like a man
surrendering at last to the agony of exhaustion. Ljoljo brought
out a tall pitcher of whey, a bowl of mashed cheese, two
onions, and then broke off a large hunk of corn bread.
Sprawled as he was, Fra Marko cupped his palms around the
pitcher and began to drink. He gulped long and noisily, his
chest heaving, and in the silence one could hear his rushing
breath and the slurping of whey through his lips; he drank so
long that the farmer, who stood by the open hearth with his
arms folded, alternately glanced at the monk and then stared in
front of himself, as if embarrassed. After what seemed like an
eternity, Fra Marko pulled the jug from his mouth with a gasp
and, as if in a trance, held it out to Ljoljo. For a while he

57

shivered and wiped his whiskers; then he began to eat the cheese, onion, and bread, quickly and with relish, like a thresher after a morning's hard work. Though it was chilly inside the house, he continued to sweat. At times he would stop in the middle of a bite, stare glassily in front of him and remain stock-still, until the farmer would stir and rouse him out of his thoughts; then, absently, he would resume eating. When he was finished, he crossed himself aloud and sat quite still, deep in thought. The farmer cleared his throat, poked around the fire, and yawned, invoking God's name as he did, but dared not speak or even smoke, although he kept shaking out his pipe and knocking it against his boot.

And in this way, hardly exchanging a word, they set out again: the monk back to the village, and the farmer, with a jug of milk, back to the cave. As they reached the spot above the riverbed where their paths divided, the friar mounted his horse while the farmer, with his head bowed, drew aside to let him pass.

"Bless me, uncle."

"May God be with you."

Ljoljo quickly descended to the rocky bed, making no sound. But then he stopped suddenly, his eyes riveted to the slope below him, and wheeled around and gave a shout:

"Uncle! Uncle!"

The monk, who hadn't gone far, reined in his horse and waited for Ljoljo. After they had spoken briefly, he dismounted again, tethered the horse to a hornbeam trunk and, together with the farmer, began to climb down the slope. Halfway down, Ljoljo halted and pointed: some distance below them, at the very edge of the brook, Ivan Roša lay doubled over a sapling that appeared curiously twisted. They recognized him by his greatcoat of foreign cut. To make certain, however, they agreed that it would be wise for Ljoljo first to look into the cave. The grotto was empty. Now there could no longer be any doubt that the man they saw by the side of the brook was Roša. To climb down the sheer rocks would have been too difficult, if not impossible, so Ljoljo made a detour upstream and found a way down that was less steep, where the slope had some shrubbery. From that point on, following the bed, he worked his way to the base of the big ledge and, clutching at stumps and exposed roots, gained the other side of the stream. The friar watched Ljoljo as he walked around the bandit and then waved his arm to indicate that indeed all was over. Fra Marko sat with his chin resting on his palm until Ljoljo's steps were again heard at the top of the slope. The farmer didn't know what to make of it; yet the situation was self-evident and clear. Having had a premonition of imminent death, which in strong creatures awakens the instinct to flee, Roša apparently had risen from his pallet and tried to get down to the brook. Half blinded by fever, he must have misjudged the precipice that separated him from the stream, or else overestimated his strength, as he started down the sheer side. What had stopped him was a young ash that grew on the slope. Under the weight of his body, the ash had bent over sharply but did not snap, and so he remained dangling from his waist over the bare trunk. The wide shoulder cape of his coat had slipped down and completely covered his head, and if one hadn't seen his blackened hands and large booted feet, it might have seemed as if someone had spread the greatcoat over the bent ash to dry. And so Roša had died.

What were they to do? The farmer was of the opinion that they should pretend ignorance; they should not touch the corpse or report anything to the Turks. The friar maintained that one ought to bury a Christian, no matter what. The farmer resisted this with unexpected vigor.

"Don't do it, uncle, I tell you! May God forgive us, but you know what they say—Where there's a corpse, there's an inquest. And where there's an inquest, there's a fine to pay.

My house is the only one 'round here—I'll never get them off my back. But when it gets dark, I'll carry him to the path on the other side, where the constables are sure to find him, and maybe later he'll get a Christian burial. Only don't do it on this side of the brook."

Wearied by all that had happened that day, preoccupied with his thoughts and too tired to speak, the monk had no stomach for arguing with the frightened and insistent Ljoljo. He said a brief, absentminded good-by to him and left.

He rode for more than an hour through juniper and hemlock woods and at length emerged on a clearing from which he could see the scattered village and glimpse the white monastery walls and heavy roof in the distance. The first dusk was already quite noticeable, as though it were seeping down from the middle of the sky. Fra Marko pressed his eyes with the back of his hand; at last he came to himself, and his head cleared. One after another, Roša's dying confessions began to flock back to his mind and take hold. As soon as he managed to push one away, another even more ghastly and frightful than the last, would appear; and each would bring with it an echo of Roša's sullen snarl. He shuddered with dread and began to fear for Roša's soul.

"Ah, he didn't repent as he should have, the child of Satan! He didn't!"

Manfully, Fra Marko tried to exorcise his doubts, but as he thus scolded Roša and with loud mumbling hoped to stifle his own anxiety, his memory kept resurrecting disturbing fragments of the bandit's confession—all of them dreadful and staggering sins, all adding up to a senseless and needless evil, one that was quite beyond understanding and should never have been allowed to exist. Day after day, year after year, that evil had bred and multiplied, ever darker and more senseless, until that twisted ash tree in the rocky stream bed had put a stop to it. How far from their path did Christian souls stray, in what unimaginable places the bodies strewed themselves!

He felt the urge to cry out at the top of his voice, but instead doubled over in the saddle. The horse slowed down. His cheeks almost in the animal's mane, he prayed fervently, "Save us, Mother of God—"

The prayer calmed him. For a while he succeeded in banishing the memory of those sins, which in any case he would never be able to understand, and to still his thoughts of the evil that preyed on the souls of all men. Yet a great sadness continued to oppress him, and he could no more slough it off than he could his exhaustion and the thickening dusk. He felt dry and spent inside, and tried in vain to find oblivion in repeated prayer.

And once again, in an access of powerful feeling, he was seized by his old urge to call out in a loud voice, to save all those who were gambling away their souls, make them see the light. Why, when God gave them this wide and splendid road, were they bent on turning aside from it? How could they fail to see? As always when he asked himself this question, the blood rushed to his head at the thought of so much stupidity and blindness, and he suddenly paused and asked in a loud, sharp voice, as if buttonholing someone:

"Why do they sin?"

With a shock, then, he would come to, startled by his own voice. In the wake of the blood ebbing back to his heart, his bitterness, too, faded quickly and he went on repeating quietly and sadly, like an echo:

"Why do they sin?"

Powerless to answer it, he found fresh consolation in the thought of God's grace, which was ineffable but all-encompassing, and which, indeed, had led even that scoundrel Roša to repentance and forgiveness at the eleventh hour. "God's grace—" he said inwardly, grasping with passionate tenderness at those two words he had spoken so many times that day. "God's grace—"

But with all that, he could not smother his private doubts

and sorrow. What baffled and embittered him especially was that unexpected, ugly, and pathetic ending. While still reciting those two words—"God's grace"—he could not resist adding in his gruff countryman's voice:

"But did You have to sling him over that ash!"

He continued to shake his head as if in a grave dilemma, while all around and above him the darkness pressed closer and the horse quickened his pace toward the monastery.

BY THE BRANDY
STILL

More than eleven years had passed since that afternoon in
Rome when Fra Marko, a student of divinity from Bosnia, was
led out with other students for a walk on the Via Nomentana.
They were to be shown the catacombs of St. Agnes. It was an
afternoon in the feverish and sultry Roman spring, full of dust,
the scent of pines, and stark light. Fruit trees were in bloom,
and Fra Marko yearned more than ever for his native Bosnia
and for his own people.

One entered the catacombs through the church itself,
which was moldy and poor. The lay brother who acted as
their guide was sullen, for he could expect no tips. The catacombs were much smaller and more run down than the great
catacombs of St. Callisto on the Via Appia. Yet they too held
cleverly arranged surprises that fascinated the visitor. In one
of the empty tombs there burned, above some crossed bones, a
tiny antique lamp of red clay that threw a clear light on a
golden medallion the size of a ducat. On the medallion was
the head of a young man, with his name engraved underneath,

and all around the head, like an aureole, was written in clear, graven letters: *Semper in pace gaudet* ("Rejoicing in eternal peace"). Fra Marko tarried by the grave so long that the guide had to call after him, and even scold him.

He never forgot that visage in the catacombs. Returning to the city that afternoon and watching the pale lights flicker on in the houses and *trattorias,* ushering in a night life that was unknown to him, he shivered at the thought that those people were unaware of the small underground light and that very probably this same evening they would lose forever the joyous, the only true life of eternity. For several days afterwards he could not eat, he slept badly, his fellow monks struck him as malingerers and slackers, the world at large as abandoned to itself and to all manner of temptations. He even forgot his beloved Bosnia. Later he calmed down somewhat, but there remained within him a powerful longing—one destined never to leave him again—for all men to realize and feel the disparity between the shortness of life and the eternity of death, as he himself had felt it before the illuminated visage of the young man in the catacombs.

Before long, Fra Marko was sent back to Bosnia. Years came and went. Due partly to a life filled with hard work and partly to disappointments that came thick and fast, which were bound to mellow even as headstrong a nature as his, Fra Marko's zeal grew, if not tepid, at least less noticeable. In his mind he saw clearly, just as he had on that afternoon on the Via Nomentana, two kinds of life and light—one great and everlasting, and the other small and fleeting; even today, he could still relive that sense of horror at the thought of millions of people who were losing the only real and true life for the sake of this brief and puny one with its wretched delights and possessions. Even now, he still almost choked with the urge to call out to people, to help, to save. Often enough these days as he cast a glance through the window of his cell and saw the fields and the roofs of houses under the early frost, bathed in moonlight, there would appear to him, in the place of quiet fields, the whole of God's earth in her breadth and length, her face covered by a rash of towns that were like spots of fire and brands of the Devil. He had seen only Rome, Ancona, and his own Travnik in Bosnia, but he knew well that the earth was full of such towns and his mind's eye seemed to encompass them all at once, to the most distant ones whose names he didn't know. In all of them alike, souls were bent on damnation and men on ruin.

Standing by the window and reluctant to light the candles as yet, Fra Marko lost sight of the darkened hamlets and fields of Kreševo and let his eyes wander instead over the great cities of the world with their streets, gardens, and houses, containing all that the Devil had built as a snare to the vanity, greed, and corruption of men. He compared his own strength with the strength that would be needed to wipe it all from the face of God's earth, from Travnik and Sarajevo to that nameless town that glowed and winked somewhere at the bottom of Europe or of loathsome Asia, where the Devil felt at home. It was a moment in which Fra Marko's yearning to save mankind swelled past all bounds and threatened his peace of mind, when this vicar of Kreševo, forgetting who he was, settled accounts between the two worlds, one of all creatures and things, the other of their Creator. He was so overcome by compassion that he identified himself completely with the man from the cities who sinned and destroyed himself, and turned against Him who permitted this to happen. The terrible thought occurred to Fra Marko—not for the first time either—that the Devil's and God's own were not clearly and fairly divided, that it was impossible to know, indeed that no one could tell, how great was the power of either or where exactly was the boundary between them.

He shut his eyes, in which the fires of all the world's cities were still blazing and turning into angry and helpless tears. Little by little, the thought that had begun as a reproach and a protest weakened and became transformed into prayer. Fra Marko ardently implored God to "draw the line" between Himself and the Devil, to show Himself more distinctly to man, who otherwise was bound to perish among the snares.

Besides such nights when Fra Marko was racked by doubts and ended by seeking comfort in prayer, there were others—much more frequent—when, exhausted by the day's labors, he would flop onto his bed with an utterly empty mind and instantly fall asleep like a child after his bath. For side by side with his secret desire to save mankind, which was uppermost in his thoughts and emotions and which, given his kind of innocence, was a substitute for those hundreds of petty and deep cravings, longings, and ambitions that preoccupied other people, there also burned in Fra Marko the farmer's passion for land and gainful work, and this drove him irresistibly to maintain and expanded the monastery lands, to use cunning when necessary, to short-change the Turkish authorities and dicker with peasants over their erratic tithe. In his absorption with these things days, months, and years slipped by imperceptibly. The plums yielded a crop on an average of every other year; corn and wheat were a thing of chance; potatoes did well only every third season. There were some years that Fra Marko would long remember either because they were exceptionally fruitful or exceptionally poor, and afterwards when another very good or very bad year came around he would start confusing it with the last similar one. And so everything finally became indistinguishable in this struggle with the soil and its fruit. Since the soil was greater, mightier, and more enduring than a man's life, he increasingly steeped and lost himself in it.

The last few years, however, had not been lucky for Fra Marko. Mishaps and disappointments, small and big, seemed to

66

multiply. The year just passed had ended with a hail, and with his imprisonment at the hands of Fazul, the Vizier's deputy at Travnik. Earlier this year, he had gone up the mountain to receive a strange and disturbing confession from a dying bandit. And during this summer yet another thing had happened to unsettle him and leave him bemused for months to come.

The daughter of one Marko Barbarez from Sarajevo had decided to become a convert to Islam in order to marry a Turk. Not the protests and tears of her parents nor the concerted efforts of the Sarajevo brothers could budge her from her decision. On the eve of the day when the girl was supposed to appear before the local Turkish judge and declare that she wished to become a Muslim of her own free will, the brothers, in connivance with the parents, packed her into a carriage and, by trick and force, bundled her off to Kreševo, where the Turks would not look for her. Two men and an old woman all but carried the girl into the monastery. Brother Superior did not wish to see her. Some of the other brothers tried to dissuade her from converting, but even threats availed them nothing.

The girl stood in a corner in the small, thick-walled room on the ground floor that housed old books, saddles, and monastery tools. With her hands clasped in front of her, her gaze fixed on the floor, her face speckled with the flush of excitement, she listened unmoved to the arguments, advice, promises, and threats of the brothers, who harangued her in turn, or sometimes in teams of two or three. Hoarse with anger at such obstinacy, Fra Peter shouted:

"Call Fra Marko! Let him thrash the she-dog until he gets through to her soul!"

A little later Fra Marko barged into the room carrying a dry dogwood switch in his hand. When he saw the girl, he halted in astonishment. Having heard the brothers discuss this would-be Turk the day before, and recalling what they'd said a moment ago when they summoned him to come and "talk sense" to her in his own way, he had imagined her to be a tall woman, burly and fierce. Now he saw before him a slender and frail young girl with hands meekly crossed in front of her, but her head held high. The most striking feature of her face were the eyelids, steadfastly lowered, a little slanting and of unequal shape, like two big leaves of slightly different size. He would have felt easier had she been hefty and insolent as he had pictured her.

Fra Peter began once more to urge her to give up the Turk and not bring disgrace upon her parents and her faith, but she remained adamant.

"Look into my eyes, you heathen wretch!" thundered Fra Peter a couple of times, hoping in this way to rattle and humble her more quickly. Each time she raised her lids and fixed her bright young gaze, boldly and without flinching, on the eyes of the blustering yet at heart good-natured Fra Peter. In fact, she did not look into his eyes but at his Venetian reading glasses, whose metal rests were broken and tied on both sides, right above the ear, with a thread. It was to this green thread that her look was directed.

"So now you want a Turk, do you?" yelled Fra Peter, disconcerted by her stare, and not really expecting an answer to his question.

"Yes, only him," she replied in a quiet and cool voice that was unusual for a girl of her years and in her present situation. It was almost as if another person were speaking through her.

"What? What! You want to become a Muslim too?"

"Yes."

At a loss for words and breathing heavily, Fra Peter was beside himself.

"Fra Marko, let her have it! She's yours!"

The girl put up no resistance; it was as if the whole thing

were but a game, in which she was an unwilling participant. Her tiny waist disappeared in Fra Marko's great paws. He laid her over his left knee like an unruly child. At the first few stripes she kicked her legs and jerked her head, but then she grew rigid and remained like that, suffering the lashes without a murmur or movement. Had she screamed or struggled, Lord knows how much longer Fra Marko might have whipped her; but now, taken aback by her strange behavior, he dropped his hand and his eyes wheeled uncertainly around the room as if in search of an explanation. The girl lay in his hands like a dead fish. It was only then that he came to himself and became aware of something he had not realized before: the small, hard-nippled breast in his left palm and, under the fingers of his right hand, the girl's belly, flat and hard, unrounded as yet.

Horrified, he pushed her away and ran out of the room, forgetting his dogwood switch, and avoiding the eyes of the other brothers. The girl picked herself up slowly and returned to her corner. There she stood quietly, exactly as before save for the twitching of her eyelids, behind which tears must have welled even though her face showed no trace of weeping or contriteness or fear.

She caused the brothers a great deal of trouble. The very next morning her Turkish boyfriend arrived and, together with a judge and a constable, led her out of the monastery. Later, at the courthouse, she was asked in front of the judge and Brother Superior whether she was embracing Islam of her own will, and she answered quietly, "Of my own free will."

When they asked her if she wanted to take the young Turk for a husband, she simply, without a word, placed her small hand on his forearm and looked evenly at the judge and at Brother Superior, as though waiting for the next question, unable to understand how they could possibly query her about something so undeniable and so apparent to the whole world. She never told the Turks that she had been whipped in the monastery, and bore herself proudly and well, although she trembled from exhaustion, lack of sleep, and from the beating she had received.

The brothers were ordered to pay a fine; and what was worse, the young bridegroom, to spite them, decided to marry her right away and to hold the wedding celebration there in Kreševo. Next evening, the brothers could see the kindling of festive bonfires on the other bank of the stream and hear the music and cheers of the wedding guests.

Fra Marko closed the window shutters in his cell and lay down on the bed fully dressed, his cowl pulled over his head. But he couldn't help hearing the wedding pipes and tambours, which seemed to throb to the rhythm of the veins in his own temples. All these things spelled only one thing to him: how mighty and hard to understand evil was, how one could sense it everywhere, even in places one would never expect it. How often God forsook his people and abandoned them to evil chance. Here Fra Marko's reveries stopped short and he lay without prayer or thought, waiting till the heathen pipes and drum tattoo spent themselves.

Next day, and for many days afterwards, the monastery was busy with the harvest and Fra Marko found oblivion in work; he no longer speculated about the origin of the world's evil, nor wondered about the hidden mysteries of woman, as he did that night long ago, but was now haunted by a faint and uneasy sense of tolerance, which he had never known before. He slept because he was tired out, and he lost himself in work, but he could not conceal to himself and before the others that he was bewildered and shaken to the bottom of his soul.

The world was without doubt full of evil, and this evil was stronger than he had suspected. Perhaps the evil was every bit as strong as good; possibly even stronger. Here he usually faltered and stoutly pushed such thoughts away. But sometimes they crept back to vex him even when he was at work, when he was least ready for them. He might, for instance, be emptying a sack of plums into a vat and, while still bending over it, freeze suddenly and become lost in thought, then quickly cross himself and flip a helpless hand at this earthly evil, muttering under his breath: "Well, there's as much of it as the Lord saw fit to send down. What can I do about it!"

The autumn turned out well. The monastery was at ease. Fra Peter was finally made Superior. With his love of jokes and hard work, and his knack for blending goodness with banter, cheerfulness with industry, he conducted the business of the monastery with great skill and success. Writing to the Superior of the Fojnica Monastery, with the request that he send him nine hundred fifty groschen which was the portion of the fine incurred by his own establishment in recent weeks, he concluded: "This, your Reverence, is the net amount of our present damage. We had to pay up to avoid worse evil. Therefore please rush this money, as things are wearing thin at this end. As for your question about Fra Marko, he is alive and in good health. He got over his argument with that Fazul in Travnik last year (true, he had to use compresses for a long time and kept sharpening a stone to kill him), but nowadays he is *valde confusus in animo* ['greatly bewildered in his soul'] on account of that fiasco of ours with the female Antichrist from Sarajevo. The poor fellow must have realized that not even his switch was of much help. I am worried about him and will try to send him to you on a visit, as *Turcae Cresevienses* ['the Turks of Kreševo'] seem to have it in for him."

However, Fra Marko would not hear of leaving the monastery and going to Fojnica now when there was so much to do. He spent long days in the fields or in the plum orchard, for the minute he came back to the monastery the brothers would tease him, pester him to tell them how he'd wanted to "dissuade" that Sarajevo female from embracing Islam, and he would get angry, call them loafers, and scamper away. The only one who interceded for him was Fra Stephen, an old man of eighty-five. Wizened and in his dotage, without a tooth in his head, hardly more than skin and bone, Fra Stephen seemed to live on snuff alone. From his large chair at the far end of the refectory, he gave Fra Marko to understand, with his hands and eyes, that he was with him against those pranksters, and he even seemed to say something, only his words were drowned in the brothers' roar of laughter.

Toward the end of November Fra Marko set up the still and began to make the plum brandy, *slivovitz*. He had a special helper for the job, one Tanasije Hrišćanin from Visoko. Always sleepy and unwashed, this Tanasije was clumsy, heavy-footed, and a half-wit, but unusually deft with the still. He made plum brandy for everyone in the district, yet when Fra Marko would call him, he would drop everything and come. The friendship with Tanasije also made Fra Marko the butt of many jokes from the brothers. In reality, the pair of them hardly exchanged a civil word, but wrangled around the still from the first day to the last, through the smoke and the sparks, their eyes tearing, covered in soot, wet and dirty from the clay that was used to line the still retort. But they could not have done without each other.

As soon as the brandy stilling began, Turkish visits to the monastery became more frequent. The smell of the "twice burned" also attracted Kezmo, a janissary who had once escorted the Eighth Regiment of the Vizier's Mamelukes into town. For the last several years, this Kezmo had been getting ready to go to war, but in fact did all his fighting in the various inns and monasteries between Travnik and Sarajevo. Fat and bloated from drink, he could scarcely walk; when he sat down somewhere, he did not rise again until he was carried out. Lately, he'd been keeping company with a certain Mehmedbeg, also a janissary, but a true warrior. In his style of dress and in his bearing, which was that of a man who had gone to school and seen something of the world, he was a complete antithesis of the coarse and illiterate Kezmo. What drew them together was drink and wanderlust. In addition to plum brandy, Mehmedbeg also poisoned himself with hashish and poppy seed, which he took in candied fruit and orange peel. This made his hands tremble and gave his face a jaundiced look; the yellow face with its drooping eyelids contrasted strangely with his athletic body.

They asked for a chicken or turkey but contented themselves with a leg of lamb, which Tanasije cut into kevaps and grilled on the open fire beside the still. Having eaten and drank, Kezmo withdrew into a corner and fell asleep propped against his saddlebag, with a stale tchibouk at his side and an empty brandy cup in his hand; while Mehmedbeg grew more and more wakeful and animated as the night wore on. Leaning on his knapsack, he stared fixedly at the fire, sipped slowly and, after every other cup of brandy, took from a round copper box a morsel of his beloved drug in candied fruit.

In vain did Fra Marko wait for Mehmedbeg to doze off too. After a while, having refilled the still with fresh plum mash, he sent Tanasije to sleep his turn till midnight, while he kept watch alone to see that the fire didn't go out. He was squatting opposite Mehmedbeg. As the retort had not cooked up yet, the celler was so quiet that one could hear the soft whistling of Kezmo's gap-toothed mouth in his sleep; Fra Marko began to despair of seeing the second man fall asleep. Mehmedbeg, on the contrary, grew more and more restless. At first he kept humming a mournful Turkish melody through his nose, over and over. (Ever since he'd grown up and come into troubled contact with Muslims, Fra Marko had felt a particular hatred for this yen of theirs to hum and wail and whine for hours on end; he saw in it a distinct symptom as it were of their restiveness and damnation.) Later, with much handflipping, the Turk began to philosophize and hold forth, like a man whose body was unsound but whose heart was brimming over, who must speak out on anything that strikes his fancy, just as he hums the first tune that comes into his head.

"Hey, padre, padre, you work so much and fuss over the still. And what is it? Just brandy—you drink it up, get a hangover, and that's that. No use slaving over it. Drink as long as you can, die when you have to, that's all there is to it."

To avoid getting into a conversation, Fra Marko set about kneading the wet clay for the next lot of mash. He worked on and didn't lift his head, yet couldn't restrain himself entirely and answered in a quiet voice, between pumping movements of his upper body:

"No use, eh? If I didn't slave over it, what would you drink and how would you let the world know of your wisdom?"

The Turk neither listened nor heard him, but went on.

"Padre, you don't know anything. You are ignorant, that's what. If you'd only feasted your eyes on beauty as I have! But how could you? You don't use your eyes except to lift a piece of food to your mouth and find a door."

"It's good to know you use them better. You've seen some marvels, I don't doubt."

"Don't get angry, friend, but that's how it is. With the cross in front of your nose, what could you see? Cross, and more cross. And there are things to see, my poor friend, I tell you."

Fra Marko cleared his throat and pummeled the clay irritably, clamping his jaws tight so as not to emit a curse. The Turk softened his tone and went on in a kind of trance, speaking almost to himself.

"There's a garden up there in Belgrade, where you go down to the Danube from the Gate. I don't know the gardens of Paradise, but on this earth, I swear, no one has that kind of shade, those flowers, those fountains and brooks. There, my friend, lives a lonely old man with his widowed daughter. That old man carried the Sultan's medal around his neck five times in that many wars. And she . . . ? The doors of her house are closed to suitors. Her husband died in the war. Vanished, no less. Perished! And when they badger the old man to give her away, he tells them: 'It's her sorrow, let her say the word.' And do you know what her word is? Here!"

At that he pulled out from his leather belt some kind of a roll in which there was an embroidered handkerchief, and, pointing at the fine work, described it to himself.

"Here—three lemons and a dead leaf. Meaning: 'I pine away because you don't come. Oh God! Better not come!' Oh padre, padre!"

His head thrown back, he kept repeating the last word and bit his lips as if trying to hold back his voice. His bare neck seemed to grow longer, swollen and yellow, unusually muscular and exactly as wide as his head. At last he fell silent, evidently realizing how improper it was to speak of these things, and before an infidel at that. Yet his urge to talk was stronger than himself; and he started off again, only this time not about the woman.

"A dark thing, the cross. All that makes the sign of the cross is dark. For a thousand years you churn this darkness and still it's nothing. You never take your eyes off the cross, so it serves you right. You're against God's bounty—against woman, a creature of God. What's one to do! Baptized folk, blind folk, blighted folk!"

He said it slowly, almost sadly, not to Fra Marko but into the distance as it were, as if looking at those who dragged the cross behind them, blind to everything that was bright and worthwhile in this world.

Fra Marko involuntarily lifted his gaze from his work and studied the Muslim. That head thrown back, the pasty face with its green shadows, the inflamed eyes, all put him in mind of something distant and exalted: of the head of a saint he had seen in a painting in one of the churches in Rome. No matter how much he tried to resist the comparison, which upset him, it flocked back to his mind and took hold of it irresistibly, like a temptation. It was the head of an unknown saint and martyr: the same rapture, the same burning eyes and expression of exalted pain. And to make the temptation complete, this head so reminiscent of a saint was now mouthing shameful, distressing, and blasphemous things. All this struck Fra Marko as a hideous dream full of contradictions.

He shut his eyes not to see him. In the incarnadine twilight in which he suddenly found himself, a yellow pool swayed before him, like the glow of the taper in the catacombs, and the pool contained the blurred male profile around which he had tried in vain to decipher the halo-like legend. Bemused by that light, he forgot the two Turks beside him in the cellar, but as soon as he opened his eyes, he was again confronted with Mehmedbeg's powerful head. Watching it and hearing unwittingly what it was saying, Fra Marko felt lost, bewildered, and small; if he had had to answer at that moment, he would not have dared or known how. The strange heathen would have had the last word.

The Turk went on talking like a man whose fancy was running away with him. His features, worn out and sallow, looked even more bloodless in the strong light of the fire, his lips bluer, his mustache sparse and dull. But his eyes were round, wise, and profound, full of a glow, both from the still fire and from another, more intense one that radiated out of him. On the other side of the room, and illuminated no less brightly, shone Fra Marko's face, glistening with sweat, round-cheeked and redder than usual; his childishly blue eyes, with barely a touch of dark in their pupils, paled and almost blended into the skin.

They sat facing one another, each sunk in his own

thoughts, the entranced Turk and the troubled brother, until Kezmo began to stir and cough fitfully. Yawning and blinking in bad humor, he got up and came to the still, then sat down and asked for water. He yawned on and on, his tongue and palate on fire from spicy food and too much brandy. Sleep had apparently not sobered him. He lighted his tchibouk and with the same thongs he had used to pick up the ember began to poke absently around the still, scraping the clay with which the retort was lined. Fra Marko glanced at him a few times out of the corners of his eyes, but Kezmo went on cracking the baked clay piece by piece. Fra Marko burst out, as only a man busy with his work can do:

"Leave it alone, man! Don't you see you'll make a leak and spoil all this mash!"

Whereupon the drunk, like a spiteful child, brandished the thongs and scraped one side of the lid clear of the clay. There was a hiss of steam from under the lid and at the same instant Fra Marko, whose blood had rushed to his head, yelled out:

"Son of a vandal, do you want to ruin all the work and trouble I've put into it!"

Saying this, he picked up a raw, barely charred log of wood from his side of the fire, swung it up and, in his rage apparently mindless of what he was doing, started toward Kezmo. The Turk, who still held the thongs in his left hand, reached with his right into his waist belt, pulled out a short-barreled rifle, a puny and insignificant-looking thing like a leg of spring lamb, and fired straight into Fra Marko's stomach. Hit at almost point-blank range, the monk jerked upright to his full height and shook his bushy head twice, as if motioning to someone in the back of the room; then all at once he collapsed with his whole weight against the still which he had tried to protect. The mash poured out over the flames with a loud hiss and the fire began to gutter. Mehmedbeg, who had meanwhile come to himself, helped the bulky Kezmo to his feet. Fra Marko writhed on the ground and tore wordlessly at his habit so that the buttons snapped.

Thoughts flashed through his head with the speed of lightning. Evil was all-powerful. If only his tongue were not so numb, he might have shouted something, anything. But he couldn't. A pounding and a reddish half-light split his head. He kept thinking, Oh God, they've killed me! They struck me with all their force, here in the middle. The blow will ravage and burn everything. Into your hands, O Lord. It's the end of everything! Everything. What a terrible pity—and darkness invaded his mind with a rush.

The liquid from the still doused the fire rapidly. The cellar grew darker and darker.

It took quite some time until the brothers, awakened by the shooting, dared to come into the cellar. The Turks had gone away. Fra Marko was dying. They all skipped around him, upset and horrified. In the middle of the floor stood Tanasije, who had run up after the shooting; awake at last, he rolled his big frightened eyes around him. The monks pushed past him; some went to fetch bandages and medicines, others tried to stanch the blood gushing out of the wounded man. Fra Peter was on his knees by Fra Marko's head; having slid his left hand under the latter's sweat-covered neck, he held his right hand with his own right. A lay brother was kneeling on the other side with a tall candle in his hand.

Fra Marko could not speak, for his mouth was full of blood, but his eyes stared in a kind of extreme and pained astonishment into the very pupils of Brother Superior. At a question from the Superior, he batted his eyes to signify that he was repenting his sins, then turned his worried gaze once more to the overturned still and the doused fire, and gave up his ghost.

For a long time after Fra Marko's death the monastery could not get over its consternation and dread, nor resume its old life. Depending on their age and temperament, the brothers wept or cursed and ground their teeth, or else prayed with their heads buried in their hands.

Fra Ivan, who had once deputized for Fra Marko in Rome, noted in Latin in the Death Register—in which every brother's death and his main virtues were recorded—that on December 2 that year the monastery vicar, Fra Marko, had died a martyr's death, and that the killer was a *Turca quidam pessimus Kezmo dictus* ("certain very bad Turk known as Kezmo"). And since the departed had enjoyed no rank or honors in the order and had not been a scholar or a man of outstanding piety, or, for that matter, possessed any special talents, Fra Ivan merely added: *Requiescat in pace!* ("May he rest in peace!").

But old Fra Stephen, who hardly ever slept, was in the habit of getting up in the middle of the night and setting straight some things done in the daytime which went against his grain but which he was powerless to prevent or change. Although they had forbidden him to do it, and hid the books and papers from him, he found the Death Register one night as he gadded about the monastery. He crossed out the frosty Latin prose of Fra Peter and with a shaky hand, in old-Church script, wrote in the margin of Fra Marko's obituary in barely legible letters:

"He loved the monastery as his own soul. Let that be known!"

MUSTAPHA MAGYAR

Just before sunrise the drum and fife lads came down from their quarters on the hill, and the mounted townsmen who were to greet the returning army also began to assemble. It was the fourth day of celebration and feasting in the town of Doboj, marking the victory over the Austrians at Banjaluka. Rejoicing was general throughout Bosnia, but especially in Doboj, since one of its men, Mustapha Magyar, had won fame as the greatest fighter in that battle. There was talk of fantastic Austrian losses, of the slaughter of Christian peasants and the spectacular bravery of Mustapha Magyar. Today they were expecting him back.

Several times during the morning and early afternoon they had been deceived by dust clouds on the open road in the distance. It was only toward the hour of evening prayer that the first cavalry approached, and then, much later, at the time of the last prayer, Mustapha Magyar himself appeared, surrounded by flags and blaring trumpets. He was slumped in the saddle and looked unexpectedly small (for in their tales and anticipation he had grown to giant size); morose, shrunken, and wrapped in his cloak, he seemed more like a fasting pilgrim than Mustapha Magyar, the hero of so many stories and songs.

Glancing neither left nor right, he rode briskly through the milling, cheering throng. Without turning or addressing anyone, he passed into the walled compound of his house, while the crowd fell back at the gate and from there watched the unloading of booty from the pack horses. This was the third time that Mustapha Magyar had come back to his neglected homestead above the stream.

With the exception of a few undernourished bondsmen, this house and these grounds were the only things which, after dividing the legacy with his brother, he had inherited from his father, a drunkard and spendthrift, even though his grandfather, Avdaga Magyar, a well-known Muslim convert from a distinguished Hungarian family, had amassed and left a large fortune. At the age of fifteen, when his father had died and his brother married, Mustapha had been packed off to the Muslim high school at Sarajevo. There he spent four hard and frugal years. On reaching twenty, he had returned to Doboj with a trunkful of books and well-worn student clothes, as well as a big ebony flute with air holes of inlaid silver; but instead of moving in with his brother, he put up at his homestead.

He had changed completely. With a new mustache above his pursed lips, stoop-shouldered, moody and unsmiling, he spoke to no one and made no friends. During the day he would read the Scriptures with the town imam, Ismet Agha, and nights he would play the flute hour after hour, filling the long marshy meadow below the house with his music. And when the army began to recruit men, he had had himself fitted out, then padlocked the house and marched off to Russia under General Delalić. For a long time nothing was heard of him. Then one year word got back that he was killed, and since he was young and had no friends, he was soon forgotten. But when Delalić came back, his men said that Mustapha was alive ("Very much so!") and had distinguished himself more than any Bosnian and gained high honor. In the sixth year he finally, and suddenly, returned to Doboj. Few people could recognize him. He was dressed like a man from Istanbul, in flowing and luxurious clothes; he had grown a beard and seemed wan and haggard. He broke the padlock on his house. Late at night, he got out his flute, which he had left wrapped in a silk shawl, and blew on it softly, at first timidly.

Tuuuu, tititataaa . . .

The sound made a nasty rent in the silence.

He saw that his breath was not steady enough, his fingers not as supple as they used to be, nor could he remember the old melodies. He replaced the flute in its wrapping and then submitted to the agony of sleeplessness that had been plaguing him ever since the fighting had ceased.

It was a torment he went through every night. He would suddenly forget all that ever happened, even his own name, and as soon as the first light slumber drowned out all memories and thoughts of the next day and there remained only the cramped body under the soundless millstone of darkness, he would feel an antlike tingle crawling up his legs, the soft part under his heart would begin to quake and terror would start coursing all through him like some chilly stream. From time to time he would have to get up, even though it cost him a great effort, to make light and fling open the window, if only to prove to himself that he was alive, that the powers of darkness had not crushed and scattered him. This went on till daybreak, when a leaden stillness overcame the body and it drifted, sinking, into a kind of sleep, fleeting but dearer to him and more merciful than anything in the world. And next morning, the day would be like any other. This went on day after day, and it would never have occurred to him to mention it to anyone.

83

For Muslim divines he had nothing but contempt, and in doctors he did not believe.

After that first night, when he went down to the coffee-house in the bazaar, the men respectfully made way for him, but he neither deigned to smile nor was capable of telling them about Istanbul and the battles to appease their curiosity. Soon they began to deprecate him and dismiss him from their minds. Then new fighting broke out in Slavonia and, leading the first column, he departed once more at the crack of dawn, as quietly as he had come.

Again there was news of his exploits in Slavonia and in Hungary and of a terrible battle at the mouth of the river Orljava. When the Austrians laid siege to the fortress of Banjaluka and the Christian populace looted the city and forced the Turks to shut themselves in the citadel, all available Turkish armies in Bosnia descended on the river Vrbas at Banjaluka. But they found the Austrians superior in numbers and armament and dared not strike until Mustapha Magyar could work out a strategy. His plan was to build rafts at a place upstream, float them down under the cover of night and, in the first light of dawn, join them in a float-bridge to enable the army to swarm across and surprise the Austrians.

That night, as the rafts were being readied, Mustapha lay down among the willows on the riverbank to snatch a brief moment of rest. Lately he had been tormented by all kinds of dreams that curtailed still further his already short sleep and oppressed him even more. He managed to doze off at first, but then suddenly he began to dream about some children in Crimea. The event had taken place so many years ago that he had completely forgotten about it.

He had been advancing with a detachment of cavalry somewhere in Crimea. Pursuing the enemy, they decided to spend the night in an abandoned summer house. As they were about to bed down for the night, they discovered, crouching

84

behind some wardrobes, four children. They were small boys, with closely trimmed blond hair, fair-skinned and well dressed. The detachment numbered fifteen men, most of them Anatolians. They divided up the children between them. In this way, half dead from terror and pain, the boys were passed from hand to hand. By morning, they were bruised and swollen and not one of them could stand on his feet. Then a strong column of Russians approached and Mustapha and his men bolted away in such haste that they had no time to slaughter the children. And now he saw them again, all four of them. He heard the Russians cantering nearer. He wanted to mount his horse, but the reins kept snarling and slipping through his fingers and the horse kept backing away.

He woke up in a sweat. He was flailing and thrashing about him, all twisted inside his cloak. It had grown chilly and the sky was overcast in the first faint gray of the morning. He put on his belt and got ready, spitting in a rage and sick with loathing at the morbid agony of treacherous and unexpected dreams.

The Turks had already assembled on the riverbank and the sky was getting light, but the rafts were slow in coming and there was trouble in lashing them fast. The noise and the sound of voices awakened the Austrians on the opposite bank. Their pickets gave alarm. Further delay was out of the question. Mustapha signaled to his raftsmen to tighten the moorings and take cover, then drew his sword and called out in a thunderous voice:

"Allah Bismillah! Followers of Muhammad, forward!"

"At the infidels!"

"On the rafts!"

"Allah! Allah!" the army took up the cry and milled down the bank.

They swarmed on the rafts after him. They saw at once that the floats were wider apart than they had thought. Some men fell into the water; a few managed to jump across, but the majority stopped short. Only Mustapha went on, leaping from raft to raft as on wings. He seemed to be flying over the water. While the advance column still wavered on the floats, he gained the other bank and, without a backward glance, fell on the astonished sentries. Seeing that their leader was out in front by himself, the other Turks started to leap across too, for in the meantime the rest of the force had begun to push forward and was threatening to shove them over the side anyway. And so with loud yelling and a great uproar the advance parties managed to cross the raft-bridge, even though many tumbled into the water and were crying for help between the rocking floats.

It had been the swiftest-won victory in many years. The huge Austrian camp, taken virtually unawares at an unexpected hour, from an unexpected side, scattered in all directions. They ran terrified, in packs. Mustapha just barely had time to overtake the laggards and pounce on them, swiveling around in his saddle like a man possessed, while his flashing saber made a fiery circle of light and spread a cold wind around him. His troops caught up with him, yelling triumphantly. The beleaguered Turks of Banjaluka came out of the fortress and this was the signal for the plunder and massacre of the Christians.

After their victory that evening, Mustapha lay in front of his tent and pressed his chest and palms into the grass, for it seemed to him that every muscle in his body was swollen and distended beyond recognition and was about to detach itself and leave him. He could see the fires and hear the cries of the looters and the shrieking of the victims.

"The world is full of scum!"

He'd had the same thought that morning at dawn on the bank of the river as he stood between the two armies (one about to run, the other hesitant and fearful on the rafts), and

86

even now something like a bitter taste remained in his mouth and he wanted to rid himself of it by repeating the words out loud:

"The world is full of scum!"

His blood kept rising, he felt gorged with it. All veins pounded away. Sleep would not come.

After that night his insomnia became all but absolute. Even those few and pitifully late hours of respite before dawn were now increasingly often destroyed by nightmares. Night after night, without warning, there rose up in his dreams hopelessly tangled fragments of his past life which he had utterly forgotten. The worst thing about them was the dreadful clarity and poignancy of every form and movement, as if each image lived for itself alone and had a special significance. He began to shudder at the very thought of the night. He would not admit this fear even to himself, yet it loomed ever bigger, gnawed at him during the day, quashed every thought of sleep, festered inside him, and, cutting into his living flesh more silently and imperceptibly than a silken thread, sank in deeper every day.

This was the third time that he had come back to his ancestral home.

Yet even now, after he had ridden through the streets of Doboj and with loathing made his way through the jubilant, dancing crowds, and taken leave of his companions, he paced the rooms restlessly so that the floor boards creaked and snapped. He could still hear the late revellers acclaiming him and the victory, but he continued to pace to and fro and dared not sit down. He glanced at the bundle of the silk shawl that contained his old flute and at the green trunk of books, but couldn't bring himself to touch them. The mountains had already swum away into darkness and the town fallen silent, while in a ravine on the nearby hill an owl announced itself.

He leaned on the windowsill. The fever of sleeplessness and of the long march, and the steady hammering of his heart, clamored for a respite. But now dreams overtook him even before he fell asleep. Had he actually shut his eyes? There now appeared before him the nethermost room of the house, full of cobwebs and some mysterious rubble, and on a chest in a corner sat his grandfather, Avdagha Magyar. His cheeks were ruddy, his beard trim, his mustache bristling. He sat there perfectly still and mute, but his very presence had an extraordinary significance and seemed to portend some unbearable grief and dismay, which tightened Mustapha's throat. He jerked himself awake. He almost died of fear in the pitch-dark room, but made no light and resumed his pacing although gooseflesh covered him all over like an armored sheath and he could not feel his legs under him.

He dared not stand still even for a moment, but was obliged to keep moving, for his dread of insomnia was hardly less intense than his horror of dreaming. Pacing like this, he remembered Sarajevo and his gay schoolmate Yusufagić and the green hill with its ancient cemetery and soft grass on which, in his student days, he had lazed away many afternoons with his head propped on his arm. Unable to endure this any longer, he saddled his horse and rode out of Doboj, stealthily, like a thief in the night.

Next day the bazaar learned to its great amazement that he had gone away and, somewhere in a field by the roadside, attacked a group of unknown cart drivers, wounding them and scattering their horses.

He traveled in turn by short cuts and through the middle of villages, beating and chasing Christians with such fury that his own Muslims preferred to avoid him. On reaching Sutjeska, he found the Catholic monastery closed. There was no sign of life anywhere. The day before some people had

88

warned the Guardian that Mustapha Magyar was coming up from Doboj, that he had gone berserk and was fighting everyone he met or overtook on the road.

He pounded the gate with the handle of his army hatchet. There was silence. He stepped back a few paces and studied the building, with its huge roof, tiny windows, and thick walls. He toyed briefly with the idea of setting fire to it, then grew weary of it, detesting the very thought of having to look for straw and kindling. In the end the whole thing struck him as ludicrous: the large dwelling turned deathly still in front of him, the friars hidden inside, tiny and gray like mice.

"How quickly they locked themselves in, ha-ha-ha!"

Laughing uproariously, he set off again. As he was riding past the monastery graveyard, the horse took fright at a white cross showing above the wall, and Mustapha reined in and stopped. While he was trying to calm the horse and angrily cursing the monks and their crucifixes, two friars appeared at the bend in the road. One carried a stack of books in a leather strap, the other a pot with food. Since it was too late for them to turn back, they stepped down into the ditch by the road and greeted the Turk. He pulled up alongside them.

"Are you priests too?"

"We are, bey effendi."

"And who gave you the right to plant these white horns by the wayside to scare my horse? Eh, pigs of pigs?"

"We are not in favor of it, bey."

"What do you mean you're not in favor? Who gave you permission?"

"The Vizier and the illustrious Sultan," replied the older friar, a tall, bluff man with a great mustache and shrewd eyes.

Mustapha dropped his left arm to his side as if suddenly appeased and no longer angry, and only glared at them evenly with burning eyes, while they flinched away and looked down at their feet.

"Ah, so you have permission, do you?"

"Yes, bey effendi. Indeed we have it."

"From the Sultan himself?"

"Yes indeed. And from the Vizier too. And one other from the mullah at Sarajevo."

"Well then, put all three of them nicely together and throw them away. Do you hear? And if anyone asks what you're doing, tell him Mustapha Magyar gave you the order, the one that crashes like a rock down the mountainside, so that he needs no sleep or bread and doesn't recognize the law."

Having already sensed trouble in his dull and witless stare, the brothers hung their heads even lower at those words. He took the coil of rope from his saddle and commanded the younger one to tie up his older companion. The latter promptly thrust his hands behind his back, while the younger one bound him awkwardly, for his hands were shaking.

"Did you tie it well?"

"I did, bey."

Mustapha bent down and felt the rope with his fingers, and when he realized that the knot was loose he swung out with his hatchet. The friar ducked in time, but the blade caught the side of his shoulder with such force that he fell to the ground without a sound. The Turk started to whip him with the free end of the rope and kept at it until the young man got to his feet and begun walking in front of him, together with his bound companion. Blood oozed down his side and left a trail on the road.

Suddenly he made up his mind to drive them to Sarajevo and hand them over to his old friend Yusufagić, a wealthy and famed prankster. But when the road turned uphill and the sun set, the wounded friar grew weak and fell down unconscious every other moment. He pounded his ribs with the ax handle, so that he echoed like a barrel, but all in vain. They halted at a tumbledown shed by the roadside. The brothers at once slumped to the floor, leaning on each other, while Mustapha tethered the horse and spread his cloak to lie on it. Almost instantly a wave of drowsiness washed over him such as he hadn't known for a long time.

No greater happiness than a swift, deep slumber!

But even this thought flickered and guttered in a mist and a murmur of waves. The murmur rose up from a stream wreathed in floats, but these were not as heavy and as far apart and blood-spattered as those in the battle, but light and bobbing imperceptibly. Then something broke the sound of the waves and he found himself on hard ground, listening to a low droning noise. He sat up and opened his eyes, with a clear feeling that they were cold and terrible taut, as bleary as if he had never slept. He held his breath. A whisper came from the corner in which the friars were lying.

Expecting to die, the wounded monk (who was still a lay brother) had confessed himself to the older brother, and although he had been given absolution he went on repeating, in his fevered transport, the words of repentance and verses of prayer.

"Merci-merciful Lord, I love Thee—Thou art the highest good—"

"What are you whispering, you sons of a she-dog!"

Mustapha snatched the small rifle and fired into the dark corner where the friars lay. There was a scream, followed by moaning. He jumped to his feet, put on his cloak and led his horse out of the shed, forgetting all about Yusufagić and the joke he had planned with the friars. He mounted the horse in a hurry, as though he were fleeing from them.

He rode through the woods and the night chill soothed his spirit though the horse shied at the spectral tree roots and pricked his ears at the distant noises. He rode on until the night paled into the first wan gray of the morning, when he lay down under a beech tree and covered himself with his cloak. The cold entered his body, the silence lulled him, and all at once he fell into a dream.

He was in a skirmish on the river Orljava. He had wedged himself between two dark-colored boulders over which water trickled and lichen grew, and had braced his shoulders against the rock while the brothers Latković, two giant and fierce brigands, lunged at him. He defended himself well, but his eyes kept sliding past their heads toward the far horizon where the sandy plain joined the sky, where now a woman dressed in black appeared, with a contorted face, her hands on her chest. He knew her, and knew also why she clutched and pressed her breasts and why her face was twisted with pain. Yet even as he thought this and watched her and remembered how at Erzerum he had surprised her all alone in the money changer's house, and how desperately she had resisted him, he still kept his wits about him and fought back the pair of brigands. Pushing the woman and the memories from his mind, he concentrated hard on keeping the two hostile sabers at bay, but fury got the better of him.

"So you brought her along too! The pair of you wasn't enough, you bandit dogs! Are there more of you!"

He parried their thrusts with lightning speed, but the outlaws pressed closer, their blade tips flashing before his eyes, so that he shrank deeper into the rock and felt drenched with moisture and dread.

He woke up icy and in a cramp, with a curse on his cloyed lips, feeling utterly numb. The sun had just come up and its light fluttered on his lids. Seeing that once again he had not slept more than a few short minutes, that there was to be no more peace and rest even in the small hours, he cried out in a helpless rage, then pitched over and started to batter his head on the ground. He tossed and sputtered like this for a long time, biting at his crimson cloak, his mouth full of froth, until the sun rose higher in the sky, topping the mountains. Crumpled and shattered, he now walked down the hill, leading the horse behind him. He paused only when he reached the level ground beside a spring. A spout of water, bright and thick as an arm, fell into a trough made of hollowed-out pine. The water overflowed, creating a wide circle of soggy ground and marsh and shallow puddles above which, in the brilliance of the morning, there was a shimmer of butterflies and dense cloudlets of flies pulsing like veils.

The horse drank greedily, soaking his hooves in the wet grass, the muscles of his flanks and croup twitching, while Mustapha sat on the edge of the trough, deep in thought and calmed by the freshness of water and morning air on his cheeks. Then he saw himself in the water and noticed his shadowy face, dark as coal; but his head was wreathed in a thick swarm of tiny flies, each shot through with sunlight and dancing, all of them fused in a trembling halo thinly laced with light. Instinctively he raised his hand and saw his clenched fingers reflected in the water, dipped in that golden, radiant quiver, yet he felt nothing on the surface of his hand, so minute and weightless were their sun-fired little bodies. The horse jerked suddenly and startled him; the swarm moved and darted away, the halo vanished.

He rode on as in a dream till about noon, strangely becalmed. That night he might have continued on his way to Sarajevo, but on the road there, at the Inn of Omar, he was held up by Abdul Selambeg from the village of Čatići, a boastful windbag with blue eyes and a scraggly beard. They were the only guests at the inn. The bey tried everything to make him spend the night there, so that next day when they reached Sarajevo his friends and the people of the town might see him riding with Mustapha Magyar, a comrade and fellow traveler. Mustapha agreed. The sultry day was coming to a close and he was beginning to feel sleepy, even though the drowsiness was more like an exhaustion in which all perception and senses remained alert. The sun was setting, yet his ill humor heaved up in his throat and began to choke him.

93

He took a drink of water and, without another glance at Abdul Selambeg, lay down, with a last threat to the innkeeper that he would kill anyone who awakened him, be it a dog, a chicken, or a man.

He dozed off quickly enough, but then all of a sudden, as always when he least expected it, those children in Crimea rose up before him, blond and short-haired and at the same time hard and smooth and resilient, and slippery like fish. There was no glaze of shock on their eyes nor were their pupils narrowed by fear; they were steady and still. The effort of trying to grab them made him lose his breath, yet his mind registered every change in their movement, even the tiniest. And as he fumbled like this, furious at being unable to catch hold of them, he heard someone mutter behind his back: "You should have roasted them . . . caught them and put them on the spit . . . but now it's too late!"

He was in a rage of anguish. That's what we should've done: roasted them! And he made another attempt to catch them, but all he succeeded in doing was to stab the air with his arms, feebly and ridiculously, while the boys kept slipping away and, abruptly, began to soar like clouds.

He came to, soaked in sweat and anxiety, panting heavily and tearing the straw mat under him. The day was over; it was getting dark. He was filled with a sense of dread; the sweat on his skin turned cold and clammy. Hoarsely he called out to Abdul Selambeg, then ordered coffee and plum brandy and a tallow candle. The two of them sat and drank for quite a while: the restless candle flickering between them, the corners of the room full of gloom and uncertain shadows, a blue snippet of night in the small window. In the empty room their voices reverberated with an unpleasant, brittle sound.

Abdul Selambeg talked a good deal about himself, about wars, and his family. He recounted his services in the field, while Mustapha, slouching over the table, kept silent and merely shook himself after each glass of brandy. To loosen his tongue, Abdul Selambeg took to discussing the battle of Banjaluka and how he had watched him, Mustapha, leap from raft to raft to reach the other bank alone and fall on the Austrians.

"And you saw all that from under your blanket?" asked Mustapha.

"What? How do you mean?"

There was a glint in Mustapha's restless eyes, and the bey's jaw slackened; he was in two minds—whether to feel offended or take the remark as a joke. Mustapha was the first to laugh out, and the bey joined him, visibly relieved.

"A joke! I tricked you!"

"You did indeed."

The bey promptly resumed his tale of how he had pursued the Austrian soldiers whom Mustapha had routed.

"By God, I must have chopped down forty of them, at the very least."

"Yes, yes."

"Hey, there was one, small and fast—he ran like a goat, but I went after him. God has made me quick-footed, you see, so I came after him, closer and closer and closer—"

"And did you get him?"

"Wait till I tell you. We came up on a slope and I saw there wasn't much wind left in him. I caught up with him and then slash—just like a chicken!"

"Hunh."

Mustapha grunted and sighed, while the bey launched into another lengthy tale. What with brandy and the late hour and the man's general witlessness, the heroic feats multiplied and swelled, extending all the way back to his grandfather and great-grandfather, and his sniping and potshots on the various fields of battle underwent a miraculous transformation.

"That's how Allah made me, without fear. I remember the night patrol near the village of Mlečići. They were all shaking and whispering in the dark, but I stood up in my stirrups and sang out loud and clear—and my voice, praised be to Allah, is like a trumpet. Afterwards the enemy wanted to know what mighty scourge of a Turk that was, but our men knew already who it was: Who else could it be?"

"Eh, you lie a lot."

Carried away by his own words and imagination, the bey wasn't sure if he heard him right.

"What did you say?"

"You lie a lot, brother," said Mustapha curtly, not really interested. He puckered his lips and nibbled at his mustache.

It was only then that the bey's fancies evaporated like a bubble. The room grew darker around him. The candle flame shook and bent in the gust of his labored breath. The blood-shot, dangerously shiny eyes of Mustapha seemed awfully close, as did his sallow forehead and deathlike cheeks above the black beard. The bey recoiled, mortally offended; he sprang to his feet. The table overturned, the candle fell with a soft, dull thud and went out.

His drunkenness notwithstanding, Mustapha backed to the wall and, with the natural instinct of a fighter, groped for his cloak and pulled the pistol from his bandolier. Between them was the upended table; on the far wall of the room the window, transformed now in pitch darkness into a luminous cutout. In the stillness, as he held his breath, he heard a soft, scraping sound: the bey was pulling his dagger out of the sheath. And now once more, as if the sound touched off num-berless memories of the past, he thought with inexpressible hatred: How much scum there is in the world! But only for a moment. And at once he took hold of himself and considered his position.

The bey is a coward and a liar, he thought, and people of that sort kill easily. He has no gun in his hands. If he intends to go after me, he must go by the window.

He raised his gun, aimed at the center of the window and

waited. And sure enough, a second later there appeared on the window first the silhouette of the bey's hand, and then the quadrant of light was blotted out by his body. Mustapha fired. In the explosion that followed, he did not even hear the bey falling. The old innkeeper Omar was either deaf to the noise or else chose to stay away.

That night Mustapha rode through the woods without a pause. The horse stumbled from exhaustion and flinched at every shadow. The rider, too, began to see weird shapes among the lone tree stumps and their shadows in the translucent night in which there was no visible moon. They both quailed at those of a forbidding or menacing shape and gave them a wide berth. All of a sudden it seemed to Mustapha as if each shape was accompanied by a particular voice, a whisper, a shout, or singing—low, barely audible voices that overlapped and commingled with the shapes. Presently they were obliterated by the sharp crackle of the whip as he lashed out at his horse. But as soon as he stopped whipping, the voices began to drone again and assail him. To silence them he shouted at the top of his lungs:

"Aaaaaa . . . !"

At that the forest sent back its reply from all sides at once, from every hollow and tree trunk and leaf, deafening and smothering him with an even more powerful chorus: Aaaooo . . . !

He strained and yelled with all his might, although his throat hurt and his breath gave out, but was outshouted by an irrepressible pandemonium of sounds and menaced by every tree and brush. He broke into a headlong gallop, insensible to the horse under him, quaking in every part of his body. He was beginning to gag, yet kept shouting without letup, until he reached an open glade where the voices dwindled and faded away.

Morning overtook him on the heights above Sarajevo, while he was trying to find his way through some plum orchards. The horse faltered at every step, his ribs fallen in, his shanks torn and bloody. The whole sky was aglow and the sun kindled the thin clouds. The town lay under a blanket of fog, pierced only here and there by minarets that resembled the masts of sunken ships. He passed a hand over his dew-moist face. In vain he swatted at a pair of dark orbs through which the radiance of the day and the town beneath it appeared to him dimly. He rubbed his temples, and turned left and right, but the orbs shifted together with his moving glance and, through those orbs, everything before him appeared misty, shivering, and dusky. The silence was deep, and in it he could hear his blood rearing and breaking and crashing with a dull roar against the nape of his neck. He could not remember where he was, or what day it was. He thought the town below might be Sarajevo, but his mind swirled and confused it with certain towns in the Caucasus that had minarets just like these. At times his sight gave out completely.

He had enormous trouble finding his way through the maze of fences and plum orchards, and as he climbed down to the nearest Muslim quarter he stopped the horse in front of a coffeehouse where, on a wide and green terrace beside a fountain and a cemetery, some Turks were already sitting over black coffee. He dismounted and went in. Rumpled, muddied, he stepped gingerly through the twilight that hovered before his eyes. He observed the faces around him, but in the next instant they had melted away unaccountably, only to reappear again greatly multiplied and jumbled. He sat down. Through the hum of blood in his ears he listened to their talk, yet couldn't make head or tail of their words. They were talking about the repression carried out by the Sultan's emissary, Lutfi Beg.

After many protracted wars, the number of loafers and drunkards had multiplied to a point where there was a marked increase in plunder, killing, and violence of every type, not only in Sarajevo but throughout the rest of Bosnia as well.

Unable to ignore the complaints of the people any longer, the Sultan had dispatched a special envoy with unlimited powers. This tall man, who rode through the streets like a hermit, pale-faced and stooped-shouldered, with thin, drooping mustaches, was implacable, cunning, and swift. Never had the severity of government been felt so strongly. If anyone was caught drunk or loitering, or denounced as a killer or looter, the emissary had him thrown into the Yellow Dungeon where his Anatolian hangmen strangled him with a hard leather cord, without examination or trial. There were times when up to sixty felons were done away with in the course of a single night. The Christian populace rejoiced secretly, but the Turks were beginning to grumble at his harshness. He retorted by ordering the arrest and strangulation of two Sarajevo merchants who had criticized him publicly, before anyone could intercede for them. In the streets one could see the corpses of those who, in drunkenness or wrath, had perished defending themselves against the envoy's constables. Blood was seen everywhere and people were terror-stricken. At no time before had death been so easy to come by.

Now these Turks in the coffeehouse were discussing the envoy's campaign of repression. Not daring to say aloud what was really on their minds, they kept lamenting the fact that so many Turks had lost their lives, among them some famous soldiers and noted fighters. One of the men at the table said ruefully:

"The Christians will swamp us, by Allah! Our own kind is dying and the baptized scum are breeding like rabbits; there's no end to them!"

As the words reached Mustapha, they seemed in an addled way to be connected with his own thoughts. He made a great effort to concentrate.

"Baptized and circumcised, both," he said. "The world is full of scum."

They all turned in the direction of the voice, which was

uncommonly hoarse and raspy, like a magnified whisper. Looking him over, they noticed his disheveled appearance and the streaks of dried mud and greenish-yellow stains of wet grass on his clothes. His face was puffed up and dark. They observed, too, that his eyes were completely bloodshot and his pupils mere pinpricks in the center, that he clenched and un-clenched his hands constantly, that his neck, uncollared and bare, was swollen, and his left mustache gnawed off and no-ticeably shorter. They glanced at one another and then back at him.

Behind his curtain of blood, Mustapha was dimly aware of the faces craning in his direction and he got the idea that they were getting ready to attack him. He reached for his saber. They all sprang up; the older men backed to the wall, while two younger ones, brandishing knives, came toward him. He cut down the first one, but then, almost blinded, missed the sec-ond. He upset the mortar in which coffee was pounded. De-fending himself, he staggered blindly into the street; the Turks charged after him. Passers-by stopped to watch. Some thought that the scramble was caused by the envoy's constables trying to run down a drunken bully, others that the crowd was turn-ing the tables on the envoy's men. In recent weeks they had gotten used to daily commotions such as this, and they all took part in them with a kind of blood-thirsty alacrity, no matter on whose side they were.

Unseeing, Mustapha stumbled between some door posts, and the Turks from the coffeehouse and those from the street cornered him at the same moment. A dozen hands clawed at him all at once. They stripped him of his tunic, down to his shirt. His turban fell, his shirt tore and gave way. Struggling frantically, he did not let go of his saber. The weight of so many bodies pressing against the thin door boards caused it to give way with a loud crash; the human mass rocked and fell, and Mustapha wrenched himself free. With his sword raised, he darted down the steep incline of the street, the mob hard on his heels.

He ran on, unable to see in front of him, bald-headed, naked to his waist, and hairy. The mob yelled after him.

"Get him! He's mad!"

"He killed a man!"

"Cutthroat!"

"Grab him, don't let him escape!"

A few passers-by tried to stop him, but in vain. He struck down a constable who tried to intercept him. Many didn't know why they were chasing him, but the pack kept growing; newcomers ran out of doorways and joined it. The crowd was egged on by the shopkeepers along the way, who also joined in the chase with clubs and chains. Frightened dogs scampered beside Mustapha, chickens fluttered and screeched. Heads poked out of windows of the houses along the streets.

Assaulted and buffeted from all sides, Mustapha's darkening mind cleared for one more fleeting moment: The scum have overrun the earth! They're everywhere!

And although he was no longer master of his strength and life, he withstood the blows and ran much faster than any of them. He was already coming closer to the wooded cemetery at the far end of the street, when out of a smithy came a Gypsy who, seeing a half-naked man pursued by a mob, threw himself at the man with a rusty poker, caught him on the temple, and felled him on the spot.

A huge comet streaked across the dark, narrow sky and the smaller stars withered in its wake. In another second the last one was snuffed out. There was darkness and hard ground beneath. Hardening. That was his last sensation. The pack was closing in.

IN THE CAMP

Detachments of hard-breathing Tartars began to arrive more frequently, billets were multiplying, and now every townsman took it for granted that the Pasha would also come and the army would be mustered here. The district judge of Višegrad, Abdurahman Effendi Pozderac, a dour and unusually fat man, thoughtfully fingered the latest official order from Travnik, the provincial capital. The Pasha had written to "all district officers, school principals, the mayor of Sarajevo, the commanding officer of the janissaries, the agas of the reserves, standard-bearers, big landowners, and all men of action and decision":

In accordance with the resolve of the Leader of our Faith, I have received two firmans from Istanbul ordering me to make known that the brave warriors and Muslims of Bosnia, who wish to do so voluntarily and thus receive Imperial Blessing, should make ready for war and put in a supply of food and biscuit and wait for me. With the help of Allah, I plan to set out from Travnik on the second day of Bairam, on

Thursday, with my escort and bodyguard, and proceed through Sarajevo to Višegrad and beyond.

O you leaders and effendis, take note of my departure. I don't ask of you any provisions or expenses for myself or for my escort, except that in each district where I shall spend the night you prepare a thousand pounds of bread and five hundred sacks of barley. Let this be ready and waiting for me and I shall not demand that you prepare any other viands. And take good care that you do not requisition in my name even a single grain from the poor peasants, or trouble them. Therefore this order is forwarded to you through the office of the governor of Bosnia, and when it reaches you be guided by the content thereof and act upon it.

As he stood by a window full of flowers, the Višegrad judge muttered to himself:

"Splendid, upon my faith! For one night he asks nothing but one thousand pounds of bread and five hundred sacks of barley. If he stays here ten days—and he might stay longer—merciful Allah, he'll eat up the ground from under me!"

Worry and anger sent the judge into a coughing fit and he flushed deeply; it took him some time to regain his breath.

The town was overflowing with refugees from Užice, Novi-Pazar, and Senica. Everyone who had fled before the Serbian rebel Karageorge sought haven here, terror-stricken, half naked, and barefoot, without food or money. And now the governor himself was to come with his whole entourage and army, to make camp here.

"Oh, oh, oh, spare me, you devil! Oh you blight, get off my neck!"

He was as well known for his stinginess as for his wealth. He did not smoke or drink, he dressed and ate frugally, and penny-pinched with everyone, even his own family. Like all true misers, he loathed all giving and was appalled at any expense, no matter where in the world, or for what. The thought of the oil burning for nothing in the mosque lamps kept him awake some nights. His favorite dream, one that seemed to him the ultimate in happiness, was of a cash sum of money deposited somewhere in a safe place and growing without ever being touched, without risk, multiplying on and on. And because in this world such a thing is out of the question, he hated the whole world and all its regulations, which made it possible for capital to change hands, to fluctuate in value, and become spent. A diabetic who suffered from coughing fits and breathlessness, he lived his days wheezing, rasping, scolding, and counting. Now he summoned several town clerks and gave them his orders. With tears in his eyes, he exhorted them to save—save time, money, and their own town.

"No, no, no, we simply do not have it! In God's name, where would we get it from? Where from—when this town isn't like other towns? Here we have nothing but misery and calamities. Flood, drought, rebellion, war! Ah, all we need is a pestilence and cholera to wipe us all out at one stroke!"

With difficulty they came to an agreement on where to billet the Pasha with his retinue and where to accommodate the army, how to collect the grain store and divide up the food. The judge kept throwing up his arms, moaning, clapping a hand to the sallow, fat, creased nape of his neck.

"Go on, climb up here, why don't you! Give them everything! Here are the keys! Take the courthouse, distribute all there is!"

Then word came that the Pasha was traveling slowly because his entourage and baggage were enormous, and people began to talk about his luxuries and the marvels he carried with him. Rumor had it that he was unable to sit down to supper until a dozen candles "as thick as your arm" were lighted, that he had with him a pair of Arabs, monkeys, and a talking bird, and also the half-wit Sheh Dedije, who could eat thirty boiled eggs for a snack. The judge fell ill at this intelligence. He ordered his sitting cushion moved from the window to the far side of the room so as not to have to look out on the street or see anyone. He moaned like a wounded man.

But the tales were exaggerated. On the eve of Friday, the Pasha arrived; with a large retinue, it was true, and a big load of field trunks, but without monkeys, birds, or Arabs. Behind him rode only Sheh Dedije, gross and red-faced, on a long-haired horse. Both the Pasha and his men took up quarters at the huge Suleimanbeg blockhouse; and the latter still had the hollow sound of near-emptiness. Cheerful columns of smoke rose skyward, marking the end of the day's fast.

As the army trickled in, the troops struck camp on the slopes around the town. They came late and in disorder. The best disciplined contingent was the one from Prozor; it numbered an even hundred and was led by Salih Agha Ramljak, a tall man with a pock-marked face, a passionate hunter, known far and wide for his bravery and integrity. These men occupied the bridge and its watchtower. The troops from Travnik, mounted for the most part, were disgruntled with their food rations and billets. The last to arrive was the Sarajevo contingent, tardy and quarrelsome as always. To spite the Pasha, who had reprimanded them for their sluggishness as he overtook them on the road, they had recruited one whole company over and above the stipulated number.

Promptly on the morning after his arrival, the Pasha received the district judge and the town elders on a sofa in front of the blockhouse. With an air of careworn dignity, he consulted with them and smartly tossed rolled-up cigarettes to each as they sat in a semi-circle around him. He asked them what they had heard about the rebel Karageorge and about the attitude of the Christian peasants in the villages, and how well the Turks were armed, how many refugees there were, and what they were saying. He told them of his intention, the moment his supplies arrived, to continue marching on Srebrnica to join up with Ibrahim Beg, whom the Serbian rebels had surrounded, and from there to cross into Serbia itself. They either kept silent, or nodded their agreement, and the meeting broke up amid deep bows, scraping, and polite mutters typical of old people.

Toward the end of the meeting, the judge nevertheless managed to broach the difficulty of feeding both the refugees and the army. Seeing that the Pasha was willing to listen, and prompted by his own concern, he hastened to mention some other troubles and expenses; he wound up his itemization with the remark that for over a month now he had been sheltering and feeding, at his expense and in his house, a certain unfortunate refugee girl, daughter of a leading Turk in Trebinje. The Pasha reassured him that he would move the army in a few days and that all levies would be reduced as soon as, God willing, he was successful in routing the Serbs; as for the girl refugee, he advised him to send her back to her father in Trebinje. The judge protested that in these dangerous times, with the cost of living so inflated, he could not afford to do it. At length, the Pasha promised that he would personally see to it that the gril was sent back; whereupon the judge took his leave. In his excitement and effusive politeness he even forgot to cough.

The Pasha and his imam, Mullah Yusuf, had a good long laugh after supper, talking about the judge.

In moments such as these, the Pasha did not conceal his loathing for Bosnia and Bosnian men. Born in Istanbul and a courtier of long standing, he saw in his appointment as governor of Bosnia a successful intrigue of his opponents at the High Porte—a misfortune which one should endure wisely.

He had nothing but contempt for these unlettered, boorish, unbelievably narrow-minded Bosnian Muslims, who spoke their inanities with so much solemnity and importance. He was also contemptuous of the Serbs, that glum, shaggy, fanatical mob of Christian nobodies, who fought with such single-minded obsession against great and ancient institutions and blindly rushed to their deaths, thus losing, in the name of foolish dreams and lies, the "good life," as he called it. And he looked down his nose on the meek Bosnian Jews, on the whiskered Orthodox priests and wily Franciscan monks, regarding them as people without honor and dignity. Once, after receiving a deputation of Franciscans, he had said to his police chief:

"When the whole world and all the states have sank and perished, these friars will be floating on top like oil on water."

He abominated the whole gloomy and mountainous country with its tortured landscape and insane climate, as he did its eternally wrangling and restless inhabitants, for he shrank from everything that was loud, shrill, and intemperate. He loved quiet work in a settled groove and moderate delights and pleasures. At times he would dream all night of the sea, dotted with white sails, and next morning he would feel a double hatred for the bearded and wide-shouldered Bosnians around him, and for the violent line of mountains that shut off the view above Travnik, his capital. He was secretly working through friends in Istanbul to regain his old post there. While he had no clear idea of the scope and extent of the present rebellion, he knew that nothing much could be accomplished with this Bosnian "army." So he planned to disperse the Serbs in quick order, or else, by delaying his punitive expedition, to wait for autumn when the contingents would disband and return to their homes. He had hopes that during the winter his scheme in Istanbul would bear fruit and he would be happily rid of Bosnia and war.

His advisers and intimates were all non-Bosnians. He had left Travnik in charge of his deputy vizier, Ibrahim Effendi, a tall and methodical man from Istanbul, and Tahir Beg, a trusted Muslim convert. With him he had taken only this Sheh.

Dedije, who under the mask of an amiable harebrain concealed quite a treasure of healthy sense and artfulness—and his imam, Mullah Yusuf.

Until recently this Mullah Yusuf had been principal of the Muslim school at Sarajevo. During a controversy between him and the Sarajevo elders, the Pasha had interceded on his behalf, and afterwards, when Yusuf was relieved of his post anyway, he had brought him to his court at Travnik to spite the old men of Sarajevo and his own enemies at the Porte in Istanbul. The man was now part of his retinue as an official imam of the army.

This wiry and brisk mullah, with a sparse beard and mustaches of uneven length, swarthy and flushed as if scorched by the sun, had been a well-known personality in Sarajevo.

Born at Edirne, he had moved to Istanbul while still a boy and there very soon won himself a reputation for learning and debauchery. Later he had lived at Brusa, spending several years as military imam in various expeditions in Armenia and Transylvania. After he came to Sarajevo, he taught grammar and speech at the high school on Čobanija. He knew many languages, and learned new ones very quickly. With great skill and accuracy, he determined the lunar periods and holidays, and forecast the eclipses and seasonal changes. Handy with writing and things mechanical, he was clever at repairing any type of clock and dismantling and reassembling guns and coffee grinders. He composed verses, instructive and easy to read, for his senior students; he also wrote (but read only to his colleagues) humorous and extremely bawdy doggerel, some of it in the "Bosnian language, for Bosnians"; and epitaphs for the cemetery monuments as well. He had no peer in this kind of thing. There was only one type of writing he refused to touch: the customary sick records of ailing citizens —which they also held against him. He had a fine voice, clear and strong, that could easily be picked out among a hundred other muezzins, and he called the faithful to prayer from the Sultan's mosque, and that only during the sacred month of Ramadan; and occasionally to mourn a dead person. He was unkempt and a careless dresser. The one piece of clothing on him that was always neat was the chalk-white hajji band, deftly and meticulously wound around his red fez, under which his narrow and swarthy face all but disappeared.

In the complaint of "Sarajevo dignitaries," in which they had demanded his removal, all the bad things that were known about him were listed in malicious and exhaustive detail. The petition alleged that he was of Gypsy origin, that he had been obliged to flee Istanbul as well as Brusa on account of some incidents which, though not fully known, were most disgusting and reprehensible. It was said that in Transylvania he had been found bending over a woman whose throat had been slit; and it was only thanks to the sudden withdrawal of the army ordered that day that the matter had been forgotten. There was also mention of a Christian female domestic who had disappeared the year before; the investigation about her had dragged on and then ground to a stop, but while it was in progress it had revolved unmistakably around the school. All in all, the mullah's manner of life was disorderly and invited derision unbecoming to a learned person and a cleric. The list of his misdemeanors included many other incidents, some hard to believe, others plainly absurd, and for all that "furor and dissatisfaction" he was finally relieved of his post.

The Pasha kept the mullah because he needed him and because he wished to spite the Sarajevo faction, but he did not like the man. Even though at Travnik Mullah Yusuf had not been guilty of any conspicuous indiscretion, the Pasha found him unpleasant and at times detestable. When he was alone with Sheh Dedije, and in a bad mood, he would call the mullah "a pig above all pigs".

Now, during the mobilization, the mullah made himself

indispensable. He kept accounts and records. In this sultry and airless valley, the mullah was unable to sleep at night, or, for that matter, stay put in the daytime. He made the rounds of the camp, received and escorted the mounted couriers; and on many an afternoon he would go down to town and, like once in Sarajevo, tear through the streets as if chased by someone, his dusty and scuffed boots creaking, the folds of his black cape gusting behind him. Women rushed to close their window shutters, and children, squatting on the door steps with large chunks of bread in their hands, simply tumbled back into the doorways. He asked to substitute for old Alihodja, the local mullah, so that he might announce the time of the night prayer. With an oil-spattered lantern in his hand, he scraped his shoulders and knees against the narrow walls as he climbed the spiral stairway to the top of the minaret. Once up there, he would cry out through his cupped palms and thrust his chin out fiercely at the invisible sky and the new moon that was melting softly in pools of murky crimson vapors. And his voice rose steadily, lashing and cutting through the darkness above the town like cold, thin, but irresistible steel, so that children awoke and whimpered and seamstresses lifted their heads from their work. Afterwards he could not sleep again.

The end of that poor, flood-ravaged spring was drawing near. At the confluence of two rivers just north of the town, naked trees poked up from the muddy banks; crows flocked in the silted fields. The days were humid and full of a trembling gray light that wearied the eye. An acrid smell of burning lay heavily on one's breath. From the ashen sky a sweltering heat continued to seep down. The seed in the earth molded and failed to germinate. The tongue grew dry in one's mouth; the eye corners smarted. There was no freshness even at night. Rain clouds would pile up in the distance, but as soon as they drew over the Višegrad valley they thinned and shrank and dissipated in a tepid mist. As for the air streams that swept down from the mountain passes, no sooner did they pour into the valley than they slackened, grew lukewarm, began to swirl dizzily in a flagging spiral, only to settle, exhausted, on the layers of humidity already stacked there.

The slopes on both sides of the river had become encampments. The army had shaken down, though latecomers were still arriving. Bakers, who were Christians for the most part, were building clay ovens and kneading bread dough. There were fires all round. Pickets began to disappear from the fences, haystacks to lose their hay. Paths were trodden in places that had never had them. Drinking fountains clogged and spoiled. Drums sounded, interspersed with loud cries and swearing. Loudest and most numerous were the reed pipes of the Sarajevo contingent; but the men from Travnik were better singers. And on an evening such as this, most of the others fell silent and came to listen to them, even though ordinarily they disliked them.

Time passed and the supplies did not come. The army was bored and grumbling over the bread-and-flour-soup rations. Chickens and spring lambs began to disappear from private courtyards. Soldiers banded in groups and went down to town, to loiter in front of shops and quarrel over prices and portions at the various inns. They roamed through the streets and peeped through fences and house gates, they ran after girls, jabbered, guffawed, and whooped. There came a rumor that a detachment of insurgents was at Staniševac. A strong column went out to reconnoiter, but they found nothing; all they brought back with them were the heads of a Serbian Orthodox priest and his brother, and those, already quite wizened, were now hoisted on stakes on the bridge.

Of the Christian inhabitants, very few ventured outdoors. At the first sign of dusk they padlocked themselves and went to bed to avoid having to burn lamps. In the big squat house at the bottom of the hill, the Orthodox priest Jovo sat uneasily, pale and with cataracts in both eyes, dressed in a dark-blue soutane and a greasy cap, waiting till they came for him. Beside him sat his wife, a portly and simple-minded woman, trying to recall a prayer that might help them, but, unable to remember it, sniveling and cowering instead. Not a soul dared to visit them. Their servant girl Ikonia had had a miscarriage and was lying in bed with fever.

All through the encampment the kneading of dough, slaughtering, cooking, and eating went on without a pause. It looked as if the Turks, through sheer idleness and long boredom, had become transformed into mere stomachs and mouths; their lapping of food, their clattering and scraping of pots could be heard long into the night. The camp stank from afar with the gluttony and loafing of the multitude. The damp and stuffy air made it seem as if the very ground under them were rotting and smelling.

Puffy, yellow-skinned conscripts from Asia, who were without equipment and money, roved through all the nooks and alleys, picking up and scrutinizing every rag they could find, after first rubbing it against their hips. They gaped with dull, inhuman eyes at the children and women, and shunned military patrols. One morning a little boy was found dead under the bridge, hideously mangled. There was a hue and cry, and the Pasha sent another courier to Sarajevo to expedite the supplies.

The judge despaired over the mounting costs and the loafing. After a vexing and exasperating day at the courthouse, he would shut himself in his home and threaten not to come out again until the camp was moved; but next morning fear and impatience would drive him out once again. His house was in the center of the little town; the only occupants of the large dwelling were he and his wife and the servants, whom they changed frequently. The old curmudgeon's home was crammed to the rafters; the cellars, granaries, and barns were

113

piled high with stores. The rooms, in which a wintry silence always reigned, were smothered in carpets, spreads, embroideries, boxes and chests of aromatic wood. But everywhere and over everything there lay that chilly spotlessness so often found in Bosnian homes that was intimidating and forbidding, that neither cheered nor served anyone. This wealth and cleanliness were guarded and protected all day long by the judge's wife, a flat-chested woman with missing teeth, contorted and rumpled from so much fussing around the rooms, from bickering with the servants, and from her excessive thrift. It was in this house that the girl refugee from Trebinje was sheltered.

She had been kidnapped from her father's estate by the rebel-brigand Špaljo Montenegrin, who then took her to the Tara monastery with the idea of having her baptized so that he could marry her. As the Turkish police were close on his heels, he had to flee with her from monastery to monastery, from accomplice to accomplice; he would leave her in hiding for a few days and go away to do his raiding, and then, without warning, in the middle of the day or in the dead of night, come back and drag her away again. Eventually, a superior Turkish force had routed him on the highway between Goražde and Sokolac, and retaken the girl. They brought her to Višegrad, where the town elders decided to send her back to her father at the first opportunity, and until then to put her up in a home where there were no children. And so she was allotted to the judge.

This tall girl was quite deranged by her terrible and disastrous experiences. She had lost her power of speech and now stared dully and fixedly in front of her, incapable of recognizing or comprehending anything.

The dreadful Špaljo, who had swooped down on her family's manor like lightning and killed everyone and dragged her away with him, had been all skin and gristle, cold and hard. Then there had been those peasant huts full of smoke and goat droppings. Then the icy monasteries that smelled of pork fat and incense, and gray-haired monks with sepulchral voices and beards yellowed by tobacco. And betweentimes, those headlong night flights when under the blackness of the mountains one's will and wits crumbled and tree branches whipped one's eyes. In that terror, hardness, and cold, she had lost all sense of herself. Since they had brought her to the judge's house, she had calmed down a little. She still did not open her mouth but did not weep either, and spent the whole day sitting in the small garden that was enclosed by high walls; it was damp there and full of fiercely tangled undergrowth. As soon as they led her indoors, she would back into a corner of a room and crouch there with her hands pressed between her knees. Days passed and the judge waited in vain till the Pasha sent for her as he had promised. Supplies had still not arrived. The army camped on.

It was only toward the end of the second week that everything suddenly took a turn for the better. To begin with, the temperature dropped sharply on Friday evening and streams of cold air soughed loudly into the valley and broke the stagnation. The sky shook with thunderclaps; bolts of lightning vaulted across the slopes one after another. When night fell, there was a heavy cloudburst. Sheets of water hit the ground with such force that they turned to vapor, swept this way and that by the wind. All things vanished and lost their voice, save for the downpour that fell all night like a dream and a respite.

Next morning, the greater part of the supplies arrived in town. The day was damp and clean-washed; the views acquired new depth, the horizons were clear. The forests on the high slopes looked like new. It was decided to break camp at dawn next morning, to move out and send a detachment for the balance of the supply train, which was then to proceed directly to Srebrnica. The Pasha summoned the judge again;

the girl was moved from the latter's house to a furnished inner room at the Suleiman Beg blockhouse. Mullah Yusuf took upon himself the responsibility of sending her that evening to Sarajevo in the company of old Avdaga and some mounted men, and from there, through his friend Munir Effendi, who was a dispatcher of mails, to deliver her to her father at Trebinje.

The camp echoed with noise, preparations, and livelier singing. After a brilliant day the dusk was gathering fast, with only a fleeting afterglow, when Mullah Yusuf came down to the blockhouse to see the girl.

The old woman Fatima had gone home. The girl sat in a corner, wrapped in a shawl. He addressed her gently, hastening to assure her that he would say a prayer over her in order to cure her and send her home; but for that she would have to take off the wrap. She rose for a moment, as if wavering.

"Better take it off, daughter. Go on."

She threw off the shawl and stood tall and motionless before him, somehow bigger and handsomer now that she was set fully against the small, low-ceilinged room; surprising and dumbfounding him with her good looks and well-shaped body. Her neck shone palely; darkened neither by hair nor shadows, it looked extraordinarily smooth and white.

"You must take off the jacket too. Yes, the jacket. Otherwise it can't be done."

His voice quavered and he smiled fixedly.

With a meek air of helplessness, the girl raised her arms (as if about to be crucified) and peeled off her short sleeveless jacket. The movements of those arms, white and ample and yet drained of all strength and will, overpowered and shattered the trembling mullah, and he came up to her to untie the sash of her pantaloons.

"This, too, daughter. Off with everything, everything!"

She resisted weakly, with gestures that were stunted and mechanical as in a dream.

116

Here the hand could wander at leisure, over those thighs and hips. No end to it, ever! It was warm there, and smooth like ice. His mouth twisted and gathered in a pucker, as if from raspberries; he felt weak-kneed and the muscles of his left cheek twitched visibly. The girl stood there absently and permitted everything with an air of grave, dull apathy that brought the lecher back to his senses and spurred a desire to prolong and sharpen the thrill, to draw forth some protest and movement. He reached up to a low shelf for a barber's razor. He was breathing hard and felt chilly from head to heels; yet kept slavering and using his hands.

"I have to shave you."

At that point, however, the girl unexpectedly slipped away, gave a stifled shriek, and began to dash around the room. She was only in her shirt, and now that she was in motion it seemed as if every part of her had swelled and was brimming and spilling. She fought back, stumbled and fluttered across the room like an unfurled banner, while the mullah, thin and darkly flushed, lunged at her and sprang after her, keeping up a disjointed mutter and brandishing the razor.

"Stop! A shave first, stop . . . !"

Her shirt split on the right side and the shoulder gleamed up, once more white, round and plump beyond belief. In the tussle and struggle, he accidentally grazed the naked shoulder with the razor, and the shallow cut filled with blood.

The mullah stopped short, his head lolling, the face ashen; his dark-blue lids came down low. A pair of teeth flashed through his parted lips. He remained like this for a second, then shivered and hurled himself furiously at the girl. She screamed, but in a choked and thin voice (a mute animal), waiting for him and repulsing him like a battlement, hard, white, and naked. She pounded the walls and rattled the locked door. And through the stampede of their feet and through their panting this sound of her big strong body could still be heard—clear, resonant, almost metallic. Disfigured beyond

117

recognition, the mullah raged on. His turban slipped all the way to the back of his head and his breath came in an exultant rasp.

"Kh-kh-kh!"

There was blood on her again, now on the other shoulder, and presently it gushed out of her throat in a spate. She doubled over, slipped to the floor and filled the corner of the room, while the mullah dropped alongside and mingled with her indistinguishably.

THE PASHA'S CONCUBINE

On the very eve of Austrian occupation, Veli-ud-din Pasha, nicknamed Circassian, came to Bosnia for the second time—this time as commander in chief of all forces on Bosnian soil. He arrived in Sarajevo early in January, without a harem and with little baggage—a fact that immediately attracted notice. In the bazaar they called him a tramp, a rag picker and beggar. "The stuff he brought with him wouldn't have filled a sack," said the men in the bazaar, "but when he leaves Bosnia, watch out for the load of trunks." But in truth, Veli Pasha's household was disorderly rather than poor. The housekeeping was done by an ailing woman, a Jewess from Bessarabia. She was thin, and bowed before her time; something dusky and melancholy in her eyes was the only trace of her former beauty. The servants were a mixed lot drawn from all parts of the world, good for nothing, thieving, and lazy. The Pasha's residence was on Alaibeg's property at the top of the steep Logavina Street.

Veli Pasha himself had changed greatly in these last eight years. He drank more, except that now he did it even more furtively and in private. He was moodier and more short-tempered than ever before. Although still agile, he had grown heavier; and the hair on his temples had become streaked with gray. His left cheek bore some kind of a red blemish, the size of a child's palm, that imperceptibly but steadily grew larger and thicker, eating more and more into the soft underpart of his eyelid. He often suffered from a pustulant rash in his mouth, and from chest pains. But there was almost no change to be seen in his Circassian profile, on which his forehead, his nose, and his heavy mustache sloped down in one line, tilted as it were at the powerfully carved chin. The eyes, too, were unchanged—dark and symmetrically cut, with a calm and earnest look, the kind one sees in clever children and in truly bold and noble men.

He came from a well-known military family and was an only son. His father had left him a considerable estate. Brave, generous, and handsome, he had advanced very rapidly. How-ever, he had spent the last few years in obscure garrisons along the Russian frontier, returning to Istanbul from time to time to sell his legacy, piece by piece.

Ten years ago, he had been transferred to Bosnia, as a colonel at Bijeljina. But since Hafiz Pasha, the commander in chief at the time, had been a good friend of his and also a distant relative, he spent more of his time at Sarajevo than at Bijeljina. He was popular with all the officers and foreign con-suls, and well known for his horses and picnics in the hills above the city. Nevertheless, even though his good command of Russian enabled him to learn Bosnian quite well, so that he had no trouble communicating with the local people, they took a dislike to him right from the start, for he could be haughty, brusque, and forbidding. And since those early days the leading Turks of Sarajevo remembered him with anything but pleasure.

In the Provincial Council, where the foremost noblemen

of the land bickered interminably with the dawdling civilian governor and with venal high army officers, he often cut short their speeches and threw them into confusion with his curt, practical, army-style questions. And so it came about that he began to feel an increasing contempt for them on account of their foolish jingoism, narrow-mindedness, and idle chatter, while they in turn began to hate him and speak ill of him. Stories were told that he had plundered all the towns in the Caucasus, that he was in debt and a friend of the Russians, that he indulged in drinking orgies with the English vice consul, and swilled wine and ate pork. And he, in his turn, gave them more and more cause for hatred and calumny. Showing no interest for anything in the world except his soldiers and his horses, he was unscrupulous and merciless and, when his army needed something, had no qualms taking it from the Turks and Christians alike. He fined the Sarajevo Jews at every opportunity; but when his soldiers helped themselves to the hay in the Sarajevo meadow that belonged to an important bey, there was hue and cry among the members of the Council. In vain did the governor, a relative of his, implore and admonish him to keep in mind the touchiness of the beys. Summoned to the Council to explain the incident of the hay, he gave a short speech the likes of which had not been heard before. To the accusations that he was a drunkard and a bully who took what belonged to other people, he answered calmly and with a sneer:

"I like to drink, but no one has ever seen me drunk. I don't look for squabbles, but, by Allah, I know how to fight. I have no money or credit, not a puppy or kitten to my name. I fear Allah and serve the Sultan—now what do you propose to do about it?"

Here he turned to the dignitaries and, with the practiced sangfroid of an old cavalry officer made an unexpectedly obscene gesture.

Soon after this he was recalled to Istanbul and reassigned to the Russian frontier.

And now, even though he had come back as commander in chief of the entire Bosnian army, he no longer showed his old interest in military affairs, or his former obduracy in his clashes with the civilian governor and the beys. At Travnik, he maintained several detachments of cavalry and two battalions of Albanian foot soldiers. These units were the only ones he was concerned with, the only ones he personally visited and inspected. He utterly neglected the Anatolian troops in Herzegovina, and had not the slightest wish to see the battalion of Turkish regulars at Sarajevo itself. Whenever the commandant of that battalion, a portly major by the name of Uzunić, came to report to him, he would gaze past him with an absent look and invariably leave all his questions unanswered. In this he was so unaffected, adept, and full of dignity that no one knew how to deal with him or dared to break his silence.

Otherwise, among the local people there were only two with whom he occasionally met and talked: Mulaga Merhemić, the oldest of four Merhemić brothers, a reputable merchant and a quiet, upstanding man; and Mullah Suleiman Jakubović, a dervish of the Mevlevi order, a devout monastic but a sincere, outspoken, and cheerful person. Jakubović had a small room at the far end of Čumurija, where that street meets Tašlihan; the room had a large window which, like a store shutter, was open to the street. Here he sat cross-legged all day long, reading and praying, receiving visitors, giving advice, or else simply gazing into the street, cordially saluting passers-by of all faiths, shouting an occasional polite greeting. And here, too, Veli Pasha often stopped his horse to exchange a few words with this lean dervish who had an unusual way with a sentence and talked freely on almost any subject with a certain wise and jovial pungency.

With the civilian governor, Vizier Mazhar Pasha, he met rarely and talked little, and then in a kind of good-humored and flippant tone that was not entirely free of contempt.

He avoided the meetings of the Council, and on the rare occasions when he was forced to attend he would sit motionless and without a trace of his old intensity, gazing over the heads of the Council members with the same absent and inattentive eyes, forgetting everything and hearing no one, while all the time, with bated breath, he would cock his inner ear to the blight that was burrowing and gnawing dully at his left cheek and spreading to the still-healthy part of his face.

A few weeks after his arrival, Veli Pasha went to Travnik to inspect the garrison. He spent there two days in all. He hardly went anywhere and completed the inspection in no time.

Although February was still in its first week, the air had suddenly grown balmy, bringing with it an unexpected touch of spring. There was a cracking of ice and a roar of new torrents, the house eaves dripped in a daylong whisper; and all night long water gurgled and ran down the streets, which began to show their underlayer of stone. The play of the new sun and rising vapors sparked a bluish, swaying radiance in the air that brightened all things.

In the forenoon of the second day, as he was returning from the drill field, the Pasha and his escort found themselves in the bazaar. They rode cautiously over the thawing ice. It was a market day, and in front of the Garić Bakery their way was blocked by some peasants' horses laden with wood. While the flustered farmers began to hop and skip around the stubborn horses, the Pasha cast a glance into the bakery. Next to the closed brick oven stood the old baker Ali, stoop-shouldered, with rheumy, wizened eyes out of which tears kept oozing on his great white mustache. At the wide-open shopwindow, among the bread loaves and pans of meat and pies, was his daughter Mara. On her knees and propped on the counter with one arm, she had stretched the other for a platter on a shelf underneath. When she heard the shouts of the soldiers and the stamping of the peasants' horses, she lifted her head, and the Pasha, seeing her wrapped like this around the counter, fell in love with her round, childish face and her merry eyes.

When he rode that way again in the afternoon, the bakery was deserted, the window half-shuttered, and on the sill was a purring cat with singed white hair.

He gave orders that the girl be found and brought to him. The noncommissioned officers and the town constables ran eagerly to carry them out. He stayed over till noon of the third day, when they reported that the matter could be arranged. The girl had no one except her father. Her mother had been the well-known Jelka, named Hafizadić after the old Mustaybey Hafizadić, who had kept her for several years and then married her off to this Garić, a quiet and simple-minded young man, to whom he had also given money to open the bakery.

The Pasha left some money and entrusted the matter to his old acquaintance Teskeredžić. And toward the end of March, on another market day, they brought the girl to him at Sarajevo.

The Pasha had not been wrong in his judgment. She was the kind of woman he had always sought and particularly esteemed, the only kind that still attracted him. She was not quite sixteen. She had big eyes of a dovelike shade and muted porcelain luster, which moved languidly. Her hair was quite fair, heavy, and thick, such as was seldom seen on women in this region. Both her face and her arms were covered with a fine, light down that was noticeable only in sunlight. What was unusual about her was that even those parts of her skin which were not exposed to the sun and air, were not uniformly white and dun, as is usual with blonde women, but her whole body glowed with a bright, burnished hue that changed only in the shadowy hollows or with a sudden and irregular onrush of blood, when it turned even richer. Her hands were perfectly childlike, short and pink.

The Pasha was buoyed up. In the first few days he was occupied only with her. He also found it pleasant to think that now too, as once before, he could tell by an outstretched hand the kind of woman her owner was, and her true worth. Had he brought her in earlier, it would have been no good; while three to four months later, it seemed to him, the bloom would have been over. This was exactly the right time. She was cut off from her own kin, frightened and isolated, dependent only on him. At times she appeared to him like a young animal which, driven to the edge of a precipice, quivers in her whole body, her pupils contracting. This fanned the passion of his love and, in the contradictory ways of the male heart, evoked in him the impulse to be generous, to make her happy, to protect her.

She lived not far from the Pasha's residence, in a separate cottage which he had rented and furnished. Except for her visits to the Pasha, she went nowhere and received no visitors, save for Hamša the Gypsy, who kept house for her, and Baba Anuša from Bistrik, who was distantly related to her and who lived with her two grandchildren in great poverty. She spent all her days in two poorly lighted rooms, doing those sundry little chores that are so inconspicuous and yet so easily fill a woman's day. At dusk the Pasha's equerry would come for her, and she would wrap and veil herself up to her eyes and then, with a bowed head, accompany him to the Residence.

In the beginning, after they had just brought her from Travnik, she felt utterly lost. Physical pain took complete hold of her; and it was only when this pain, after the first few nights, began to fade that there arose in her mind, like a torment, a vague yet dark and nagging thought of sin and shame. She was afraid of the Pasha, she loathed that Jewess of his,

Sarah, and shied away from daylight and from people. She could not sleep, yet even in her dreams felt herself damned.

Nevertheless, she gradually came to terms with Sarah, who was taciturn and good and who did her work and helped in everything with a kind of melancholy friendliness. Getting accustomed to the Pasha and his caresses was harder; even after the initial pain and fear had faded, she accepted those numbly, in childlike bewilderment. But after a while she began to get used to them. She grew especially fond of the smell of his skin. It was seldom that she could look into those unusually steady eyes without a certain timidity, or into that face with its dreadful patch of blight on the left cheek and its dark drooping mustache that was always a little damp and quivered when he spoke like tufted grass in a dark forest pond. But the waftings that his body sent out attracted her more and more, they thrilled and delighted her; and she inhaled them for hours with her eyes closed, her head resting on his chest or in the palm of his hand.

The anguish came back to haunt her only at night when, as it often happened, he sent her to sleep alone. She would then wake up several times with a clear realization—such as can only come in the dark—of what and who she was now, and with a mouth choked with sobs she would press her face between the quilt and the pillows and stammer:

"Turk . . . !"

In the darkness, the racking thought would assume the shape of eternal punishment and hellish torture, not of earthly shame and ruin as in the daytime. But the next evening she would again face the Pasha with blushing cheeks and a wordless smile that seemed to be made entirely of glistening white teeth and sparkling eyes.

So it went every evening. He would come from an army exercise, or from a ride, flushed and a little sweaty, and she would wait for him with her hands crossed on her breast. He would then undress; Sarah would bring cold water, and a maid would take away his boots. After he had washed and cooled off, he would ask them to open the door and all windows that commanded a view of Sarajevo and the Trebević mountain. He would sit like this in the cool draft until Sarah brought a bottle of *mastika* and a tray of olives and thin strips of bread. Later the equerry Salih would come in with the *nargileh* on which the lighted tobacco heap would smolder a dark red, while in its crystal bottle, on the limpid surface of water, there would float two crimson cherries. Then Sarah and the equerry would vanish, and from an adjoining room Mara would return, prepared, and sit on his lap. Between the two of them, this was called "sitting in the box." And next to him, indeed, she was so small, and would snuggle so closely, that all of her could fit comfortably between his crossed legs.

While it was still daylight, she would, sitting thus, rummage through his box of pictures and photographs, in which she found unusual delight and excitement, and which he explained to her only on rare occasions.

Here there were many photographs from the time when as a young officer he had taken part in the various commissions that set the common frontiers with Russia. On all of them she indentified him easily—slimmer, with a smaller mustache and a face not yet disfigured. She admired the Russian officers, splendid men in white blouses and caps, and timidly inquired about them. These questions he answered more willingly, for through them she would touch his weakness for everything that was Russian, a partiality he had acquired during long years of life in the garrisons along the Russian frontier, and in consorting with the Russians, and which all his life he had harbored like a secret foible. Among the pictures were also lithographs of hunting scenes and ships, sent to him by an English friend, whose snapshots, invariably sporting a pipe and a pair of dogs, kept cropping up. There were street scenes, too, and views of Istanbul and Smyrna, and of the gloomy town of Akka with its ruined battlements.

And even when twilight began to deepen, they would be sitting quiet and motionless like that; she inhaling the familiar smell, he feeling the imprint of her small ear, with its invisible ring, on his bare chest. They would hardly stir, and talk little; save for an occasional smile and mock threat on his part when she would start to nibble the hem of his shirt. Over her inclined head he would drink glass after glass of *mastika*, or blow rings of whitish smoke from his *nargileh*, in the restless water of which the two crimson cherries kept bobbing. So he drank and smoked and, over her blond nape, watched the slow darkening of the town below and the guttering of cloud after cloud on the mountains.

And when the dark was complete and on the steep roads of Bistrik and Megara clusters of tiny lights flared up, and the stars surfaced in the sky, she would get up, light a candle, and remain waiting by the door. If he said, "Are you sleepy?" she would nod and withdraw into the other room, leaving him by his bottle and candle. But if he said, "Shall we, daughter?" she would go up to him, help him to rise, and they would go together into the room to lie down. Except that this happened less and less often. Usually he sent her in to sleep alone, while he stayed behind to drink, sometimes for many long hours.

Lying in the dark, she would listen to every sound from the glazed verandah and wish that she could be with him, and not have to sleep; at the same time she trembled at the thought that he might enter.

Often she would get up and, shivering all over, peer through the keyhole. (No sooner was she thus a few paces away from him, than he seemed to her strange and forbidding.) She would watch him abandon his *nargileh* and put away his amber bead-string, then reach for an oval mirror with an inlaid handle and a frame of gilded bronze, and take a jar of

128

silver nitrate from a box and dress the purple bruise on his face for long minutes, scowling from pain. Before his crossed legs there lay a long, gleaming knife, resting on its back, the sharp side uppermost. And this carefully placed knife, which looked as if it might tip over at any moment, seemed to have the effect of further subduing and mesmerizing his already cramped and infrequent movements. After which he would once more resume his frozen posture, staring into the night and draining his glass at ever shorter intervals.

Seeing him so glum and stiff, with the string of beads, the knife, and the mirror beside him, she felt as though he were performing an inexplicable rite and making an offering to something arcane, horrible, and utterly evil. She would shudder and grit her teeth, yet wouldn't budge from the door until her breasts turned cold and her feet fell asleep. Only then would she slump on the pillows, exhausted, crushed by a feeling that there, behind that door, her soul had also perished.

On waking next morning, her sense of dread would be undiminished. But as the day advanced and the afternoon drew nearer, her curiosity and desire would wax stronger and stronger, until at last, fully dressed and wrapped, and with a kind of aching impatience, she would start waiting for the evening, for the night, for the torment, and for all that had to be. And the dusk would find her "in the box," with a lapful of scattered pictures, timidly asking, "What's on the other side of the sea?" "What kind of people are the Russians?" "How's it that you can take pictures of saints and people?" And everything would be repeated over again.

One other thing troubled her greatly: that she didn't go to church. She dared not and didn't know how to tell him that. But in the veiled and never openly acknowledged give and

129

take that was now developing between them, he remembered it himself and told her, one Friday, that she ought to go. She blushed deeply and only nestled closer to him. And the following Sunday a special attendant of the Pasha's accompanied her to the foot of the church walls, and there waited for her until the Mass was over.

She came back with her head bowed even more abjectly, shaking with muffled sobs. She had often enough, during the day and at night, mused about her life and her shame, but none of it had ever been quite so real and dreadfully clear as during those two brief hours which she had spent in church.

As she had appeared on the church portals, all heads had turned toward her. Old and young women, under red or multicolored kerchiefs, looked her up and down and then resumed praying, their chins on their chests. Hatred and scorn closed in from all sides; so much so that she froze and stopped in the middle of the church. No one wanted to step aside and make room for her. She fell to her knees as in a dream, not daring to lift her eyes either at the altar or at the wall above it on which there was a painting of a haggard and sallow saint—not of Our Lady, as in her church at Dolac. Even the sexton going the rounds with his copper collection bowl gave her a wide berth. And Fra Gregory, during the service itself, gave her a cutting, wrathful, implacable look whenever he turned around. At the end of the sermon, he added several words which she did not understand but felt clearly were meant for her, and which signified the climax of her shame. And so she had knelt in the middle of the church, doubled over, her clenched fists on her pounding heart, burning with a fire that almost scorched her eyes. She could not remember when and how she had managed to walk out, or found the attendant and followed him home.

Afterwards she vainly tried to calm herself, and bathed her face in cold water; her eyes were swollen from crying, the face full of red blotches that would not go away. The Pasha noticed the change right away, but couldn't draw a word out of her; all she did was tremble and press her tightly clamped mouth into the muscle of his arm. In the end he understood what had happened. Early next morning, he sent for Fra Gregory.

Fra Gregory was summoned for midday, but as the times were troubled and full of uncertainty, and he himself was curious and apprehensive, he dropped in at the army riding school at Kršlo much earlier than he was due. Just at that moment the Pasha was standing in the barrack yard and studying the canter of a horse which a syce rode around the ring. He waved his hand, and the syce took the horse away. To the friar's greeting, he answered without any introduction:

"And why don't you let that creature of mine come peacefully into your place of worship and pray to God according to her law?"

Fra Gregory mumbled something about his vocation and about the girl's soul, but Veli Pasha interrupted him sharply:

"What've you got to do with her soul? I don't want to hear about her soul, and I'm not asking about it, but about your church and about last Sunday."

After this Fra Gregory, frail and gaunt, his head barely level with the decorations on the Pasha's chest, mustered his old nimbleness and eloquence in which there was always an equal measure of wheedling and threat, of humility and pugnacity, and which seldom failed to achieve some success. But this time nothing was of any avail.

That morning the Pasha was fresh, alert, and quick with thoughts and words, as he had not been in a long time. He held his whip under his arm, and in the light of the forenoon his big white hands showed brightly against the black uniform. Fra Gregory vainly exerted himself with long Turkish phrases; he could not finish a single one.

"Never mind, no matter—I didn't call you for that. She will come again next Sunday, when it's time to pray, and if you don't make room and receive her like any other female—"

The friar again began to speak about religious rules, and about the folk who kept to their ways.

"Never mind, never mind. I can't wrangle with your folk around the church. You are their headman—it's you I know."

Fra Gregory made pointed allusions to the foreign consuls, to the political situation in the country, but the Pasha broke in decisively:

"Go and tell that to the Vizier!"

And he clapped his hands for the syce to bring his horse out of the stable. Two other young men appeared and got busy around the horse, inspecting the girth once more and holding the reins. First the Pasha mounted his horse, and after him his sergeant-major. The animals started to prance, and Fra Gregory stepped aside. Before riding out of the gate, the Pasha turned over his shoulder once more:

"Let it be as I say, priest, so that you too will be at peace and alive and healthy on Sunday."

He spoke this more softly, though firmly and from a great height, as seagoing men on ships and riders on horses are wont to do.

Fra Gregory, in his tough and indestructible doggedness, wanted still to say something more, but the riders vanished beyond the gate, and he remained thus, with an arrested gesture and unfinished words, beside a couple of soldiers who were wiping their palms on their canvas aprons and looking at him dully.

Yet Mara not only didn't go to church any more, but was incapable of praying even at home. As soon as she would think of God and prayer, the incident in the church would be resurrected in her memory and at once the old cramp would stiffen her jaws and chill her breast, so that she would break off praying and give herself entirely to fear and to her shame. The Pasha at first urged her to go, but later even he forgot about it. For he too, in the last four days, had become more withdrawn and was apt to retire into pensive silences.

In this way the spring months went by.

In the meantime, unknown to her, strange things were happening in the city, and there were changes afoot that would alter the course of her life.

2

Summer arrived, and with it warm showers during the night and clear skies and sunshine in the daytime. The bloom on the hillsides was over, the gardens were blending into the dark greenery. The market stalls blushed with the Konjić cherries, which were big and watery and cracked, as always when the year was rainy. The summer gave every indication of being mild and fruitful.

Yet the bazaar was worried and restive. Business was slow, money scarce and its value unstable; imports were irregular and beset with difficulties. The peasant avoided buying what he needed, and hesitated to accept Turkish paper notes for his produce. Among the Christians there was an ominous silence. Rumors constantly spread that the Austrian army was poised on the river Sava and was only awaiting orders to cross; and while the Austrians were so deployed, four Bosnian battalions had been idling for many months on the outskirts of Istanbul; other Bosnians, prisoners of war and scattered at all points of the compass, were writing home from Russia, Transylvania, and Bessarabia. The bitterness of the populace was turning against the Ottoman authorities—against the Vizier to begin with, and then against his chief army officer. The people gathered in shops and cafés; there was a growing chorus of whispering, the kind that usually precedes action, and which kindles a vague excitement among the masses and kills every desire for work. In the shops, surrounded by worried and attentive listeners, the hodjas read Turkish newspapers, translated and explained the news. In Hajji Ivo Livajić's warehouse, Fra Gregory Martić secretly translated the Budapest newspaper *Pester Lloyd,* while in the commercial center of the city Stevo Petranović, a former teacher at the Serbian school and now in the service of the Italian consul, went from office to office, his pockets bulging with Italian newspapers. Following a few paces behind him went the clerk of the Austrian consulate, Herkalović, a well-dressed and portly man from Lika, telling everyone in the dignified manner of a bureaucrat about his Empire, its might and its order. Storekeepers of all four faiths listened, smoked, shook their heads, but said nothing themselves. Courteous to the point of insincerity, and used to many evils and changes, they heard and noted every word, but when their turn came to express an opinion they steered the conversation to health, which, after all, was the main thing and the greatest boon, and to this year's crops, or else took cover in vague reminiscing about the past. And meanwhile, each thought his own thoughts, thoughts that were nursed in private and remained unvoiced, but which every man lived with, and for which, when necessary, he would fight, spend whatever he possessed, even give his life.

Toward the end of June, rumors of an imminent Austrian occupation came so thick and fast that the jitters, especially of the Turks, could no longer be disguised.

On Friday morning, a deputation of some thirty Turks, representing merchants, agas and artisan guilds, went to see the Vizier to seek assurances about the critical situation and draw his attention to the grave Christian danger from Austria, and to demand the return of Bosnian troops to Bosnia and the recall of Veli Pasha.

Hoping to soothe them with a long speech, the Governor kept them at the Residence an unusually long time. Seeing that the deputation had not returned, the bazaar, distrustful and irritable for many months past, could not contain itself but flared up like one man. There was a sudden banging of store windows and stanchions. From all the lanes and alleys artisans came milling and marching, as if by a previous agreement, toward Sultan's Bridge. The general bitterness and exasperation were at last set in motion, and found expression; everything happened as if by itself; the crowds melted together as if into a ready mold.

At the head of the throng marched Salih Vilajetović, named Hajji Lojo, flanked by his escort of some ten fugitives from Nikšić, homeless desperados. He was bony, haggard, and tall, with legs and arms that seemed much too long for his body; his face was creased with deep, sensual wrinkles and overgrown with a sparse beard, and the gaze of his big blue eyes was disconcertingly rigid. He wore tattered student pants of a dark satin; his chest was bared and hairy, the shirt ripped and stained with mulberry juice. He was muttering some sort of prayer; from time to time he would stop and reel around to face the mob, which would halt also. The men from Nikšić would then fire their rifles into the air, and a thin cloudlet of smoke from their shots would hover, as if unfurled, above the head of their leader, as the myriad tiny bits of paper with which their rifle barrels had been crammed would flutter down on him like snowflakes. Following the silence that followed the volley he would, with arms outspread, intone several words in a deep voice, to which the crowd answered with shouts of acclaim; and then he would continue on his way. He stopped and turned around like this several times.

"We don't want the Istanbulis to fatten their bellies on us!"

"Noooo . . . !"

"We don't want traitors to sell Bosnia to the infidels!"

"Nooooooo . . . !"

And this word, which apparently suited the crowd's temper and mood best, caught on with lightning speed and the men kept repeating it furiously, in a quickening rhythm, not even listening to what their leader was saying.

"Noooooo!"

In this fashion they reached the Residence. Here the shooting increased and the whine of sharp bullets could be heard. Most of the shouting was against the two hated pashas.

Hearing the running fire and the noise, the frightened Mazhar Pasha promised the deputation all they had asked if only they would go out and calm the mob. And indeed, when the deputies walked out, the crowd began to subside and go home. But the more restive among them marched around the Residence and gathered in front of the army riding school. There the yelling was confined to protests against Veli Pasha, and the mob called for the disbanding of the Bosnian battalion and demanded that the people be supplied with arms.

In the large balconied hall that sometimes served for receptions and celebrations, Veli Pasha was sitting with his adjutant, Major Saffet, silently puffing at his *nargileh*. When earlier that morning the Governor had asked him to come and attend the deputation, he had declined. Now he sat as if he didn't hear the yelling of the mob. His face was pale, and the lesion on his left cheek had turned purple. To the excited Ismet Pasha Uzunić, commander of the Travnik garrison, who kept asking what was to be done, he replied that everything needful had been taken care of. Ismet offered to go out and pacify the crowd, and wanted to know what to tell them.

"Tell them that I have hauled out my field guns, that my cavalry is ready, and that at the first attempt to enter the barracks I shall order fire."

Whereupon Uzunić did something unexpected. It was an

instance of that sudden and unpremeditated bravery that appears in ambitious men when their vanity overcomes both their fear and their common sense. He ordered that the gates be opened and rode out to face the astonished mob. He was in parade uniform, on a white horse, with a drawn sword in his hand; behind him rode two other officers. Taking advantage of the crowd's momentary astonishment, he began to tell them how the Sultan's eye never closed but kept a steady watch on security abroad and on the internal peace of the state, and how they, although acting in the best of faith, would make a terrible mistake if they tried to anticipate the Emperor's thoughts and outbrandish the Emperor's sword. Here, somehow, he managed to weave in an obscure victory of his in a skirmish on Black River, and mentioned the ancient glory of the Sarailis, and requested them to disperse and wait for the Sultan's call.

Since none of their leaders were present, the crowd faltered and started to go away.

Breathless with excitement, Uzunić came back to the hall where, without having changed their postures, the Pasha and Major Saffet were smoking. He wanted to boast of his success and tried several times to recount his speech, but the Pasha maintained a stony silence and didn't wish to show even with a glance that he was listening.

A couple of days after this incident—it was a Sunday, the last day in June—Governor Mazhar Pasha convened the Council.

Forty-two of the city's leaders took off their sandals on the steps in front of the Residence, and sat down, according to their years and rank, in the great hall. No one spoke, save for an exchange of greetings. At the head of the hall sat Mazhar Pasha, even sallower than usual, full of high-sounding, empty words; and indecisive as always. On his right was Kostan Pasha, a tall and sickly Armenian, his face set, as always, in an expression of grave and tense attention; on the left was Veli

Pasha, and right next to him sat Brigadier Ismet Pasha Uzunić, fat, red-faced, looking pleased with himself.

After a lengthy and undistinguished introduction, the Governor admitted that he had called them in order to give them "grave and fateful news," namely, that yesterday the Austrian consul had informed him that at a meeting in Berlin it had been decided that Austria should occupy Bosnia, "perhaps even Herzegovina," and that Turkey had agreed to it.

In the back rows loud muttering was heard. The Vizier, who never once in his life had spoken a single truth, clear and whole, began, as if alarmed by his own words, to modify and soften them with the statement that this was only a consul's advice and that he had received no information of any kind from Istanbul; rather than make any decisions now, they should discuss possible courses of action in an emergency and meanwhile pacify the common folk.

The muttering grew louder, and out of it rose the voice of Hajji Hafiz Kaukdžić. He had a pink face set in a short, thick, and pitch-black beard, and pudgy white hands like a woman's, and these provided a strange contrast to his booming voice and ever-burning, severe eyes. There hadn't been a vizier in Sarajevo in the last fifteen years with whom he had not clashed and whom he had not accused of slackness; and he never let pass a meeting of the Council without making a speech against the neglect of religious precepts and against dangerous concessions to the Christian populace. In talking to him, everyone chose his words and took care not to provoke and anger him. Many could still remember one such Council meeting some ten odd years ago, in which it was debated whether or not to allow Christians to install bells in their churches and to ring them in towns where there were Turks. One young Osmanli, a scribe of the Governor's, maintained that they could do so without infringing on the laws of the holy Koran. Hajji Hafiz, quoting from a huge book, argued that they couldn't and that no Muslim should live in a town where "bells were banging." The scribe cited his reasons, the sputtering Hajji Hafiz his own, meanwhile bristling more and more at his opponent. At the end of it all, in front of the Governor and the whole assembly, he whacked him with that book over the head so hard that the frail scribe had to be splashed with water and doused with sherbet before he came to himself.

Now, also, Hajji Hafiz spoke at great length about the jeopardy of Islam, about enemies within the land and without. Glaring steadily at Veli Pasha and at Uzunić, he demanded that the "Sultan's generals carry out those things for which they are appointed, and which the Faith and the Sultan ask of them," and that they equip and mobilize the army and organize popular resistance.

He was abetted in this by the hodjas and poorer members; the wealthier and more distinguished ones sat still, with an air of inscrutable dignity. The assembly was particularly eager to hear the words of Mustaj Bey Fadilpašić, a portly and ambitious nobleman who sat at the head of the hall. Ordinarily, he would go around like a goatskin full of laughter, always spouting jokes and epigrams, and shrewdly hiding behind them what he really thought, or what he didn't know. But now even he sat in worried silence; the fat on him was quiescent, and only the cunning small eyes on the full pink face never ceased flitting.

After the Governor had spoken briefly, there was an embarrassed silence, interrupted by Ismet Pasha Uzunić, whose disjointed sentences didn't make much sense. He was followed by Kostan Pasha the Armenian who, like all clever and timid people, seemed to be torn between his timidity and his irrepressible wit and could not come to a realisitic conclusion.

There was another pause; one heard only the mumbling of those in the last rows, and the fidgeting and rasping of Hajji

139

Hafiz. At that point the governor himself looked across at Veli Pasha, but the latter was gazing fixedly through the windows, at Bakia, where white summer clouds were peering over the hilltops. Mazhar Pasha cleared his throat.

"Esteemed effendis, let us hear the opinion of the military commander."

At that Veli Pasha turned slowly in his direction and began talking without any preliminaries.

"Honorable Vizier, you will understand that I cannot explain to these people and to this overwrought hodja"—and here he pointed to Hajji Hafiz and waved at the Council, then at once turned back to Mazhar Pasha, not bestowing another glance at Hajji Hafiz during the rest of his short speech—"I cannot, as I say, begin to explain what the army needs, and what the imperial army can and should do. This is neither their business, nor would they understand it—"

This created an uproar, in which Hajji Hafiz was again most vociferous. When the voices quieted down, Veli Pasha finished his speech: In the defense of the country he would undertake only what was ordered by his superiors in Istanbul, and he would put down all meddling by the bazaar in military affairs, and all rebellion, with guns and cavalry. That was all— and nothing could again budge him out of his immobility.

Once more Mazhar Pasha held forth in long, learned sentences of which less than half of the assembly understood every other word; but if his oratory did not salve their souls with its lengthiness and vacuity, at least it wore them out. The Governor wound up the meeting by saying that they should await clear orders from Istanbul, and until such time try and quell the excitement of the people.

Meanwhile, the majority of the assemblymen were more inclined to rebellion that pacification. The insulting words of Veli Pasha had veered the undecided ones, whose number was always great, to Hajji Hafiz and the malcontents. They were now in the majority and were plotting, by signs and whispers, to organize another meeting that same evening. The few beys and wealthier men who were not for drastic measures seemed anxious to get home as quickly as possible, and avoided giving any opinions or promises. As they were leaving, only Salih-aga Šahinagić, a rich and reputable man, known for his sincerity, generosity, and honesty, spoke his thoughts aloud:

"You are a learned man," he said to Hajji Hafiz, "and you know that in all things the leaders have to be ahead of the people, and that without it there's nothing. How could loafers and riff-raff make war on their own? That has never happened, and never can—"

Still excited, Hajji Hafiz interrupted him and again said something about the ruin of Islam.

"But I too can see, my dear Hajji Hafiz," Šahinagić went on, "that there's nothing good in the air as long as the imperial army and the beys sit on their haunches while refugees from Nikšić, naked and barefoot, stomp and brawl around Sarajevo, and coopers and gut cleaners take it into their heads to recruit an army. I simply wonder at you and those monastics of yours. Where do you get your confidence? What are you thinking of? May the Allah help us!"

Not deigning to reply to him, and surrounded by a throng of men who shared his views, Hajji Hafiz was concerned only with one thing—to arrange a decisive meeting with Hajji Lojo and Muhammad Effendi Hadžijamaković, which would depose the Vizier and all Turkish authority and put together an insurgent government.

So ended the session of the Council that marked the beginning of rebellion, and decided the fate of the girl from Logavina Street.

Some days previously—when the Turkish merchants had sought an audience with Mazhar Pasha and complained about the grave situation, about the Bosnian army units, and the danger from the Christian riff-raff, or from a certain Christian country—they had, without mentioning names, hinted at two leading culprits, Kostan Pasha, an Armenian and thus a Christian, and Veli Pasha, a despot and drunkard who cared nothing for the security of the land. Even then Mazhar had telegraphed the High Porte, demanding the recall of both. Now, after the last meeting, he telegraphed again insisting that at least Veli Pasha be removed. As it happened, this telegram crossed another one from Istanbul, in which Veli Pasha was recalled and replaced by Hafiz Pasha, who was supposed to arrive any day from Novi Pazar. Mazhar Pasha breathed a sigh of relief. He perked up even more when he saw that Veli Pasha had taken the news calmly and was all set to depart at once with no intention of interfering in Bosnian affairs. He wouldn't even wait for Hafiz Pasha's arrival; he knew that "desk officer," and "diplomat on a horse" quite well. When told about the squadrons of horse which the new commander in chief was bringing with him, he only smiled and told Mazhar Pasha:

"If he brings more than twenty mounted men, I will personally groom all his horses for a whole year. You'll see."

From Friday till Tuesday, Veli Pasha made his preparations for departure. He visited all the consuls, but made a point of spending more time with the English. Among local people, he took leave only from Hajji Mulaga Merhemić and from the Mullah Suleiman Jakubović, in the latter's own cell.

At home everything was being moved and packed, but Mara continued to come every evening as before. The Pasha said nothing, and she dared not inquire. At night she got even less sleep than before, fretting and asking herself what had happened and what was to become of her. She understood

142

nothing of what was going on. During the day she listened fearfully, as to a distant echo, to the clamor of the mob that gathered in the city below, and at night to the shooting and calls of the sentries as they mustered and changed. She realized that Sarah and the inmates were getting ready for a journey. All this merely deepened her dread and bewilderment.

It was only on Monday afternoon that Veli Pasha spoke of his departure for the first time. The house was already completely dismantled and it echoed with a hollow sound. That afternoon, he was sitting as usual on the glazed verandah, in the draft, wearing his lounging clothes, when she came in, as she did every day, shut the door, and sat in his lap. It was only after he had smoked his *nargileh* to the end, and after an exchange of small talk (during which her ear was cocked tensely to the clatter of the maids' sandals and the creaking of the baskets that the houseboys were roping in the large room on the ground floor) that he told her he was "going away" tomorrow morning, and then promptly passed over it as though it were something trivial and incidental; he started to tell her how she would be "well off," how the house rent had been paid for a whole year, and how he had arranged for her to get whatever she needed in the Merhemić store, and if there was something they didn't have, Mulaga Merhemić would give her the money to buy it elsewhere.

"And if you would rather go back to your father in Travnik, just tell Merhemić. He will make it his business to send you. But no matter what, you won't be too badly off. Until this blows over—and later we'll see—"

Here he paused, as if at a loss for words. She had hung her head low, but the moment he stopped talking she looked up again for fear he might think that she was crying. And until now he had used the word "daughter" only once in addressing her, at the very beginning (the way he used to say, "Shall we, daughter?"), and had made it sound as though it were a slip of the tongue, for from then on he spoke dryly, matter-of-factly, without changing either his tone of voice or his facial expression. And with all that she neither heard nor understood him; everything that was happening and being said these days she saw and heard as if through a dream; to her, all of it together was one single blow—a blow that took away her breath and sight. Would she still continue to eat and pay for things as if nothing had happened? After all this, was there anything she could still do or say? Here, he was going away, but the shame remained. Taking the horses and servants and the dogs with him, but leaving *her* behind.

Going—leaving behind.

She felt a great emptiness in her breast, something hushed, abruptly stilled, throughout her body. Only two points, in the two temples, beat fast and out of rhythm, misting her vision.

Going—abandoning.

They stood facing each other. He spoke a few words and, holding her left arm, stroked her hair and cheeks briefly, after which he quickly pulled away and clapped his hands. Sarah entered, led her out, and gave her a box with some presents. Resting her hand firmly on Mara's shoulder, Sarah led Mara through the large room downstairs, while Mara, unable to hide her trembling any longer, clutched the box to her body in an unconscious cramp.

One of the houseboys appeared, and they loaded all of her bundled linen on his back. Sarah accompanied her all the way to the courtyard gate, leading her and supporting her, and there kissed her on both cheeks with her thin, cold lips. As in a dream, Mara began to walk down the street, most of which lay in the shade; behind her went Salih, the one who always used to call for her and take her back home, and another young man who, bent low, carried her pillows, a bulging eiderdown, and her house robes. Salih helped her to unlock the door of her cottage and remove the bolt. The porter sat down on the

144

threshold, blew loudly, and untied the carrying rope. The bedding fell open. They put the box next to it on the floor, exchanged glances, greeted her awkwardly, and then vanished.

She looked around the room and, when nothing stirred or made a sound any more, fell first to her knees and then, with all her weight, face down to the floor. The cramp that had tightened her jaws until that moment let up suddenly, followed by a spate of tears that all but choked her. She wanted to cry out, to call a high and sacred name, as she used to when she was a child, but through her lips there came only a howl—drawn out, hoarse, and quaking—and her tears mingled with saliva on her chin. She wanted to catch her breath a little, but the tears welled up again and again, from her very innards and up into her throat, and, choking, she clutched at the bedding with her fingers and upset that box from which baubles scattered in all directions, all the time struggling vainly to utter Our Lady's name.

She remained like this till the following morning. She just managed to drag herself to the window, lean her head against the wall, and close her wakeful eyes. Around her everything lay unpacked and in disorder until Hamša the Gypsy arrived at her usual hour.

That same morning Veli Pasha was leaving town. The baggage cart, together with Sarah and the houseboys and maids, had already set out from Bakia at dawn. They were escorted by mounted men. The Pasha meanwhile rode off to the riding school, and there once more inspected his horses and the detachment that was to go with him. As always in the early morning, he was fresh and alert, his eyes sparkled and he talked easily.

The day was well advanced, the people were leaving their

houses and the shops were being opened, when the wooden bridge on Čumuria rumbled under the Pasha's horses. There were twelve mounted men all told, and they rode in a long file. At their heads was the Albanian sergeant-major with two buglers; five or six paces behind him came the Pasha, followed immediately by his adjutant, Major Saffet, swarthy and dull-faced; then came three junior officers and, finally, four Albanian horsemen. They were all neatly turned out, fully armed and equipped, with bulging saddlebags and capes folded in tight rolls behind them. Before riding through the narrow Čumuria, the Pasha halted to greet Mullah Suleiman Jakubović once more.

The day before when he had taken his leave of him, the man had looked pale and oppressed. His usually wrinkled face had been drawn and pinched, and his bright, ever-smiling eyes had had a sad and uncertain look. He was evidently very sick. He hadn't complained about anything, but had spoken about the "transience of things," about death, and the vanity of this world. When the Pasha mentioned his departure, he had become upset.

"All of you are quitting! To whom will you leave Sarajevo, and us in the boiling cauldron? Off you go, each on his own, and may Benevolent Allah grant you ever good, but we here can't look forward to anything good any more. We've become heathen, at loggerheads with each other. Now we're waiting to see who'll come from beyond the borders to set us aright and baptize us!"

"But the beys are debating in the Council and Hajji Lojo is collecting an army," Veli Pasha had said with a smile.

"That's just it—the time of the Hajji Lojos has come! In the good old days they went around in chains and pounded stone—they didn't sit in council or recruit armies. But then, I suppose, if one just lived long enough, one might see the end of them too. They'll shout a bit, fire a shot or two, then run home to their wives, who'll lock them up in the storeroom. And should the Austrians remain in Sarajevo even a couple of years, they'll be the first ones to put hats on their heads and scramble for crucifixes and stuff themselves with pork. Ah, my good Veli Pasha, there's hardly a man left here any more, just hungry ragtag and bobtail, and greedy beys. Now each one will have his fling, and as for us, dear friend, what has been—has been."

And lowering his voice as in prayer, he had recited Ibn Abass's prophecy about the terrible "last times when the heart of the true believer shall melt as the salt melts in water, and nothing shall be of any avail."

This morning, too, Mullah Suleiman sat on his narrow window sill, and when he saw the Pasha, he rose to greet him. The Pasha reined in his horse and gave him a military salute; and after he had ridden past and turned the corner, Mullah Suleiman remained standing like that and prayed with open palms, asking Allah to "help and protect this traveler, a true Muslim and man of noble heart."

They rode on through Tašlihan and Predimaret. Most of the shops were still closed, especially those belonging to Christians and Jews. Here and there a Turk was squatting in his shopwindow, but the merchandise had not yet been arrayed on the window shelves, and was inside the shop, so that, if it proved necessary, the place could be shut in a hurry. In Baš Bazaar, there were some bread and sweetmeat vendors and a crowd of loiterers, and they all turned to look at the horsemen who rode slowly and solemnly as in a parade. In the Coopers' Market a few hammers could be heard, and from Green Maidan, where the troops used to assemble daily, came a growing murmur and muffled yelling. It was impossible to make out what they were shouting; one could only hear occasional single voices and the answering roar of acclaim from the mob—a drawn-out chorus that hovered above the town, waxing and waning one after another.

"A-a-a-a-a!"

Riding up through the Kovači, they slowed down and their horses came closer together. Gripping the back of his saddle, the Pasha swiveled around and spoke to Saffet in an undertone:

"The Austrians will pound them into the ground, and I'm only sorry it won't be me who'll do it."

They kept climbing and the city gradually spread itself out beneath them, with its blue smoke above the houses and thin mist above the plum orchards, and every few moments the air shook with the cheering of the insurgents.

"A-a-a-a-a . . ."

They rode out beyond the Višegrad Gate. In a green sward beside a spring some ten armed Turks were sitting on the grass. They were insurgent pickets. The sight of the horsemen threw them into confusion and set them whispering. A few rose to their feet; the brass-edged butts of their new Winchester rifles flashed in the sun. Thus they glared, without saying anything, until the horsemen rode past.

The city disappeared from view, all sounds faded away. In the peace of the morning, all that was heard were the gurgling of springs and the cascade of Mošćanica Brook in the gullies. The path was straight and soft, partially vaulted by sagging oaks and trees of late-ripening pears. Acorns, still green, lay on the ground and burst under the horses' hoofs. They halted by a spring to water the animals. Way down below they could see the last tiny Sarajevo café, carved into a steep slope. On the clearing in front of it were sprawled several men, beside their cartridge belts, rifles and, presumably, brandy cups hidden in the grass, for they were obviously drinking—another good-for-nothing insurgent picket that had sought haven here, for the insurgent government in the city had prohibited all drinking, vagabondage, and loitering. A couple of the men were holding a red bitch for a shaggy dark-haired dog that was hopping around her, and were having their coarse soldiers' fun. Seen from that height, the spectacle had something particularly loathsome and unnatural about it; perhaps because at that distance one could not hear their voices and guffaws, and it seemed as if they were going through their motions in complete silence and dead seriousness.

The officers talked quietly among themselves, scoffing at this Bosnian army engaged in mating dogs. The Pasha was quiet. The morning was well advanced and, as always, he was beginning to lose his feeling of freshness and to succumb to his habitual ill-humor. He grew more and more irritable. As the sun rose higher, it seemed to him that the gloom and bitterness within him were also waxing. Words came harder to him, and lifting his lids needed more effort.

The path rose again and became stonier. The sun began to burn; the path heaved upward more violently. The horses snorted and sweated. Thrashing their tails, they picked their foothold gingerly and slipped every few seconds on the smooth stone, sending up sparks with their hoofs.

Two of the officers began to curse, mopping their sweaty faces.

"Fuck their sisters and their Bosnia! What kind of a country is this! You climb and climb and break your feet like you were trying to reach the sky, and when you get to the top, there's nothing! More rocks and mountains!"

"Phew! A foul country!"

And they would fall silent again and ride on, sullen under the broiling sun.

3

On the same day that Veli Pasha went away, Mara moved to Baba Anuša's house in Bistrik.

Earlier in the morning, when Hamša had arrived and

149

found her weeping and disconsolate beside her scattered linen, she had barely managed to raise her up and force her to wash her face and take hold of herself. The good-hearted Gypsy even cried herself, as, at the slightest provocation, do those women who have worn themselves out with hard work and frequent child-bearing. And, through her own tears, she comforted the girl with countless petty and contradictory lies: how the Pasha might come back; how she would go to her father in Travnik; how she would get married and settle down quietly here in Sarajevo; how she was young, pretty, and fresh as a dewdrop; how she still had Baba Anuša, and herself, Hamša.

"A-a-ah, if I were your age I'd do nothing but sing and dance."

In the end she managed to persuade Mara to change and go with her to Baba Anuša's, where, if she felt like it, she might stay for a few days to calm herself and recover a little; while she, Hamša, would look after the cottage.

After midday, she set out with Hamša and her youngest son, who carried her bundle. As they were crossing the Miljacka by the Latin Bridge, they met some armed Turks marching briskly. She bowed her head in fear and her eyes fell on the shallow, pea-colored water and on the small pebbles at its bottom; the sight made her yearn for a whirlpool that would swallow her up without a trace.

They found Baba Anuša in tears, and the house full of women. Under a threadbare quilt whose stuffing was falling apart, lay her grandchild, a girl of about ten. In a corner sat a small grandson, slightly younger, with a big belly, gnawing on a wet cob of cooked corn.

Because both her son and daughter-in-law had died last winter, within two months of each other, Baba Anuša had taken the children into her house. She had always been fond of tippling, but since the death of her only son she had become a complete drunkard. Her poverty prevented her from buying as much plum brandy as she needed, so she bought a cheap spirit in the bazaar and melted her own sugar and made a kind of drink that was called *sagrdan*. She ate hardly any food, but walked around the house all day with pouchy eyes, her head tied in a kerchief. She neglected the children, with the result that they spent their days loafing in the streets, coming home only to sleep. This was particularly true of the girl, who had freckled cheeks and a hint of something cunning and brash in her eyes, and was developed beyond her years.

That was how yesterday, already in the early morning, she had gone out to mope around the refuse heaps and steal fruit from other people's gardens. Dressed in a long shirt of coarse calico, she had separated from the other children and sauntered to the top of Bistrik. The streets were deserted and all house gates shut, as people stayed indoors on account of the rebellion. There she met two young men. One was Salčin, from Bistrik, an epileptic and a thug, pock-marked, burly, with a crippled left arm and a forehead that was always bruised. The second was from another district, a slim young-ster, well dressed, strapped in a massive cartridge belt, and armed. When he saw the girl, the epileptic called out "Hey little one!"

Standing by a fence, she watched him without batting her eyes, rubbing one foot against the other, and she did not move. He then produced from his sash a big lump of sugar and showed it to her.

"Come here and I'll give it to you."

Glancing from the sugar to his face and back again, she came on slowly, holding four fingers of her left hand flat against her mouth. But as she approached, he backed away up the street. She faltered, with distrust in her eyes and move-ments. He stopped, too, and stretched his hand out even more.

"Here's the sugar. Here."

Seeing that she did not stir, he took out of his shirt a heavy black key and, with its heavier top part, knocked off a small piece of the sugar. She came up gingerly, like a magpie, and took it. As she bit on it and crunched it, she kept gazing at them. When she was finished, the epileptic held out his hand again.

"Here's some more."

The girl approached, and he backed away, only to halt again and knock off another few morsels and give them to her. So he lured her, as one lures a stubborn ewe with corn. The other young man walked by his side a few paces away, glancing around him every few moments. In this way they finally reached Berkuša, where there were no houses but only a deserted stone quarry, now overgrown with nightshade and thistles.

Salčin climbed a stone mound, from which a part of Sarajevo could be seen. The other young man stood in a ditch below him. The girl alternately looked behind her and then lifted her greedy eyes toward Salčin, who squatted on an overgrown rock and held the sugar in his hand. He broke off one more lump and she came closer to take it, but as it was too far up, the second young man reached for it and gave it to her. And as she stood there with her mouth still full of sugar, he threw himself on her, pulled her down and vanished with her in the undergrowth of the ditch. At first nothing was heard but the scraping of the gravel and the creaking of his bandolier; but very soon the girl began to sob, then scream and call for help. He must have clapped his hand over her mouth, for the screams were muffled and came intermittently.

Salčin meanwhile continued to crouch on his rock. His mouth was agape; the calves of his legs, on which he was squatting with the full weight of his body, twitched and trembled. He remained like this for a long time, staring wide-eyed into the hole under him. All of a sudden his eyes glazed over, he let out a dull, smacking sound, threw out his arms and fell into the ditch beside them. From down below one could hear the noise of his gagging and of his trashing legs. The little girl had fallen completely silent.

When, some time later, the other young man reappeared in the sun, his face was blanched, his knees and elbows coated with brown soil. He put on his cartridge belt and dusted himself off, then went back into the hole and pulled out Salčin, who put an arm around his shoulders to support himself. There was blood on his nose, his lips were blue and twisted, the hair matted, and on his chest were specks of froth and saliva. He had trouble breathing and his eyes lolled helplessly; he could barely drag one foot behind the other. Thus they vanished among the houses.

The sun rose higher, flooding the quarry and the weed-tufted pits with ever more light. In the hollow of that ditch, the girl lay on trampled grass and torn earth. Her shirt was pulled back over her head, and her child's body, resembling a small object, squashed and lifeless, seemed of a piece with the sharp, near-white rocks basking in the sun. Above it the flies were buzzing. In the sun-drugged silence one could hear how, in the city down below, the mobs were rumbling and threatening and how from time to time hundreds of voices blended into a long, indistinct cheer:

"A-a-a-a!"

That afternoon Baba Anuša, having waited long and vainly with her lunch, sat down to eat with her grandson. The boy sipped the thin broth with a good deal of noise, but refused to eat the barley bread, which was hard and leathery, made of a coarse-sifted flour and full of prickly chaff. To tempt him, the old woman crumbled the bread into the soup and, using a spoon, quashed it into pulp at the bottom of the bowl.

"This is how a Turk sinks in hell, there!"

The little one liked the game; he helped his grandmother and pressed piece after piece to the bottom of the bowl, then fished them out and ate them mashed like that. Occupied thus with the child and the meal, Anuša never even heard the steps on the stairway. The door suddenly flew open and people brought in the little girl.

She had been found unconscious by some Gypsy women from Berkuša who had gone to gather wood, and the district clerk had recognized the child and ordered them to take her home. Now she lay wrapped in wet rags soaked with vinegar, and did not regain consciousness. She was full of blue bruises, mumbled deliriously and from time to time moved her arms, but from the waist down her body was numb and stiff, as if paralyzed.

The women came and went, shed tears of sympathy with Baba Anuša, debated among themselves, but not one of them knew what to do. A few suggested getting some medicine from the Jew at Predimaret, others recommended calling a doctor, while a third group was all for calling a priest, or reporting the matter to the authorities. Outside, in the city, there was open insurrection; the stores were shuttered, the officials had run away, and Lord alone knew where the priest and the doctor were hiding. Everything was cut off, left to its own devices, and everyone felt helpless.

Mara stood by the oven and looked about her in bewilderment and fear. They were all busy with the little girl, and no one seemed even to notice her.

In the end, after a long and futile palaver, the women left. It had grown dark, but no one thought of lighting the candles. The little boy had fallen asleep in his corner, with an uneaten crust of bread in his fingers. Baba Anuša was sitting in the middle of the room and, with practiced movements, preparing her drink, decanting it from one pot into another. The room filled with an acrid and unpleasant smell, as from sour bread. Lying cramped on a narrow, hard sofa in the dark, Mara could make out the quilt that covered the little girl and which was silhouetted against the window as a round, still mound. Thus she fell asleep.

She woke up some time at night. The room was bathed in moonlight. The old woman was still sitting in the middle of the room, with a compress on her head, but she was strangely animated, rocking and flailing around her with her arms. She took off her compress every other moment and soaked it in water, while mumbling some disjointed and meaningless words.

"Bless and cross—bless and cross—"

She put on and took off compress after compress in this manner, and then all at once she would begin to sway her upper body and sing in a low voice:

"My Jesu-u-us—sweetness mine—"

Tongue-tied and chilled by fear, Mara listened to the whispering and watched the demented movements. She could not understand anything, but felt that something ugly and dreadful was being done here; it was again as if a rite were being offered to something that was evil, something that struck numbness and terror into one. She could not sleep, and dared not reveal her presence. And she made up her mind to flee as soon as dawn came.

Before the women started to gather again, and before Baba Anuša had sobered up, Mara stole away with her bundle and ran down to Bistrik. There were no women in the streets. In front of the huge building of the Austrian consulate there was a row of carriages guarded by armed horsemen. She set off in the opposite direction, staying close to the shuttered stores. As she reached the bottom of Bistrik and was about to pass by the military riding school, she heard a clamor and, from the top of the little knoll on which she happened to be standing, saw a large crowd of people below her. In the center of Atmaidan, the corpse of a Turkish officer lay on its back. His uniform was in tatters, his chest bared; around it was a litter of torn-up papers, a sword sheath, a fez. Cursing and swarming around the corpse like wasps, angry insurgents were kicking its flanks and groin. Mara quickly averted her head and set off in another direction, toward the Latin Bridge. There, still trembling from what she had just seen, she looked once more at the yellowish water with its pebbled bottom and decided at last to do what she had contemplated during the night as she lay on the hard sofa at Baba Anuša's: to go to see Fra Gregory. To do what was hardest and most terrible, and thus forestall every other evil.

In the Latin Quarter everything was quiet. She knocked on the door by the side of the church; but for a long while there was no answer. Eventually, from the adjoining house, an old woman shuffled out, led her into her own courtyard, and from there, by way of two small doors, one through a fence, the other through a wall, they came into the courtyard of the Franciscans.

Here the gravel was white, the hedges trimmed. The old crone led her up a steep stairway, and they found themselves in the spacious reception hall, draped with curtains of white cloth. Suddenly Mara saw Fra Gregory before her, and she faltered, not letting the bundle out of her hands. He was walking diagonally across the hall with a brisk and firm step, and held an open breviary in his left hand.

He walked to and fro several more times, as if not seeing her; while she remained stock-still, with a single thought in her head: This was it—that most terrible thing! Finally he stopped, closed the breviary with a snap, and turned to her.

This is it, the most terrible thing, she kept thinking as she looked at him and saw, as if through a mist, his clenched knuckles rapping the breviary, his spreading arms and the agitated whipping of his white waist cord and heavy rosary, and his eyes boring into her, brown, cutting, implacable beneath their thick brows.

"Do you know what you are now in the eyes of God and in the eyes of Christian folk? Dung, dung, full of stench and maggots!"

He thundered on, telling her how with her own hand she had reopened all the wounds of Jesus, which had already healed, how she'd made Our Lady weep, spat on the cross and the Holy Host. He glared at her, terrifyingly close. And before those eyes and words she felt as if all of her were shriveling and whittling away, as if there were no ground under her, as if before so much shame her body were disappearing, melting away, existing only in her consciousness, like a dark spot that no amount of effort or pain could wash out.

So she swooned and foundered more and more, as in a miasma, in this thought of damnation and eternal punishment that was the ultimate solution, almost some kind of a respite. And when she thought the end of everything had come, he startled her and rallied her once more with words about the Savior's endless mercy, which was greater than all the sins of mankind, greater than all evil and shame. He spoke about a long penance, about contrition and forgiveness; yet even then his eyes did not become milder, or his words softer. And this penance appeared to her so harsh and inaccessible, and she herself so helpless, that it seemed to her it would be easier to sink utterly in that darkness of damnation and punishment than to think, say, or do anything. But the friar kept darting around her, lashing her with words, and jolting her out of her swoon.

"If you were to bathe the church crucifix with your tears year after year, and live on bread and water, you could not wash away your shame nor make up for the evil you've done."

After which his talk would again take on a vague note of conciliation, which indeed had to come from some quarter, at some time, but which, she felt, was incapable of lifting or comforting her.

She was recalled out of her faint by the rumble and clicking of the clock; a colored Turkish clock, with leaden weights, chimed the hour of noon. Fra Gregory stopped abruptly, knelt down on a *prie-dieu* by the window, crossed himself, and started to pray aloud.

"Hail Mary, full of grace, the Lord is with thee, blessed art thou among women, and blessed is the fruit of thy womb, Jesus—"

When he reached the middle of the prayer, he paused and shouted at her without looking over his shoulder:

"Why aren't you praying? Tell me!"

She obeyed mechanically; took up the prayer and, stammering and swallowing, recited the second half, as was the custom during vespers and vigils.

"Holy Mary—Mother of God—pray for us sinners, now and at the hour of our death."

He joined her once more:

"Receive this servant of our Lord. Let it be as Thou commandest. Ave Maria."

When it was her turn again, she prayed a little more loudly and collectedly. And when in a sharp and clear voice he began the concluding prayer, she felt bold enough to lift her eyes.

Bowed, with a wreath of grizzled hair on his head, his hands clasped around the dark, leather-bound breviary, above the rosary which had pleated itself and become entangled with the white cord of his waist string—he, too, it seemed to her, was doing something mysterious and serving someone, he alone knew whom. This now seemed less unfamiliar and less dreadful, but in its own way just as baffling and upsetting, like those weird night watches of Veli Pasha and Baba Anuša. What was more important—here, too, her soul had been humbled and crushed.

When they had finished praying, he called the housekeeper in a steadier and quieter voice and told her to take the girl to the kitchen. And so she walked out, shivering and stumbling from hunger, from lack of sleep, too much crying, and from utter incomprehension of all that was happening to her.

Fra Gregory also was getting ready to abandon his apartment and seek shelter in some consulate or other. The night before a group of insurgent Turks had looked for him and called his name, but he had hidden himself in the Pamuković house, in the neighborhood. That day also, as soon as the sun went down, he walked over to the Pamukovićes, by way of the garden and through the back fences. There, in conversation with the old Pamuković, he decided finally to move in the next few days over to the French consulate, since the consul, Riveux, a talkative and unusually amiable man and a good Catholic, had offered to give him shelter. The same evening Mara's fate was also decided. She was to come to the house of Pamuković and work there as a maid until the rebellion quieted down and the church could be opened again, so that she might perform her public penance, on a Sunday, during High Mass, in front of the people.

4

The Pamuković houses were not far from the church, in the same Latin Quarter, but close to the edge of it, with the result that they faced in two directions: one toward the Latin Quarter, the other toward Čumuria. There were two of them, whiter and considerably larger than the rest of the homes in the Quarter. The main entrance faced the river Miljacka, and opened into a great courtyard. In the middle of the courtyard grew shrubbery, planted in a rectangle, and within it, at the center, were clusters of small flowers; along the edges of the yard, by the walls, there were evergreens and bushes of a silvery flowering plant called *igda* that gave off a heady and stifling fragrance. Here was the main house of Pamuković, two stories high. Jutting out the entire length of the house, and resting on white pillars, was the large drawing room, its windows painted a pale blue.

Under this main house there was a passage into the second courtyard, which was even bigger, though spread with a coarser gravel, lacking flowers and decorations, where wreaths of onions and drying red peppers hung on the walls. There was the second Pamuković house, smaller and more squat, but just as clean, immaculately whitewashed, with colored windows. At the far end of the yard was a building called the *mutvak*, a simple one-story dwelling containing the kitchen, storerooms, and servants quarters. Behind it, separated by a fence, was a third yard, small, dark, and damp. This was the place for the unloading of hay, wood, fruit, and of everything that the tenants and share-croppers brought in. Stables, too, were there, and vats, barrels, and all kinds of scrap.

All this Mara saw but could hardly register, for her knees were wobbly, her head swam, and her lids drooped from lack of sleep. But one thing she sensed right away: this was a great, splendid, and rich household that could not be compared with anything she had seen thus far; not with the ramshackle house of Alaibegović, nor the half-empty rooms of Veli Pasha, let alone the house of her parents in Dolac or the awful hut of Baba Anuša from which she had fled that morning.

They led her into the kitchen in the last courtyard, where

the maids and daughters-in-law were preparing dinner. Here she put her bundle on the floor and stood, like one condemned, by the door jamb. The women studied her with unabashed curiosity. Old Jela was the only one who found a word for her and tried to make her feel less unwanted. When the time came for supper, she sat down with Jela and two other maids at a low, round table. She kept lowering her eyes, misted from shame and lack of sleep, and her hand trembled; and at the same time she was embarrassed before them for not being able to eat, and picked at her plate every now and then, even though she didn't have enough strength either to chew or to swallow. She was relieved when the meal was over and she gathered that she would sleep with Jela in the same room.

She lived through the first few days in a state of wonder and confusion. She helped in the work, both in the kitchen and in the yard, although both Jela and the maids preferred to observe her and question her than to give her work. And she kept pushing and hiding her thick, unruly hair in the kerchief and feeling ashamed of her body. For that reason she liked it best when they gave her a long chore which she could do alone and withdrawn from others; like shelling peas, pleating onion wreaths, or combing wool. Sitting in the corner of a cubicle next to the kitchen, she would then watch the Pamuković house with its lofty drawing room, which was not built of wood and sagging but stately and resting on arches that tapered down to white columns. She tried to imagine how the interior was furnished, what sort of people were they and how they lived. But she rarely saw any of the Pamukovićes; and the less she saw of them and knew them, the better she liked to watch those white columns and windowpanes which were never thrown open and behind which, as it seemed to her, life was better and people were of another kind, the kind that knew no poverty, no misfortune, and no shame.

As time went on, she had the opportunity to see one or

the other of the Pamukovićes; but there were many of them, and from those she met she never heard a word or received a smile; they simply walked through the courtyard, or stalked quickly through the drawing room.

That was how she got to know Auntie Andja, sister of the old Pamuković, who had her apartment in the smaller house. She lived there alone, for she had no children, and her husband, Simeon, kept an inn on Kiseljak and only occasionally came to Sarajevo. She was fat and red-faced, with dark pouches under her eyes and incipient wrinkles; she wore shiny loose pantaloons of heavy black satin, which rustled when she walked.

Later she met the two unmarried daughters, and also the daughters-in-law and sons as they chanced to go by. The older daughter was in her late twenties, willowy, rosy-cheeked like all the Pamukovićes, but past her bloom. The younger was still an adolescent. She still laughed loudly and stammered in her speech; her face was pale, with dark rings under her eyes, and her look restless. Yet she, too, was losing the marks of childhood with each new day and in her gait, visage, and accents, beginning to resemble the other Pamukovićes. The two older daughters-in-law were already like them in every respect. It was strange how they'd taken on all their characteristics: the steady and disdainful gaze, that frosty edge in the voice, the ramrod walk and gestureless speech. Only the third and youngest daughter-in-law was different and a contrast to all the inmates. She was called Nevenka.

One day Mara had a fleeting glimpse of the old woman Pamuković in her drawing room. She was walking slowly, flanked on one side by her younger daughter and on the other by a daughter-in-law; but she was not leaning on them. She was huge, heavy, and could hardly move. Her hair was swaddled in several dark scarves, and her big breasts hung loose in a thin shirt of a silky fabric. The face was laced with red and bluish veins, and bloated with a double row of thick pouches, above which there stared a pair of vacuous, completely round eyes without any lashes.

It was less often that Mara could see the men, who spent their days in the shops, came home late, and went away early. In them, also, as in their womenfolk, one could see that gloomy and ponderous dignity of movement and glance. But Mara believed that those things, like some kind of a shadow, were inseparable from wealth and being a gentleman. And as she combed her wool she continued to muse about their life beyond those windows and columns, full of security, order and dignity, quite different from her own.

Then Jela and the youngest daughter-in-law, Nevenka, took to dropping in and working with her. From their talk and the stories each of them told, the truth about the Pamukovićes begun slowly to dawn on Mara: she learned that they, too were beset with trouble and misfortune, like all the other people she had known till then, like her own mother, Hafizadić, and the old Elias Garić, like Veli Pasha and Baba Anuša—save that they bore it and concealed it in their own fashion. Some of the things the two women told her made her blood run cold, even though frequently the details escaped her, or she happened to listen with half an ear and spent the time thinking about herself. All the same, their long tales and laments made her realize more and more clearly that even behind those big windows and columns life was not good, that this home, too, concealed the same inexpressible thing that was driving her from house to house and tormenting her day and night.

Jela was short but corpulent, with a sallow and puffy face. She was past her fiftieth year, and had never been married. There was some kind of a secret behind this, which, for all her garrulity, she took care to hide. She had served the Pamuković household for thirty-seven years, and now virtually all of it depended on her. Wrapped up to her chin in a great many scarves, in summer and winter alike, she bustled in the kitchen all day long, preparing things and giving orders. At the age of sixteen, she had been seduced by the younger brother of the old Pamuković, an impetuous and beautiful young man who later went abroad and perished somewhere. Since then she had remained in this house, as a maid. Never leaving the kitchen, forever scurrying on the same round of chores, she had withered early and become quite dull. She was in the habit of talking aloud to herself. The Pamukovićes and their household were her whole life and her whole world. She remembered when the old Pamuković had married, when the daughters-in-law had come into the house, when the children and grandchildren were born, when anybody died or was sick. All of them, from the day they were born, had gotten used to her as to an object. She worried about everyone, but nobody worried about her; no one knew whether she ate, slept, or was ill; and if they didn't have to call her, they might have forgotten her name too. In her talks with Nevenka and Mara, she spoke of the Pamukovićes and their lot as of some evil that could not be changed, and which had to be put up with.

Much more alert and eloquent was the daughter-in-law Nevenka. Mara found it hard and unpleasant to look into her fevered black eyes, and talked to her always with a certain sense of unquiet and fear. She was, indeed, not afraid of her, but of the Pamukovićes. And Nevenka, in turn, connived to remain alone with her more and more often, and told her increasingly detailed stories about herself and about the family.

Frail, pallid, brisk in her walk, Nevenka loved to talk, yet always took care to lower her voice when one of the Pamukovićes approached. A poor girl, daughter of a mason, she had come to this house against her will. No one, including herself, knew how it came about that the youngest Pamuković boy saw her in church one Sunday and promptly fell in love with her, or how he managed to overcome his parents' objections and bring her to the house as his bride. She was childless in the first two years, and became pregnant only this past spring; she was now in her sixth month. In that same little room behind the kitchen where Mara combed wool, they had furnished an apartment for Nevenka, in which she now wove cloth for her baby. She was preparing a swaddling outfit, and humming all day long. The song was typical of women at work; neither the tune nor the words had a beginning or an end. When the yarn snapped or the shuttle stuck, the song would cease too; as soon as the shuttle moved again and the loom clattered on, the song was resumed, in faster time. When she got bored with it or her back began to ache, she left off work, sat down next to Mara and, while combing the wool, started to talk: of how she got married, of how she had lived these last two years in the Pamuković household as a barren woman, and so forth. The wool crackled and scraped, the teeth of the carding comb chattered, and Mara, with her chin on her chest, listened as she singled out and dwelt, with a certain bitter satisfaction, on the ugliest and most shocking incidents of her married life. Mara was terrified by what she heard, and even more by the thought of having to hear something more dreadful yet. She would have given anything if the young woman had suddenly burst out laughing and told her, chortling, that none of it was true, but only a horrible tale. And still the daughter-in-law talked and talked, and interrupted herself only from time to time, when she burst into tears. Since her hands were in the wool, she did not wipe her tears but simply averted her head, so that the tears streamed soundlessly to the floor. At those moments the embarrassed Mara bowed her head even lower, while the young woman, having cried herself out, would go on with her story.

The tale Nevenka told was this: After they had seen each other in front of the church two or three times, young Nikola Pamuković had come with his father and old Matan Boštor to ask her hand in marriage. It was the afternoon of Annunciation Day. When the suitors had departed, her mother, who had been ailing for several years, called her to her bedside and embraced her. Although her legs were paralyzed and she lay motionless on her pillow, the mother spoke with her usual calm and an unwavering strength in her voice and eyes.

"Child, I'm not giving you away so that you will have it good and easy, but because it's fated like this, you understand. That house is hard and wicked. You will not starve for bread but for a good word and a kind look. Still, you must go through with it, and a time will come when you'll tuck them all in your waist sash. You won't have it worse than I had it with your father. Be obedient to them and look after your husband, but hold your own. If things ever get bad and you really can't go on any more, you know where our doors are."

Then she kissed her on both cheeks and on the hair, and made a quick sign of the cross over her, as if forestalling danger. And the girl was on her knees by the bed, in her light pantaloons and dark waistcoat—frail, tiny, her head lowered. She did not cry, but she was pale and clenched her teeth with an effort, so that her chin would not tremble.

In the next few days the usual formalities and courtesies were exchanged, all rather hasty and lacking spontaneity, as when a rich house condescends to receive a poor mason's daughter. Four weeks later, she was married at an early Mass and taken to the Pamuković house. She was received by the sisters-in-law with that cool, wounding civility peculiar to rich people.

After the wedding, she waited the customary seven days, not saying anything to anyone, and on the afternoon of the eighth went to her mother, all wrapped up in shawls and bowed

down, accompanied by a maid. Quietly she entered the house
and her mother's room, but the moment the latter put her
arms around her, she slid to her knees in a fit of sobbing that
threatened to suffocate her. An unexpected, harrowing, and,
for that small body, unbelievable howl filled the room. No
matter how much the old woman tried to soothe her, she
could not come to herself, but only beat her face on the floor
and drenched the old carpet with her tears and spittle. When
she calmed down a little, she wanted to get up, but her mother
wouldn't let her and pulled her closer instead; and as the girl
vainly tried to wrench herself free, the old woman loosened
her dress and began to examine her. Then she gave a cry and
started to curse.

"Oh God, what did that heathen Turk do to the child!
Oooh, that Pamuković beast! The monster!"

She wailed and cried like this over each bruise she discovered, while the young one shivered under her fingers, tiny and
naked like a shorn sheep. They remained together till sundown, and then the old woman called the Pamuković maid.

"Go home and tell your mistress and Auntie Andja that we
have no one but this one child, and that I thought I was marry-
ing her into a Christian house, not to a brigand. And if their
son wants his wife, let him come for her, so I can ask him
where he learned to break a poor mite's bones."

And her large, shiny face blazed in the evening light.

He came the very next day, looking pale, and left looking
even paler, leading his wife behind him. And so Nevenka returned and stayed among the Pamukovićes as a "domestic
enemy," a secret adversary and a mute victim. In the course of
time, that flight of hers was forgotten. She went to visit her
mother only on Sundays, and by no means regularly. She
began to help in the housework and gradually got to know the
Pamukovićes, and their home, and the life in it. This became
for her a source of many miseries, which not only gave no sign

of diminishing but gave rise to new anguish.

From the day they had brought in her dowry chest—cheap, gaudy, brass-shod, and secured with linchpins—and placed it among their furniture, which was bulky, dark, and without a touch of brightness or color, she had always felt before them, and before every one of their things, a sense of shame that gnawed at her very innards, but this she would never admit or show to anyone. She saw their strength in all they did and said, and saw that everything on them and around them was theirs, grand and fine. Yet she couldn't bring herself to give them credit for anything. All through the day, and even at night, she mentally quarreled with them and made comparisons; and this need to compare herself with them ate at her, consumed her, and never quite left her. Yet, racking and torturing herself in this way, she slowly got to know the Pamukovićes, and learned many new and terrible things.

She saw that they wronged everyone, gave quarter to no man, that they liked no one, and were hated by the whole world, even though the house was frequented by the town notables and the priests. They fought even among themselves, though with "silent gunpowder," as the saying went, and the daughters and the in-laws stole from each other, dickered, and taunted one another long after the lights went out at night. She learned that the old Pamuković sometimes stayed up till dawn over his ledgers and accounts, arguing with his eldest son, so that throughout the next day he would be incapable of touching anything except coffee and tobacco. She saw that each of them, on reaching a certain age, developed an open wound on his leg or arm, and secretly bathed and salved it nights. That was the reason they tried to marry off their young early. She learned that the old woman Pamuković had seizures almost every month, that she locked herself in her room, allowing no one to come in, and howled and raved and threw herself on the floor, and afterwards lay in bed five to six

168

days, moaning like someone mortally ill. She saw a great many hidden evils, until one night there was revealed to her, in all its terror and beyond a vestige of doubt, "the thing about Simeon."

He was Auntie Andja's husband. In her fortieth year, she had felt a passion for him and had married him; he was her third husband. Born at Travnik, he was considerably younger than she, of a sallow complexion, a loafer and blasphemer who drank night and day all over Sarajevo and the outlying suburbs. She loved him as only women in her years can—morbidly, maternally, unconditionally. She concealed and glossed over his outbursts, and gave him money for fresh carousals.

One night Simeon came home in such an uproar that it was impossible to hide it. He babbled and kept crashing to the floor like a piece of timber. Sprawled on the ground, he rolled his eyes, his face alternately yellow and ashen, and babbled on even as they tried to hush him and raise him up.

"Oh, oh, pray to God! Make an offering of holy salt! I met a Turk in Ferhadia—squint-eyed, with crinkly hair, in a hansom cab. Black horses and black driver—black, the lot of them. Get into the hansom, Simeon, says he. But I didn't feel like it. Come on, get in, sit down. So I get in. And he breaks into a gallop right away—"

Here Simeon twisted to one side and scraped the floor with his forehead.

"Oh, oh! He rides and rides, till we come to Miljacka. Then up and over the dam and right into the river! I yell and try to stand up, all for nothing. And he gets me across to Čumuria—more dead than alive! Then he disappears, with his cab—into the thin air!"

And again he beat his forehead on the ground and shook in his whole body, while the women sprinkled water and made signs of the cross over him, whispering prayers, coming and going on tiptoes, humming like bees.

169

"Save us, Virgin!"

"Immaculate Mother!"

And Nevenka, paling and shivering from the cold, from interrupted sleep and fear, watched it all from her window. And in all that horror and disgrace she could not help noticing the fine pleating on Simeon's pantaloons and the elegant way in which his embroidered shirt sleeves settled around his bloodless wrists; and how slender and handsome the sisters-in-law looked in their thin nightshirts of silken cloth.

Some time after this, the Apparition began to follow Simeon to the very gate of the courtyard. Jela told her that she had seen It with her own eyes, that It was really a Turk, cross-eyed and frizzle-haired, with his fez askew and his left eye half shut. Nevenka thought about It all day long; and her sleep became fitful from so much thinking and fear. She would wake up suddenly during the night and listen to Andja and the other Pamuković women struggling over Simeon as over a fallen soul. The Apparition tugged at his brocade waistcoat to get him out of the courtyard, calling him back to more revelry, and the women pulled him back into the yard. Andja was the boldest. She swung at It with her rosary and its crucifix, using it like a whip, cursing in a shrill and choked voice.

"Away, infidel scum, leave my man alone! In the name of Holy Trinity, don't touch this baptized soul! Back to hell with you, devil!"

Simeon teetered like an upended log of wood between the flailing women and the motionless Turk, who stood in the shadow by the gate. And Nevenka leaned out over her window sill and pressed her face to the wooden bars to better see and hear, although she shuddered from cold and terror and bristled with gooseflesh every other moment. For long hours afterwards she would be kept awake by her fear and, even more, by her gloating and selfish thoughts.

In this intimate contact with the Pamukovićes and their

relations, yet actually quite isolated and left to herself, Nevenka brooded increasingly about everything about her. Her as yet callow mind took her off along paths that were too complex for her, and which until then she had never dreamed existed. Her first and most persistent thought was: Where did so much evil come from? Without a spark of goodness, without compassion, devoid of tenderness for anyone or anything that was not the Pamukovićes'? She waded through this evil of theirs as through a darkness, and couldn't see the end of it, nor the sense, nor the reason for it. Pure evil. And when she was through thinking such thoughts, which she was adept at starting and expanding but not at disentangling and solving, she would slump helpless and crushed before the realization that the Pamuković depravity and ugliness would never be denounced and made public, but that they would remain like this, respectable, powerful, redoubtable, each in his place, till the end of time.

"No one can ever touch them!"

Look, they sin, poison each other, rot away; they humiliate and are contemptuous of everyone, and they hate each other; they are greedy, shameless, and owe money, yet each one of them holds his head high, steps boldly, looks around him undaunted, eats well, wears fine clothes, is not abashed or afraid of anyone, does what he wants, takes whatever he fancies.

"No one can do a thing to them!"

And when the lot of them, the way they were, at last found themselves in the other world (her weary imagination often traveled as far as that), she felt quite certain—no matter how much they had sinned—that not a single one of them would cast his eyes down before the radiance of God's face, and that even up there they would find their way to the top, separate themselves from others, and carry on as they pleased, obeying their own laws. Vainly she tried to think of a way in

171

which she might put them out of countenance and topple them, justly, as they deserved. And when she tired of such brooding, when the flagging thought coiled into a circle and began to eat itself, another, contrary thought would suddenly appear above it: that, despite all of it, this state of affairs could not continue, that somewhere there had to be someone who will unmask them, punish them, annihilate them, and accord justice to her, to her mother, to Jela, Mara, and all those whom the Pamukovićes scorned, devoured, and trampled. With these thoughts she racked and mortified herself to the point of utter exhaustion, and still they kept returning and jarring her out of sleep and rousing her to new torments.

She could find peace only in prayer. Here there was no solution either, but prayer spun a kind of sheath around her, in which she was, if not safe, at least protected, though the thought of them and their evil would penetrate even that. It occurred to her sometimes that they, the Pamukovićes, might be saying the same prayers and speaking the same words, and she resolved to find words and prayers that would apply only to herself, and which they would never be able to find out and speak. And she would often lull herself to sleep breathing such prayers in a hot whisper into the edge of the quilt—prayers made up of new, grave and sweet words.

It was only here that she found what she craved so very much, a realm in which one truly and honestly knew who was right and who was wrong, and could tell the mean and foul from the good and pure—except that all of it usually melted away somewhere between sleep and waking. And next day the rankling thoughts would start again.

But even at that, having discovered "their true face," she found it easier to suffer both their contempt and the hitherto unbearable gap between her own simplicity and poverty and their lordly ways and haughtiness. The more she learned and suffered, the more comfort and relief she found in her musings and prayers—relief that she never suspected a person could find in himself. Realizing what kind of people they were, she got used to looking at the problem in this way: on one side the Pamukovićes, in their wicked strength and comeliness, and on the other she herself, with God and God's justice as allies. And so she toughened inwardly.

Her greatest bane was her husband. Before his spite and rancor she was still terrified and dumbfounded, though ready to defend herself. At first he had not drunk much and had kept early hours, but she knew and felt that he hated her, secretly, deeply, ever since that day when, after her initial flight, he had brought her back from her mother. And when the first year had gone by and she had not conceived, he began to drink more often, to return home at dawn, or even the following day.

Once he went to Kiseljak to join Simeon, and came back only after midnight of the third day. Not expecting him any more that night, she had gone to sleep. She was startled awake by a hoarse voice. Jumping up and flinging a wrap over herself, she helped him into a chair. He was muddy, covered with soot, spattered all over with wine and food. She strained hard to pull off his soaking boots, while he, blinking, stared at her with eyes that were not so much drunk as vicious. Suddenly he jerked his leg and drove his booted foot into her chest. She crashed backwards, cushioning her fall with her hand.

"Nikola—"

But he interrupted her hoarsely and wrathfully, drawling the words through a mouthful of spittle.

"You barren bitch!"

"Niko, what are you saying—"

He snarled out an obscenity, involving her mother, but never finished his oath, for she hit him right across the face with the loose boot. With his arm raised to protect himself, astonished more by her unexpected boldness than by the blow itself, he remained stock-still. But then, as if suddenly sobered up, he sprang to his feet and, the way he was, one foot bare, the other shod, started to chase her around the room. Rumpled, bent, his arms outspread, he staggered about as if trying to catch a bird. Since she was quicker than he, she gained the door, rushed across the hall and stopped in the shadow of the stairway. He came after her, muttering unintelligible oaths. She ran down the stairs and into the yard, where the first light of the day was already noticeable, and crouched behind the waterwell. She heard him shuffle and stumble down the steps, his one boot thudding as he went. He stomped around the yard.

"Where are you? Come out, I tell you!"

After discovering her, he started to chase her around the well. She was faster and more nimble, but he went on darting and lunging even though he kept banging himself against the corners of the stone well. At times he would stop and wait in ambush with his arms open. So they faced each other—he on one side, she on the other. In the silence, only their panting could be heard.

"Jump into the well, bitch!"

He kept growling this, but under his breath, almost in a whisper, until suddenly she found her tongue, too, and replied in a changed voice, much clearer than his.

"Your old mother Pamuković is a bitch!"

"What!"

After which the furious chase around the well started afresh. But when he lost his balance and stumbled, she took advantage of it and fled to the smaller courtyard, where she hid between the vats and barrels. Barefoot and lightly dressed though she was, she waited till the sun rose and then went back and lay down. Next morning life went on as if nothing had happened. Yet, from that day on whenever he took it into his head to rush her either in drunkenness or for any other reason —and this he often did without any provocation—she would defend herself stoutly, then run away and lock herself in until he had sobered up or calmed down. And their combats were neither seen nor heard by anyone.

It was only in the third year, this past spring, when she had already begun to lose all hope, that Nevenka suddenly conceived. She was overcome more by the joyful unexpectedness of it than by the pregnancy itself. It was as if the three years of secret tears and desperate vows had come back once more, metamorphosed into an excruciating rapture of victory. She said nothing to anyone, but went around the house with bright eyes, doing her work with unaccustomed zeal. The barren woman was jubilant. And the inmates noticed the change, and understood. Her exulting heart sometimes all but choked her, and she had to clamp her mouth with her fingers not to scream from defiance and joy. In the end the long waiting, terror, and reproach, followed by sudden happiness, made the whole thing more of a pain than delight.

One day the old dowager Pamuković called her in and started to tell her, in a roundabout fashion, that it was time for her to begin worrying about swaddling, cradle linen, and little frocks, and to leave off heavy housework. Pale and resolutely calm, Nevenka made as if she didn't understand. The old woman bit her lips. The daughter-in-law exulted. Nevertheless, it was agreed that an apartment would be furnished in the small quarters behind the kitchen, where from now on the young woman would weave until her seventh or eighth month, after which she would only sew. And so here she was now, spending the greater part of her day beside Mara, while in the big house in front they were content not to see her, not to have to avert their eyes before that gravid belly and expectant air of hers.

———

175

Evening came on as Nevenka finished telling her story, and it was only then that Mara summoned enough courage to look her in the eyes. In the gathering dusk her sallow face was quite colorless, the lips thin and drawn, while the eyes, darker yet and more glowing, full of hatred, stared absently through the window. Her look, as if piercing through both the Pamuković houses, was lost somewhere in the distance.

Seeing her so rapt and still, her legs oddly spread out with the empty, naked, and sharp-toothed carding comb in her lap, Mara had the impression that Nevenka was plotting something that she, Mara, could not know but which she guessed was to bring vengeance, unquiet, and endless trouble in its wake. She was afraid of all the things she had just learned about the Pamukovićes, and of the young woman herself, even of the child that was yet to be born. Oppressed by her dread and incomprehension, she contracted inwardly, pressed her hands to her chest and hung her head even lower. But Nevenka seemed not to notice her, and went on staring absently through the window, utterly engrossed in her memories, and thoughts of revenge and of the child.

There were other things as well, new and unfamiliar to her, that bewildered Mara. Those visits, above all. Although she lived in a small room in the kitchen building, she nevertheless saw, when her work happened to take her to the front yard, the people who came and went. As soon as the daylight faded, Fra Gregory would arrive; and even though he never spoke a word to her, his presence always disturbed her. Another visitor was old Hajji Ivo Livajić, thin and clean-shaven, his hair trimmed short as though he were a Muslim priest; then the brother of the Pamuković dowager, Matan Boštor, a huge and stout old man, gray as a sheep, with a blotchy face. He once came across her alone in the yard. Stopping, he gave her a long look which she could not understand, but from which she shuddered all night. What did they tell him about her? What did he want? Was he sent to question and punish her with that look of his jaundiced old eyes which, like those of predatory animals, veiled over languidly every other minute and yet saw everything with terrible clarity? And if not that, why did he stare so long and hard? All this was beyond her, something she did not know how to unravel. She knew only her sleeplessness and torment.

One of the visitors of whom she was not afraid was Dr. Ketchet, a Swiss in Turkish service. Small and gray-haired, he would smile already from the courtyard gate and greet her cheerfully. She had not seen such a reassuring smile either among the Christians or the Turks—on no one, in fact, save this foreigner. And she felt that she didn't have to be afraid of him. In recent weeks, however, he came less and less frequently, and disguised in Turkish clothes of all things, which gave him an absurd appearance and a diffident bearing. But she was always pleased to see his face, with its smile and an open, somewhat worried look.

On the whole, however, she feared all these visits, no matter who came, for she was wont to connect them, like all the other things that happened around her, with her own person, or with incidents and changes that might develop and embroil her.

Besides these visitors, she saw another foreign and unusual face. Right behind the stables there was a high fence that separated the Pamuković yard from the garden and house of the family Telalović. In that Telalović dwelling was the English consulate. Through the cracks in the board fence one could see the building and the wooden porch erected on columns overgrown with bougainvillaea. One day Jela and Nevenka showed Mara, through the fence, the English vice consul walking up and down the porch. He was young and sturdy and pink of face. He wore some sort of a long house robe of dark satin with lapels and piping of maroon silk.

177

The two women told her that this vice consul was crazy, that he often sang and woke up the neighborhood at night, that he collected Gypsies, beggars, and half-wits. All that was deranged, cretinous, maimed, all that crawled naked and bare-foot in the alleys, he collected and brought home; there he gave them presents, dressed them, forced his houseboys to bathe them and cut their hair, and played strange games with them. Some of those fools had the temerity to come uninvited, while others wouldn't come near a second time for any money and would run the minute they saw him or his boys. And he often roamed through the most Godforsaken alleys, in high rubber boots and a long leather coat, and invariably led several leashed dogs that were very old and ugly, "as if they'd been bred in hell."

After that Mara used to go alone behind the stables and watch the Englishman through the board fence. She was afraid both of the foreigner and of being found out by one of the Pamukovićes, but still she went, especially in the late evening. The porch was then in a glow of the setting sun. The consul strolled briskly up and down. Sometimes he would pause and throw his head back, and she would see the sun kindle his purple robe and his eyes flash as if with a kind of madness. But the most outlandish thing was his hair, light brown and lux-uriant, streaming over his temples and cut in a straight line at the nape of his neck, as on a schoolboy. Observing how, with his unnaturally tilted head, flooded with sunlight, he gazed toward the west, she imagined that he, also, was performing some kind of a rite whose meaning she could not divine, and which filled her with the familiar dread associated in her mind with everything she had seen at Veli Pasha's, Baba Anuša's, Fra Gregory's, or Nevenka's—and, beyond that, with a peculiar and aching curiosity.

Presently, one after another, the visitors stopped coming. For a while yet she saw Matan Boštor, but then he too dropped out of sight. In the city, the rebellion was in full swing, the bazaar deserted, and all houses shuttered up. Marijan, a syce of the Pamukovićes, who used to go with the horses to Kiseljak every Sunday, went no more. Lolling and smoking around the servants quarters, he talked about the Austrians who had already reached the town of Jajce, with artillery and a great deal of equipment, and about the Turks who were planning to wait for them at Klokoti. They all listened to him attentively and in fear, but to her the whole thing seemed so distant and unreal—those towns as well as those people getting ready to go to war—that she hardly felt any dread. Then she began to be awakened at night by the calls of sentries from one shore of the Miljacka to the other, and by the bagpipes and yells of the detachments marching through Čumuria. Occasionally she would sit up with a start and jump out of bed with a scream, so close seemed to be the one who yelled. Once it was a man somewhere outside the front gate, shouting in a thin and terrible voice:

"*Ya hayun—ya kayun!*"*

In the silence that followed both the footfalls and the low murmuring of those who echoed the cry could be heard. Then the quiet was again shattered by the calls of the patrols. Pair after pair of dissimilar voices would chorus one another, as if in some kind of a game.

"*Yek dur Allah!*"†

"*Yek dur, yek!*"†† a second one would answer, as if to prove he was awake.

As her heart pounded away, she waited for new voices and tensely stared through the darkness in which Jela's shadow could be made out. Jolted out of her sleep also, Jela was sitting on the edge of her bed, praying with her rosary and trying to calm the girl.

"Cross yourself, child, so that the Lord may humble the

---

* *Thou who art from the beginning:* one of the epithets for Allah, that also serves as a battle cry.
† *Allah is one!*
†† *One and only!*

179

Turkish fiends. Then go back to bed and sleep."

But she could find no peace for hours, what with that ceaseless shouting, and it was only toward dawn, when the voices grew less frequent, that she curled up and, overcome by tension and fatigue, drifted off into a profound and sweet sleep.

Once, just before daylight, she dreamed an unusual dream: that she was playing with a ball in some kind of a strange and spacious meadow. Dark-green grass grew over the meadow and underneath the soil was soft like on a day after a generous rain. The ball was small and blue, quite like the color of the sky, so that up aloft it blended into the light of the sky and disappeared in it. Thus each time she tossed it she felt an anxiety: would she catch it again? This fear sent a tingle through her breasts and brought on an aching and delighted laugh that she was powerless to stop, and which made her quite dizzy. All of her interrupted childhood and stunted youth came now to cavort down the length of the meadow. And as she careened along and lifted up her arms and eyes toward the ball and the sky, she felt as if her innards were straining to take wing and soar aloft somewhere. This made her pant and swell throughout her body, so that it seemed to her she would burst at any moment and float away into the distance. Yet she continued to run, to toss the ball and catch it, laughing and almost blinded by ecstasy; and in the midst of laughter all of her seemed to scatter into the radiance of the huge day.

Next morning, she was still under the spell of the dream. She still felt a little of that pleasurable tingle and lightness in her breasts, and something bright and restless behind the eye lids. Indeed, she hardly remembered just what she had dreamt, but only felt a great relief, as if in the darkness that surrounded her a bright window had been sprung open.

That same day, as she sat in her room and combed wool,

she heard Jela and Nevenka talking in the kitchen about Simeon, Auntie Andja's man, and gathered that because of the uprising he too had fled from Kiseljak and returned home. In the afternoon, she remained quite alone. There was no one in the kitchen either. Since the building was low and the window in the small room rather tiny, and the courtyard enclosed with a high wall, the room grew dark early. Outside, it was still daylight; the red glow of sunset fell directly from the sky and filled the entire yard. At that moment the door opened slowly and unexpectedly, revealing an oblong of crimson glow on the yard gravel and, in the door, a red-haired man with a puffy and flushed face. He hesitated for a second, then shut the door behind him. In the careful and soundless way in which he closed it there was something that froze the blood in Mara's veins. It was Simeon.

"You're the little one from Travnik, eh?"

His voice was hoarse and deep, he had difficulty enunciating words, but he made an effort to give his watery and bloodshot eyes a set look of amiable kindness.

"A little compatriot, eh? Look at her."

Seeing how he was slowly pushing the wool aside with his foot and trying to come closer, she got up frightened and backed to the wall. There she stood up to her knees in wool, her palms pressed desperately into the wall, the blood drained out of her cheeks, eyes dilated. He was still mumbling words that made no particular sense, while awkwardly shoving the wool out of his way, when the door opened and the crimson light of the courtyard fell in a shaft across the wool and over the pair of them. Auntie Andja stood in the doorway. With his back turned, Simeon could not see, nor did he hear the door open, and he went on mumbling:

"Little one from Travnik—now don't you be afraid," while trying to edge closer.

Not bothering to shut the door behind her, Andja

grabbed him around the waist and pulled him back. After the first shock of surprise, the drunk tried to wrest himself free, while mumbling on. But his wife was stronger and she dragged him away cursing under her breath:

"Come here, you philanderer! You don't need a Turkish concubine!"

Left alone in the semi-dark room, the girl did not move from the spot for some time, then slid down into the wool heap and repeated, inwardly, the word—*concubine*. Only once in her life had she heard that word: When some woman, during a quarrel, had hurled it at her mother across a street. Since they had taken her from Travnik, she too, in her bad moments and during sleepless nights, had been thinking of that word, in which she felt there was something as if blue, giving, and evanescent, but at the same time deadly; she had thought of it, it was true, but had never heard it flung at her by anyone, nor had she dared to pronounce it aloud to herself; it had not been spoken even by Fra Gregory in his worst anger. Now it had been voiced, and she reeled under it as under a final blow.

She was startled by Jela's voice; back in the kitchen, the woman was calling her to come and lend a hand. She rose, shook the wool off her dress; she worked and moved around the kitchen till late in the evening, feeling chilled all over.

That night, sleep would not come. Through her numbness she heard the clatter of some horses, the shouting of patrols, the clamor of the insurgents. Jela, who had no inkling of what had happened that afternoon, got up twice, tried to soothe her and fetch water to wet her temples and chest.

Next morning she could scarcely drag herself into the kitchen. No one noticed that her face was changed and her eyes restless and strange. That same night Simeon tried to hang himself twice. As the day was dawning, Auntie Andja no longer knew how to contain him and called in the young

Pamukovićes to take turns watching him. The whole house suddenly withdrew into itself and fell silent, more oppressively so than usual. But Nevenka brought the news to the kitchen, and talked quietly to Jela. Mara could not make out what they were saying and only caught a remark of Nevenka's as they were parting.

"Satan put the yoke on him long ago!"

In a lower, but hard and dry voice, Jela added:

"When the Devil puts his rope around a man, it stays on for good."

Hearing this, Mara could not bear to eavesdrop further, but fled to her little room, full of uncarded wool, and banged the door shut after her. The moment she was alone she slumped into a chair, let her arms drop at her sides, and hung her head as if for a blow. She made no sound and shed no tears, but merely froze in the dread that enclosed her like air. After she had rallied a little, she began to pick up the wool with cold fingers and stick it on the comb. Working slowly and vacantly, she felt at times as though she were seeing herself on her knees, with outspread arms and a bowed head, voiceless and without tears. Every now and then she could feel her blood in turn coursing and freezing in the nape of her neck, the muscles twitching on her arms and chest. There was a steady hum in her head; her sight in turn darkened and flashed with painful and unbearable sparks. She was seized by a terror she had never known; as if someone had shut the door behind her and there with her, in the darkness, was the terrible Simeon and her mother Hafizadić. She strove with all her strength to think of something she might clutch at and which would guide her back among those whom the devil had not roped in. She wanted to call someone, but could not remember anything any more; neither Jela's nor Nevenka's name, nor her dream of last night. The only thing that occurred to her was that yesterday, when she was in the stable, she had seen a rope

dangling from the rafters. It was the loose end of a halter, thin
and sturdy, made greasy and smooth by the drovers' hands.
She sprang up and set off toward the stables. She crossed both
courtyards without meeting anyone, but before she reached
the stable her strength gave out and she stumbled in that narrow, damp and always murky enclosure into which all kitchen
slop was emptied, where the cobblestone was usually wet,
greenish and mildewed, and where some kind of white and
repulsive toadstools grew along the fence. This was the most
outlying and hideous nook on the Pamuković property, and
here she slumped to her knees and burst into tears once more,
without warning, in a copious, heartfelt, childlike fit of crying.

Blurred by the welling and unstoppable tears, the resurrected images passed before her in a streak: her mother Hafizadić, the old Elias Garić, then Veli Pasha, with red epaulettes
and a silver-inlaid dagger hilt; then Fra Gregory, quick to
work up an anger; then Sarah, Anuša, Jela, and Nevenka . . .
Picture dissolved into picture and faded away, and over them
appeared that haggard and austere saint from the altar in the
Sarajevo church; but he too melted away in a tear and was
replaced by Our Lady from the chapel at Dolac. Holding a
fold of her blue gown in each hand, she walked toward Mara,
but slowly and with a strange air of gravity. Unable to wait till
she came near, Mara fell prostrate on the stone and reached
out toward her; resting the weight of her body on one hand,
she stretched the other to clutch the hem of the gown and pull
it over her head.

"Cover me, Sweet Rose, shelter me! Hide me from all of
them, all of them. They've dragged me all over—the Turks
and our people, both. They've pulled me apart. I don't know
anything. I'm not guilty. Don't let me out of your hands!"

She cried out through her tears, at the top of her voice.
And the voice was not the same, but rose up from the base of

her throat, clear and firm, as it had never been before.

One of the maids working in the kitchen heard the sobbing and the voice and glanced through the window. She ran out immediately and called Jela. In the yard they were joined by another maid and by Nevenka; together they hurried behind the stable. Finding the girl prone on the ground, they stopped in horror. She was pitching from side to side, her face on the muddy cobblestone, her tiny hand grasping convulsively at something above her, as if trying to pull it over herself. They called her name, but to no avail. On the mud-smeared and utterly distorted face there was not the slightest spark of consciousness or understanding. She did not cease her disjointed wailing and moaning, and showed no restraint or embarrassment. They led the pregnant Nevenka away, to spare her the sight. Jela rushed back to the house for the holy water and the consecrated salt, while the maids, crossing themselves, averted their heads and backed away, dismayed, step by step.

5

From that day on the daughter of the Travnik baker and Veli Pasha's mistress struggled almost continuously with apparitions and hallucinations.

The times were becoming more difficult and turbulent. It was hard to know what to do with this girl whose mind was rapidly distintegrating, and so she remained in the Pamuk-ović house, kept there on sufferance and out of pity. She was quiet, except that she wept a great deal and for no apparent reason. Both Jela and Nevenka cared for her as much as they could, but the girl refused food, didn't want to wash or change, and, like a cut sapling, wilted and withered with terrifying speed, shriveling and disappearing before one's eyes. Her face, whose beauty had once seemed indestructible, grew haggard and coarse, her eyes lost their luster, the mouth grew ugly. Only the hair, thick and fair, kept its old sheen and luxuriance; and rumpled and unkempt though it was, it looked like the adornment of an imperishable beauty. But with time it, too, began to coarsen at the ends, to mat in sweaty knots and lose its color. It seemed incredible that so much beauty could waste away in so short a time.

In a few weeks all that remained of this girl who had combined in herself the charm of a child and the beauty of a woman, was a pathetic, dull-eyed wretch, dressed in rags, after whom urchins would have scampered in the streets had the Pamukovićes only let her out of the house.

And even Jela, who in her time had seen a good deal of evil and had become inured to sickness and slow death, was shaken and baffled in the face of such a disaster. But there was something in this misfortune that perturbed this hardened and prematurely aged homebody even more: the demented wisp of a girl, "wrecked by a Turk," as she put it, was about to give birth to a child. There could be no more doubt about it. Right after that first fit, as she had washed and undressed Mara, Jela had realized that the poor girl was pregnant, and no longer in her early months either. Jela, who had never had a home of her own or known happiness and family, who had experienced man once in her lifetime, and only as a brutish horror, became all concern and excitement at the prospect of children and births. Now all at once she had to do with the moody and embittered Nevenka who was about to start her labor, and with this sick girl who was only a few weeks away from it.

So much evil and suffering, and all of it still breeding and multiplying at every step!

Staggered though she was by it all, Jela did not lose her presence of mind. She looked after Mara, soothed and comforted Nevenka, who was in her last days and apt to be an intolerable burden to herself and others. All this Jela did and bore alone, not saying anything to anyone, knowing from way back that words were useless, that she could expect no help from the others.

Meanwhile, in the Pamuković house the women were whispering and the men were making arrangements. They filled the house with grain, dried meat, and all kinds of provisions. According to the advice conveyed by Fra Gregory, they prepared two large bed sheets in order to hang them out as flags on the two house gates the day the Austrians entered Sarajevo. For, the latter had already marched past Klokoti and it was clear that they would continue unhindered all the way to Sarajevo. And Sarajevo was getting ready to put up resistance.

The city, which for a long time now had resembled a camp and a chaotic anthill, was receiving its first wounded, whose tales injected new excitement into the inhabitants. It was as if everyone were filled with an awareness of the importance and solemn greatness of each day and each hour. Everyone went his way with a dark face, armed and dignified, and each man felt prompted to carry this solemn rigor to the others. The Council forbade the sale of brandy. Constables were arresting young loafers on the streets, marching them off to the arsenal fortress to unload and pack ammunition there, or, when that was done, to loll around there similarly unemployed. Except that each man was eager to do something for the common cause. The mosques were thronged with people, alms were given out generously. No one kept track of lunch or dinner; one ate wherever one happened to be, and somehow there was plenty of everything. Few men slept in their own homes, but, rather, at various picket posts and assembly points; and the one who managed to doze off couldn't even finish his catnap for he would be jolted awake by a rifle-shot or a drum or a cry of *Yek dur Allah!*

Still, little more than a distant echo of all this reached into

the servants quarters where Jela was caring for the two pregnant women. Nevenka had grown so heavy and weak that she
could hardly move. It looked as if she would never part with
the child. The members of the Pamuković family grew noticeably kinder and more solicitous toward her, as if they were
only waiting for her delivery in order to announce her complete equality with all the other Pamukovićes. But the daughter-in-law was getting to be increasingly sullen and less accessible; she refused to accept the least favor from them, and their
attention. And had she been able to follow the dictates of her
own heart, she would have hidden herself, when the time of
delivery came, in some remote and forsaken nook of the quarters and there given birth without a sound and without their
help, and never even shown her baby to them.

At long last, in the middle of August, Nevenka bore a
male child which, though tiny, cried in a strong voice and
greedily demanded food.

Two days later, the first guns boomed out above Sarajevo.
By noon, the artillery fire came thick and fast. The air shook
ominously. Since the Pamuković house towered above the others, its high roof ridge stopped many a stray rifle bullet.
Through the steady roar of the field guns one heard clearly
from time to time how the lead shot hit the roof boards and
how the latter crackled under it. The entire family moved
down to the ground floor of the big house, and was ready to
descend to the cellars if necessary. The servants were particularly terrified. Only Jela scampered unafraid now and then
across the yard between the house and the quarters.

Since the artillery fire had started, Mara had been scream-
ing and sobbing without letup in her room. This frightened
and bewildered the Pamuković servants even more. It was only
in the afternoon that her wailing ceased. Jela, who throughout
that time had not rested for a moment, rushed into the main
house and whispered something to the old dowager Pamuković:

although barely in her seventh month, the Pasha's concubine had given birth to a child.

As the day drew to an end, the guns fell silent, while small arms fire grew scarcer and more distant. Even before dark, loud music of the Austrian Jaegers could be heard in the city. Both gates of the Pamuković homestead were flung wide open, and the older men went out into the street.

In the quarters, water was being heated, herbs and medicines readied, and Jela shuffled around briskly, preoccupied with tending the baby and its mother, as if inside the house and outside it, and in the whole wide world, there was nothing greater or more important than what she was doing now.

Delivered before its time, Mara's child responded weakly to the cold and light of the world in a feeble voice and with a few puckers and twitches, and promptly expired. Old Marijan rummaging among the wooden cases in the storage bin, chose an empty box on which the stamp of some Austrian nail factory could still be seen, and in that box he and Jela buried the child whose life had lasted a bare half hour. Since the presence of the army made it impossibe for them to go to the cemetery that day, Marijan tucked the box under his arm, carried it into the garden, and buried it under the tallest plum tree along the fence.

As soon as she would complete her ministrations to Mara, Jela would immediately go over to Nevenka and continue working by her side with the same zeal and efficiency. The child was healthy and Nevenka was feeling well, but she had no milk to give. Jela fed the child skillfully, as well as she could, but seeing how Nevenka's milk would not come, she took the baby one morning, carried it into the small room where Mara lay in bed and placed it on her swollen breasts, holding it with both hands. The sick girl neither resisted nor touched the child, but with closed eyes and averted face let them do what they wanted with her. In this manner Jela fed

Nevenka's child twice a day, until she noticed that Mara had fever.

From that moment, Jela nursed the sick girl for six days and nights. On the evening of the sixth day, Mara breathed her last, without a word or prayer. They buried her next day in the cemetery in Carina.

The funeral was attended by all the servants—three boys and two maids. When the rites were completed, the sickly and embarrassed chaplain wrapped his books in a piece of cloth and went away. The boys put the finishing touches to the grave, while the maids whispered prayers and gazed absently at their clasped hands or at the fresh earth. Marijan erected a makeshift cross and then sat down beside it. A little farther away sat Jela; her eyes were still glued to the mound in front of her, as intensely as if she were looking at something in the distance. She was about to finish her brief prayer for the soul of this girl from Travnik when all of a sudden, from the invisible road that ran behind the cemetery wall, they heard voices, footsteps and a clatter of arms and chains. First the boys, and then the two girls too, broke off their praying and went up to the wall. The boys at once climbed over it, while the girls, after mounting a stone heap overgrown with thick and scorched bramble, watched the scene on the road from inside the wall.

Muhammet Hadžijamaković, the dark and sinewy Kaukdžić, and another pair of reputable townsmen, all fettered to the same chain, were walking past as fast as they could; they were flanked by Austrian soldiers in full equipment, and at the head of the column there rode an officer on a white horse. They were taking them to the place of execution. In a carriage that brought up the rear sat a hodja and some people from the Council.

The boys went forward to the edge of the road to see better; the girls leaned over the wall, holding hands and clinging to each other in fear.

By the grave, which already lay in a summery shade, there remained only Jela and Marijan. Jela had finshed her prayer and wanted to get up and call the others, but found it hard to abandon the grave. She thought of Mara and her fate, and of that tiny creature buried without a name and a cross under the plum tree in the Pamuković garden. Absently she went on praying. The words came welling by themselves, and they in turn deepened her melancholy. It had been many years since anyone had seen her shed tears; now she wept and loudly prayed to God to protect and keep safe all women, unhappy companions, and martyrs.

Marijan, who had learned to drink in the company of Simeon on Kiseljak, was quick with tears, and also with words. Seeing Jela cry and whisper, he too began to weep and talk.

"Oh, oh—" he sighed, not quite knowing what he wanted to say. "Oh, we buried a sinner, we buried a poor soul. Each of them took something from her, and now there's no one to feel sorry for her and shed a tear over her. Oh, shame!"

He hung his head and was silent for a while, then suddenly burst out and with a heavy tongue, all twisted with emotion, cried, almost yelled out, as though revealing and admitting something unexpected and dreadful:

"Jela, we buried one of God's angels—an angel!"

Jela came to with a start, interrupted him gruffly and, wiping her wet eyes, called to the girls who were still watching the procession of condemned men marching down the road. In a quieter voice she admonished them not to forget anything by the grave, and to close the gates of the cemetery properly.

On the way back, Jela walked in front of them, with Marijan at her side, and talked with him about housework and about the need of finding as soon as possible a strong and healthy woman who would be able to suckle Nevenka's son, the youngest Pamuković.

THIRST

Soon after the Austrian occupation of Bosnia, a post of the *gendarmerie* was opened high up in the mountain village of Sokolac. The commanding officer brought with him, from somewhere abroad, a lovely fair-haired wife with big blue eyes that looked as if they were made of glass. With her brittle beauty, her Western dress and outfit, she was like a precious and frail thing mislaid on the mountain heights by some travelers en route from one great city to another.

The village had hardly gotten over its first shock of astonishment, and the young woman was still busy furnishing her new married quarters, filling the rooms with little cushions, embroidery, and ribbons, when bandits were reported in the vicinity. A company of special scouts arrived at the post, doubling the barracks population. The commandant spent his days out in the field, deploying and supervising his patrols. His young wife was left, bewildered and fearful, in the company of village women, so that, nominally at least, she would not find herself completely alone. Her time was spent in waiting.

Even her sleep and meals took on an aspect of waiting and no longer refreshed and nourished her. The village women coaxed and begged her to eat, until in their nudging and wheedling they themselves ate up all the food and drank all the milk. At night they sat by her bedside and told her tales of village life to lull her to sleep. In the end, exhausted by their talking, they would doze off on the red carpet while she, from her bedstead, would gaze at them with her wide-awake eyes, sickened by the heavy smell of milk and coarse wool that came from their peasant skirts. And even when, after several days of such waiting, the commanding officer would return, she had little cause to feel joyous and relieved.

The man came back dead-tired from marching and lack of sleep, his face hidden behind a thick stubble, his clothes dirty and soaked through. His boots, which he had not taken off in several days, bulged with mud and water and it took a pair of orderlies to pull them off; and with the woolen putties bits of skin came off his sore and swollen feet. His lips were chapped, his face weathered by the sun, wind, and mountain air. He was worried and distracted by his lack of success, and in his mind would already be plotting his next expedition. Tense and wound up, he literally burned with zeal and anxiety. In those short intervals of rest at home his wife nursed him like a wounded man, only to send him off again two or three days later, at the crack of dawn, into the mountains. And so all her thoughts and prayers were animated by a single wish, that the wretched brigands be rounded up as soon as possible and that this dreadful way of life might finally be brought to an end.

And then one day her greatest wish came true. They caught the chief bandit, Lazar Zelenović, the most cunning of them all. After him, according to the barracks talk and village gossip, it would be easier to catch or scatter the other petty bandits who were less skillful and experienced.

It was by a fluke that Lazar was caught. A patrol that was

on the trail of another, younger bandit stumbled on him accidentally. Some two months previously, when he had moved into this region from Herzegovina, Lazar had been wounded in the chest by a bullet. This no one knew. In order to tend his wound, Lazar, with the help of younger bandits, had built himself a shelter beside a mountain stream; it was made up of dry branches and driftwood and washed-up silt. He lived in that hole out of sight of the paths that traversed the hillside high above the stream, yet was able to reach water by stretching out his hand. In this way he could bathe his wound all day long while the patrols looked for him everywhere, scrambling up the crags and mountaintops. And he might have recovered had he dared to look for a more comfortable shelter and had the weather just then not turned unseasonably warm, which made his wound much worse. He did his best to ward off mosquitoes and flies, but the wound grew bigger and, deep down under the skin where the water could not reach, it was beginning to fester more and more. And his fever rose.

Such was the condition of the bandit when one of his younger companions decided to bring him some wax and brandy to use as medication. A patrol spotted the young man as he was leaving a shepherd's hut on his way down to the stream. Noticing them only at the last moment, the boy scampered down the stream bed and vanished without a trace.

The commandant who had left his horse in a meadow below and was running at the head of the patrol after the young bandit, stumbled into a patch of soft mud and grazed his feet against something soft and lifeless, before sinking up to his waist in the silt. And he might have gone on ahead, after extricating himself with difficulty, and might not have discovered Lazar's small and deftly camouflaged hideout, had he not smelled the terrible stench of the bandit's wound. After pulling his legs out of the mud, the commandant glanced through the parted branches and saw a sheepskin. Sensing that a live man was hiding in the burrow underneath, he never even dreamed that it might be Lazar himself; he thought that it was the younger bandit or some accomplice of his. To hoodwink the concealed man, the commandant gave loud orders to his patrol:

"He must have run ahead. Go after him and I'll follow you slowly. I've gashed my leg on these thorns."

As he was shouting this, he cautioned them with one hand to keep quiet and with the other signaled them to form a circle around him. When three of the men came near, they threw themselves all at once at the shelter and pinned the bandit down by the shoulders, like a badger. Since his only weapons were an old long-barreled rifle and a big knife, he had no time either to fire or reach for the knife. They tied his hands with a chain and his feet with a rope and carried him thus, like a log of wood, down the hill and to the meadow where the commandant's horse was waiting. All the way down they were aware of the heavy stench, but it was only when they put him down that they saw the ugly wound on his bared chest. A certain Živan from the village of Goražde, who had joined the patrol as a guide and scout, recognized Lazar right away. They were from the same village; both their families honored the same patron saint, St. John.

The bandit rolled his big gray eyes, which had grown clear through his living out in the open and beside the water but which now were aglow with fever. The commandant asked Živan to confirm once more that this really was Lazar. They were all leaning over the bandit. Živan addressed him for a second time.

"It's you, Lazar!"

"I can see you know me better than I know you."

"You know me, Lazar. Sure you know me."

"And if I hadn't known you before, I'd sure know you now. I would know who you are and what you are. And so would every last village from here to Goražde . . . every man who calls himself a Serb or a Turk would know you. If you came with a stupid child who'd never seen us, and he saw us now just the way we are, he'd say, 'The one lying tied up on the ground, that's Lazar, and the bastard that's bending over him, he's Živan."

The bandit had a fevered need to talk and mark time, while Živan wanted to assert his authority and buttress his reputation before the company, and who knows how long the two of them might have dickered in this fashion if the commandant had not interrupted them. But the bandit met all further questions with silence. He would say nothing about his accomplices and contacts, using the excuse that he was wounded and in pain. After consulting with the patrol sergeant, a strapping man from the province of Lika, the commandant issued strict orders that the bandit was not to be given a single drop of water no matter how much he begged for it, but was to be referred to the commandant.

While they were readying a stretcher on which to carry the wounded bandit, the young commandant sat down some distance away to rest and collect himself. Planting an elbow on his knee, he leaned his chin on the palm of his hand and gazed at the mountain, which had only just turned green and seemed as endless as the sea. He wanted to think about his success, about the citation that awaited him, and about resting up in the company of his wife. But he could not concentrate on anything. All he felt was a leaden exhaustion, which he resisted and fought as a man caught in the snow at night fights against sleep and freezing. Wrenching himself up from the ground, he stood erect and ordered his men to move on. A second patrol overtook and joined them. Now there were nine men in all. The litter they had improvised for the bandit was rough and made of gnarled branches. One of the gendarmes threw his tunic over it, averting his face as he did so, almost as if he were abandoning his coat forever.

They traveled by slow marches. The sun was beginning

to burn in earnest. The commandant, who rode in the rear of the litter, was forced to move to the head of the column because the stench from the wounded man had become unbearable. It was only after midday, when they had climbed down to the Glasinac Plain, that they managed to commandeer a cart and oxen from a peasant. In this way, shortly before sundown, they reached the broad valley that stretched out before the village of Sokolac. They looked like a party returning from a hunt, save that these huntsmen were lost in thought and their game was extraordinary.

In the meadow in front of the barracks the women and children of the village had gathered. Among them, too, was the wife of the commandant. At first she gave no thought to the bandit, and was simply waiting for her husband, as always. But as the women began to chatter more excitedly about the man on the litter and their tales grew more and more lurid, and as the procession came nearer, slow and drawn out like a funeral, she too was filled with a sense of misgiving and suspense. At last they arrived. The men noisily threw open the left wing of the barrack gate, which ordinarily was done only when a cartload of wood and hay had to be taken in. Here the commandant dismounted, hitting the ground with a thud, as exhausted riders are wont to do. The young woman felt the scratch of his sharp stubble on her cheeks and smelled the odor of sweat, earth, and rain which he always brought with him from these official raids.

While he gave his orders, she stole a glance at the bandit who lay bound and motionless. Only his head was raised a little on an improvised cushion of straw. His eyes didn't seem to see anyone. The acrid stench of a wounded animal spread out around him.

Having ordered all that was necessary, the commandant took his wife's hand and led her into the house, for he didn't want her to witness the unloading and untying of the bandit.

198

After he had washed himself and changed, he went out once more to see how they had settled and secured the man. Lazar was locked in the cellar under the commandant's apartment, which was to serve as a temporary jail. The door was not a strong one; the upper half had iron bars, and the lock on it was the usual kind. Thus a man had to be detailed to stand guard in front of it all through the night.

The commandant ate sparingly, but talked a great deal with his wife. He chatted about trifles and was as lively and cheerful as a boy. He was well satisfied. He had caught the leading and most dangerous bandit, after five months of strenuous traipsing up and down the mountains and after undeserved reprimands from his superior officer at Rogatica and from the headquarters at Sarajevo. He would find out from Lazar about the hiding places of his accomplices and so earn a respite and an official commendation.

"What if he doesn't give them away?" asked his wife timidly.

"He will; he'll have to," replied the commandant, unwilling to discuss it further with his wife.

Presently he grew sleepy. Exhaustion weighed on him heavily, overcoming his joy, his hunger, his desire for his wife. The freshness of the bed linen went to his head like wine. He made an effort to speak, to show that he was not sleepy, but the words became raveled on his tongue and the pauses between them grew longer. He fell asleep in the middle of a sentence, the fingers of his left hand still resting on his wife's small white and rounded shoulder.

The woman didn't feel like sleeping. She was contented and thrilled, and also frightened and sad. She gazed long at the man sleeping beside her, his right cheek sunk in the softness of the down, his lips slightly parted as though he were greedily drinking in the pillow. Between a person who is wide awake and his sleeping mate there is always a great and chilly chasm that grows wider with each new minute and becomes filled with mystery and a strange sense of desolation and tomblike loneliness. The woman tried to fall asleep. She closed her eyes and breathed evenly, but was startled out of her first light sleep by the changing of the guard in front of the cellar door. As if she had never slept or thought of anything else, her mind returned to the bandit.

The new guard was Živan, Lazar's countryman. Now she realized that she had not been awakened so much by the change of sentries as by Lazar's crying and calling. The prisoner was asking for water.

"Which of you is out there now?"

There was no answer.

"Is it you, Živan?"

"That's right. Shut up!"

"How can I shut up, you infidel, when I'm dying of thirst and fever. Give me a little water, Živan, for the love of St. John, our common saint. Don't let me die like a beast!"

Živan made as if he didn't hear and gave no answer, in the hope that Lazar would get tired of begging. But the man called him again in a low, hoarse voice.

"If you know what suffering is about, and prison, don't play deaf with me, Živan, in the name of your children!"

"Leave my children out of it! You know I've got my orders and I'm on duty. Keep quiet! You'll wake up the commandant."

"Let him wake up. He has no right to sleep. He's worse than a Turk . . . letting me die from thirst, on top of all my troubles. I beg you, in God's name, hand me a little water through the bars."

As they went on talking in muffled voices, the woman learned that he was being kept off water on the orders of her husband, who was determined to force him to betray his fellow bandits and helpers. And Lazar, racked by unbearable

200

thirst and the fire in his blood, apparently found a certain relief in obstinately repeating the word: Water. He would lie still for a few minutes, only to heave a long and deep sigh immediately afterwards and follow it up by a spate of words.

"Ah, Zivan, Zivan . . . May you never taste my salt and bread again, that you make me suffer like this, worse than a Gypsy. Give me a jigger of water and then you can make short work of me . . . and no one will be the wiser in this world or the next. Oh-h-h-h!"

But Živan had stopped answering him.

"Živan . . . Živan! I beg you . . . I'm burning up!"

Silence. Afterwards, a ragged last-quarter moon bobbed up in the sky. Živan had backed away into the shadows and when he spoke his voice was an indistinct mumble. The bandit was now loudly addressing the commandant.

"Oh, Captain, don't torture me needlessly! May the Emperor's bread rot in your mouth!"

After each of his imprecations the silence closed in more thickly. In that silence the bandit growled and moaned heavily, no longer bothering to lower his voice and heedless of what he was saying.

"Oh-o-oh! Heathen sons of bitches! May you drink blood through all eternity and never slake your thirst! I hope you choke on our blood. Where are you, Captain, you son of a werewolf?"

He shouted the last few words in a smothered, helpless voice that peeled strenuously off his parched palate. Once again Živan tried to silence him, promising that he would call the commandant first thing in the morning and that they were sure to give him water, if only he would tell them what they asked; till then he would have to be patient. But Lazar, in his fever, forgot everything after a few moments and started wailing again.

"Živan, I beseech you, in the name of God . . . I'm burning! Water!" And like a child he repeated the word a hundred times, his voice and speech waxing and falling with his uneven, fevered breath.

Wide awake and trembling, sitting on the edge of the bed, scarcely aware of her body and of the room around her, the woman heard it all. She was overwhelmed by a new terror, a kind she had not known till then, touched off by the prisoner's groans and by Živan's hissed warnings and by the deep, exhausted sleep of the man beside her.

When she was still a child in her parents' home, sometimes during the nights when she could not sleep, in the spring or in the autumn, she had spent the whole night listening to such monotonous and frightening sounds from outside: the wind rattling the metal vent at the top of the chimney, or the banging of the garden gate which someone had forgotten to latch. As a child, she had endowed those noises with a special meaning, she had imagined that they were living creatures who were struggling, rasping, and sobbing. Life often transmutes on a larger plane the imaginings and terrors of our childhood, and out of petty fancied fears weaves some real and potent ones. She thought how wonderful it would be if the innocent horrors that once had disturbed the sleep of her girlhood were true and the reality of this night, in this godforsaken village, in her marriage bed, and the dreadful talk and moans of the bandit down below, were nothing more than a dream and will-o'-the-wisp.

And during all this time—just like the soughing of the wind in a tinny chimney vent or in a crack of the attic trap door—there could be heard, almost at regular intervals, the steady, labored breath of a man in high fever and a weary human voice as it gasped in fits and starts through a parched, wide-open mouth over a thick and coated tongue.

"Water, water! A-a-ah!"

Živan's watch presently came to an end and he was relieved by another gendarme, yet the bandit's appeals for water did not cease; they merely grew feebler and more tired. The woman continued to sit up stiffly, listening to every sound from below and thinking the same thought over and over, endlessly and inconclusively. How was she to fathom and understand this life and these people? All she could see was that on the one side were the gendarmes and on the other bandits (two aspects of the same misfortune), that they both pursued each other without mercy and that here, caught between the two, a person was certain to pine to death from sorrow and pity.

For months past there had been a lot of talk in Sokolac about this man Lazar. She had heard awful tales of his cruelty, how he tortured in the most brutal ways the peasants who wouldn't yield to him, and shot gendarmes from ambush, stripped their bodies to the skin, and left them naked on the road. And now she was witnessing how the gendarmes repaid him in kind. Could this possibly go on forever? It seemed to her that they were all rushing toward some kind of abyss and that they would all perish together in a night just like this, destined never to see the light of dawn, in blood, in thirst, among unspeakable horrors.

She thought now and then of waking her husband and begging him to dispel, with a word or a smile, all of this horror as though it were a hideous dream. But she could not bring herself to move nor to arouse her husband, and remained stock-still on the edge of the bed almost as if the body beside her were that of a dead man, and listened to the voice in the cellar, alone with her terror and her questions. She even thought of saying the prayers they had taught her in childhood, but those were the prayers of another, forgotten and vanished life, and they gave her no clue or comfort. As if making peace with her own death, she resigned herself to the thought that the wailing man would go on wailing and imploring forever, and the man sleeping and breathing beside her would thus sleep and remain still forever.

The night kept pressing in from all sides, growing thicker and more ominous. This was no longer an ordinary night, one of the countless ones in the string of days and nights, but a long drawn-out and perpetual desert of gloom in which the last man alive was moaning and crying for help, begging hopelessly and in vain for a drop of water. Yet in the whole of God's wide world with its waters, rains and dew there was not a single tear of water, and among all living creatures not a single hand to offer it. All the waters had run dry, all mankind pined away. Only the frail rush-light of her consciousness still flickered, like a solitary witness to it all.

At last came the dawn. Not daring to trust her own eyes, the woman watched the slow paling of the wall, at the same spot where it always paled at daybreak, and saw how the morning twilight, first pearly and then pink, spread through the room bringing shape and life to all the objects in it.

If she strained hard she could still make out the bandit's voice, but from a great distance as it were. The cursing and oaths had stopped. There was only an occasional dull "A-a-ah!" And she inferred that rather than actually heard it.

Although the daylight was growing brighter, the woman had no strength to move. Doubled and rigid all over, with her chin cupped in her hands, she was crouching on the edge of the bed and never even noticed that her husband had woken up.

He opened his rested eyes and his gaze fell on his wife's curved back and on the milky white nape of her neck. At that moment, when the haze of sleep first cleared from his eyes, a sense of joyful reality flooded back into him, washing over him like a warm, luxuriant wave. He wanted to call to his wife, to sing out her name, but changed his mind. Smiling, he raised himself a little, making no sound, then propping himself on his left elbow reached out with his free right hand, and without a word, suddenly took her shoulders, pulled her over, and brought her down under him.

The woman struggled briefly and in vain. The unexpected and irresistible embrace was dreadful to her. It seemed blasphemous and unthinkable that she should betray so quickly and easily, and without any explanation, the world of night in which up to that moment she had existed and suffered alone with her anguish. She wanted to hold him back and convince him that it was not possible, that there were grave and painful things which she had to tell him first and over which one could not pass so lightly into everyday life. Bitter words rose to her tongue, but she could not speak a single one. Her husband never even noticed this sign of her resistance, this fragmentary sound that never hardened into a word. She would have pushed him away, but her movements were not nearly as strong as her bitterness, or as swift as her thoughts. The very heat of that awakened and vigorous body crushed her like a great weight. The bones and muscles of her young body gave way like an obedient machine. Her mouth was sealed by his lips. She felt him on her like a huge rock to which she was lashed, and together with which she was plunging downward, irresistibly and fast.

Losing all recollection not only of last night but of all life, she sank into the deaf and twilit sea of familiar and ever-new pleasure. Above her floated the last traces of her nighttime thoughts and resolutions and of all human compassion, dissolving into air one after another like watery bubbles over a drowning person.

The white, gaily draped room quickly filled with the vivid light of day.

THE SNAKE

On the white road that cut through the Glasinac Plain as far as the eye could see, an elegant yellow phaeton was moving slowly, drawn by two rather small but lively blacks in a spanking new harness. Seated in the coach were two young girls wearing identical gray mantles of light silk and wide-brimmed straw hats on which the veils had been raised and drawn back. In front, with a pipe between his teeth, sat the driver, a native of Kranj. His red beard and whiskers and bushy eyebrows were coated with dust of a flourlike whiteness.

The girls, Agatha and Amelia, were daughters of General Radaković, traveling from Sarajevo to Višegrad. A month ago they had both arrived in Sarajevo, where their father had been on duty since spring.

Their father, a gray-haired but slim and red-cheeked man, belonged to the Viennese family of Radaković that, for more than one and a half centuries, had supplied the Austrian Empire with high-ranking officers. Orginally from the province of Lika, they had long since become Germanized and had, in the fifth or sixth generation, come to regard themselves as genuine Viennese. With a certain archness, they claimed that they were descended from some Bosnian princes, and in their family coat of arms, which each of them wore engraved on a massive ring, were supposed to be heraldic indications that bore out their claim. Beside his Croatian surname, it was possible that this legend too had contributed to the general's appointment that spring to the post of division commander in occupied Bosnia, with headquarters at Sarajevo.

Now that the mild September weather had set in, the general had begun an inspection tour of his garrisons on the eastern border. Višegrad was to be the base from which this tour would be conducted. He planned to remain there two or three weeks. The Višegrad commanding officer was an old acquaintance from Vienna, a veteran bachelor and an amiable rake who had long given up the hope of advancing his career and was now assigned only to easier duties in outlying garrisons where he might gratify his passion for gardening and organizing mess rooms and officers' quarters—the one passion left to him from so many foolish and expensive ones, which had earned him a bad name among his superiors while at the same time making him popular with fellow officers, with women, and with moneylenders. It had been his suggestion that the general bring his family, and he took it upon himself to arrange their quarters ("the best available, considering the place and circumstances"), and to furnish house help, organize the hunts, and plan suitable diversions for the ladies.

So the general had set out with his wife, two daughters, and his son, a cadet at the military academy and now on furlough.

They had left Sarajevo early the day before. The general, his portly wife, and cadet son were riding in the heavy black landau which the Sarajevo firm of Saračević rented only to leading notables and for grand occasions. The daughters, both grown up, had connived to travel separately in the general's coach, which was light and gaily painted. They were thrilled at the prospect of spending two whole days together and of being able, while passing through wild, unknown country, to talk undisturbed and to their heart's content; they were unusually fond of each other, even though the only thing they had in common was their beauty.

Agatha, the older sister, was of a quiet and sober nature, even-tempered and dependable, always occupied with some business of the family or home. Her Viennese friends jokingly called her Caritas, for she had, while still a young girl of sixteen, founded her own society for helping the poor. She was one of those girls for whom personal happiness was not the first and last thing in life, and who in seeking happiness would find it in the service of others.

Barely a year younger but just as lovely, Amelia was somewhat frailer and paler. She had been nicknamed Ophelia. She was very musical and fond of books and entertainment. Ever since her "coming out," she had suffered (there is no other word for it) from a complicated and hopeless love for a childhood friend, a cool and self-contained young man who would have driven into a convent even a hardier type than Ophelia. Amelia did not enter a convent, since those things were not done any more—the year was 1885—but she continued to suffer because of the young man, or, more accurately, because of her love for him, as from a secret and lingering disease. Hidden wounds take longer to heal, and the one person in whom she could safely confide was this sister of hers. Agatha responded with patience and genuine sympathy, and was ever ready to understand, soothe, and offer comfort.

The girls had been inseparable since childhood. When their father was stationed in small garrisons in Hungary and Galicia, they had gone to the same boarding school near Vienna. Later, he had served five years at Prague and Vienna, and they had spent their first adult years in those two cities. Now this remarkable and breathtaking ride over the wild Romania Mountain and along the endless Glasinac Plain gave the younger sister a rare opportunity to confide in the elder. After a lengthy and particularly agonizing whispered confession, she broke down and started to cry. In the middle of that sun-baked plain, sketchily edged by blue mountains in the distance, her anguish sounded even more distressing and hopeless than usual.

The older sister gestured at the hulking back of the driver, reminding her that one should not give way to emotion in front of servants and that there would be time enough to cry later, then drew her gently to herself in order to calm her. After a quiet cry on her sister's shoulder, the blond girl lifted up her head. Her face seemed transfigured in the September sun. They exchanged smiles that were almost identical in the beauty of their teeth and lips and shiny eyes, but one seemed to say, "Isn't it better and easier now?" and the other, "Yes, it is, my dear, but it hurts all the same and always will."

Now, as their carriage continued on its course, they were enchanted with the air and the wide expanse of the changing landscape. The landau carrying the rest of the family had fallen behind by almost an hour's ride.

It was getting toward noon. The road dipped imperceptibly. Here the plateau appeared to sag a little and for the first time they felt the mugginess of the day, which seemed more like midsummer than early autumn. On both sides could be seen scattered cattle sheds built of dry gray logs. The lonely and empty structures gave an impression of utter neglect. There wasn't a human being or dwelling anywhere in sight, not a tree or cultivated field or cattle, or a single bird in the torpid air. From this shallow lowland the road began to ascend again in a wide curve. The horses slowed down and their breathing grew more labored. And when at last they had pulled the carriage to the highest point of the rise, the plain reappeared once more, though no longer as smooth and uniform as before. Now it was tilting slightly and was fringed on both sides by small mounds and dimpled ridges covered with low undergrowth in the hollows.

On a little flat to the right side of the road they saw a small knot of people. Two of them were peasant women, bending over something on the ground. Both sisters saw them at the same moment. As they drew nearer they realized that the women were busy with a small prone child. Next to them stood a small boy. The women and the boy turned to stare up at the girls as if they were apparitions.

It was obvious right away that the small girl who lay on the grass beside a fire was feverish and very sick. The sisters knew only how to say "Good day" in Bosnian and beyond that they were unable to make themselves understood. They called the driver. He was reluctant to leave the coach, but after securing the team he went up the rise and began to act as interpreter.

The child had been bitten by a snake while rounding up her sheep in the bushes. (Both sisters froze in momentary confusion and fear as if they themselves had stepped on a snake.) This information was conveyed by the weeping younger woman, the child's mother, who gasped between words as though she were laboring uphill with a heavy burden. The older woman was a charm healer from a nearby village. She squatted beside the little girl, whispering.

The charm healer was known as Smilja the Serbian. A ruddy, powerfully built woman with big dark eyes, she was the healer and fortune teller for that entire region. The sudden appearance of the two foreign ladies did not disconcert her in the least. She went about her ministrations with perfect composure, yet also with a total concentration that brought to her features the calm and compassionate expression seen on the faces of good doctors. Her patient would undoubtedly have found her presence reassuring, were it not for the fact that more than three hours had elapsed since the accident and the child had already passed into that typical state of utter apathy common to snake-bite victims—eyes shut, lips tightly compressed, face of an earthen color, breath short, skin cold and clammy. The sorceress had observed all this at the start, and was concentrating all the more zealously on the tiny, all but invisible wound on the girl's swollen leg. Calm and unruffled, she was gazing at the wound as if it were some secret text. From time to time she would trace, with the long thumbnail of her right hand, a wavy line around the wound resembling a spiral thunderbolt that was supposed to represent the broken black stripe on a snake's back. In a low but steady voice, she recited some verses in which it was possible occasionally to make out the rhymes, but the rest of which was lost in a prayerful whisper. Then, lifting her head and rocking over the wound, she recited in an undertone:

> Early on Sunday Lena made her way
> to the meadow for a sheaf of hay.
> In the hay a yellow snake
> bit Lena and made her cry,
> Her mother tried to soothe her:
> "Little Lena, fear no harm,
> your mother will find a charm:
> Milk from the wild doe yonder
> and apple milk to seal the wonder."

This was followed by a rhythmical chanting of jumbled and meaningless gutturals, punctuated by a solemn blowing of her breath first directly into the wound, then into the distance, and finally in all four directions of the compass. When it was finished, the sorceress calmly rose to her feet, as though all were now in the best possible order, and began to untie the knotted end of a short towel and take out some dried snake herbs that were to be wetted with saliva and then applied to the wound.

The older sister watched the stern, matter-of-fact woman with disapproval. She felt that one ought to protest against such superstition, make a determined stand against this witchery and offer instead some sensible treatment and genuine medication. But she remained standing as if chained to the spot, as if on climbing down from the coach she had immediately stepped into a tepid and sticky quicksand in which one moved only with the utmost effort and where every thought foundered and vanished the moment it was born. She had to brace herself and summon all her strength to move closer to the scene.

The child lay on her left flank now. Her long white shirt was thrown up over her knees, her left leg thrust out sideways and already noticeably swollen. The bite could not be seen, though it must have been somewhere just above the ankle, for that was where the blue-green circle was, fiery around the edges. The child was moaning softly and every once in a while her whole body shook as in a hiccup.

After moving closer, the older sister gazed long and fixedly at the inflamed leg. Her fine dark eyebrows had come together, which gave her face an altogether new and unnatural expression. Disturbed by it, the younger sister joined her and asked in a hushed voice:

"How does one treat a snake bite?"

Still staring at the sick child, Agatha seemed not to hear the question.

She had seen illness and poverty in the slums of Vienna, on her periodic rounds in the company of other members of her organization. But this—this was something new and quite horrid. There, one had always known what was lacking and also the possibilities of help, at least as far as practicable. There it had been a problem of saving children from bad parents, alcoholics, or from an illness that was easily diagnosed and prescribed for, in which only the money for the pharmacy was lacking, or of patients who needed a better diet or a change of air. But what was one to do here? This plight seemed to be beyond anyone's grasp and intervention. Scowling as before, Agatha asked question after question, which the driver translated haltingly.

What had they done about it so far? It turned out they had squeezed all the blood they could from the wound and tied a tourniquet above the knee and then sent a boy, the little girl's older brother, to the village for brandy. Wiping her tears and sweat, the child's mother motioned vaguely at a point in the distance where the village was supposed to be. Now they were waiting. There was nothing else they could do.

"Do you have any rum or brandy?" Agatha asked the driver.

"No, miss. I don't drink or carry the stuff when I'm on the job."

Agatha would best like to have sent both of them packing, the spellbinder with her unctuous face and the driver who seemed as if he were secretly gloating over the fact that there was nothing anyone could do, and to roll up her sleeves and do something useful. But she stood there helplessly, fretting at herself and at everyone around her.

"One can't let a human being die like this," she said under her breath, not knowing herself whom the rebuke was meant for. She went down on her knees, poured some cologne water on her handkerchief and gently began to mop the child's forehead and face. The girl only moaned louder.

"Alcohol, of course! Only alcohol can save her," she said under her breath, as though it had only just occurred to her. Then she turned to the driver. "Please turn the carriage around at once and go back as fast as you can to meet father and mother. Ask them for the cognac flask and come back quickly. Quickly, do you hear?"

But speed was not congenial to this driver from Kranj, who was wont to regard the young mistress's activities among these Bosnian peasant women as something exaggerated, slightly unreal, and altogether senseless, much like those drunken cutups of gentlemen officers when they urged him to drive faster at some ungodly hour over rough and tricky roads. But he turned the coach around and started back. To Agatha it seemed that he was crawling.

Throughout this time Amelia had stood to one side and, with a sense of uselessness, watched her "big" sister. Now that they were alone they could look around and take stock of the situation. In the oppressive heat of midday the little peasant group appeared wretched and pathetically lost on the scorched plain. The women stood there as if made of stone. The child's mother kept glancing westward, toward the village where the life-saving brandy was supposed to come from, but the glance was tormented and empty of hope, as if the village were half a world away. The spell-woman quietly waited for her work to take effect. The little boy stared on dully, while the stricken girl lay in her dirty, grass-stained shirt, her swollen leg stuck out stiffly.

"Will she die?" asked the younger sister in a voice full of fear.

"Not if we can give her enough alcohol in time," the other replied in the tone of an expert.

The silence was complete—broken only by the child's muffled, continuing moans. The sun beat down mercilessly. The vast gray plain seemed to have swallowed the coachman. Time stood still, hot and immovable, like the misery and suffering that surrounded them.

"My God, Agatha, what kind of a life is this! What kind of a country, what kind of people!" whispered the younger

THE PASHA'S CONCUBINE

sister, trying to still her own deep unease.

Agatha's eyes were on the horizon, on which the carriage was supposed to appear momentarily. Steadily, mechanically, the child's mother was drying her invisible, inexhaustible tears.

Suddenly the child gagged and doubled convulsively, then vomited without lifting her head off the ground. The mother leaned down and propped up her head, while Agatha wiped the child's mouth with her lace handkerchief. The spasm racked the tiny body a few more times, after which she grew still and deathly pale. Her breath sounded shorter. Agatha pulled up the shirt and saw that the belly was also beginning to swell. There came off her a rank and sickening smell of excrement, as the food had poured out of her from all sides.

Agatha rose and asked by sign language if they had any water. On the grass lay an earthern jug, and from this they drained the last few drops, indicating that there was no more to be had for miles around. When she asked for a small spoon to pry open the child's tightly clamped teeth, it took quite some gesturing for them to understand each other; and again the answer was in the negative.

"Nothing—not a blessed thing," Agatha said as she wiped her fingers on the handkerchief her sister had handed her. In the face of so much helplessness her goodwill began to fail her too.

She folded her hands and with a mounting sense of impotence looked querulously at the sorceress who crouched on the dry and parched ground, unshakably calm and confident in her nostrums and magic which, judging from the looks of her, were already at work and were bound to help, if God willed it. Agatha began to relent toward her and was in half a mind to ask her to get on with her spells and charms, seeing how there was nothing else to be done, anything but slouch there so impassively while the venom raced through the child's body and spread havoc with every passing minute.

The younger sister was apt to imitate the older unconsciously. Now they both stood with folded hands and waited, like the two peasant women, for the help that was supposed to come. Now they, too, were beginning to feel a little as if they had always stood forlorn like this, helpless and superfluous under the vast sky on this interminable plain of stunted pastures that was empty of any vestige of human habitation or activity save the dingy, ramshackle cow sheds which looked for all the world like a discarded stage setting. They felt as if they were poor and squalid themselves, embroiled for untold ages in some drama of primitive shepherd life, with a leaden weight on their heads, on their eyes and all their limbs, rooted in a cosmic seizure in which only the hidden evil in the child's body continued to live, pulsate and ravage unimpeded.

In silence the mother wiped her tears and sweat and then, between expelled breaths, began to emit short laments of which the sisters understood not a single word and yet perceived the full meaning.

"Oh, poor unhappy me! Hoo-ooh, everything comes down on my head. Hoo-ooh, what a cursed wretch I am!"

And again she would lift her head and scan the horizon for the boy who some three hours ago had gone for the brandy and was dawdling as if he were fetching Death itself.

Finally, the bright-yellow coach reappeared on the highway. Agatha nervously waved her handkerchief at the driver, urging him to hurry, but the man was a congenital laggard whom nothing could change. He brought along a flat crystal flask with a silver cap that served also as a peg.

They barely managed to loosen the child's cramped mouth. Into it Agatha poured the cognac slowly and carefully, afraid lest the girl bring it up again. As soon as the child would start to choke, she at once withdrew the flask and waited. In this way the flask was gradually emptied of cognac. Some ten minutes later big drops of sweat broke out on the child's forehead, her eyes cleared and her cheeks came out in a flush.

Through the driver Agatha explained to the women that the child should be kept awake at all costs, that they were to massage her forehead and chest and raise up her arms periodically to encourage breathing and stimulate the heart. They nodded and promised to do it, but in their awe forgot either to thank her or bid her good-bye. The little group remained unchanged, save for the two extraordinary foreigners in their bright city finery.

The girls quickly took their seats in the carriage, which promptly started down the road of the plateau. Some distance behind them the dusty and lumbering landau had just come into view.

The terrain grew more and more uneven. The plain heaved and sloped downward at the same time. The swelter grew more intense. Thin spurs of red earth began to border the road on both sides and low, scraggly undergrowth became prevalent: dwarf juniper, hellebore, briar, hawthorn, and nameless tiny thornbush close to the ground itself. The landscape rapidly lost that grandeur and melancholy beauty usually found in a plain that meets and joins the sky in a soft unbroken line; it began to look somber and frayed, poor somehow and lacking proportion. The horses trotted faster. The driver spurred them on, anxious to outdistance the landau to spare their honors the dust he was raising. With a forward tilt, the light carriage fled along the dust-filled ruts making hardly a sound.

The sisters gazed ahead in oppressive silence, lost in the languor of the landscape and of the stuffy afternoon. How different, how crisp and invigorating had been that morning on the same Glasinac Plain when they had chattered about this and that and Amelia had eased her heartache with a good little cry!

Her eyes riveted on the driver's shoulder buttons, Agatha continued to scowl just as she had done over the sick child a while ago. Now the expression gave a new cast to her features, both aloof and alarming. It cowed Amelia, who, glancing mutely and anxiously at her sister, longed to be able to say something, anything, that would break the heavy encompassing silence, yet dared not for fear of making her wise big sister sadder yet. Shyly she put a hand on Agatha's. As if she had been waiting for the gesture, Agatha bent her dark head to her sister's shoulder and closed her eyes. Observing her from the side, Amelia saw the quivering lips and the long dense eyelashes straining to hold back tears. Touched to the quick, she gave her an awkward hug and said:

"No, don't cry. There's nothing to cry for. Please don't. A fine big sister you are, carrying on like this."

In an unconscious echo of her older sister's gesture earlier that morning, she drew her attention to the driver and wordlessly implored her to control herself. Agatha quickly checked herself and dabbed her eyes, but just then her tears came welling with an unstoppable force and she again dropped her head on her sister's shoulder and said in a smothered, trembling voice:

"Oh, I told you in Vienna what kind of a country we were going to. Now you've seen what it's like. Not a wretched thing under the heavens—I kept telling you about the poverty and wilderness—the ugly, indescribable squalor. I did tell you, didn't I? It's awful—absolutely awful!"

"Darling, calm yourself, please." Flustered, the younger sister tried to comfort her. "Don't be a child. Remember how Count Prokesch used to say you exaggerated everything—and that Turkish proverb he used to quote to you: He who weeps for the whole world won't have any eyes left. He knew what he was saying, he'd lived long enough in the East. The world's full of misery and backwaters like these, and there's nothing you or I can do about it."

"Ah, nothing—really nothing. But one should at least make an effort. Somebody ought to try—at least a little—because like this it's impossible, impossible for them and for us to live. It's too horrible for words."

"But that's neither your fault nor mine," said the younger sister with an edge of exasperation in her voice, herself close to tears.

"No, of course not," answered the older sister dully. But she immediately corrected herself. "Really, I don't know any more. Not our fault—that's very easy to say. In the end it turns out it's nobody's fault, but look how the people live and what they do. You saw it with your own eyes. Somebody must be to blame or else how could this horror exist? Such horror!"

With a tenderness at once childlike and grave, the young one put a hand first over her sister's mouth, then over her eyes, as if to snuff out the tears. In doing that she herself dissolved in tears, brought on by a vague sense of shame, anger, and grief over her sister's outburst, impelled by the instinctive egotism of young, beautiful, and spoiled women who understand and endure tears only in relation to their own pain. Her feelings presently coalesced in one urgent wish: That this weeping of her sister's cease and that all talk of misery and bad luck be silenced forthwith. In a chiding and irritable tone she whispered through her own tears, even while pressing her sister's head to hers:

"Don't cry, Agatha. Calm yourself, I beg of you. The driver is listening. Really, I don't understand you. Bosnia isn't worth crying about. Please don't! I can't bear to see you crying. I can't."

Huddled like this and mingling their tears the sisters crossed the Glasinac Plain, oblivious of the driver and of the whole world. The plateau soon came to an end and was replaced by steep mountain country. The road began to drop noticeably and the vegetation on both sides thickened. The brakes made a harsh scraping noise against the coach wheels.

THE SCYTHE

On market days the town throbbed with all kinds of voices and noises: bleats, bellows, the bedlam of trade and human clamor. But in the main square metallic sounds predominated: farmers testing the scythes they were thinking of purchasing by banging them against the stone steps of the shops. Dun, dun, dun . . . tsen, tsen . . . tsen! The clangor filled the market-place all day long.

A peasant does not worry beforehand about a job to be done, but when the time comes for it he applies himself wholeheartedly, with concentration and perseverance, with all his strength and his entire body as it were. Buying a scythe is such a job.

At the first crack of dawn, from his village on a high, steep hill, Vitomir had gone down to town and there sold his produce, and now the rest of the day still lay ahead and he was preoccupied with the thought of one last errand: the purchase of a new scythe.

He first talked with several peasants and consulted with

them, then spent some time window-shopping along the hardware row, at last deciding to enter the store he knew best. When the storekeeper asked him what he needed, he answered vaguely, evasively, merely sliding his eyes over the merchandise that hung from the ceiling, looking for the scythes. At last, after partly betraying his secret, and after the storekeeper had divined the rest, a boy apprentice set in front of Vitomir a bundle of scythes wrapped in burlap and tied with bass, like so many swords.

The peasant began to pull them out one by one, to examine the curve of each, and its color and temper, testing the blade with his finger, grasping it with both hands, raising it to his cheek like a gun and peering down its ridge as if taking aim. He spat on the steel, scratched it with his nail, and felt it with his tongue. The apprentice, some of whose front teeth were missing, hovered around him during that time, his small eyes already flickering with a sly light one would not have expected in a child.

As soon as he had picked out and put aside two or three blades that he considered better than the rest, Vitomir carried them out of the store and began to knock them on the stone steps, one by one, slowly and deliberately.

The apprentice went after him, not letting the goods out of his sight. The peasant would have given anything to be able to free himself of the runt and to stay alone with the scythe he was testing, for in this way, he believed, he might sooner detect its hidden flaws. He made an effort to push both the boy and the surroundings from his mind. He banged the blade on the stone and at once put it to his ear like a tuning fork, listening carefully to the pitch of the steel and following it long after everyone else had stopped hearing it. His face wore an expression of rapt vacancy. In his deep preoccupation with the sound, he forgot that he was in the market, where, in any case, he had little to do and which he ordinarily visited only in case of need, and felt as though he were already up in his field, when the mowing was at its height, his ear cocked to this same scythe, now hafted and hammered, as it hissed through the grass like a snake and toppled the swaths down the incline of the meadow in a pattern of half-moons.

Several farmers passing the store halted and watched him, and some listened attentively and put in a few words of advice, or else volunteered the opinion that all the knocking and testing couldn't make up for the fact that the good old Varcar brand of blade was no longer to be had. Vitomir gave each one his due, but, in fact, listened only to his own ear and formed his own judgment.

He banged like this and deliberated for a long time, until even the storekeeper lost his patience—the ample and inherited patience of the marketplace—and came out through the door and set to advising him in a voice of thinly veiled irritation, urging that he make his choice between two of the best in the bunch. "You don't have to worry, Vitomir. Whichever you pick, it'll be good. We've no duds here."

"Yes," said the peasant, marking his time rather than agreeing, for he needed a few more minutes to deliberate leisurely, without paying any attention to the merchant's words.

One of the blades carried the large gold-lettered signature of its maker: Boehme & Son, Wiener Neustadt—the one farmers called Goldie. There was another kind, too, nicknamed Tyrolean, that shimmered all over with the dark-blue iridescence of tempered steel; the letters on it were small and silvery, and its trademark was a picture of a four-leaf clover, also engraved in silver.

"No need to rack your brain any more," the storekeeper insisted. "You can see the letters and the clover for yourself."

"Yes," said the peasant absently. "Hm—" He was thinking that even those who could read were sometimes deceived by inscriptions, and that pictures often fooled a man into not seeing the very thing he was looking at.

"Hm—"

He said no more to the storekeeper, but continued his private debate with himself and with the blades in his hands, and this pre-empted his thoughts and occupied his eyes to the exclusion of everything else, engaging all the attention he could muster in this double-faced and prevaricating anthill of a market.

"Don't I know it," he said to himself. "Fine and dandy they are, these words and pictures, couldn't be dandier—but all this beauty lasts only until you put down your money. And then, look out, brother, because that's the end of fine words and the start of trouble. And trouble is what they make their money on. Devil take their fine words and gold letters—I need them like a horn adder! Still, I've got to get me one of these. Sure, the tough grass up at Dikave don't know the difference between letters and pictures, all it wants is a scythe. A scythe, my friend. And that's something I know—this one here's not the first one I've bought. You see it here in the store and, by God, you'd think it's a saber. But take it up to that no-good field at Dikave, put a handle on it and start mowing, and it just melts away in the grass and under the manure like a bloody icicle. Oh, I know it all!"

Talking to himself, Vitomir went on knocking one scythe after another on the stone doorstep and wished that his blows could force them to speak the truth about themselves, the truth now buried under colorful lies and obscure printed words.

Again he picked them up one by one and studied them unhurriedly. It was as if in the curve and the blue-and-gold sheen of each blade he could read its story and see the entire distance it had traversed from the far-off outer world in order to reach *him*, a farmer from Dikave. He saw—or imagined that

226

he was seeing—the mine from which they had taken the iron ore and the furnaces that had smelted it, and the forging works that had given it shape and a name, and the hundreds of hands through which it had passed from the works themselves, through importers, agents and wholesale merchants in Vienna and Sarajevo, across countries, mountains and rivers, transported, carried, and loaded again until, via Romania and Semeć, it wound up in a horse-drawn cart at Višegrad. And in each one of those hands something had stuck—everyone had made some money on it. Everyone!

All this Vitomir guessed in a dim and vague fashion, but it was as real to him as a physical pain. And here now, at the tail end of it all, he was supposed to buy the blade and wield it until either he or it reached the end of their roads. It had to be done, there was no other way. "Ah, you little tramp," Vitomir said, exasperated, and struck the blade so hard on the stone that the storekeeper behind the counter jerked up his head, and he himself, awakened from his fantasies, paused in some embarrassment.

After another long interval of testing, brooding, and wavering, he finally cast his lot with one of the two scythes, and did so abruptly, like a man plunging into cold water. Then came a lengthy haggle with the storekeeper. (This exhausted the latter, used though he was to endless, ceremonious, stubborn, and insincere bargaining. After getting home that night, after he had washed and sat down to supper, he would probably tell his wife with a deep sigh, as indeed he had done so often in the past: "Ah, those peasant rascals are a pain in the neck. It's tougher to get their pennies than someone else's paper money!")

The bargain sealed and delivered, Vitomir mounted his pony and stuck his purchase through the empty sack fastened to the pack saddle behind him.

On his way, he stopped at an inn and had a drink of

brandy. He met and chatted with several people, and his conversation was mostly about the scythe he had purchased. He also bought drinks for a couple of his godfathers, who were demanding a "treat." He himself had one, then two and three, over his usual quota—all on account of the scythe. And when dusk fell, he set out on the road up the mountain, toward his village.

The trusted old pony clung to the steep side of the hill like a beetle. Vitomir's befuddled head was clearing, and the brandy he had drank, far from clouding his reason—at least, so it seemed to him—gave a curious new lease to his flagging strength and his courage, stimulating all kinds of thoughts, filling his chest to bursting, clamoring for talk and a song. Only now did he begin to see and understand things with perfect clarity; only now, it seemed, was he quite ready to tell the pitch of the blade with absolute accuracy, and talk to the storekeeper as one ought to talk. It was always like that: While he was down there in the market he felt bewildered and on the defensive, full of a helpless distrust of all and sundry, even of himself, but the moment he got away from the throng and the hustle of the bazaar and began to climb back to Dikave, everything at once fell into its proper place, he regained his confidence and his belief in himself. He then perceived and understood everything. And yet when the next market day rolled around, the whole thing would happen all over again and there would be no improvement.

There, that always annoyed and vexed him.

Spurring the horse, he turned to look at the scythe that had cost him so dear and had given him so much trouble that day, and which at this moment, tied behind his back, was as inseparable from him as a lawfully wedded wife. Still, how was one to know fully and truly the nature of a lifeless thing? Who knew whether he'd picked the best possible scythe? How was he to tell whether or not he'd overpaid it? He saw again the expression on the shopkeeper's face at the moment when they'd finally come to terms, and he still could not un-riddle it—any more than he could decipher the maker's name on the blade. He would now never know whether that stained and speckled blade which he'd turned around and around and finally abandoned might not have been harder and better than this one, even though this one did look "louder" and "keener." Well, it was over now—a man simply had to make a choice in the end. But his doubts lingered on, prompting him now and then to turn around distrustfully and glare at his purchase with a beady and reproving eye.

If he glanced over his right shoulder, he saw the dark heel of the blade; if he tried it from the left, its top appeared as a steely half-moon to which the real moon, rising in the sky at that moment, lent a gentle silvery sheen. Each time he swiveled around in the saddle he would apostrophize his new possession in words that were both tender like a lover's and gruff like an enemy's.

"Go on, give yourself airs if you want to! It won't be for long. Wait till you find out what kind of village you married into, my pretty bride! You think somebody's going to gape at you in wonder and moon over your fine gold letters? They won't, never you fear. Where I come from, they don't go in for finery and clever writing. No horsing and playing around up there—not for you, or the grass, or a living man . . . I remember the way my grandfather Ristan—a hard man, as hard as they come—the way he shoved us all out, young and old, to gather hay. The stars were already up and the kids were dropping down left and right. Mothers begged him to let the children go home, but he went at them. 'Get on with it, little good-for-nothings! There's plenty of flesh left on you, I don't see any skin coming off your good-for-nothing fingers. What are you on this God's earth for if not to work . . . !' I can remember it all. I remember even worse than that—"

Vitomir grinned at the scythe, which shone back at him with the borrowed light of the moon, and then wound up zestfully through his clenched teeth:

"Ay, ay, my beauty. First thing in the morning I'll have you on the anvil, and by the time I'm through hammering you'll sparkle like a star and they'll hear you all the way down in the valley. And when you start squealing under my whetstone, you'll know what Dikave is! Your airs and finery will drop off like magic. Just you wait and see. It's a mountain, this is, my little lady—a tough big mountain, not one of your soft and flabby lowlands!"

Peering ahead through the pale moonlight Vitomir caught sight of the hollow called "Under the Small Hornbeam." At once he felt nearer to his village and sang out at the top of his voice, then let out a long wolflike howl, without words and to no particular melody, as though singing a song of defiance, or of revenge.

WOMAN ON THE
ROCK

Hotel Marina, built only a few years before the last war, small
and hidden away on a green island, is bound to be remembered
by those who had known it. (Alas, it was gutted completely
during the war and today only a charred ruin marks the site.)
Its beach, enclosed by greenery, consisted almost entirely of
pale-yellow and reddish rock tumbling unevenly into the sea.
The guests took their sunbaths on the flat slabs of these giant
cliffs, as if they were specially devised beds of stone. Off these
rocks they dived into the sea, which was deep at that spot, and
rose out of it on cement steps or by climbing an iron ladder
built into the steep rock. Around most of the bathers, especially the women, the stone was littered with colorful odds
and ends that they had brought with them for the swim.
Large, gaudy beach towels, jars and *flacons* of lotions, balls,
newspapers, books, cigarette packs, and a motley of Sunday
magazines in various languages. The guests left each other
alone. The majority had their steady places and occupied them
day after day as if by unspoken agreement. Each lowered

himself on the seething stone in a posture that answered his body's needs, much as a drop of liquid takes the shape dictated by the laws of its physical composition.

For the most part the guests didn't know each other, and when occasionally there was laughter among the younger couples and friends, this occurred without noise and without noticeable commotion. Only now and then, usually on a Sunday or holiday, bathers from the big nearby strands would arrive in their motorboats and ketches and step ashore for a while, disturbing the quiet and upsetting the established routine. But as soon as they had left, the beach would lapse into its usual quiet. Occupied each with himself, the bathers read on their stony bedsteads, gazed through their sunglasses at the blue horizon of the sea, or else, with their eyes firmly closed, gave themselves up to the glare and fire of the searing sun in the high blue dome, each relaxed in the knowledge that no one paid him the slightest attention, just as he wasn't expected to pay any to the others. From time to time one of the bathers would get up like a sleepwalker and descend the steps, or jump from his perch into the sea, only to hasten back afterwards and take up his old position.

On the craggy shore that was raised above the water and completely exposed to the sun, peace was a thing of dazzling incandescence, bruised only fleetingly, peripherally, by a lone cricket in the hotel garden and by an occasional broken-off cry from the water. In that torrid, brilliant, and blue calm of the land, the sky, and the sea lay the motionless, fakir-like bodies of the bathers as if stilled by an unknown drug, surrendering their pores to the sun.

One of the slabs—the same one day in and day out—was occupied by a middle-aged woman; she may have been closer to the upper limit of that age than to its uncertain beginning. Without the radiance and freshness that only youth can give, yet well-formed and preserved, she invariably came at the same hour of the day, always alone and unobtrusive, spread a large towel of a fluffy orange fabric under her, arranged her colorful trifles around her, and lay there for hours, now on her back, now with her face on the towel, offering every side of her body to the sun like a person submitting to a sacrifice. Now and then she rose and jumped into the sea in a smooth but unspectacular dive, then returned to her place after a short swim. She was among the last to leave. She made herself quite inconspicuous, save perhaps with this marked eagerness to remain unnoticed. Still, her swim suits, towels, scarves, and toiletries gave one an idea of her tastes and sense of color.

There are those women, like this one, in whom the feeling for color and chromatic harmony is highly developed, as if inborn. Like plants, they live and talk in color. Around such women colors sing, as it were, inaudibly and yet in such unison that they seem to be part of cosmic harmony scaled down to a woman's being and the power of human senses. Women like this seem to gather new colors from nature, and to create new relationships between them, and new iridescences; actually, all they do is to uncover them to our eyes, which otherwise wouldn't know how to see them. Slowly and calmly, as unerringly as nature herself, they spread about them, according to their age and possibilities and the circumstances in which they live, their *own* colors, as if that were all they had to communicate about themselves to other people.

Very little more could be said about this woman who lay at some distance from the rest of the bathers, her hands clasped on her breasts, stretched out and slender, with her eyes shut, like one of the stone duchesses on a sarcophagus.

We know next to nothing about people who pass by us or lie next to us. Was there anything more one might have added about this woman, laid out like a statue, Martha L., an opera singer on her vacation, in her forty-eighth year? She herself was trying to forget who and what she was, and how long she

233

had been around. Drowsily she gave herself to the sun's fire and to the dim memories and daydreams that welled in her aimlessly and against her will. Vague stirrings, words clearly spoken and yet unintelligible, silences of an unknown meaning, all this mingled inside her, ebbed swiftly and came back again, refusing to fade into limbo. Though not asleep, she was dreaming. And now she saw clearly: a strange image out of her past life, one that she had never suspected was still alive in her memory. She was sitting on a garden wall.

It was the high wall that enclosed their rambling garden. It was built of a hard stone, thick, some six or seven feet high; almost a rampart, that gave the passer-by a fair idea of the size and richness of the garden hidden behind it, and of the substance of its owners. Along the wall ran an alley strewn with the needles of big old pines. In the distance was the sea, with two small islands floating on it. When she was still a moppet, not allowed to leave the garden, she had got into the habit of secretly climbing the high wall and, from up there, watching the sea or the occasional passers-by in the alley below her. The habit stayed with her even later when she was already free to come out, when such infantile squatting on the wall, always in the same spot and position, was no longer becoming to her.

She was fifteen, if not older, when one day she again settled down in that favorite spot of hers. Letting one leg dangle over the wall, she raised the other and folded it until her heel rested on the very edge. A strong wind was blowing. She felt the cold stream of air wash her naked thigh above the stocking on the crooked leg and seep through her body with the same shivery chill that also filled her eyes, which were glued to the dark-blue and furrowed sea. She tingled all over, in a gooseflesh that was both aching and pleasant; she barely stirred. It was much like the moment at night when, after she had uncovered herself in her sleep, the chill would grow stronger and threaten to grip her completely; she would want to reach for cover but couldn't part from the lovely dream, and so kept putting off the actual movement, which unconsciously she had already made. She endured the cold with pleasure. Entranced, as if soaring on the bright crest of a wave at great and exhilarating speed, she never even noticed whether anyone had come down the alley or was looking at her. Only belatedly, and with a start, did she see old Matthew down on the ground below her.

The man was about fifty, homeless and without a wife, a good-natured eccentric. A part-time day laborer, part-time beggar, he worked for the wealthier families. Because he was valuable and utterly indifferent to money, everyone was fond of him and wanted him, especially for garden work. He did his chores as though he were bound to the soil, talking very little, his mouth set in a small fixed smile whether he dealt with people, animals, or the plants he hoed. Afterwards he would wander around for days, at loose ends, along the shore or down the paths between garden walls.

For a moment the girl looked at this man as if she had never seen him, her eyes batting as though she'd been caught in some light mischief, recalling with difficulty which side he had come from and how long he had stood there by the wall, his head lifted up like someone whose name had been called. As soon as she'd collected herself and realized that it was only the harmless "old Matthew," she grew quiet and reassured. But when she saw the direction of his stare, she dropped her raised leg in instinctive haste, only to pull it up again a second later, a little uncertainly, to its original position.

Rooted to the spot and gaping at her, Matthew furtively snatched off his cap, as though he were standing before a roadside shrine. She then saw that his eyes had opened wide and that they were unusually shiny. It was a new kind of stare, hard and unabashed. Overcoming her shyness and ignoring the chilly airstream, she lifted her leg a little higher. He thrust his head out and echoed her movement with his whole body. His eyes were round, clear; on the burnished, unshaven face their gleam seemed to be all of a rich and precious fire that was quite unconnected with his workman's bent body and his shabby clothes. (What is it they see, the eyes with that kind of look?) Again she moved her leg a little higher, feeling a vague sense of numbness and dizziness. Matthew leaned still closer to her, as if tied to her movements. It didn't seem possible that he could hold that position for long; he was bound to lose his balance. By now chilled to the bone, she pulled her leg higher yet, pressing it to her chest and tucking the knee under her chin, and he, in turn, tilted forward even more, pressing the cap to his body, frozen in his unnatural pose, deep in a rapture that seemed to overcome the very laws of physics.

Everything was changed. Her posture, the expression of her face and her whole bearing were no longer those of a little girl from a good home, nor was Matthew a day laborer and a crackpot. The wall, too, had ceased to be a wall and the wind was no longer what it usually was. Everything became nameless, unimportant, and weightless; it floated about like some kind of thistledown, neither rising nor falling, boundless and measureless, without a destination, swept by an anonymous, inexplicable force. And whether all of it happened in that precise way, or how long it actually lasted, she could not have accounted to herself even then, let alone today, some thirty or more years afterwards. But she knew today, just as she had known then, that she made a sudden end to that exceptional moment which had seemed utterly unbelievable while it lasted, and remained so forever afterwards, but which all the same, between those two implausibilities, must have taken place and existed as vividly and surely as any other public and acknowl-

WOMAN ON THE ROCK

edged event of her life. With a swift and fluid move of her body she pivoted around and shifted abruptly to the other side of the wall. (The skirt fluttered brightly. The two silk stockings rubbed together, producing a low but sharp hissing sound, like two wires passed quickly one over the other. Once more, around her naked thighs and into her very groin, she felt the spurt of the cold wind from the sea.) And now everything was changed again and restored to its erstwhile, everyday place. She already stood with both her feet on the middle rung of the wooden ladder in the garden. Not climbing down right away, she turned her head and, hidden up to her neck behind the wall, studied the man in the alley a while longer. He stumbled at first, as if her sudden movement had deprived him of a foothold, but remained on his feet. Then all at once he shambled away, in his gait and appearance once again the old, commonplace Matthew. The only other thing he did was to mutter:

"Thanks, *signorina*."

His voice faded. He turned once more.

"And—well—thanks!"

And he vanished behind the greenery. She sprang from the ladder and landed on both feet with all her weight, so that her teeth chattered and from the parched earth, which now appeared unexpectedly hard and unbelievably close, a painful tingle shot up her legs and all the way to her hips.

Some years later (soon after she got married), she learned accidentally one day in February that old Matthew had died in his drab room in an attic, in such monastic poverty and want that they had to get up a collection for his funeral. The young man and the girl who came to ask her contribution told her that the dead man did not have a shirt in which they could bury him. She gave them money and, as they thanked her and were about to leave, asked them to wait and then hurried into the bedroom. From there she brought one of her husband's fine new white shirts and gave it to them, so that poor Matthew might be laid to rest.

And now, with cap in hand, elongated and huge, he was drifting slowly, ghostlike, over the rocks and the blue sheet of the sea and across the sky; hovering, indeed, like a giant shadow rather than moving. And as he turned over his shoulder, he spoke his parting words over and over with an ambiguous smile on his face.

"Thanks, *signorina*, thanks!"

She twitched angrily and made an effort to shake off the distressing vision. Still oppressed by the daydream, she struggled against it with the alert part of her mind. Where did this sudden memory, twisted into a nightmare, come from? Was the curse of growing old so strong that it not only warped the present and darkened the future but also dominated the reveries of the past? Where did this apparition come from, and why—this image of more than thirty years ago, absurd, tarnished, splayed, and yet so morbidly fascinating?

Aware that she must resist it, and bracing herself for the effort, the woman half-rose and quickly turned. Now she lay with her face in her palms, as on an open book. But what she might read in the russet twilight behind her lids was again the same thing, one and the same thing always: the tortuous, appalling, and secret course of her battle with the advancing years, a futile and never-ending strife without allies, without a moment's rest, and without any hope of success.

Everything that had happened to her lately was opposed to her whole nature, to all that she had ever been; it was completely contrary not only to her wishes, her feelings, strength, independence, and personal dignity, but also to her whole understanding, her sensibilities and, in a way, to her familial tradition.

238

At this point she thought of her father—and only of the father—for she never thought of her mother, a soft, pale, colorless woman with that passive sweetness of people who are good because they could not exist in any other way. She thought of Father, who had loved more in her than an only daughter; in whom she had always, in all things, had not only a parent but also the best and most trusty of friends, to whom ineffable ties had bound her, ties that did not depend on tender words and sweet nothings (or on words altogether), nor on wistful parental caresses, for those things would never have expressed adequately what the father and daughter felt and thought about each other.

A man of great physical strength and a well-rounded mind, simple to the point of apparent coarseness, he had loved this daughter of his ("an engineer's child") especially for her strong will, her uncomplicated spirit and resoluteness of thought and conduct, and also because she seemed to temper her rich zest for life with an inborn restraint. While still a child, she once overheard one of his crude though amused and good-natured "engineer's" quips. Somewhere in the gathering dusk of the terrace, speaking not to her but to one of his companions, he had observed as if in an afterthought: "A woman's machine is always in repair." (His taste had never been too fine and his tone never particularly delicate, just as those playfully caustic and overemphatic opinions seldom were actually and wholly accurate; but they were marked by a naturally bold and cheerful brightness that helped the listener to get the point sooner and grasp it better.) She overheard, but didn't dwell overly on the meaning of the words. The world of her senses was then still intact and of a piece, not yet open to outside influences, and her body, womanly and frail, was still without a trace of dull weight and softness, of excessive juices, unburdened by tears and the need of support; in short, without any of those signs of weakness that so often hamper the bodies of even the most beautiful women. It was and remained for years harmonious, strong, and marmoreally pure, nimble as a light and finely built sailing boat. While not conscious of it, she used it and controlled it like a vast and immensely varied fortune; she never felt the need to think about it, much less talk. She lived its life, which was luxuriant, free, consistent, unclouded, sufficient unto itself, and seemingly incapable of being anything else, free of petty scruples and vulgar reckoning.

And now for some time past everything had been changing for the worse, grading into something unlovely and shameful, quite unfamiliar and fiendishly alien to her.

It had started about three or four years ago. "About"—because when it comes to big and difficult changes in one's life, one can never say exactly when they had started. Sometimes it seems as if they had always been present, and then again as if they had only just come to light and become visible to one's eyes. Moreover, they are deceptive and treacherous. This anguish seems at times to be hard and palpable, a single overmastering one, like some dark mountain that hides the world and will not change or budge from the spot. Afterwards, there are days and whole weeks when the mountain seems not to be there, seems never to have existed, when it is altogether unimaginable that it might exist. Until one day, at a certain moment, it springs back to life and looms before us, real, larger than life, darker than it had been before that short and illusory truce and respite.

That was how several years ago she had begun to notice the first outward and inner changes and signs of age, and, after each discovery, to debate with herself the hellish question: Is it—or not—is it? She took pains not to answer either yes or no, and to silence her questions, to forget them. But they came back again, now sooner, now later, when least expected. And the sea which had always been the greatest joy of her life became now her main and foremost antagonist and tormentor.

Born and reared by the sea, she had abandoned it soon after her first marriage; since then she had always lived far away from it, except during the summer months. Lived! What did that word contain? Two marriages, both rather brief and without any real meaning, and not in the least memorable. Next: ten years of a great love for a real man in which everything, even the unavoidable end, was good and fitting. And finally, the twenty years of her career as an opera singer, a quiet and secure career, free of the bluster and humiliations that often accompany this kind of success. Even now she was still in good voice and her interpretations were subtler and profounder than ever.

Throughout those twenty years she had never failed to spend the summer on some beach or other. It was her best time, the glorious climax of each year, one that promised still better things for the next; carefree, poised, harboring no misgivings, she accepted the crowd of people around her in no way differently than she did the sand and the sky and the sea that were necessary to her summer vacation.

And this went on from year to year. To others and to herself it appeared as if the laws of nature had no power over this body. People talked about it as about a small miracle; they talked too much. She herself hardly ever gave it a thought, accepting it all as if it were the most natural thing in the world. And it was only now, it seemed to her, that she saw herself as she must have appeared in the eyes of others during the many years of her exceptionally long youth. For doubt and worry can see what happiness and confidence never can.

Until that summer four years ago, everything had gone passably well. But then, unexpected and unbelievable, the thought of change appeared for the first time: a faint cloud between her and her summer at the seaside, a portent that accompanied her home and stayed with her all through the winter. And having invaded her, it smoldered there like a hidden sickness. What at the outset had seemed like a horror that was hard to believe, a hideous dream bound to scatter itself, awaited her at the beginning of the next summer already as a part of reality and a festering dread. And it kept growing and taking hold of her with each new year. She found it almost impossible to face. Sickened by her own question, she would ask herself: Could it be, dear God? Is it possible?

There was no answer—there couldn't be—to that question of hers; nor did she expect it, knowing that she was addressing a hopeless void. All the same, she knew perfectly well that these questions meant: Was it possible that she was aging and losing her looks visibly and irrevocably, that soon there would be no more blithe summers for her, no more sun and murmuring voices and bright hues of the seashore? Was it possible that this wretched body, having betrayed her and become her enemy, had reached the point where it was no longer fit to be exposed on a beach, where she herself could no longer look at it without a pang, let alone take it into the sun, into the gay and sham dazzle of the world?

This was why in the last few years, starting in the early spring, she had begun to query and observe herself, to study her complexion feverishly, as a lost traveler studies his map, to preen herself naked between long mirrors, scrutinizing every movement and asking herself uneasily whether this one more summer, at least, she might show herself on some modest beach, quietly, without any flashiness or real joy, yet also without shame. At least without shame! For weeks and months on end she would busy herself with the question of an appropriate swim suit, a problem that once she used to settle in the manner of a youthful athelete—simply, quickly, casually, but always with the happiest results.

Such had been her life in recent years. Indeed, one could hardly call it life; it was a madness that hung between her and the world and life and made of her a solitary being, racked by insane thoughts which she had not known before, and by an endless, muddled dialogue with age and aging. Even now, here in the sun and air, these thoughts and the awful, witless reproaches coursed inside her like some dark and sour juices. She carried on a wordless private debate with herself. Every word burned and hurt her, but there was no way of stopping them. She talked with herself as if dickering with another, invisible person.

No, there's no goodness or grace in old age! Not in any part of it. It's not even clean! It's not only that one's attention wanders, consideration becomes blunted, interest dulls, so that one tends to neglect one's dress and posture, but it's as if the body itself were harder to keep clean and were more easily dirtied. It gets dirty by itself, from inside. And even when a person who is getting old manages with the utmost effort to keep himself neat and clean, it is the sterile cleanliness of a pharmacy, not of a flower. Youth is clean because her sap renews itself, but the fluids of advancing age are stale even when they hadn't yet dried out. And what was so venerable about gray hair if one had to hide it like a shame, yet could not? It was the same thing with the wrinkles on one's face. Wrinkles inspired respect in most people and lent a certain charm and warmth to modest old women and dignity to a thinker's forehead, but those same creases on the face of a lovely woman who is beginning to age are like a brand of defeat, something misshapen and almost disgraceful, since in the eyes of the beholder they evoke the same feelings as those in the woman who bears them. Cosmetics can't gloss them, massage can't erase them; sometimes, in fact—damn them!—it is as if one can't even wash them properly. The shadow of age seems to have settled in them for good and ever, just as on those marble and bronze busts in the provincial museums there always remains some dust in the wrinkles of the faces and the folds of the dresses. And from these barely perceptible but always visible—above all, visible!—lines on the face of a beautiful woman who is beginning to fade there wafts a bleakness and chill as from deep-sea weed and mountain gullies.

And what was she to think of her eyes? There is nothing harder and more painful than to look at the world around you with the eyes of a former beauty. The glance of such a woman grows more and more restless, hard, distrustful, and vindictive, for she wants to see only one thing in the eyes of others: the impression which her appearance makes. Even in a mirror she timidly catches this new glimpse of herself, smiles at it, trying to iron it away or at least soften it, but the visage slips even through the smile, wretched, full of misgiving about other people and its own diffidence, hesitant and at the same time keen as an inquisitor's. (Never again the old carefree sparkle!) And if at times it manages to recapture a little of that youthful dazzle, this gives the whole face an expression of something giddy and frivolous, almost indecent, and to herself so repulsive that she would best like to snatch the nearest lotion jar and smash the big mirror together with its vision.

Such is the horror of old age that all things turn against the person who is already at odds with everything because she is growing old.

She no longer simply mused about old age; she conjured it up, magnified it, and reviled it. Her warped, poisoned thoughts gave no quarter to anything: not to the weakness, or wisdom, or dignity of old age. These struck her as self-delusion and a cheap comfort, and she didn't want them because her eyes had been opened at last to what is called the truth of growing old, and she refused to deceive herself, could not be satisfied with her own deceptions. She wanted no part of it, and cared not the slightest about anything else. She would have wanted only one thing at that moment: to be able to squat as she once did on that wall which had encompassed the garden of her youth, to have the power once more to experience that wordless and blind soaring on the cool wave of air. Just that.

But this was something she could not do—would never again be able to do.

Such were the thoughts and the inner debate of the prone, unstirring woman on the rock. (And as often when we decide in this way that our eyes have "opened" to something, what it usually means is that we have shut them to a hundred other things.) She felt alarmed and tried to stop her errant mind. No, you shouldn't dwell on it, at any rate not here in the sun! Close your eyes firmly and be carefree, at least try not to think.

This is good. Like this. Screw the eyes down tight, forget that you have them. Forget who or what you are, how much space you occupy, where you came from, or where you are going. Give yourself to the basic and simple things that do not change, or at any rate not so swiftly; to the rock on which you lie, to the sun and the blue sky above the darker sister-blue of the sea. Wipe out every thought and all carping and fault finding, drift away beyond the reach of desire and comparisons. That's good. Good—but it doesn't last long.

From time to time, turning over from one flank to the other like a bed-ridden patient, she would open her eyes and experience a quick stab of pain as from a pair of wounds. Her short glance would alight on a young woman, or a girl, sure of herself and without a thought of her body, emerging from the sea with a toss of her wet hair, or else getting ready to jump in. All at once she would think again: Ah, if these women knew how quickly it all goes—how soon— And just as abruptly she would break off in the middle of the thought. "What am I whining and crying here for! What do I care about other women, about the whole world for that matter!" But her mind would be off on the same old merry-go-round, the thoughts would chase back and forth and whirl so sharply that each conclusion would be the opposite of every other. And why shouldn't I care? This thing that's happening to me happens to every woman on earth. Surely not one of them remains young and beautiful—they all go through it! Once more, there would be a subtle shift in the logic. Yes of course it happens, how wouldn't it? It happens. But maybe not to everyone, and not in this way? Not like this! And then she would realize with a kind of bitter and surprising clarity that such aging was typical of people who were ashamed of growing old, that a body living only for itself and because of itself was unfortunate, that the full extent of its misfortune became apparent to it only with the onset of old age.

She tried to push these thoughts away, but couldn't dispel the insane one that stood out and apart: Not like this! She felt it as a steady weight on her chest, a hard, dark bell-clapper swinging to and fro with a sound like a never-ending moan, since all the attics of her mind only swelled its echo. Not like this! She beat her forehead on the soft padding of the towel, beneath which there was the eternal stone.

Not like this! Merciful God, not like this!

With a shock, she caught herself whimpering inwardly. Her failure to smother, or at least muffle, the "miserable helpless devil" in her made her frantic. Lately, she had fallen into the habit of picking some such meaningless word and repeating it over and over until it became a gloomy refrain, a wail that sent her whole body quaking and which only she could hear. She hated this whimper of hers, yet caught herself at it every other moment. She trembled at the thought that one day it might grow audible, pass her lips, and that one of the people around her might hear it.

The quiver made her flesh creep. Her body grew colder and icier, despite the warm rock under her and the August sun above her. The chill started in her toes, real and excruciating, then climbed and spread, numbing her innermost tissue, and joined finally with similar icy waves that had started out of her elbows and the nape of her neck. Soon she was a piece of ice, her skin encased in gooseflesh. With a last effort she asked herself: Where could all this blood have drained to? The only thing still alive in her was her mind, and this mind informed her that she was lying somewhere among people, like a strange oasis of darkness and frost in the white heat of rocky ground and seething air. The thought made her want to run, to hide herself from the world and this daily exposure. But it was too late for retreat; it would only fan the shame and the horror. The last way out was to vanish. To vanish unnoticed, completely, for ever, in this ice age of the earth, together with all the earth's oceans and continents.

But this powerful and bitter urge to vanish would set off, in the very center of her body, there in the vault of the parting ribs, an infinitely tiny spark that would presently quicken into a flame, minute in compass but terrible in its intensity, which would spread gradually and push out the cold as it grew into a fire. At last, the frost inside her would be transformed into a blaze. Through the mist and the heat waves she would ask herself: Where does all this blood come from? Where is it gushing out of, and why is it so hot? I'm going to burn up!

Yes, this too was a way to limbo. There was nothing left but to vanish—yes, to burn up, to scorch this body that had let her down so abjectly, twisted her whole life into the very opposite of what it had always been, of the only thing it was capable of being. To consume oneself utterly, to the last particle, beyond recall, in the all-powerful, clean, honorable, irrevocable fire! To burn oneself without a trace, to annihilate oneself in the general conflagration of worlds, like a blaze within a blaze! But still, she remained conscious and did not vanish.

She lifted her head languidly, opened her eyes. Everything was still there. Everything was the same. With difficulty she summoned her strength for a few crabbed movements in this reality which neither cold nor fire could deaden and destroy. She unscrewed the jar of cream and mechanically anointed that body which had died twice in the same moment, once from ice, the second time from fire, but which was still alive and moving and demanding something. The act of motion calmed her, her gaze came to terms with the familiar landscape and with the bathers scattered over it, with the world that existed unchanged outside her thoughts and independent of the changes in herself. In this world there was room, there had to be room somewhere, somehow, for everyone. For everyone.

In the wake of the insane fire and dreadful cold she now felt the living warmth of her blood and its measured beat in the veins of her neck, like the pulse of a clock that ticked the time for living people and slowly bore her to the regions where there was no suffering.

This brought on the soft lassitude of sleep. Will I really doze off? she asked herself with the fainter part of her consciousness. Right here, in full view of everybody? Will I? But her questions grew fainter. In the last instance what did "here" mean? Who was "everybody"? None of it really existed; all was spirited away by the gentle and yet overwhelming power of sleep, before which the color of the sky and the sea and the light tang of the brine-dusted rock faded away in a cosmic mist, in which colors no longer had names, nor scents any meaning. The mist wrapped her from outside and filled the hollows of her body as if she were an unresisting valley, lifting and lowering her at the same time—wafting her somewhere as the ocean of air wafts an immeasurably tiny mote, without a perceptible movement or sound or any sensation familiar to human beings. At the bottom of that mist she discerned a pale blush, the last vestige of a life in which, she vaguely remembered, there had been unfair comparisons, changes, and questions about youth and age, numbers, names, and visible signs of some picayune human existence. There had been, but they were no more. She knew only one thing: That she was falling asleep on the rock. Sleep—on the rock. What did "sleep" mean? What was "rock"? Presently that, too, melted into the ocean of nonbeing. She slept. Eternity.

She didn't wake up from her short nap with a start but glided lightly to the surface. Transformed and invigorated. The scene around her was unchanged. One heard the waves lapping, and the voices of people that meant nothing and could make no difference. There wasn't anything to be afraid of. No confusion, no bad thoughts! All was real, simple, almost gay. The sight before her was attractive; it gave her a strong sense of well-being. Slowly and lightly, she rose with the movement of a deathless goddess loosening the sandal from one of her feet, as she stood, in perfect balance, on the other. The sandals fell away, first one then the other, weightlessly, making no sound.

She stepped forward, upright and natural, her breasts lifted high (though neither too much nor too little), tucking her hot hair under the rubber cap and fastening the strap under the right ear. She approached the edge of the sheer cliff and, with head slightly bent forward, her arms raised high, dived off in a perfect arc. The sea was cooler, harder and darker than would have expected. Still, she was not expecting anything. She hadn't thought about it at all. She sank.

When she came up her face bore the bright mask of liquid shimmer. The two slits on the mask reflected the blue, endless and ever-lasting sky, in whose center the sun was blossoming—a fiery bloom that one could not look at. She swam out, climbed the vertical iron ladder, reaching up for the higher rungs with strength and ease, while at each step of the climb there waxed in her a sense of calm satisfaction which had no need either to hide or show itself, which did not think of a goal, and knew no end. Mounting the rock she had abandoned a short while ago, she glanced in absent wonder at the pair of carelessly dropped sandals and then lowered herself (smoothly, like a sea creature) on her knees on the big orange beach towel, almost as if she had come across it unexpectedly. She buried her face in the moist softness of her crooked elbow. Her whole body, together with all it had ever been, or desired, or thought and felt, poured itself into this small nook and found there a moment's peace and sanctuary. Somewhere deep in her entrails she could feel a nameless bliss germinating and sprouting, then growing and branching through her entire trunk, spreading at the same time like a palm leaf, its points fine and keen and reaching all the way to the eyes, pressing and teasing the closed lids from inside like a welling of healthy tears. Perhaps everything was all right after all.

She felt as if she were completely enveloped in a bright, feathery, and yet impenetrable sheath, without a name, unknown to herself. Her wet flanks rose and fell to the rhythm of her still agitated breath, gleaming on the rise, darkening as they fell; gleaming and darkening. She felt herself as light and big and powerful as the world which itself changes and remains always the same, calm and happy in the lap of the benign, momentary respite.

BAR TITANIC

1

In the quarter between the electric plant and the tobacco factory, which at one time was called Hiseta, there was a honeycomb of forlorn little streets containing several cafés and tiny bars, even though the neighborhood was stagnant and not particularly noted for its human traffic. Some of these cafés had bad reputations, which meant that they were well known and well frequented; they were regularly patronized even by people from the other parts of the town.

On the very edge of the park that enclosed the tobacco factory, in Mutevelić Street, was the hindmost of these bars. It was a two-storied house with peeling plaster that reminded one of a loathsome skin disease, and its windows, flowerless and bare of curtains, were like some festering eyes shorn of lashes and brows. Its building style harked back to the middle period of Austrian rule, and was a bastard offspring of the architecture of Central Europe and of the Near East of that time, suffering from anemia and weak breath. Its visage was one of poverty, but poverty stripped of all charm and picturesqueness: the architectural expression of a life without thought or vision. Beside the main entrance on the ground floor there was another, narrower one, topped by an overlarge green board with a red-letter sign on it:

BAR TITANIC
Prop. Mento Papo

This little bar-café, boasting the name of the tragically capsized English transoceanic ship, was a dark hole-in-the-wall some six yards long and two yards wide, without any chairs, so that the five- or six-odd guests it might accommodate always stood at the bar counter, though the owner would produce a crate or a beer barrel as a seat for his more elderly customers. Men given to drink and bar life are fond of just this kind of bare and cramped space, which gives one the sense of being a casual visitor, forever in transit; the kind of room in which none of the furnishings can distract a guest's attention from the essential business at hand—drinking and the exchange of maudlin conversation. At the far end of the bar, a green drape concealed a door that led by way of a corridor to two larger rooms. One of these was Mento's quarters, the other was empty, save for a bare table and several rudimentary chairs. This was the gambling room. Its windows faced onto the garden, which in reality was a combination of hen coop, stable, garbage heap, and children's playground. The pair of windows were always covered with cotton curtains, mildewed and already quite stiff with age and dust, which were never drawn aside as all gambling was done by electric light.

The customers of the bar and the gambling room were an assorted and motley lot. They included the poor and lowly inhabitants of that district, petty clerks, workers, baggage porters from the railway station, who came for a break and an hour's distraction; and also idlers and barflies from the whole city, who spent their lives in pub-crawling and in a perpetual quest for fresh stimulation, yet always settled for the same old one. The gambling room had its special patrons. Those, indeed, were not bar visitors in the usual sense of the word, but passionate players among whom there were both professional gamblers and erstwhile house owners and government officials, as well as artisans and waiters, who dropped in only after the cafés in which they worked had closed for the day.

In the other room, Mento spent his nights, and there, too, lived his common-law wife Agatha, when she wasn't feuding with Mento and tramping around the other bars of Sarajevo and the suburbs.

Mento was a short, stunted man, still young, with a squint in one eye, and a flushed, puffy face. He was always both a little drunk and nursing a hangover, though never quite one or the other. Son of a small merchant, and a onetime student of the School of Trades, he had started, while still at the school, to drink and gamble with loafers like himself in the various small bars on the town's periphery. A convivial fellow and a tosspot, better known among his acquaintances by his nickname, Herzika, than by his own proper name, he had quickly traversed the road that led to this bar-café and gambling den in Hiseta. All the efforts of his parents, relatives, and other Sephardic Jews of Sarajevo to steer him from that road had proved unsuccessful. In the town's Sephardic community Herzika was looked upon as a lost man, a black sheep, a renegade and an outcast such as the local Jews had not known in a long time; and they were wont to quote on his account the old saying: "There's nothing worse that can happen to one of our people than if he takes to drink and mischief."

As for Herzika, he set little store by the judgment of his community, and by public opinion in general. He lived cut off from his family, from his co-religionists, and from the entire class of people whose ranks he had deserted. He looked after his lilliputian "shop," organized parties of *frische Viere*, wrangled with the police and internal-revenue inspectors, amused his guests with songs and witticisms, quarreled, fought and made peace with his girl friend, and whatever money he made on the drunks at the bar, or at cards in the back room, he gambled away with his clients, or spent on drink, or frittered away by selling on credit.

Agatha, who in her own circles was called "Titanic," after the bar of her friend, well deserved this name, for indeed her movements were like those of a great, strong ship. She was blond and tall, an athletically developed woman, with a pink face that looked as though it were continually flushed with excitement, and with big, pale-blue eyes—"eyes of a devil," as Mento would say in his moments of bitterness; their expression of childish and laughing mischief would often grade into a mad and menacing light that flashed up every now and then, to disappear at once somewhere beneath the dense lashes and heavy eyelids. She came from Vareš.

The life of these two people, the frail Mento and the giant half-peasant woman, was truly unusual even in this sort of crowd in which there were many unusual lives. It consisted of a fitful alternation of wild quarrels and dizzy love ecstasies; save that the days of love were discreet and inaudible while the quarrels were noisy and common knowledge. Their fights were familiar in the neighborhood and among the steady patrons of the bar. As a rule, they would start fighting at the bar, then retreat to their own lodging and there settle the argument in their own fashion.

Often they would remain locked for hours in those untidy, Gypsy-like quarters, arguing and flailing away at each other. Mento would stand in a corner of the room and shout angry words at Agatha, lacing them with grotesque and insulting names. The number of these words was great, and so the number of their variations and permutations seemed endless.

He said whatever occurred to him, while she hit him with anything that was handy, whatever part of him she could reach. And so it went: curse-blow, blow-curse. Except that each curse found its living target, whereas not every blow did, for Mento knew how to defend himself, taking shelter behind pieces of furniture, shielding himself with cushions and other objects that were close at hand; he knew how to jump deftly between the things hurtling at him and the massive arm of Agatha.

They fought and cursed like that, then grew tired and paused for a few minutes, after which he would again launch a fresh insult, a scurvy epithet he had just thought of and which he could not have suppressed even if he knew that it would cost him his life, and Agatha would flare up anew and take aim at him, in a fresh lease of strength, with some objects that up to that moment had not been employed in the battle. Understandably, these frays sometimes ended up in the police station or in the emergency room of the city hospital. But each one was eventually patched up in a dark and ecstatic truce, which in turn led to more fighting.

Prior to that time, during the years that preceded the German assault on our country, so much had been said and written about Hitler's persecution and destruction of the Jews in Germany, as well as in the countries which he took over and subjected one after another, that this was bound to percolate even to the customers of the Titanic. They looked at world politics, and at the world at large, through the atmosphere of this narrow room, heavy with the breath of brandy, dampness, and tobacco smoke, and so the reports of that persecution, too, were to them simply fresh material for jokes on Mento's account. (In Bosnia there is more wit and humor than a foreigner observing the country from a train might think, but the wit is often coarse and grave; uncheerful, if one may say this of wit; hard on the person for whom it is meant, and revealing the uneasiness of the jester himself.) There was joking at the bar, but the jokes and laughter were even freer and more riotous in the gambling den.

Here were half-drunk kibitzers without a penny in their pockets, resentful of life itself; half-sober gamblers for whom the fickle card was the last possibility of any kind of gain, or, for that matter, loss, since in life they had long lost everything —if indeed they themselves were not already lost when they came into the world. And between the deals of *frische Viere* or *Eins*, they needled and riled each other, especially those among them who were more timid and weaker, and did so with an unconscious cynicism, with the callousness of thick-skinned people who always take it for granted that the other person is utterly devoid of feeling. And they viewed world events from their own low, dark vantage point.

"Do you see, men, what this Hitler is doing to the poor Jews," said one of them, who had heard something about German concentration camps in newly conquered Poland.

"Looks like their black Friday has come!"*

"And there's an even blacker Saturday on the way." This came from a humble railway worker who had been retired on account of heart disease and alcoholism, and who had nothing against the Jews but a great deal against the world in general.

Mento heard, and did not hear. He would have preferred not to. But this was hard when one was being personally addressed by people who liked to put their finger on the sore spot of another man.

"Come on now, what are you, Herzika? You're not a real Jew, and not a Christian either. What religion are you?" asked a young man in a thick voice, a loafer and wastrel son of a well-to-do family from Vareš.

Mento, who even in better times had not cared to discuss

---

* An unlucky day—a colloquialism.

religion, answered with studied lightness and made a joke of the whole thing.

"I'm the captain of the great ship *Titanic*."

"Hear, hear!" Shouts of acclamation came from the twilit back of the room. "Hear, hear! Long live Captain Herzika!"

It seemed as if the unpleasant subject would be buried under this bantering, drunken clamor, but it refused to die altogether. For another customer began to relate, with a boorish lack of compunction, how Hitler went from one country to another and wiped out Jews everywhere, to the last man.

"Just suppose they start this thing with us, then, God forbid, it's Herzika next!" someone remarked in a tone of mock concern.

"Eh, by God, once the wheel starts rolling—"

"Don't you worry your head about Herzika. Hitler looks after his shop, and Herzika after his," said Mento, who up to that moment had been humming quietly, wiping a glass and squinting through it against the light. And he went on humming.

They laughed until the players began to hush them—those inveterate gamblers to whom all this was a distraction, who cared neither for talk nor laughter, in fact, for nothing in the world save the monotonous shuffling of cards and banknotes in a game which to all appearances never varied but which contained the possibility of all manner of sudden turns.

Mento Papo found such jokes strangely disturbing. Separated from the rest of the Jews, he was not accustomed to sharing their fortunes, either good or bad, yet the jokes once again connected him to them. He therefore affected an indifference and did what in such company was the best tack: accepted jest after jest, and returned them with another jest. But even as he joined in their laughter, unconsciously longing not to be set apart from them, he would feel a hitherto un-

familiar tingle crawl up and down his spine. Some atavistic
sense forewarned even him of the danger that was in the offing.
In those moments he would laugh incontinently, trying to
hoodwink his companions, to draw their jokes away from himself and turn them to another subject, and to drown out this
inner voice.

In the opening months of the year 1941, the mood of
nervous expectation, worry, and ominous silence began to
thicken and darken throughout the city. Even at the Titanic,
humor grew thin and laughter more subdued. People came as
before, each drinking his own portion, and the gamblers still
arranged their parties, but they all talked noticeably less and
confined themselves to trivialities; and with all that, conversation flagged every other moment, and their eyes sidled uncertainly and haltingly around the room.

And when in the month of April the "rolling wheel"
came as far as Sarajevo, that is, when Germany attacked Yugoslavia and smashed its resistance easily and quickly, and when
the puppet Ustashi government settled down in Sarajevo and
began to take the first steps toward realizing the plan for the
annihilation of Serbs and Jews, Mento Papo was more bewildered than frightened. But before he could understand the
true nature of his bewilderment, the latter had turned into
dread. It was the kind of dread Mento could never have imagined when hearing the tales of fear in other people in other
parts of the world.

One after another, his customers began to stay away.
Some vanished as if the ground had swallowed them up, while
others walked by the Titanic without dropping in; they either
lowered their heads or else cast a quick glance over the house
that contained the bar, as if the building itself had been razed
and the site were now a vacant lot, devoid of memories. When
Mento, pretending ignorance as he stood in the door of the
empty bar, tried to hail one or the other of them in a jocular

and comradely voice, the erstwhile customer and drinking companion would be mysteriously preoccupied and would barely acknowledge the greeting with his eyes, as if deaf and mute. Even those who used to have all the time in the world, were now in a hurry.

One day Agatha ran away, although they had not quarreled or fought; she vanished quietly and inconspicuously. The morning when Mento, obeying the general summons to all the Jews, had gone to the police to register himself as an "Israelite," to surrender his bar license and to receive the yellow armband with the Star of David, she gathered all the money, clothes, and valuables that could be found in the house, and disappeared without a trace. That treachery of his Roman Catholic wife, who had made no bones of the fact that her brother was an Ustasha, was for Mento, at long last, a clear sign and a blow from which he would never again recover. He saw that the people were running away from unpleasantness and risk. The thin protective envelope that so far had shielded him from the world was peeling off him, scale by scale, and at the center there remained Mento Papo, a Jew without any ties with Jewry, alone, without money, without respect, without property, naked, mute, and helpless.

In his dread and confusion he even decided to visit a few respectable Jews, simply to ask them: What is happening? But they looked at him dully and had nothing to say to him. And it was not lost on him that they, too, had no idea of what to do with themselves and their families, and that even the reputable, upright Jews could see no way out, no salvation. Coming back to his deserted house he realized again that the circle of emptiness around him, a Jew, was growing wider, and that this new power which day by day appeared to him more almighty, more relentless, and inhumanly cold, made no distinction between good and bad Jews.

Bar Titanic became quite deserted. Even the beggars

avoided it. The only person who dropped in these days was Nail Plosko, a railway porter and old customer, for whom Mento had always found room, even when the bar was crammed full, and a little brandy and tobacco for a cigarette when he was sick or without money. He was a man of giant stature, but twisted from rheumatism, ravaged by drink, and always in tatters; his hair was unkempt, and his face covered by a thick red beard out of which shone a pair of big, blue, and cheerful eyes, the only part of that great body which had remained unspoiled and pure.

In the old days, when he used to return from the station, sweaty and covered with dust, or else swathed in rags and frozen to the bone, he would never pass by without looking in at the Titanic. As late as a few weeks ago, he had sat on a crate in a corner and, fussing with a poorly rolled cigarette which kept shedding tobacco and going out, cheerfully taunted a younger guest:

"Look who's talking! Even today I can lift with my teeth what you carry on your back!"

How faraway that wonderful and carefree time seemed to Mento! As if it had been another age, on some other planet. And now . . . ? Nail was the only man, the last one, who dropped in. Perhaps he too felt uncomfortable about it, but shame would not let him walk past. Mento produced a little brandy from somewhere. They drank together and tried to converse like before, ignoring what was happening before their eyes; but they could not. Mento spoke in a changed voice that trembled as though it were about to snap and break into sobs. He appeared even more shriveled, his unshaven face wore a blank expression, and his squinting eyes, inflamed by insomnia and fever, seemed to be staring into empty space. He told Nail that the bar was closed to customers, but since it provided the only access to his quarters, he was obliged to keep it open for himself. The worst, he said, was that he had remained without anything. He talked on, about trivial business worries, while his voice shook from quite another kind of anxiety and dread. He was not afraid of going hungry, he said, but minded not having at least a little money, or some valuables in the house, with which to bribe hostile people and so keep worse evil at bay.

With an unsteady right hand, Nail clutched the glass in front of him, while with his left, in embarrassment, he twisted and tugged at the greasy baggage rope that dangled from his shoulder. He knew nothing, and could do nothing, like the rest of them, but seemed anxious all the same to convey this and somehow explain it to Mento. He snorted and hemmed and hawed like a debtor, or a culprit.

"Well, Herzika, let me tell you—this is—Herzika, brother, it's some kind of big and rough politics or something . . . It's one of those—those—those—God forbid, Herzika. One of those—how d'you say—those, God forbid—"

He kept murmuring like this but could not finish a sentence or indicate what he meant by "one of those," or what it was that God should forbid, and in what way. Except that he, in contrast to the other former companions, looked evenly and straight at Mento and his big blue eyes seemed damp, moistened not only by brandy fumes but also by a deep, helpless compassion.

The pair of them sat like this and presently fell silent, since neither knew how to explain his anguish to himself, let alone to the other. Mento would have wanted at least to smile at this good fellow who alone had dared to visit him, but he lacked the strength to smile; his eyes kept stealing toward the narrow slat of bright light stretching into the dark room through the not quite closed door. And he perceived that this thing he was seeing as a thin and straight blade of gold was a brilliant, high September day above Sarajevo, in which at this moment walked and milled a great many people who, like himself, wanted to live with as little suffering as possible, live as well, as quietly, and as long as possible.

It was through that narrow, golden passage that Nail also vanished, after they had sat together long and silently, after he had awkwardly taken his leave.

Mento did not stir from his place. The shaft of light left at the door in Nail's wake turned russet, then paled, and at last faded altogether, without his becoming aware of it. Sunk in darkness now, he sat on crushed, his head hanging, but under a vivid impression that someone had opened his door—the same one that had not been opened since this misery had started—that a living creature, an acquaintance, had dropped in for a visit, to see him and ask him how he was. And Mento suddenly lifted his head, took hold of the small glass containing the rest of his last brandy, raised it solemnly as if toasting an invisible guest, in the darkness, on the vacant stool opposite, and smiled for the first time in what seemed to him like ages; smiled sadly and gratefully, like a man whose troubles had eased at least for a moment.

That visit was the last one. After it, even Nail stopped coming.

Before long, it finally dawned on Mento that this was indeed Black Friday, after which, as far as the Jews were concerned, there would be no Saturday but only a black and certain end. He knew of no reason for it, and couldn't see how it might happen, but he could sense it in the quiet and desolation around him, just as some days ago he had felt it in Nail's look and his awkward mumbling. In truth, the only thing he felt clearly was dread, which now had become for him the measure and expression of everything.

Fear in these countries was sown like a crop, according to a planned schedule and with a thorough knowledge of the soil and other factors, then carefully nurtured and maintained; and now the seeds were bearing fruit. Fear was ultimately responsible for the plundering and slaughter of people like Mento;

fear numbed their minds and bound their hands, so that the Ustashi found it easy to perform the actual plunder and slaughter.

Mento Papo was one of those who so lost their head that they failed even to ask what kind of lethal power it was that pursued them and whether its blow could be averted, and instead they simply waited for their turn to come. And how could he escape fear, he with his shallow brain and debauched life, when so many cleverer, more reputable and stronger people were frightened?

In those few months Mento became a changed man. He ate little and all but stopped drinking. Not till the evening would he toss back a double jigger, simply to deaden his fears. He no longer had anyone to gamble with, and couldn't care less; the japes and the gallows humor of the old Titanic never even entered his mind. He grew haggard, thinner, and somehow more refined in appearance; his face was now pallid and lean, his eyes seemed bigger, and the moist veil of dread that constantly lay across them gave his look a new expression of sorrow and dignity.

From time to time he, too, was led with a larger group of Sarajevo Jews by the local train to Ilidže, to remove the rubble of aerial bombardment. The Jews returned his greeting, but he failed to draw any of them into a conversation. This oppressed him greatly, for he saw them conversing among themselves, and he longed greatly to talk to someone, anyone, about what was happening, about all that might lie in store for them yet. It was difficult and hopeless to have to ponder these things alone, to ask questions of himself and vainly search for answers. But the toughest of all was the physical work, to which he was not accustomed. During the day, partly carried away by the team spirit and partly driven by fear, he managed to hold out somehow, but in the evening when, dirty with sweat and dust, he returned to his lonely quarters, every muscle in his body ached so that he could have cried out aloud from pain, like a child.

The hard life and constant danger exhausted Mento Papo. The little sound judgment and power of resistance that he had possessed drained out of him, and their place was taken by a panicky, hallucinatory fear.

And when one evening there really was a "knock" on the door of the Titanic, Mento was not surprised but only more terror-stricken. The whole scene had long been staged in his head, rehearsed during the long hours of trepidation, loneliness, and sleeplessness. He accepted it as inevitable "Fate," saw it as a simple matter of accounting. It was clear to him that somewhere, in certain mysterious, immaculate, and smoothly run German institutions, dossiers had been compiled and studied, that every person had been investigated down to the smallest detail, and that finally a decision was made as to when an individual would be arrested, in what manner he would be tortured and stripped of his property, whether he was to be killed forthwith or sent to a camp. Written orders were then prepared, and the Ustashi—whom Mento imagined to be men of steel nerves, deliberate, cool, and implacable, punctual as a clock—carried them out inflexibly, like a fate which one could not oppose, let alone defend oneself against. In this great master plan of his, Mento Papo's turn had now arrived. All that remained for him was to open the door and do what was demanded of him. And so he opened it.

There entered, imperiously and with hunched elbows, a man in Ustasha uniform, with an Italian cap tilted over his forehead, bearing Ustasha insignia, and a leather gun holster bulging from his left hip. In Mento's eyes, there had entered— at long last—that ineffable punishment and terrible Fate.

Actually, the man who entered was Stephen Ković, a recent Ustasha from a special detachment that had just been transferred to Sarajevo, otherwise a well-known loafer and Jack-of-all-trades.

2

Stephen Ković was born in Banjaluka, but his family came from somewhere in central Bosnia. At one time they were successful artisans, but after the Austrian occupation, in 1878, their workshop went bankrupt and with time the Kovićes scattered all over Bosnia as day laborers or, at the most, petty government or municipal clerks.

As a young man, the father of Stephen Ković had been a court messenger in Banjaluka. His name was Augustine; he was a pinched and seedy-looking man, dissatisfied alike with his life and his job. His burning ambition was to be transferred to the Banjaluka prison "Black House" as a warden, *Kerkermeister*, and to have the ear of higher officials—to belong to that part of humanity that carried the saber and maintained authority, even if that authority was no bigger than a winnowed grain. With that ambition he was destined to go to his grave.

His wife—Stephen's mother—was the daughter of a poor widow who used to wash the officers' linen. As a young girl, Stephen's mother sometimes delivered the laundry to the officers' apartments. Tall and neatly turned out, the girl then suddenly and unexpectedly married the lowly court attendant —Augustine Ković. She bore him one child, a baby boy, not quite seven months after the wedding. The women of the neighborhood, who always kept a count of months and an eye on everyone's movements, whispered that the child's father was an officer. Augustine himself denied this heatedly and maintained that the baby was his. And with the passage of time the gossip was forgotten. But during the evenings when he had drunk a little more than usual—and he was a secret drinker, one who drank only at home—he carried on bitter, vindictive, and interminable fights with his wife, asserting that he knew full well he had been palmed off "a jackdaw under a dove,"

265

that he was feeding and buying clothes for "strange blood." This would usually go on until exhaustion set in, until he fell into a leaden sleep from weariness, quarreling, and brandy.

The boy was pale-skinned and thin and, in fact, resembled neither his father nor mother. The father wanted at all costs that his son go to school and become a gentleman so that, at least through the child, he, Augustine, might get his own back on life. The boy, however, had no head for study. He muddled somehow through the first two years of Gymnasium, but then bogged down in Latin and algebra, as in a sticky morass. The father alternately beat him and implored him, but to no avail. Physically, the boy developed very quickly and matured before his time, becoming utterly absorbed in his body and in the vague desires with which it filled him—distracted, dull, unreceptive to anything else.

Meanwhile, Augustine Ković died, and the widow had to take her son out of the Gymnasium and apprentice him into a trade. He started working in a manufacturing plant, but didn't like it and soon changed for a job in the leading book and paper supplies store in Banjaluka, owned by a Jew. There again they wouldn't keep him, because they caught him stealing. What he stole were petty, meaningless little things; and in accordance with the established trade custom and the dictates of his Jewish sense of caution, the owner neither reported the thefts nor asked for the return of the stolen items but dismissed the boy on the spot, with the warning that if he ever saw his face around the store he would call the police and have him arrested. The only person the shopkeeper confided to, in strictest privacy, was Stephen's mother.

After this, Stephen Ković joined one of the Banjaluka photographers, but even there didn't last long. Taking advantage of the upheaval of 1918, he left both the shop and his native town. He wrote home from Zagreb, then from Belgrade, where eventually he completed his apprenticeship in a photographer's store. In those stormy years after the First World War it was easy to get a trade license, and jobs and money were easy to come by.

Stephen began to travel all over the country as a salesman, booking orders for enlargements and sending them to his company in Zagreb. Now and then he would turn up in Banjaluka, and, after a short visit, resume his travels. In due course he got married, somewhere in the province of Bačka, where nubile girls were quick to marry, and received a considerable dowry in cash. But he refused to settle down in Bačka, and his wife would not hear of moving to Banjaluka. So he returned alone to his native town, dressed like a dandy, affecting a jaded, man-of-the-world air. There, with the money he had brought, he set up a photographic studio—*Photo Studio Helios, Stephen Ković*. The actual work was done by a gymnasium classmate of Stephen's, a drop-out from the Academy of Arts at Zagreb, who was a talented draftsman, a Bohemian, and incorrigible alcoholic. Ković merely "supervised" the shop and spent the income.

When, after a couple of years, the alcoholic would-be artist died of tuberculosis, Ković's studio began to decline and lose customers; and finally he had to close it. Once more he went back to work as a salesman for picture enlargements and photographic materials.

Yet no matter what business he took up, or how widely he traveled, Stephen Ković remained a figure of fun to his own native town. He was one of those jejune, barren men who neither withered nor grew to maturity; incapable of resigning themselves to a petty and humdrum way of life yet lacking the energy and talent to change it; men who, since birth, were doomed to torment and frustration.

For Stephen, going into the street invariable meant that he must exhibit himself. He envied those who could walk quietly and naturally down the main thoroughfare, could go about their business with an unself-conscious air, heedless of other people's glances or opinions; he envied and hated them, for although he believed himself better than they, he somehow also felt inferior to them. Neither as a youngster, nor later in life, had he been able to stroll empty-handed through the bazaar, because he always had the oppressive feeling that he would come apart, that his knees would turn to putty and he would stumble, if he didn't carry at least something in his hand—a newspaper, a cane, a book, or a package of clothing. And the more unusual the object was the better he felt, the lighter and more assured his step.

Talking to other people about virtually anything was for him a hard and complex task, for underneath the topic he happened to be discussing there always flowed a second stream of his thoughts. He made conversation, but inwardly he kept asking himself what his companion thought of him. Is he contemptuous of me . . . ? Why is it that his eyes slide over my face in that bored way, with that offensive air of indifference? Meanwhile he himself would be talking and listening absently, and his look would be unsteady, his speech unsure.

Ever since adolescence he had been afflicted with a morbid vanity, with an irresistible craving to be what he was not. To be anything else, as long as it was different, or at least looked different! It didn't matter what, just so long as men's eyes didn't flit over him coldly, just so long as his lot in the world was not like everyone else's—that is to say, work, worry, and struggle—but gave off a glitter and radiated a sense of ease, the kind that attracted attention and dazzled the eyes of onlookers. Yet how was he to achieve that, uneducated and untalented, lazy and diffident as he was . . . ?

And so from his earliest days as student and apprentice Stephen Ković had felt impelled to challenge, amuse, or astonish the populace of his native town with the eccentricities of dress, speech, and bearing. What had he not tried in the course of years to amount to something in the eyes of people! He would take the canvas slipcover of a tennis racket, for instance, and stuff it with strips of wood and carry it proudly through the bazaar; on another occasion, he would borrow an empty violin case and take it for a walk. Or else buy a pipe, which he would pass off as an English import, and clench his teeth on it as he sauntered down the street, puffing away ostentatiously while his mouth felt bitter and his stomach heaved. Then again, he would buy huge dark glasses somewhere, or a pair of small round ones with blue lenses and a white plastic frame. From each one of his trips he returned with something more outlandish. He would come in a suit of a strange cut and color, the likes of which Banjaluka had never seen; or bring back a dog, for which he dreamed up a fantastic breed and pedigree, and a name that no one could pronounce. But a few days later even that would become familiar and commonplace, and he would have to think up something new. As time went by, he thus changed his hair style, shaved off his mustache, grew a beard or a goatee, and shaved it off again. He varied his oaths and wisecracks, his walk and gestures, according to the latest motion picture he had seen.

When there was nothing he could find or think of, he would, on his return from a trip, pretend that he had just undergone a difficult eye operation and that his right eye was now of glass; he would walk down the main street batting his left eye, patiently keeping the right one wide-open and, as far as possible, perfectly still. He often boasted of vices he did not have and pleasures he could never have afforded, and for which, in truth, he cared very little. And so in the end there was hardly an aspect of him, inward or outward, that was honest, true, and his very own.

The town became inured to these antics of Stephen Ković His supply of lies and fads seemed inexhaustible, With time, however, the shamming began to decrease—just as an animal leaves off playing once it is past its youth. It was the onset of drab and lackluster years. He grew tired of and came to detest this naïve and transparent game of youth. Truthfully, he had always hated his "English" pipe, for it had been made in Slovenia and was spurious and incapable of deceiving anyone; and even if on occasion it did deceive another person, him it would never deceive, not even in his sleep, not even for a moment. He realized now that he had hated all these cheap masks which over the years he had used to set himself apart from the crowd, to raise himself in the crowd's esteem; hated them in the first place because they had been indispensable to his goal, but especially because in reality they had failed him and only made him appear ridiculous. How often had he felt this as he awoke in his pauper's room, naked and vulnerable, bathed in sweat, on the threadbare quilt that had not been aired in ages, and which sent out a torrid heat and a hideous reek of old wool! (This reek followed him everywhere, and often appeared to him like an olfactory expression of his penury and impotence.) Knowing it all so well, he was driven to seek new masks and eccentricities; yet because he sensed beforehand that those, too, would be of no avail, his hatred of the world and of his own behavior and of himself grew ever more intense.

After long years of this sort of life, Stephen Ković, discouraged, was beginning to lose interest in his play-acting and his masks. Less frequent now were the surprises that he prepared for his fellow citizens, feebler and feebler the inventions with which he tried to distinguish himself before them, and their effect correspondingly weaker. He exhausted himself, grew weary in his fevered quest to attract glances and attention, to gain people's wonder and laughter, if not their admiration and respect. And yet, in giving up the effort, it was as if the sap of life were draining out of his body. He began to age before his time—indeed, not so much to age as wither and mold. His luxuriant brown hair that once had commanded attention with its exotic styles and evoked smiles from the citizens, thinned out visibly; the top of his head developed a premature bald spot. For days and weeks now he would go through the bazaar without carrying or wearing anything in particular, or imitating anyone's gait; walking with a slouch and a diffident look. He had no real occupation and took any job that called for no effort or skill, or one that was temporary. While it was apparent that he still earned his keep, the source of his income was less clear. And always at his side, in good and bad times, there was his mother—dressed in black, sickly and thin as a reed, more silent than a shadow. She saw what the others did not see; that her son, who had never been a heavy smoker or drinker, let alone a drunkard, now spent all his evenings at home, putting away his quota of brandy. She watched him slumping down on the same little bench on which once his father had sat, in the same private corner, as glum and solitary, without a companion, joyless, wielding the bottle like a man condemned.

A year or two before the war, Stephen Ković again resumed his travels and began to improve his income, but he no longer made himself conspicuous. A new generation of young people were coming into their own. The town gradually forgot him. He turned forty. It seemed indeed as if at last he would sink into oblivion.

Then came the year 1941, and the Germans and Italians invaded the country. That month of April, which was to bring to light so many strange and unexpected things, also revealed a new side of Ković's personality. It became clear that the long years of his play-acting and affectation, telescoped all in one, had a dark and menacing aspect, and that during the recent lull in his private life they had ripened for the worse.

While the Yugoslav army was still being mobilized, Stephen Ković went into hiding, but immediately after the defeat, as the first Ustashi began to arrive in Banjaluka, he popped up again, this time in uniform. At first it seemed as if the old days were back—the time when, returning from one of his trips, he had caused wonder among the people in the streets with some outlandish suit of clothes or pair of shoes. This time, however, despite his unmilitary posture and bearing, Stephen Ković was pale and drawn with the importance and gravity that apparently filled him, and which he was anxious to spread all around him. He wore no decorations of insignia of rank, but gave out that he had been connected with the Ustasha movement since 1938 and that in the last two or three years he had undertaken several crucial and dangerous missions for them. Yet from all appearances, he served them only through his firsthand knowledge of the town, its people and their relationships—in other words, as an informer and spy, a scout for those who performed the actual house searches, arrests, and committed violence. He also took part in the "expropriation" of the big Jewish-owned book and paper supply store from which he had been sacked as an apprentice; with relish he kicked and crushed underfoot the empty boxes and cartons. The son of the owner, the "young master," had hidden himself somewhere in the town or else had run away. They found the "old master" in the apartment on the floor above the store—the same one who once had quietly dismissed the apprentice Ković because of theft. The old man was past his seventieth year and was fast losing his sight. They tried to force him to disclose the whereabouts of his son and of the money, but the knowledge that his son was not in Ustasha hands gave the old man courage. He answered all questions calmly and freely, and would not be shaken by threats or even blows. His inflamed eyes shone with a rapt, almost gay light, and gave his whole face an absent and carefree cast. That same night he disappeared without a trace.

After the initial pillage and killings, authority was restored in the town and an Ustasha hierarchy established. The latter got to know the local setup, and Stephen Ković, who had been of some small use to them until that moment, now became superfluous. He swaggered about in his new uniform, but in the general bustle and preoccupation of the Ustasha functionaries no one asked or called for him. Increasingly often now he would boast of those trips on behalf of the Ustasha movement, when he had walked "on a barrel of gunpowder," yet it was also beginning to dawn on him that the real reason why they had picked him for those jobs was that he was a man of no substance and weight, in other words a person no one could possibly suspect.

As he strolled around the town it seemed to him that nothing had changed, that he had somehow been cheated of his triumph. People's glances still skimmed over him lightly; when he spoke, they listened with a vacuous air, and very few waited till he was finished talking. It seemed that even this great and bloody masquerade had made no appreciable difference. Among the Ustashi, too, he felt like a fish out of water. These for the most part were younger men, more forthright and martial than himself, men who knew well how to strike, terrorize, loot, and kill when necessary—without too many words or any hesitation. He simply could not keep pace with them.

After a while someone in the Ustasha headquarters must have tumbled to the embarrassing conclusion that the town, which still remembered all the metamorphoses of Ković, now saw the same Ković as a Ustasha, and saw him constantly, since he was incapable of discreet and unassuming behavior. So they transferred him to the special detachment that was being sent to Sarajevo to terrorize the Jews, before the latter were shipped abroad. He, too, found the change of scene more to his liking. For, as long as he was on the streets of his own town he would always have the feeling that he must distinguish himself in some way, while knowing full well that his efforts would come to nothing and that no one, apparently, would ever take him seriously.

No, he realized more and more clearly that his old dream of an exceptional life, of those things that were born of pluck, luxury, and strength, would never come to pass, for he was dogged by his own true nature as by a shadow. Even in these terrible and extraordinary times, which to men like himself opened up unexpected vistas, offered boundless opportunities and complete immunity of action, his share of life could not be anything but mediocre and wretched. Here he was—an Ustasha, a great thing!—yet he was feeling almost apprehensive about it! He had got mixed up with young men, rapists and hooligans, of whom he'd always been leery and in whose midst, to be truthful, he still felt like a back-alley mongrel among the wolves. The uniform he wore gave him a sense of embarrassment before many an acquaintance; his own mother, who never once had questioned anything he had done, now looked at him with pitying and troubled eyes, saying nothing, shaking her head in mute reproach and worry.

And what did all this get him? He listened to the tales of other Ustashi, younger and more brazen than himself, and how they broke into Jewish homes like tigers among rabbits; he watched them carry away Serbian and Jewish property and saw how overnight they acquired certain new, free, and ample gestures—gestures of men who denied themselves nothing, who didn't have to account for what they did or finger a coin before they spent it; altogether, they were devoid of any consideration, of any sense of measure either for themselves or others. He listened to them and observed them, and his feelings of admiration and envy mingled with the desire to learn once and for all how these things were done, how best to achieve that kind of commanding presence, become as clever, evil and inconsiderate as they; but in the same breath he also felt a profound and baffling fear of such a change. During the raids on Jewish homes he did try occasionally to bark at an inmate, to stamp his boots and wave his revolver, but what was the use when there was no real conviction behind it? He felt that he was missing the mark somehow, that his actions were not sufficiently brusque and terrifying, his words not the kind that stopped further argument, that even the gun in his hand seemed to carry little authority. In the presence of the other Ustashi the Jews wrung their hands and died of fear, but to him they appealed with tearful trust, seeking help and sympathy in his eyes. He could not help feeling that the Jew he was trying to cow with his abuse and shouting looked at him more in wonder than in fear, that in those barely alarmed eyes there was a faint, tentative glimmer of an imperceptible smile, as if the man were waiting for the moment when this morbid incubus between them would vanish like a foolish dream. He had a sneaking suspicion that the elderly Jew at whom he was growling would all of a sudden wave his hand, and speak up in a dry, matter-of-fact voice:

"Now then, on your way, loafer!"

This attitude offended and exasperated Stephen Ković, and alarmed him more than the prospect of resistance and fighting. It happened sometimes that in his fury and resentment he would actually cuff an old Jew, but cuff him so effeminately, so clumsily and unnaturally that he staggered under his own blow and was left helpless and bewildered at his victim's side, haunted by the thought that the whole world had witnessed it. And he would turn around to see if one of the Ustashi had been watching.

Because of all this, Stephen Ković welcomed the idea of leaving Banjaluka and going to another town where the people didn't know him, and he himself knew no one. It seemed to him that there everything would somehow be better and easier.

But Sarajevo turned out to be more of the same. He was assigned petty, errand-boy chores. As for the night "operations" which the young Ustashi organized on their own, he was not only ignored but openly excluded. Often, on an evening, he would be left without a single companion in the large dormitory of the improvised barracks. He would then get some brandy, sit down on a stool in a quiet nook and start drinking, alone and embittered, trying to find comfort in the addled and fitful visions of greatness which the liquor brought on. Even that somehow fell short of expectations in this accursed town which appeared to him like a trap laid between two mountains.

One night, as he sat like this, he heard a small group of Ustashi discussing the plan of a raid. The air was thick with Jewish names and street numbers. He got up and, emboldened by brandy, firmly demanded that he be allowed to take part in the raid. A silence followed, in which he all but sensed their contempt and boredom; he could swear that their eyes flitted over him in embarrassment, then sidled away into the distance as if looking for something that promised more interest and excitement. Finally one of them, as if out of charity, gave him a street address and the name of a Jew. He wanted to ask who the man was, in what sort of style he lived, but they shrugged it all off and went out one by one, laughing and making coarse jokes. Someone said cheerfully, going by:

"Get in, little brother, and ask no questions. Don't be sorry for the Jew! You haven't signed a receipt for him."

Stephen Ković walked down to the Miljacka embankment and, in his fuzzy head, through the pounding veins in his temples, kept repeating to himself: Mutelević Street, number four, Mento Papo, owner of the Titanic Bar. At the same time, he was thinking how to tackle *his* first Jew in the sternest and most official manner possible. Then he grew impatient with his own rehearsing and planning—as if he were going in to sit for an exam, not to collar and interrogate a Jew! He would enter, as they all entered, and announce that he was there to get information about him and his family, then drop a hint about arrest, internment, or worse things yet. Papo was sure to offer some money or jewelry, or both; and if he didn't volunteer it himself, he would remind him in no uncertain terms. And then he would leave the whole family in dread and confusion, anticipating the worst, resigned to the thought that they must continue to bribe him if they wished to postpone their destruction.

When he got to the electric plant he saw, in the milky light of big windows behind which greasy machines were throbbing, a man with a red fez on his head. He gave him an Ustasha greeting and asked him the whereabouts of the bar Titanic. The man answered promptly and politely that he was not of these parts and didn't know. Ković then asked about Mutevelić Street; the man didn't know that either. Stephen felt an angry rush of blood to his head, but there wasn't anything he could do since the man spoke with that honeyed courtesy which the natives of Sarajevo affect when faced with a question they don't wish to answer, from someone they don't like.

He had to find the street and the house by himself. At the main entrance, he met a small and poorly dressed man carrying an armful of firewood. To his query about the bar, the man dropped the wood in astonishment and, evidently struck dumb by fear and yet relieved it was not him they were looking for, pointed to the small closed door on the street side.

Stephen Ković knocked, and then, remembering who he was, at once began to pound the door with his fist. He did not wait long to be admitted.

3

First he demanded to see all the premises and the rest of the family. At this Mento recovered some of his courage. There was no other family, Mento informed him. (He wondered whether or not to say something about Agatha, but remembered in time that this had better be kept quiet.) As for the premises, showing them was no problem: there was the bar, which was no longer in operation, the empty room which once had served as a gambling den, and his lodgings. There they paused.

"Is that all?" asked Stephen Ković in a suspicious voice that was yet heavy with barely concealed disappointment. More boldly, almost cheerfully, Mento suggested that, if he felt like it, he examine the apartments on the second floor for comparison. In the same breath, he bade him eagerly and humbly to sit down. The Ustasha sat down and began his interrogation.

"Name? Surname? Occupation?"

Mento obliged readily.

"Jewish faith?"

"Yes."

"Sephardic?"

"Sephardic."

The worst seemed to be over.

The examination went on. Mento answered standing on his feet and after each statement made several short and almost gay nods in all directions, as if approving the simple question and his own prompt and clear answer. He betrayed some awkwardness only when trying to address the Ustasha by name, to assign him a rank and a title. "Yes, Mr.—", "No, Mr.—" Finally he settled on "Mr. Officer." From then on, he spoke with more confidence and ease, using the title as a prop.

At one stage, when the Ustasha reached for the water jug that stood on the table, Mento plucked up enough courage to offer him a glass of liqueur. This, he said, was something he used to keep behind the bar counter for special guests, for better people. With a daring and an agility that was typical of people frightened to death, and not waiting for an answer, Mento set on the table the potbellied *flacon* of liqueur and a small glass. The Ustasha declined it with a curt flip of his hand, but the bottle and the glass remained on the table in front of him.

The interrogation continued.

Had the bar been frequented by Communists? Who were they, and what did they talk about? Mento's lips parted in a grin and he was about to laugh out, but controlled himself and then, quickly and timidly, wiped the grin off his face. Nevertheless, the voice in which he made his answer was still colored by that suppressed laugh.

"No, there was nothing like that in my place, Mr. Officer. Just plain citizens—looking for a bit of fun, sure, but decent people, if you know what I mean. No, there was no such thing."

The questioning went on. Did he have any relatives? Who were his friends? Who did he work with? Who were his pals in the black market?

Mento's answers became even more forthright and composed, nor was it hard for him to find them. He really had no family and no business ties, no property, not even personal effects, save these few odds and ends. As for the Jewish community, they no longer recognized him as one of their own. He could name any number of witnesses to that, not only among his neighbors but among his customers as well.

"Ask anyone about Herzika—that's what they call me, you see. They'll all tell you, Sure, he's a skylarker and all that—but as for mischief, or any kind of business under the table and such like, well, he's not that kind. No, sir, Mr. Officer! You just go and ask."

Again he felt like mentioning his wife, albeit unwedded, but shrank back from the thought and bit his tongue. Yet even after this, the temptation to speak of her came back strongly several times. He knew that it was better for him not to declare this liaison with a woman of the Aryan race, but he couldn't help thinking that it would be useful if he could inject that Catholic name in some way—Agatha—to hold it up like a talisman, as a shield and a defense. Still, he restrained himself.

At one point in their lengthy conversation, Stephen Ković unconsciously emptied his glass of liqueur, and Mento promptly filled it up again.

As the interview dragged on, Mento grew livelier and bolder with his answers, and Stephen Ković more hesitant and sluggish in his questioning. There were long and awkward pauses in which one heard the ticking of the cheap, tinny alarm clock—an implacable, mechanical warning. Like an actor who had not learned his part, Ković cleared his throat, harrumphed and, not knowing what to do, kept reaching for the glass. And when he thought of a new question, he would drawl it and pad it, deliberately stressing certain words and syllables as if they were cleverly set traps in disguise. He had a vague notion that this preamble had gone on long enough and that it was time to get down to business, but he didn't know how to cut short the preliminaries and get on with it. What hampered him especially were the other, private thoughts that kept passing through his mind. He forced himself to ask questions and at the same time watched the enlivened Mento and thought about him, about himself, and about things that had no connection with what he was saying.

Stephen Ković studied *his* Jew, dissatisfied both with himself and with the Jew. (This is what they left for me, wouldn't you know! he thought again and again). And his displeasure shaded into a bitterness that tightened his throat and made his head whirl, creating an inner need to say something, to yell out, to act.

Obviously, this was not the authentic kind of Jew he had always imagined, nor was he himself the kind of Ustasha he would have wanted to be. The small *parterre* was messy and wretched, like his own in Banjaluka; and the Jew himself was a pitiful nonentity, dressed in a worn and greasy suit, given to bowing and scraping, to blinking and shaking, hemming and hawing; fear had so sapped him of blood that he was ashen, even a little green, like a drowned man. In no way did he resemble those people the newspapers were now writing about, the type shown in the caricatures: the rich, well-padded parasite Jew who sucked the blood of naïve working people of Aryan stock. There was no big belly here, no golden chain, no jingling cash till, no plump white Jewess who fed on goose fat and was weighted down with jewels, no misshapen progeny. Not a trace of that wealthy, arrogant Jew he'd dreamed of and whose appearance might have roused him and spurred him to act like a genuine Ustasha, to shout, to hit, to plunder.

He tried to recall everything they'd told him about the Jews when he was still a child. He remembered his mother telling him how as a small girl she had been led to church with other youngsters at the first chilly crack of dawn, while the last street lights were still on and before the sun had ever risen, during the Holy Week, there to "whip Barabbas," the accursed Jew on whose account, they said, Jesus Son of God had been nailed to the cross. They gave them fagots of willow switches, and the youngsters lashed the church pews in a frenzy of delight, so that the dusky nave echoed to the farthest nook and cranny beyond the altar, in front of which a barely visible priest was mumbling incomprehensible prayers.

He remembered—a strange power drew the veil from

281

those distant, forgotten regions—he remembered how as a child he had walked one Friday evening through the bazaar with his paternal aunt. It had only just begun to grow dark, and the Jewish merchants were already lowering the iron shutters and closing the doors of their stores. In one of these a door had been left ajar—the other wing was still open—and inside, almost leaning on it, stood the owner, a Jew, in a Western suit of clothes and with a fez on his head. One could barely make him out in the shadowy interior; his hands were folded over his belly and he was rocking lightly with the upper half of his body, as if lost in prayer. His aunt explained to Stephen that this was the way the Jews, after closing shop on Friday evening, prayed to God on the threshold of their store that He may send them, every day of the following week, a "blind customer," an oafish and inexperienced buyer who would be easy to confuse and cheat.

And that was all. In vain he racked his memory to recall other items that were worse and graver yet, which might stoke his anger against the Jews and prod him to strike and torment this wretch, and at the same time justify such treatment. In the last few months he had read the Ustasha newspapers that accused the Jews of being responsible for all the woes and evils of mankind, but none of that stuff was either explicit or definite, and it was convincing only in so far as you were already willing to hate the people called Jews and to do them harm. In general, the printed word did not, and never could, make an impression on StephenKović; he was one of those people who were unable to see clearly, or for that matter feel properly, what they were reading, and who perceived and admitted only what was tangible and bound to immediate personal desires and interests in life.

It looked as if neither the recollections of old wives' tales nor brochure reading would suffice to make a person terrible and daring in his actions, or teach him how to crush the weak and the humble. No, what was needed was another, stronger kind of goad.

And again he was angry at having to excite himself artificially and work up a fury to deal with a Jew, and was only too painfully aware of the poor figure he cut against the other Ustashi. Exploiting his own anger, he lashed out at Mento.

"Listen you, get out your money and gold at once, or else—"

As he spoke, he heard his own words as if from afar; and each word sounded too drawn out, like a word in an ordinary conversation, not a sharp order to which there was no appeal. He wondered, too, how one of the younger, real Ustashi would have said it, while at the end of the sentence, in the pause, after the words "or else," where there should have been a threat of torture or killing, or both, he heard only an echo of emptiness. Or else—What else . . . ? The impotent craving to appear mighty and forbidding, to be rich and enjoy one's possessions, to be someone and amount to something, and, in the same breath, a fear of it all, a sense of loss and unease, the wish that this burden would pass from one, vanish so thoroughly as if it had never existed—even those feelings had now left him, the "Israelite," as it were, no longer stood in front of him, he himself was not there; he felt as though he were another person, in another place, one who never even dreamed that such things, such conduct and confrontations, were possible.

Nevertheless, having already voiced the demand and the threat, it behove him to proceed against this Mento, and do so coldly, incisively, thoroughly. Yet this he could not do. And how could he, torn as he was in opposite directions by these contradictory thoughts of his! Now he felt a consuming hatred of the Jew, hated him as much as he hated his own impotence.

While this conflict was swirling and raging within him, he did not look at the man in front of him; and when he did, he hardly saw him. After the last unexpected and blunt command, Mento had grown pale and there was cold sweat on his neck and forehead. He'd been fool enough to think that the questioning had been an official matter and that his answers were important—what an imbecile! All of it had been nothing but a preamble to this: money and jewelry! It was what he'd most dreaded. To be left without money and valuables in a situation of this kind meant courting arrest, torture, and those other things his fear had whispered to him in his dreams and waking hours. The only way out was to convince the Ustasha that he truthfully possessed nothing. Taking advantage of the pause and the silence in which the Ustasha pursued his own thoughts and moved his lips as if he were chewing unspoken words, Mento pulled himself together a little and began to talk. He spoke like a man defending his life.

He maundered, quibbled, and ranted, trying to convince Stephen that he had neither money nor jewelry. How hard it was to prove the truth when it was not believable! Especially in times like these and to such a man! Tears mounted to his eyes from a genuine fury with himself at being such a wastrel and gambler that he really didn't have a farthing to his name— which, of course, the Ustasha didn't believe, and never would. People spun so many lies amongst themselves, especially when it was a question of money, that no man could believe another even when the issue was the barest, clear-as-day truth; so much so that he himself, knowing full well that he had no money, that he could not possibly have it, ached and sweated a deadly sweat in order to make this truth credible, to think up something, anything, even a lie, to make it acceptable to the Ustasha.

And so Mento kept talking, haranguing, invoking everything on earth and in heaven; he explained, promised, begged, and flattered, stringing word after word and interpolating entire sentences that had neither head nor tail, he flailed his poor brain and worked his dry mouth because he knew: as long as he kept talking, and the Ustasha let him, it was still all right, he was not being tortured, and there was still hope that he might save his life. Talking meant putting off torture, meant living.

He was not, said Mento, like his other co-religionists—no, he didn't put money away in a bank or in a strongbox. In his case the strongbox was the little pocket of his waistcoat, and no coin ever spent the night there. He'd eaten and drunk up everything with cronies and friends who for the most part were not Jews, among whom, in fact, there were Catholics. And quite a few at that! No, he had no money, he could swear that on his own eyes, his life, the peace of his dead mother. Still, considering it was a question of a personage like Mr. Officer, he would try first thing tomorrow to get some, to borrow, and give it to him. He would sell the furniture; he would work and save and pay him monthly. He would kill himself with work and die of hunger rather than deprive Mr. Officer of his due. And this would be good money, as safe as if deposited with a pass-book in the Land Bank.

After he had said this, silence reigned once more in the dusky room; all the words together had not been enough to blanket that interminable night stretching naked, cold, gloomy, like a fateful corridor to which there was no end. Everything that could possibly be improvised and said had been spoken, and yet, it seemed, he had to keep talking as best he could, irrespective. So Mento resumed talking. He lied with an ardor that only a flight from suffering and a terror of death can inspire in a man. He told a long and detailed story about a court action over some kind of an inheritance, which until recently had been pigeonholed by corrupt officials, but which now, under the new, more efficient government, had been re-activated. It was quite possible that even tomorrow morning the court might pass the judgment that would, beyond any doubt, void the testament of his wealthy relative, and Mento would find himself one of the lucky heirs.

And after this tale had been told, he dreamed up others,

more farfetched and less believable yet. His slow and limited imagination ran on, stumbled and, driven by fear, performed weird and pitiful and improbable leaps. It became harder and harder for him to find words and put sentences together; one could see plainly how he tacked one to another, making little sense, each new one less convincing than the last; and still he continued, afraid of one thing only: of the end and of silence. His whole body quivered in a chain reaction of tiny movements, everything on him twitched noticeably, more or less constantly: the muscles of his face, the fingers of his hands, the legs under him, while his eyes sought the Ustasha's glance so as to meet it with a smile. Stephen Ković had meanwhile withdrawn into himself, appearing quite remote to the agitated Mento; in reality he was much closer than he seemed, closer than the hapless Jew would have wanted. While Mento was talking and improvising and babbling, Stephen, not listening to him, thought his own complex thoughts.

Stephen Ković's entire countenance at that stage was likewise troubled and unhappy in its own fashion. His face was sickly pale, and on it were three dark spots, three blurs of gloom: a pair of black eyes, joined by the brows, and a drooping mustache hiding an invisible mouth. Hunched over the table, his chest in the shadow, he seemed lost in his Italian uniform of a billious and ill-omened green; the sleeves were too long, the breeches much too wide, the black shoes and puttees new, made for soldiers of medium stature. But Mento could not see the man as he was, and only saw the Ustasha of his nightmares.

How would it be, thought Stephen Ković, if I lashed out with my knife just to see how he would take it, what it would look like? To swing out—maybe even hit him. And why not hit him? Why? I can do as I want—hit him, or not hit him.

The alcohol in him was fast doing its morbid work. Mento's breathless babble was beginning to grate on his nerves in real earnest. His mind was in a vindictive whirl.

Yes, I can do what I want. There, for all his grovelling and bootlicking, the Hebrew is not answering my question, not carrying out my order, just trying to get away with a lot of talk and promises. That means he considers me a fool, a weakling, he's not afraid any more and doesn't think he's in any danger. How come he's lost his fear, and when did that happen? I've no idea, but I can see it's like that. How am I to strike him now when it's too late? He's no longer afraid, that's pretty clear. Not of *me*, that is. If he were, he wouldn't delay another second, he wouldn't have the nerve to spin these insolent yarns. At the outset he was in a funk—scared of the Ustasha—and then he saw through me. Behind all the weapons and through the uniform he sensed StephenKović, the bungling, insignificant weakling over whom people's eyes skimmed lightly, whose questions no one bothered to answer, of whom no one thought very much, and before whom, naturally, even the likes of him had nothing to fear.

Here Stephen suddenly felt the sour, familiar and loathsome whiff of the stale and lumpy wool, the fiendish heat of the quilt and the whole weight of his old despair, which threatened to choke him.

"Money!"

This cry of Stephen's rang around the gloom-shrouded room like the shriek of a drowning man, like a single, drawn-out *ooeey!* At the same instant, he banged his fist on the table with all his strength, like an avenger. The glass of liqueur overturned, the flagon rocked on the bare table, the bulb swayed on its cord and dimmed. Along the walls and on the low ceiling there was a fitful play of shadows thrown by the swinging light, which to Mento's almost sightless eyes appeared like wolves and bogeys. For after Stephen's cry he had jumped, upset a chair behind him, and found himself in the corner of the room, as if flung there by an explosion. For a while it seemed to both of them as if the room were still filled with the deafening noise and shadows. Although everything had been quiet and still for some seconds, they were both frozen in the same postures; Stephen Ković with his fists clenched on the table, his head low, face twisted, as though he were aghast at his own movement and trying to collect himself and understand it, while at the same time divorcing himself from it; and Mento in the corner of the room, unbelievably shrunk and disfigured with terror.

Strength and resourcefulness were gone out of Mento, he could no longer summon words, all that was left in him was the desire to escape torment. But how . . . ? Never had he so regretted his failure to make money and save it, to accumulate the kind of baubles and gold with which many a Jew now saved his head or at least put off the evil day. Never had he so hated those who had money and knew how to get it. He would never be able to give what he did not have. This meant he must perish. Once more he raised his arms as if in supplication, no longer knowing whom he was entreating, or for what.

"I beg you, Mr. Officer—as soon as it's light, I'll—"

At that Stephen Ković abruptly uncoiled himself and sprang to his feet. The talk of first light and next morning again sent coursing all the blood, fury and alcohol in him. It was as though he'd only just realized that the Jew, cunning and persistent, was setting the next day as a trap, a decoy to a blockhead and a milksop whom he underrated and was contemptuous of. One recent night just like this he had seen some reputable and proud Banjaluka Jews hand over their prized heirloom jewelry to a band of teen-age Ustashi—beautiful, heart-warming things of gold, platinum, and precious stones of unexpected colors and brilliance—and they surrendered them without a murmur, cheerfully, as if they'd found them on the street that morning, while those young numbskulls and ignoramuses took the stuff gleefully, as though it were the most natural thing in the world.

And here was this paltry little Jew asserting that he had

nothing, prevaricating and deceiving him because he thought: no need to be afraid of *this* one, *he* doesn't count, I can wrap him around my little finger. He was trying to pull the wool over his eyes with "tomorrow," but Stephen knew that tomorrow did not exist for him, that he was committed to this night and to this Jew, that he had to prove here and now who Stephen Ković was. There were more things at stake—many more—than money and jewelry. And he began to advance slowly, like a bear, heaving and twisting his shoulders like a man squeezing through an invisible fence, and then, reaching behind him with his hand, pulled out a heavy revolver, like some sort of ultimate and decisive evidence, then raised it vaguely in the direction of Mento and fired.

Aiming at random and thrusting the gun away from himself while his fingers twitched convulsively against the trigger, Stephen emptied bullet after bullet, like thunder and lightning, into the corner where Mento waved his arms about in an unnatural and fantastic fashion, and skipped and leaped as if trying to dart between bolts of lightning and jump over them.

A SUMMER IN THE SOUTH

When Professor Alfred Norgess and his wife Anna arrived in the little town on the Adriatic coast, they were met by sweltering heat and petty disappointments of all kinds. Everything looked crude and forbidding. Everything—beginning with the porter who brought their luggage and took his money without even saying "Thanks" to the ailing landlady who, standing in front of them with her arms limp at her sides, answered all their questions with helpless shrugs. The room was like a darkened and suffocating oven, for the green wooden shutters had been kept closed. What was worse, the town's water supply had run low; instead of water, the little faucet above the wash basin emitted a sadly mocking hiss. The landlady assured them with a perfectly straight face that the water would be turned on before dawn and would run for a couple of hours; one would have to catch it then. In the air, and over the furnishings, lay an odor of neglect and lassitude.

The professor watched his wife as she took her things out of the valise, and wished he could run far away from there, in any direction, for it seemed to him that the place lacked not only water and freshness but was devoid also of order and life. Still, in his usual old way, he didn't say a word.

After an hour, this first impression underwent a change. In the last glow of the afternoon sun, they had a short swim in the sea and felt refreshed, then took a short walk around the lighted town square, and after supper lingered a long time on their apartment terrace, which was fringed with flowers and partially roofed over with a dense vine arbor.

In the morning, after getting up early, they had breakfast on the terrace, with a view of the sea, in the freshness and shade of the summer morning. That early hour promptly displayed for them all the radiance and glory of the region, and won them over completely. In the wake of this came an unexpected and swift transformation. Their bad humor of the day before disappeared without a trace, as did the thought of running away; and they wished only one thing: that this beauty would last as long as possible. The evening before, they had met their old friends from Vienna, who spent every summer in this place and who, in fact, had recommended it to them. Nothing seemed important or difficult any more, not the sweltering room nor the water system that produced a tepid dribble during a few short night hours, nor the slow service in the restaurant. On the contrary, they now began to discover fresh beauties in this sojourn by the seaside.

Frail and woebegone though she was, the landlady turned out to be a good woman after all, ready to meet all their wishes; the natives of the small resort town proved friendly and helpful; while their own interludes on the flower-decked terrace became a source of steady enthusiasm and inspiration.

They would rise early, around six, and bathe for a couple

of hours. Afterwards, Mrs. Norgess would go to town to buy fruit and do her own small errands, while he would remain on the terrace, sitting at the table with his papers. (These were the galleys containing the final revision of his monograph on Philip II of Spain.) Refreshed by the swim, sun, and sea water, he felt as though he were dressed in light and yet festive clothes—daisy-white and fragrant—as though he himself were blooming and growing in unison with them and with all things around him. Inside him as well as around him everything seemed clear and lambent. His work was just one of a hundred delights. He found it hard to concentrate fully, since everything else drew his attention and fascinated him: the spreading trees below the terrace, of which he saw only the glistening crowns, the sky with clouds in it, the sea with its gulls, ships, and constant changes of color. All of it radiated harmony and pleasure; not only that, but you knew that tomorrow would be even better.

That was how he waited for his wife to return, enjoying his own sense of anticipation. You waited for her, you looked forward to her return as though it were a nice surprise, yet knew with absolute certainty that she would come. You experienced that special thrill that preceded happiness. And even before she appeared, you heard her, still unseen, quietly calling you from the bottom of the stairs.

Breakfast would follow, with strong tea, fresh fruit, milk, and rolls. (Sparrows fluttered down to the terrace in the expectation of crumbs.) And after breakfast his wife would quietly withdraw and leave him alone, to enable him to work undisturbed. With all that, as the days went by, he found it harder and harder to apply himself. Everything conspired to make him restless. A plain cigarette produced a heady feeling like a passion, and left him breathless like an exertion. The food and the air and the scents entered him as innocent momentary delights, but once inside him, they seemed to generate, with each and most minute of their particles, a kind of powerful glow and a hundredfold strength that would not let him in peace. More and more often now his work would be interrupted by daydreams and rapt gazing at the distant sea and the sky.

These reveries took increasing hold of him. He felt them as a soft but heady tyranny that cut him loose from his inner self and from the reality around him, yet kept him utterly subordinate to itself; presently, the sensation would turn into a strange kind of game that changed the relationships in the world around him, as well as the energies and proportions of his own body. Which was near, which was far? What was airy, what liquid, what solid? What was he—he of the day before?—and what were these beauties and raptures that so tumultuously filled his inner being and also encompassed him from without . . . ? This—in moments when the game was at its peak—was hard to make out. All things were veiled in cigarette smoke, and in that smoke everything moved. Tobacco became a potent and perilous thing.

He squinted in one eye. In the waving portal of smoke there stood a frail, gray-haired man. He knew him. It was the local fruit vendor from whom his wife bought fruit every morning, and whom every evening, as she went by, she "bribed" with a special smile that evidently was not displeasing to the old codger. Only that now he was a little more solemn, like a portrait of Philip II, and he batted his eyes and motioned him to enter with a light wave of his right hand. After a moment's hesitation, Norgess went in. In actual fact, he entered the landscape which up to that moment he had viewed in perspective, and became one with it and with each of its parts.

The sea was breathing. The bewitched motion went on to embrace the bare rocks of the shore and the wooded mountain above it, then passed on to the clouds and the blue tent of the sky. All things were on the move, on the point of taking off.

Unbelievable and impossible though it seemed, the terrace also was about to float away. If it did not, he himself would take off and leave it behind, for he belonged to all that was moving. It was unusual, even dangerous and a little frightening, but it could not be otherwise. Marvelous it was, too. And the old man seemed to have abandoned his fruit shop for good and was now some kind of a guide, perhaps even master of the worlds on the move. He winked slyly and, as he drifted among the clouds, between the blue of the sky and the almost liquid gray hulls of the mountain range, he pointed out convenient and safe places which one might use as a foothold and a springboard for further flight.

"Here, if you will. This way!"

One met with no resistance of any kind. The law of gravity was suspended, and so were the old norms of distance and solidity of things. Everything was transformed and staggered. If he climbed to the top of the mountain that rose steeply above the town, it would be no problem at all, it seemed to him, to step right off into heavenly space. All things were possible.

Somewhere at this point he would be jolted out of his strange reverie by the voice of his wife who was returning from her walk. As she came up the stone flight that connected the street with the terrace, she would call up to him in a voice that was confident of an answer.

"Fred? Fred!"

"Yes, yes—" he would reply quietly, until first her head and then her upper body and the rest of her, her arms full of fruit or flowers, emerged on the terrace.

All at once the surging elements around him would steady, revert to their appointed realms, distances, and scales of proportion, and become again what they were throughout the rest of the day to all people and to himself. The exhilarating and hazardous bliss of animated space, and the witching effect this was having on his summer, would be replaced by the joy of the actual, down-to-earth summer vacation in the sight of familiar objects and in the company of people who had always been close to him. And this would be repeated every morning, accompanied by that steady, intimate sense of certainty which is the true mark of every happiness. He would relive all those sensations, each time more intensely. The dream on the terrace thus burgeoned and grew like every fruit of the region at that time of the year, waxing ever closer to what was bound to come one day—final ripeness.

That day arrived like any other in the procession of days of his summer holiday. On that particular morning, the world appeared gay and more memorable than usual. A brisk south-easter was blowing. The sea was agog. Long and powerful breakers rolled up one after another and, with a crash and a boom, shifted wide surfaces of clinking pebble and wreathed the shore with white foam, each flattening and vanishing under the next one, bigger and stronger yet. The rearing whitecaps knitted a silvery stairway that bound the surf to the sky on the far horizon. A few bathers romped on a beach that was skeined with froth, reluctant to venture into the water. Women splashed in the surf, now wading in to meet the waves, now running away from them, and under the flying shower of white froth they screamed with an uncertain, nervous joy for which no one either saw or needed an explanation. The air was heavy with the smell of brine and the tang of some distant storm, of which the rushing surf was a dwindling echo.

On that morning, too, the professor and his wife went down to the beach. He felt strangely elated. Everything seemed to goad him to try what none of the bathers—a handful of foreigners—dared to do: throw himself on the rocking waves and let himself be lifted and carried aloft and passed from one crest to the next. But his wife stopped him from doing it. In this she was firm and determined, as she seldom was in other things. Holding him by the hand, she called to him through the din of the breakers, implored him not to go farther, and told him how just a few minutes ago she had heard from local people that these seemingly playful waves could be dangerous, and how last year in this kind of weather, on this same beach, a man had gone under and drowned; careless and not used to the sea, he had vanished in the foam in full view of the bathers who were unable to help him. That was why no one now ventured out.

He gave in to her. After cavorting gingerly with the waves that splashed them to the top of their heads, they went back home, intoxicated with the wind, tired, and relaxed from laughter and exercise. When they had dried themselves and changed, the woman as usual went to the market to do her shopping, while he remained on the terrace, at his table, on which the ears of his spread-out papers fluttered like some miniature whitecaps out of their element.

Work went slowly and gave him much trouble. Something constantly seemed to flicker and twitch on some part of him—a strand of hair, or the hand, or an eyelid—like a series of calls overlapping one another. He was still enthralled by his unfulfilled desire to push off on the streaming pale-green waves whose clamor reached up to him on the terrace. Like a boy plotting mischief, he tried to imagine what would happen if he quickly ran down to the beach, hurled himself into that forbidden sea and let the waves bear him and whip him; and then, before his wife arrived, came back to his place on the terrace. Or, better still, set off along the path that ran above the house and straight uphill, and explored those heights and views that seemed to draw nearer of their own accord?

The thought of this made him lift his head from the papers every other moment.

His gaze was suddenly drawn to the stone balustrade of

the terrace on which at that instant, as if by arrangement, a plump sparrow alighted, his feathers ruffled by the wind. Judging by its cheeky air and general appearance, it was some sort of a winged adventurer and vagabond. He made several of those fine, twitching head movements typical of birds and then all at once—as if realizing he had landed at the wrong address —took off again, disdainfully and with dignity. It looked for all the world as if he had flown directly into the sky and blended with it. The man followed the flight with his eyes as far as he could. The sky was clear and dappled along the edges with thin white clouds that kept changing color, as if getting ready for a celebration. The outlines of the far islands that mingled and fused with the still more distant shadow of the mainland at the extreme end of the view also grew softer, and their gray stone, capped by scarves of darker pine woods, turned pink and hazy and began to sway. The sea, looking shimmery and becalmed in the distance, appeared, in its hues and shapes, more and more to resemble the festive air of the clouds, sky, and shores, and even there where the open sea merged with the horizon and stretched mistily toward infinity, it looked quite accessible and no less firm than the line of the shore. So did the airborne clouds, the flowing sea, and the solid land, exchanging their basic qualities, float to meet and embrace one another.

Everything was unimaginably deep and at the same time near at hand and touchable, and everything conspired to lift the professor from his seat, to make him light, nimble and, above all, receptive to the festive elemental surge. Everything beckoned and urged him to climb and fly, and his resistance was weak, almost nil. He could, at all events, move with perfect ease up to the stone parapet of the terrace, as if in a game, and to lean on it and then mount it and jump down to the path which led steeply uphill toward the ranging heights, and thence to wing into space like that vagabond sparrow.

The dense crowns of green trees, already far below him,

had the iridescence of that same sheen that had joined and blended together all things on land, sea, and in the sky. That sheen—it was a marvelously sheer and swaying bridge which one ascended without any feeling of weight, on and on forever! It was a true wonder, yet so effortless and simple; the anticipation of bliss had already begun. Everything was one and the same, you could lean on every blessed thing and use it as a foothold—each one merely served as a take-off point for the next weightless and natural flight. All that lay below the eye level magnified what lay above it, the softness coalesced into hardness, the dark things helped to furbish the bright ones. All was endless, and its beginnings were forgotten beyond recall. The old man with the face of Philip II was no longer there to show one where to pause, because now tongues of light bore the professor onward like a moving stairway, more and more effortlessly as the distance increased, toward a billowing rose-colored threshold up aloft; and beyond that one could already glimpse new tiers of airy and luminous stairs that would transform a man's walk into an accelerated flight of sound. He could surge far and climb high, he became momentum itself, and in that momentum was his whole existence. He walked, but his motion was winged.

On her return from town, his wife, as was her custom, announced herself already at the bottom of the stairs in her low warbling voice, a voice that expected his customary absentminded echo of "Yes, yes."

"Fred?"

There was silence.

"Fred?" she said again, having gained the terrace and caught sight of his empty chair and the table with its papers aflutter in the wind.

"Fred—" she repeated in a near whisper, but more insistently, as she walked into the shuttered and already cleaned room, where more silence met her.

"Fred!" She gave a smothered cry, frightened by her own strange voice and by the chill of dread along her spine.

The landlady came and managed to explain somehow that as recently as a quarter of an hour ago, more or less, the professor had still been sitting on the terrace. She had seen him through the window as she tidied up their room, and had noticed that he kept getting up and then sitting down again.

"Fred! Fred! Fred!"

The young woman ran down the steps and into the street, repeating her husband's name under her breath, getting no answer. She walked around the town's small square and through several nearby stone streets, then trudged to the scattered and deserted beaches, and finally came back to the house. "Fred? Fred!" But her husband was not there. In the sunlight that now flooded almost half the terrace the professor's work sheets were furling and unfurling with a rustle. The landlady, as always, kept shaking her head.

The young woman set off to the villa of their Viennese friends. They had only just finished breakfast. Wiping their lips with an air of satisfaction, they assured her that her husband had gone for a walk somewhere that he would return, if not sooner, then certainly in time for lunch. She found their sated good humor and lack of concern hard to bear.

She visited the parks and cypress groves above the little resort town, interrupting her search every now and then to rush back to the pension; and each time as she mounted the steps to the terrace she would try to kindle new hope in her heart ("Fred? Fred!"), like someone attempting for the third or fifth time to coax a spark from his cigarette lighter. The hot terrace lay in hopeless, unbearable silence. From the sea came the pounding of breakers and the grating of pebble which the waves steadily heaped into parallel bars along the shore. When the lunch hour came and went, and the end of the day began to draw near, still without any sign of her husband, she went out again, her face flushed and her eyes glazed, to find that friendly couple, and together with them she set off to report the matter to the militia.

In his cool office, the young man on duty was just getting ready to leave. He promptly returned to his desk, inserted a sheet of paper into his typewriter, and wrote out a report on the disappearance of Professor Norgess; he, too, reassured the young woman that her husband had very likely gone for a longer walk and was bound to show up soon. All the same, he ordered his militiaman to start a search right after supper.

The militiaman, the only one at the post, was a burly, kindly young man, who in fact had very little to do in the small township, where nothing of any importance ever happened, either among local people or foreign visitors. Now he straddled his official motorcycle with an earnest air and rode off along the shore road with a great deal of noise, at low speed and with much confidence.

The professor, however, was not found that day or the next. The militia organized a thorough search up and down the coast. The newspapers also published a notice about the vanished tourist.

Meanwhile, the professor's wife spent her time at the far end of the beach where the two of them had bathed until recently. With her hands in her lap, she squatted on her haunches like one of the fishermen's wives waiting for her husband to return. Her light-colored dress blended into the white pebble and became indistinguishable from it. When night was about to fall, her friends would barely manage to persuade her to leave the spot and go home to sleep. But sleep was one thing she was incapable of.

Three days later, her mother and younger brother-in-law arrived and took her back to Vienna.

.   .   .

The days passed. It was already the end of August, the finest time of the year on the coast. The long investigation of the professor's disappearance had still not produced any clues. Neither the sea nor the land had yielded up his body. The authorities continued to inquire and search. The tiny seaside resort lived under the shadow of the mysterious disappearance. Walking along the street one would often hear a couple of housewives, on their way back from market, ending their conversation with a shake of their heads.

"Still nothing. What do you make of it?"

One guessed right away that the topic was the hapless vanished professor. And the other townsmen, too, when chatting amongst themselves or with the visitors, remembered the fate of the missing man. From the sudden embarrassed pauses in their conversation and the troubled glances they stole unconsciously toward the sea, one could infer, even without words, that they were all anxious to have some kind, any kind, of explanation of the baffling disappearance, that they were waiting for it impatiently, as though it were something on which the inner peace of every single one of them depended.

A Note About the Author

IVO ANDRIĆ was born in 1892 in Travnik in central Bosnia. At the outset of the First World War, while he was still a student, Andrić was arrested for his participation in a revolutionary movement which opposed the Hapsburg regime and sought unity and independence for the South Slavic peoples. He was in prison for three years. After his release, he completed his studies and received a doctorate in history from the University of Graz in Austria. He then entered his country's diplomatic corps and served in a number of European capitals, including Berlin, where he was stationed at the outbreak of hostilities between Yugoslavia and Germany in 1941. During the Nazi occupation of Yugoslavia, Andrić remained under virtual house arrest in his Belgrade apartment and devoted himself to writing. One of the products of this confinement was his fictional narrative of the Napoleonic wars, *Bosnian Chronicle*, published by Knopf in 1963. Another and earlier novel, *The Woman from Sarajevo*, was published in 1965. In 1961 he was awarded the Nobel Prize for Literature by the Royal Swedish Academy of Letters.

A Note on the Type

The text of this book was set on the Linotype in Janson, a recutting made direct from type cast from matrices long thought to have been made by the Dutchman Anton Janson, who was a practicing type founder in Leipzig during the years 1668-87. However, it has been conclusively demonstrated that these types are actually the work of Nicholas Kis (1650-1702), a Hungarian, who most probably learned his trade from the master Dutch type founder Kirk Voskens. The type is an excellent example of the influential and sturdy Dutch types that prevailed in England up to the time William Caslon developed his own incomparable designs from these Dutch faces.

Composed, printed and bound by
The Haddon Craftsmen, Inc., Scranton, Pa.
Typography and binding design by
JEANNETTE PERTZ

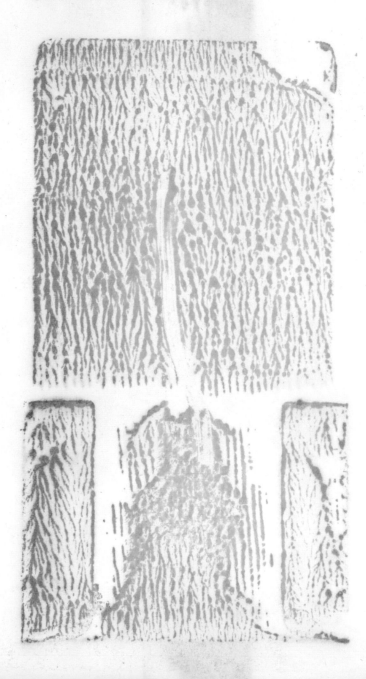